Potentially Settled Scores

By Jovana Iv

© 2022

The World Cup taking place in this story is in no way connected to the World Cup 2014 that also took place in Brazil. The author only used the schedule of matches and their delegation across cities to make the events of the book as realistic as possible. The participating teams in the book unrelated to the plot are chosen randomly by the author.

The sad events in Eastern Europe in 2022 did not in any way influence the author or the plot of the book or its end. The entire story about the characters in this book from the first part *There Are Other Ways to Score*, published in 2020, until the last part, publishing date of which is yet unknown, were thought up and devised in 2006.

TABLE OF CONTENTS

CHAPTER 1

I hated Paris. I still do. That city is overladen with memories of the worst two years of my life. To this day, I still refuse any job offers that would involve a shoot there. Madrid was better; at least there I could speak the language. Sure, I could've learnt French, too, but I hated Paris too much to give it more than the bare minimum. I resented it for everything, particularly that it was the location of my career's absolute downfall after the World Cup in Germany.

The fear and confusion I felt while seated next to Alex during that short flight from Berlin to Paris continued after we landed, like it had settled in my bones. It followed me out of the airport. It lived in my body for weeks. And then it continued for the following two years.

Alex hadn't touched me since I'd cried on the bed that damned night, in that damned hotel in the German capital. (Though I cried many more times, on many mornings, days and nights after that.) Only once, in an emotional moment on our first Parisian New Year's Eve, did he try to make love to me – but he retreated when he was most excited. He couldn't make himself do it, he said.

In the meantime, I was dying, inside and outside. I barely ate, stomaching food only to survive, and even then, it was difficult. I subsisted on blended fruits and vegetables that Agnes, our maid, made for me.

Agnes was amazing. She spoke perfect English without French accent. Most of the time it was only the two of us—Agnes and me—at home. She was invaluable, the thread that stayed taught and kept me from insanity, although she never knew that. We didn't talk much, but she still knew something was wrong between that perfect couple Alex Yanov and Jane Andersonn. At home, Agnes saw how they didn't resemble the happy, smiling faces that still appeared in newspapers and at events. She didn't let that slip to anyone, though. I don't know if Alex had advised her in her confidentiality – tipped her or anything like that. Nonetheless, I was deeply grateful. I probably owe my survival in France to her.

It was an enigma why journalists kept writing about me. I didn't do anything. I hadn't completed any of the projects I had signed up for before the tournament. That was out of any question. Physically and mentally, I wasn't capable of any of them. It was as if all of my energy and talent had been depleted during that month in Germany. What I was best at couldn't put me back to a whole, couldn't help me focus or fight my battle. Everything that used to galvanize me, drained me. I felt more like a collection of weak, writhing body parts than a woman or a person.

On the other hand, Alex's career was soaring unstoppably. I was nowhere to be seen, except for at parties and dinners organised by his club and the Ukrainian national team – events he still wanted me to attend with him. Whenever somebody would ask me what was going on with my life, I would robotically reply that Alex and I were getting used to living together in a completely new place, how it wasn't easy, how I chose to commit myself fully to him and create a wonderful life for us, and if it meant putting my career on hold for a while, I was gladly doing it.

They took everything I had, those parties. Those learnt-by-heart words, fake smiles, acted-out emotions, false reactions. I was constantly surprised that I, a person who had been capable of lying so well – to my boyfriend, my dad, people who knew me better than anyone – was now summoning all my energy to pretend for a couple of hours.

It looked convincing, though. If you looked past my terrible appearance – I had lost a significant amount of weight since leaving Berlin – and some occasional stutters in my statements, you would think Alex and I were happy. He was the best goalkeeper in the world, and I was his perfect girlfriend who waited faithfully for him at home, taking care of everything.

I did it all for him. I had to. I was ready to do everything, anything, just to get back the man I had fallen in love with. The graveness of what I had done in Germany pressed on me, mercilessly, every day. I wanted desperately to reconcile, although I knew I would never entirely be able to. I knew there was no forgiveness for what I had done.

And I was right. Despite all my efforts, my Alex wasn't coming back.

He didn't let me travel. Or meet the girls. He had never really explicitly prohibited either, but the first time I expressed wanting to go to London and see Bea, Angie and Lana, he said "I don't think that's a good idea." I opted against going and never mentioned it again; I also told the girls not to come and visit me. They were shocked and worried at that, of course, but what could they do? We kept in touch, but only through text messages. I didn't want to make any video calls and risk them seeing the state I was in or, worse, me falling apart in front of them. I knew if they did, they'd immediately raise the alarm to my parents, who'd come within hours to take me home.

I didn't want that. I didn't want to be pitied or saved when I didn't deserve it. But more than anything, I didn't want to leave, because I was terrified that there would be nothing to come back to – that Alex, with me gone, would have realised he actually could live without me.

So I stayed. Day after day, night after night. Each and every entirely the same, without any hope of change.

It was such a terrible paradox — before the World Cup, we would meet three or four times a month, sometimes less, and we were so happy with each other. Now we lived together and yet were more distant, physically and emotionally, than ever. In my whole life, I had never experienced such pain and discomfort. I'd always had everything; all circumstances worked in my favour. Now I was in an inescapable situation where nothing conspired to make me happy. Technically, I could have left. But I chose to stay. Every morning, after every uneasy night, I got up and faced another gloomy day, still determined to stay.

We never really had visitors. While Alex had made a few friends in his new club, they always met outside. Those nights out with his club, when he wouldn't show up home until late, were another level of agony. I knew it would be the same regardless, with or without him in bed. But for the first time in my life, I was afraid of another woman having him. Never before had I been jealous or scared that some woman other than me could take what I wanted. It was after the first few late nights, with Alex slinking in around four in the morning, that it occurred to me – whatever he wasn't getting at home, he could be getting elsewhere.

The first night I thought this, I didn't tell him anything. I just lay in bed alone, studying the ceiling and swallowing my tears, until he got home. He crawled into bed softly, and I stilled my shaking and screwed my eyes shut so that he didn't notice I was awake. Two more nights of this, and I couldn't go to bed and wait for him there. Instead, I sat in the living room next to the fireplace, wrapped in two blankets because it was late January and my body couldn't take any heat from the fire.

Alex entered quietly. He always did – though whether it was more about not waking me or not giving himself away, I didn't know. Reflexively, I jumped from the armchair to face him. There was nothing suspicious about him at first glance, so I approached him.

Wafting around him was a clutter of aromas – the smell of cigarettes, a mixture of perfumes, none of them familiar. Scenes flashed through my mind of him with another woman, some skinny, pale, blonde Parisian chick, or maybe a couple of them.

I wanted to scream at him, but I knew very well I had no right to, not after what I had done in Germany. The thought of him with another girl unbalanced me, sickened me (a taste of my own medicine), but I couldn't say a word. I felt my face distort, and I let out a desperate cry and ran upstairs to the library.

"Jane!" he called. "Jane, wait!"

But I couldn't. I slammed the door shut and shrank onto the wide windowsill. I looked down at the garden, a blanket of muddy snow glowing faintly in the ambient light of Paris at night. I couldn't breathe from sobbing.

I heard the door open, and he entered.

"It's too late. You shouldn't have stayed up."

I didn't say anything.

"Let's go to bed," Alex said quietly.

"You go. I'll stay here," I replied sternly.

I heard him approach me. I didn't dare look at him now, not when he was so close. I was afraid of what I'd see – perhaps a golden hair, or a smudge of lipstick on his collar like in a movie.

He inhaled and exhaled deeply. "Jane, there was no woman tonight."

I shivered, goosebumps bursting up my arms, and I finally turned to face him. For a second, I saw a glimpse of *my* Alex. My heart jumped.

"Has never been," he added.

All the pictures I had created in my mind dispersed under the warmth of his eyes. I looked at him longingly and with relief. Of course, there were no other women. He wasn't like me.

We went to the bedroom together, but nothing changed. Some deep, foolish part of myself hoped that this night would be different – that we would make love, or that he would hold me, or even that we would fall asleep apart and wake up in the morning with our limbs intertwined, having reached for each other in the night. But instead, we slept on two sides of the bed, not touching each other, not even in our sleep.

*****

Instead of bringing some joy, the visits from our respective parents were torturous and exhausting. During meals, I had to force food down my throat and keep it there so that nobody suspected anything strange, struggling not to vomit my soul out.

The first time he saw me, Dad was furious. Mom was crying.

"Don't tell me you've started representing one of those idiotic fashion movements that argue for bones! I'll put an end to your career and put you in my office!" Dad shouted while Mom was hugging me.

They never suspected Alex. Together, the two of us managed to convince them it was just a phase. We repeated numerous times that I was a Londoner, that I didn't like Paris, that things would be all right once we truly settled in. It was suspicious, of course, that it would take me so long to settle – me, who has never struggled to acclimate, who takes joy in new experiences – but we stuck to our story and they believed us. Why would we lie?

*****

The European Championship in Italy came and went. I didn't go; Alex didn't want me to. I lived vicariously through Bea's exploits at the championship, since she and the English national goalkeeper, Harold Dare, were still together. They had great fun in Italy. She enjoyed travelling with Harold from city to city, along with her parents and Angie and Lana. Every day I wished I was with them. They had a true Italian experience, Bea recounted to me through regular text updates. Bea's mother, Sarah, was of Italian origin, so they used this opportunity to pay a visit to all the cousins they had neglected over the years. I wanted so badly to share it with them, but knew it was all my fault that I couldn't. They constantly sent me photos and videos, but, of course, it wasn't the same. And each new message, however much I wanted to see it, was another twist of the knife.

I noticed a suspicious radio silence from the media on my absence from the championship. Surely they would never miss an opportunity to speculate, especially about me. At first, I thought it was strange that newspapers weren't full of articles trying to gauge why "the most popular football girlfriend" wasn't attending one of the biggest events in football, but later I saw my father's invisible hand in that silence. He must have had to pull out all the stops to threaten and convince his media houses connections not to meddle with slandering me. I was extremely thankful. Yet again, my dad, now the second most important man in my life, saved me from additional suffering and pain.

I did watch the championship, tuning in to both Alex's and Matthias's matches from our ghostly empty villa – though I concealed the latter's games from Agnes. I didn't want her to catch me red-handed, even though I knew she wouldn't mention anything to Alex.

On one occasion, Bea, Lana and Angie met the German Four. (That's how the media still referred to Germany's most popular four footballers: Michael Krimm, Ben Schwimmer, Lens Petrov and Matthias Beller.) They pushed my girls to go for a drink, so the seven of them ended up in a hotel bar alone, where Matthias demanded to be told what was going on with me, and why I wasn't attending the championship if everything was "fine". Poor girls, they couldn't say much, simply because they didn't know much.

What shook me to the bone was what Bea told me afterwards.
"I shouldn't be telling you this, 'cause it won't make anything easier for you, but...that man is still persistently and hard-headedly in love with you. He was mad with worry. We all felt so sorry for him."

She was right. It didn't help. I only felt worse. *Great job, Jane,* I thought. *You've properly messed up the lives of two wonderful men.*

The tournament ended well for Ukraine, although not as great as they wanted. They took home bronze, having lost to Spain in the semi-finals. Alex was again awarded the best goalkeeper in the competition – nothing unexpected by now.

As for gold, that went to Germany. Again.

Neither the German media nor Matthias had let me rest for quite some time. In the days that followed the World Cup final between Germany and Brazil – when I ran to the pitch and Matthias kissed me under a German flag in front of millions of eyes – the local media couldn't stop thundering about the two of us being secretly together. I had to allow a French homestyle magazine to interview Alex and me in our villa in Paris three weeks later to make the rumours recede at least slightly.

Nevertheless, Matthias didn't stop. After a couple of months, he began sending me letters, which Agnes (bless her) noticed before Alex did, and passed to me discreetly.

What's going on? Where are you? Give me your new phone number.

You look terrible. What's he doing to you? If he's maltreating you, I swear I'll come and kill him.

Don't torture me any longer, Jane. Tell me where you are and I'll come for you.

Needless to say, I never replied to any of them. The "Matthias and Jane" story was over for me, and it had better be over for him, too. I told myself this every time a letter arrived. But a shameful part of me couldn't help but be impressed. He'd stood up to his word – his promise when we separated at the Olympic Stadium in Berlin, when he told me he'd never want or love any other woman. He hadn't been seen or noticed with any girls. I didn't know if I was supposed to be happy about that or not.

I had feelings for Matthias, as crazy and illogical as it sounded. In some unreasonable, unexplainable way, I cared about him. I had since the night before the semi-final between Ukraine and Germany, when we'd spent five minutes hugging each other while Alex slept peacefully a few rooms down. I had planned to tell Matthias everything was over, but instead, I ran into his arms heedlessly, like a teenage girl.

I hoped my feelings for Matthias would stop if I saw him move on. I felt I could bear to care less if I knew he did, too. But he still loved me, and that just preserved my feelings – and deepened my torture – despite how hard I was telling myself that we could never, ever, in any universe, *be*.

I thought many times about just running away from Alex, from that damned villa, from Paris. Run to Munich, to Matthias's doorstep. I knew he would take me in. But what I didn't know was whether I would be happy there. That night after the World Cup finals, the night Alex shouted all those gross truths, I knew I would never be able to be openly, freely, publicly happy with Matthias. The fantasy of my life with Matthias was only that – a fantasy, which can be only sullied by making it real. So if not Matthias, then Alex. If I could not have one, I must have the other. Because how could I have put them both through that, if I chose neither?

That was, of course, only half true. The other truth was the obvious one. I loved Alex. I loved him more than anyone or anything. I loved him more than Dad, more than myself, more than living. It couldn't have been any other way. After he decided to stay with me, despite all the atrocities I'd committed, how he chose us over himself…if he hadn't been the most important thing in my life before, he certainly was now.

I knew he loved me, too. I fully understood his behaviour, even if it hurt me. I knew it wasn't him punishing me (though I deserved to be punished). He just didn't know how to love me anymore. That was why I stayed for over two years, despite decaying physically and mentally in the absence of his care. It was natural that he kept his distance from me. I had no right to complain about anything. We were to stay together, as long I held at least a trickle of hope that one day he would be the old Alex – the Alex who loved me and adored me. It would all be worth it to feel that again.

I didn't know that there would be a time when I would not be able to endure the coldness anymore.

It was late November, two years after the World Cup. Alex's parents were visiting for the weekend. They didn't know the whole truth, but, like everyone else, they knew something was extremely wrong. During dinner on their first evening, Tanya broached the topic of my health. She was almost as concerned as my parents. For the millionth time, I repeated myself, saying the same meaningless words like a parrot: I had difficulty adjusting to France, and I didn't like the city that much. Tanya pushed me to talk more, asking me for the reasons, offering up ways I could give Paris the chance to make me happy. That familiar cold sweat crept over my body, and my chest felt tight.

"It's been two years, and you haven't even been shopping on the Champs Elysses!" Tanya said. "Maybe we could all go this weekend, get you some fresh air and good food. I just worry–"

"Don't worry, Mother," Alex intervened, his voice taking on that horrible glacial tone that I had only heard that night in Berlin. "She well-deserves everything that's happening to her."

My face went white, and his parents' did the same.

"What do you mean, dear?" Tanya asked him, validating that he actually had said it; this wasn't a nightmare.

"She knows what I mean," Alex replied. His rage was not dampening under the scrutiny.

"Alex!" I screamed in fear, not knowing where that strength came from.

I was terrified at the idea that his parents might find out the truth. My eyes filled with tears. He looked at me and understood what was on my mind, as we always wordlessly understood each other – I was begging him not to tell them. The thought of the Yanovs knowing what I had done to their son made me close to fainting in trauma. If that happened, I knew I would be over. They would beg him to leave me, and their love towards me would turn into immeasurable hatred. Even if he decided to stay with me, even if he explained his reasoning to them, they would still hate me. I wouldn't be able to live the rest of my life with that. *Please give me this one mercy, Alex*, I begged him silently. *Please don't tell them.*

I couldn't have stayed at the table any longer. Tears were swelling in my eyes, and I couldn't let the Yanovs see. Alex, only Alex, was allowed to see me cry. I ran upstairs to our room and went to the window, pressing my forehead against the cold glass. The evening outside was terrible, just like every other in that gruesome city. It felt like my soul was twisting its way out of my body, riding the current of my tears, coating my lungs and forcing every painful breath. As I fought for air, I allowed myself to realise it. Things would just get worse.

These last two years, I had been staying, hoping, praying, that my Alex would return. Tonight, I understood he wasn't on the way back. The pain this time was incomparable to anything before. It was too physical, too strong for my body to endure. I had to leave. There was no other way. I had always been too weak for suicidal thoughts. No matter how terrible my psychological state would get, it wasn't an option. I couldn't put that on my father's name. His only daughter, dead by drugs, or cutting her veins, or jumping off a balcony. Gruesome. I could never do that to him. Selfishly, I was also scared of the physical pain that was supposed to take me away. What if I did something wrong and didn't die instantly, instead ending up forever tied to a bed? No, I could never do that. Not to myself, not to my family.

I would do what I should have done immediately after Germany.

I don't know how long I stayed there, motionless, staring. I could hear them shouting downstairs. Strange. The Yanovs never raise their voices at each other. After some time, everything went quiet, and soon afterwards, Alex entered the room.

I didn't turn. I was half-afraid that his look of rage would kill me and half-afraid that I would lose my courage and change my mind.

"Jane..." he started hesitantly. His voice was blunted, the fury replaced by something else.

"This is it, Alex," I interrupted him. "I'm sorry. I cannot do this any longer. I wish I could, but I cannot. I'm leaving on the first plane to Dallas."

For a while, he didn't say anything; he was probably as stunned at what I'd said as I was. I don't know what I had wished for. Perhaps for him to ask me to stay, which I would, undoubtedly, even if he uttered one sentence, even if he didn't beg. Or perhaps that he let me go, which would at least relieve me of the constant fear and dread I was living in.

Finally, he stuttered, "That's probably the best for both."

It hurt. It hurt like I hadn't expected it to. Up until now, the greatest pain of my life had been the moment Alex had found out about my outings at the World Cup, when he'd shouted at me that I was the worst thing that had happened to him. But this was another animal. This was the pain of being let go, of looking in the eyes of somebody you loved – and who loved you – and that love wasn't enough for them to keep you around. It threatened to devour me there on that spot. My heart ached, my lungs, my stomach. I didn't even have the strength to turn and look at him, so I kept staring out that damn window, focusing on that gloomy, gruesome weather until I heard the door close.

When I finally managed to rise from the windowsill, turning to the now-empty room, my bones clicked and groaned, as if straining under a great weight. My whole body felt compromised, heavy, like water-soaked planks of wood.

I did no packing or preparing. I figured the best thing would be to do as we had in Berlin – to take only my documents and leave. And if I saw him one last time on the way out, well...he was just another thing I was leaving behind.

*****

When I went downstairs at 5 a.m., he was in the living room. Wide awake and swollen-eyed, he stood up as I was descending the stairs. I wondered if I shouldn't talk to him. Maybe I'd give up my plan. What was there to say, anyway? I figured I would just walk past him as if he wasn't there.

"You don't have any suitcases?" Alex asked.

A hurricane of thoughts ravaged my head, and my reply was a reflex, involuntarily said.

"No," I said quietly. "I don't need anything."

Another silence, during which we only stared at each other.

"Do you need a ride to the airport?" Alex broke it.

"No, a taxi is waiting for me outside. Thank you."

So polite. The quiet civility of the moment was punishing. No tears, no begging, no wretched words we'd regret. Was this really happening? Two lovers like us? Jane Andersonn and Alex Yanov, breaking up for good? Impossible.

Everything beautiful we had done together was flashing in front of my eyes. Nine months of a perfect relationship – walks around London when we'd hide from the rain, his games in Kiev, long phone calls, the heart-pounding excitement I'd feel before we'd meet, his silhouette in Texas on my birthday, the Ukrainian anthem ringing out through the stadium as I sang along and he gleamed with joy and love, all those nights hugging in love and care and peace. Nine months of that love. And two years without it.

Because of me.

All over.

"You should sleep," I said, speaking through the rock in my throat. "You have training soon."

"Yeah, I will." He didn't look away from me.

I couldn't discern what was in his eyes. Was he reminiscing like me, or did he finally feel relief?

I had to go.

While I still had the courage, I said, "Goodbye, Alex."

He looked at me for another long moment, his expression inscrutable.

Finally, he replied, "Goodbye, Jane."

I should have been released then. I should have felt a huge burden falling of my back. I should have breathed in the new freedom. But I didn't.

When I saw myself in the rear-view mirror of the taxi, the ghostly face that looked back at me scared me, and I was hit by a wave of immediate nausea. After begging the taxi driver to pull over, I vomited all the food I had forced into myself the evening before while pretending for the Yanovs that everything was fine. I composed myself enough to go through passport control at the airport and board the plane. Thankfully, I had found a first-class suite available last-minute; I don't know how I would have dealt with all the curious looks and glances from passers-by. Even fifteen kilograms lighter, I was still easily recognised by people.

I immediately made an alliance with the flight attendant, asking her to check on me regularly but not to give me anything except for water, since I confessed I was in a terrible state but couldn't postpone the trip. She was wonderful and helped as much as she could, including holding my head during one of the vomit fits. Both of us knew that something was gravely wrong, worse than the food poisoning story I told her.

*****

It was terribly cold in Dallas, so I hid myself in a big scarf and cap, and a coat that was now too big for me. When I arrived at the Andersonn Ranch, everyone was more flabbergasted than happy at my first appearance in more than two years. Sophie – who hadn't seen me since my twentieth birthday, when I was the happiest girl in the world because my wonderful boyfriend had taken a week off training to come to be with me – screamed and began crying, attracting everyone's attention. Arnold, our foreman, came first and found himself shouting, too.

"Dear goodness, Child, what's happened to you?" Arnold clearly wanted to hug me but was afraid I would break under his arms, so he just observed me, hesitant as to whether he could touch me or not.

Dad was the next to see me. Although he knew I had lost weight, my sickly complexion added to my terrible appearance, so he went white and started swearing. I had never seen him as worried as he was that afternoon. When he hugged me, I couldn't hold it in anymore. I started crying – ugly, gruesome tears, loud sobs interspersed with gasps. The urge to wail had come over me when the pilot announced our descent to Dallas, and every second since had been devastatingly difficult. At first, I thought Dad would step back, disgusted, because I hadn't cried in front of him since I was five, but he didn't. Instead, he held me tighter, and I cried even harder.

Dad took me to his office while my cheek was still on his shoulder. I didn't have the strength to open my eyes and face anyone. We sat on the comfortable leather sofa I had always liked as a child. He still hadn't released me from his hug, and that encouraged me to snuggle up and cry more. His arm over me was what I desperately needed at that moment.

After a while, the river of tears started to dry up. When he felt I had calmed down enough, Dad asked demandingly to know what had happened. I appreciated his patience; I knew he had wanted to ask that since the moment he saw me.

The first sentence I could form was, "I couldn't stay there any longer." That wasn't really smart – or fair towards Alex.

"I should've guessed it had something to do with Yanov. How could I be so stupid?" Dad hissed. "But, he is over. In a few days, he'll be just a fading name. That bastard. How dare he kill my beauty with his sick jealousy!"

"No, Dad, it's not him," I tried to interrupt, but he was too furious to listen.

To my immense relief, I heard the door open.

"Sophie," my dad said, equally relieved. "Get Jane some sleeping pills and that calming tea. She needs rest."

Sophie returned in a matter of minutes. She fussed over me briefly and left me with a steaming cup of tea and two small pills.

"Dad, please," I said once Sophie had left again. "Promise me you won't do anything to Alex before I wake up."

"Jane, Sweetheart, I have been silent for too long. Look where that brought us."

"No, Dad," I sobbed, "*Please*, wait until I am capable of talking to you. I want you to know everything before you act. Trust me on this. Please."

In another show of restraint, my father acquiesced. That soothed me more. When I finished the tea, I took the pills and fell into a nineteen-hour sleep.

*****

I didn't tell him everything, of course. I never will. When I woke up the next afternoon, groggy, it took me a couple of minutes to comprehend everything that had happened. I looked around the room in confusion until it sunk in that I was in my bedroom in Dallas, at the ranch. The last time I was there, Alex had been with me, and we were happy together. I cried for another half an hour.

When the crying spree was over – for now, at least – I washed my face with cold water, knowing that I would now have to meet my parents and present them with a sensible, credible story. The full truth was not an option. I was too embarrassed, and I couldn't face my father's rage and rejection when he heard that his only daughter was a world-class slut. At the same time, I had to protect Alex. Knowing him, Dad wouldn't calm down until he'd settled everything with *that guy who hurt his precious daughter*. I had to prevent that.

Therefore, just like I had done many times at the World Cup in Germany, I opted for semi-lies.

"Nonsense!" Dad shouted after I said Alex had nothing to do with my condition.

The three of us were in Dad's office. Mom had been at work yesterday and missed my arrival, but from her eyes, I could see she had been crying, too. She had covered me in a thick, warm blanket and held my hand while I talked. I looked like an escaped hospital patient.

"Let her talk, Brad," Mom said.

"It was all my fault," I continued. "I hurt him back then in Germany. I did some...very bad things there, very inappropriate and disrespectful to him. He had all the right to withdraw his emotions for me."

"Then you two should've broken up in Germany!"

"She didn't say he'd stopped loving her," Mom said. "She wouldn't have stayed if he had."

I nodded in agreement. She understood me.

"But, Honey." My mom put her hand on my back carefully, afraid to break me. "What is it that you did in Germany to make him so upset? I remember you became friends with that funny group of Germans, and that Matthias was, and apparently still is, very fond of you. Of course, it would've been smarter to stay away from him, for his own good, but..." Mom pursed her lips, unsure how to say it. "I thought you knew what you were doing. That Matthias was all right with you being around, with you not giving him any hope."

I almost cried in despair at this, but I knew very well I couldn't tell her how much more than hope I had given Matthias.

I took a deep, shaky breath. I had been expecting that question and preparing for it.

"Then you know most of it." I chose the words carefully. "You remember that I went to watch German matches – almost all of them – despite what their players had said about me and the girls earlier that year. That was the first thing that didn't go down well with Alex. Dad, you know that we met them very soon after the tournament started, and I realised they were not as bad as we had thought. Plus, after Gottfried advised them, they stopped saying vulgar things in public. So the girls and I...we really enjoyed those games, hanging around the guys." I couldn't help defending myself, this hypothetical Jane who did wrong but never took it too far. "I mean, of course I wanted to enjoy the tournament. Most of the time, Alex was busy training and prepping for the games."

They listened carefully, without interrupting me. I took another deep breath.

"What you don't know is that Bea, Lana, Angie and I attended some private parties the Germans organised. I can't lie – we had fun. Alex knew I liked going to those gatherings, and most of the time I wasn't honest with him. I would tell him I was going only for the game, and then, the girls and I would go on and meet the players in their rooms—"

"For god's sake, Jane!"

I knew this would upset my father, but I preferred him being angry at me for being at parties over him finding out what I had done before and after them.

"I know it wasn't the right thing to do, but at the time, I thought that as long as nobody found out, we were fine. They were always very nice to us. Not to Alex, though. They flirted with us, and they would make fun of Alex and the other Ukrainians until we and, well, Beller would stop them."

"That boy really cares about you," Mom said sympathetically, which made my heart cramp in pain at the thought of Matthias and how difficult those few weeks with me were for him.

I continued with my well-thought-through story. "Yes, he actually kept hope all that time, especially because I was coming to their games. I never gave him or any of them reason to think that something could possibly happen, but..." I felt shame all over my face. "I cannot say that I didn't respond to some of their flirting, although I knew it wasn't really appropriate. It was funny, and flattering, and hardly seemed harmful."

Dad was about to again say something disapproving, but Mom stopped him with a hand on his shoulder. I had never been so grateful to her as I was that day.

"I know that was a mistake. That's why my conscience has been killing me." I swallowed hard at the next heavy lie. "Matthias was always kind and stopped his teammates whenever they went too far in their mockery, but, you understand that wasn't enough for Alex. He knew how the Germans talked about him and his friends from the team. I couldn't deny it. The disrespect...it really got to him. I shouldn't have gone to those gatherings in the first place. I shouldn't have attended any of the matches without you, Dad. What happened with Gottfried in the semi-final just confirmed that."

There was silence for a while before Dad spoke.

"I understand Alexander's anger. You made mistakes by seeing those boys in their rooms. If I had known about it, we would've had a serious discussion." I lowered my head, wishing for the first time in my life that I'd faced my father's wrath. At least he would've prevented me from making the other mistakes that I willingly ran into. "Still, that is not a justification for the condition his behaviour has put you in. If he didn't like what you were doing, he should've told you then – he should've done something about it."

"Like what?" Mom asked. "What would you have done?"

"I would've prevented my girlfriend from going anywhere. I would've prohibited it!"

"Oh, would you really?" Mom said with a loud scoff. "You would've stood up and confronted Brad Andersonn?" Dad didn't answer. "Apart from that, we both know how hard-headed and persuasive Jane can be when she wants something."

My heart panged. Despite the restrained distance in our relationship, my mother still knew me well.

"On top of all that," I continued, "there was the final match, and what I did with Matthias. I was reckless and stupid and surging with adrenaline. All I wanted was to congratulate them on the trophy. But it looked totally different to everyone, to Alex, even to Matthias. Everyone thought I had dumped Alex for the golden boy. It was only when Matthias tried to kiss me that I understood what I was doing, what a show I was providing the world. But it was too late."

"Yes, that was one of, if not *the* worst things you've ever done."

"Brad!"

"It's alright, Mom. He's right."

"I had to personally deal with the consequences of your whim. It took weeks to clear our name as much as possible. And still, those scavengers keep writing about you two." My father referred to the numerous articles about Matthias and me, even after all this time.

"I know. I cannot express how embarrassed I was, and still am, for that. I'm sorry."

"Being sorry is not enough." Dad's voice was level, but I could tell he was raging. "The word 'sorry' can never compensate for all the comments and questions I got from my partners at every business dinner. Same with Josephine at her company. They were all like vultures on us." I could feel tremors of fear rippling through my body, paralysing me. Maybe I would lose my name and family after all. Mom tried to interrupt Dad, but she didn't manage this time. He continued, "Do you know how many contracts I broke before summer even ended? All because I didn't want to tolerate those intruding, unprofessional bastards that I could benefit from?" He wasn't shouting; he sounded quite calm, actually. And that terrified me even more. I didn't know what to expect. "Thankfully, the inquiries dried up by September – on that end at least – and everything has been alright since then. But it was too close, Jane. Much too close for comfort."

I mustered the courage to look at him. "Dad, I don't know what to say except that I am aware of how stupid, reckless and inconsiderate I was, and that I will do everything I can so that you regain your trust in me."

Our eyes met, and in his I saw warmth. He put a hand on my shoulder. "It's all good now. It's over." He sighed, forcing the anger away in a familiar move. "Go on, Jane. Why didn't Alexander leave you after the incident in Berlin? Why did he take you with him to France?"

"Because, well, I hadn't cheated on him. It only looked like that. If he had broken up with me, it would've been admitting that I had. And he knew… he knows that I love him…" I started sobbing again. "And… and I know he loves me, too… But…"

"But sometimes, love is not enough," Mom said, pulling me into a hug.

I fell into a million pieces at the thought of two of us, Alex and me, once a perfect picture of how a couple should behave, look, love – and now, we were nothing, with thousands of kilometres separating us and light-years between our hearts.

*****

It took me a couple of excruciating days to convince Dad not to do anything to Alex. He understood me – he understood Alex, too – but he asked me to put myself in his shoes: His only daughter had spent the last two years physically and mentally derelict, in a terrible state, beyond recognition. Any parent would go after the culprit, regardless of where the blame truly lay.

In the end, I negotiated Dad into promising he wouldn't do anything without consulting me. Mom was right when she said I could be extremely persuasive. "Andersonn women always get what they want" was a legend in our family, which Mom and especially I stood up to.

Dad's promise didn't calm me as much as I'd hoped. I stopped taking sleeping pills for fear of getting addicted, and while I managed to fall asleep without them, I usually cried until I did so.

Bea, Lana and Angie came to see me as soon as they heard that I'd left Paris. The four of us cried together for days. They blamed themselves for not helping me, and no matter what I told them, they wouldn't change their opinion. They understood Alex – especially knowing the full story – but, just like my parents, they didn't think it was the right thing for him to have tortured me mentally all that time. Nevertheless, I knew I deserved it all. I tried endlessly to persuade them to that effect, that Alex actually hadn't done anything to me. He never shut me in the house, he never prohibited me from doing anything. He only behaved in a way that was justified after what I had done.

At the very beginning, I asked Bea not to tell Harold why Alex had been cold to me. Again, not because of myself, but out of respect to Alex. I didn't want people to know his girlfriend had cheated on him, especially since he hadn't told any of his friends, not even Luca Ferreira, his best friend. Since leaving France, I hadn't seen anything in the news, although I woke up every day expecting to see the title "*JANE AND ALEX SPLIT*" on my phone. Alex hadn't given any statements unrelated to sport, nor had he mentioned me in any interviews. As far as the public knew, everything was still alright between us.

Harold knew I had done something very bad. Not because Bea had told him any specifics – he would have been blind not to have seen how much I enjoyed myself at the German matches.

The girls stayed with me as long as they could. After ten days, Bea had to go for a shoot. Lana and Angie stayed for one more week, after which I persuaded them to go home and not neglect their jobs. They organised a plan to come and be with me in shifts, which cheered me up significantly.

Oscar, my oldest and dearest friend in Texas, was invaluable, too. In the beginning, I didn't want to see him. I was ashamed of my appearance, and he knew me too well not to suspect something grave had been going on. I couldn't lie to him. However, when I saw him the first time, I felt I could tell him everything.

I waited, though. I couldn't tell Oscar the truth in the house, where I might risk my parents or anyone else overhearing me. While the girls were visiting the ranch, I slowly started eating and going for short walks. By the time they'd all left, two-and-a-half weeks later, I was strong enough to go for brief horse rides.

I also understood that I had to tell Oscar everything for one more reason: I would've exploded if there was no one at the ranch who knew the full truth. I needed somebody who could completely understand me, entirely know me.

During the first ride Oscar and I took together, I confessed everything. Once we were far from our houses, deep into my property, I lit a fire and I opened up. I talked for ages in a nearly unbroken stream. The late-December cold started seeping in, so we snuggled under the same blanket, and I talked on. And on. Oscar listened carefully, patiently, without interrupting or judging. When I finished, gasping in tears, he hugged me.

"Oh, Lovely, you've always had all the attention from men. Didn't you know that? You will always have it. There was absolutely no need to share your body with them to confirm that. That Yanov is a great man."

I sobbed into Oscar's shoulder, so glad I had told him. He understood me and why I still loved Alex with all my heart – even though it was broken in suffering for him.

CHAPTER 2

Nothing much changed over Christmas and New Year's, except that I managed to put back on four kilograms. I also agreed to start doing some office work with Dad to divert my thoughts from Alex, at least for a while. I hoped that time would help me to begin not thinking about him every damn minute I was awake, but it seemed that every day was worse than the previous one.

Working in the office did help. I met people who didn't ask questions, who assisted me when I asked and who tried to make me feel comfortable there. I translated some contracts and prospects from Italian and Spanish, which was highly effective at diverting my thoughts for some time.

Oscar was immensely helpful. He spent all his free time around me, and also kept Vanessa and the Stevenson brothers at bay. I wasn't ready to talk to them, to face their concerned looks or hear their questions I couldn't answer. For the time being, the best path forward was for me to spend time in the office, at the ranch, and with Oscar.

By January, my parents and friends seemed optimistic that I was taking steps forward in my mental health. But one bit of news popped up early in the month that surprised me and entirely displaced me: Ben Schwimmer had moved to Paris to play for Alex's club. I knew how uncomfortable that would be for Alex, playing with someone from the German team – and a friend of Matthias's, at that – but I was grateful to every force in the universe that it wasn't Matthias himself who got transferred.

Fortunately, one week later, another headline took the world by surprise: Alex was moving to Madrid. He was to play for the best team in Spain. I knew his contract with the Parisians would expire just before the World Cup in Brazil (still a year and a half away), which meant that he had come to this decision abruptly. Nothing and no one could persuade me that Ben Schwimmer wasn't the reason. What could he possibly have told him? That question hounded me, hung over me. The stress resurfaced with a vengeance and I lost the kgs I had gained; my body felt too weak again.

I didn't watch Alex's games, of course. I knew doing so would further deteriorate my already fragile state, and I wanted to be better for my parents because every day I could see how much my bad health hurt them.

Another thing that surprised us all was that no one seemed to know that Alex and I had broken up. Journalists had no way of reaching me, and I didn't want to say anything or show up anywhere. When the press asked Alex about me, he simply didn't reply. I loved him more for that. Even when separated, he didn't want to damage my reputation. Dad and Mom noted that, too, and I couldn't help seeing on their faces how sorry they felt about us. They weren't angry at him any longer. They knew Alex cared like no man would normally care after being hurt like that. They believed again that he was the best man for me; they felt sorry he wasn't mine anymore.

In February, Mom suggested that I travel somewhere; maybe the two of us could get away, or at least me and the girls. I refused. I dreaded the idea of being surrounded by strangers, whether at airports or restaurants or anywhere beyond the fences of Andersonn Ranch. Instead, we went camping with Alejandro and Maribel, Oscar's parents. It was a lovely weekend. They were respectful and didn't ask much, but once we returned, I again plunged into a depression. My parents and friends didn't know any longer what to do with me.

Only the evenings with Dad helped. When we returned from his office in the city, we'd have dinner with Mom and then the two of us would head to the library. Dad would walk me through some financial books that helped me understand the graphs I had dealt with earlier in the day. I was embarrassed at how little I knew about the job that had given me the life of a princess. Even with all my effort and newfound appreciation, though, I couldn't make myself care about those numbers and figures, statistics and share management. I preferred modelling and acting, but whenever I thought about my career, I'd start sobbing again, knowing I couldn't go back. Reason #1: I was a corpse. Reason #2: I wasn't capable of even holding back tears in my daily life – forget posing attractively for a product.

I had to do something with my life. I knew that. It was now approaching late March – nearly three full years in which I hadn't done anything with my career. *Ha, my career! As if such a thing still existed.* But I wasn't capable of anything. The only thing I loved doing, I couldn't do. And most of the time I was awake, I was thinking about Alex and the life we could have had – but that I had destroyed. Would I ever forgive myself?

*****

Soon, spring was blossoming its way through the ranch, pulling some of the chill out of the air. I went for a horse ride. Dad let me go alone, under the condition that I had to have a meal before. I managed. I was willing to stomach anything to have some time alone with my horse, Honey. She seemed to understand everything I felt; every time I started crying, she would put her head close to my heart.

I went to the lake nearby, where I'd had so much fun with my Texas friends over the years. I'd never had a chance to show it to Alex. I was sure he would like it, too. It somehow soothed me to think that, bringing nice memories to the surface.

I remembered how almost three years ago Alex had surprised me by showing up at the ranch for my twentieth birthday. I was the happiest woman alive then. And now, my twenty-third birthday was approaching and I couldn't have been more miserable. Me, the famous Jane Andersonn! Who would believe such a thing?

I cried for what felt like hours. I wondered if all the tears I had been pushing down for years had really been collecting deep down inside me, and now they were surfacing in uncontrollable waves. At the end of every day, I would dry up as the tears ran out, and I would hope that was it – no more tears left from the reservoir, and tomorrow I would have nothing to cry out. But each morning I was mistaken. Every day it hurt more. What else could I do? I had seen Angie, Bea and Lana suffering for ex-boyfriends. I remembered them starving themselves, sobbing, spending nights on the couch watching action movies until dawn to divert their thoughts. But their pain receded within a few weeks. The longest sad spell belonged to Angie, when she couldn't put herself together after spotting the guy she was seeing at a bar with friends, behaving as if he were single. She was seriously down for a month, but then it was over. Time healed her, and soon she was even able to make jokes about him.

With me, it seemed completely different. Was I so much weaker than them? There were times I begged God to relieve me of the pain, to make me stop caring, to help me move on. My parents looked at me with worry and fear. I wasn't their confident, independent daughter anymore. Now they were afraid that any minute I could stumble over something and break into shards, as if I were made of glass. *Weak*.

In dark moments, I even thought of reaching out to Matthias. Perhaps his affection would make me feel better, make me feel loved, cherished, appreciated. Perhaps we could be together, and I could imagine that he was Alex – close my eyes and let him take care of me, and when I was almost fully recovered, I would open my eyes wide and start loving him. After all, it was my Mati. He would do anything for me. And I was sure that he had been troubling himself with questions over where I now was. I prayed Agnes still collected and threw away his letters so that Alex wouldn't find them and think we had been talking to each other. At the ranch, I had no cell phone. I used only the landline or my parents' phones to talk to the girls in London. Matthias had no way of reaching me.

But I couldn't reach him. I couldn't put Dad through more shame. Going to Matthias would be an admission that all those articles about us were true, that we had fallen in love from Day One of the tournament in Germany... that Alex was only a nuisance. The media would be on our side. Alex would be presented as a cruel and vengeful monster who kept us apart. This time my dad, I was sure, couldn't forgive me. And I hadn't forgotten the effort Alex made that last night in Berlin to save me, him, us, my family, from colossal shame. All that would amount to nothing. I couldn't do it to him. Not when he still was protecting me from afar by not mentioning me in the news except to say that everything was fine. I couldn't turn the world against him now.

Honey rested her head on my chest as I wept in front of the lake. When I dried up this time, the golden hour had just begun. The silhouettes of the trees in the distance seemed to have caught fire, struck by the gold of the sun and shaking gently in the spring breeze. Perched in the fiery branches, the birds chattered joyously, swooping and skimming the water. The water, too, shivered and swirled as the sun cast its last beams on it. Honey sniffed in approval. I stared. It was beautiful. Alex would find it beautiful, too. I missed him terribly, so much that I again felt that fist clenching my heart, twisting my lungs. I tried to inhale, but my breath was cut short by the pain. The colours of the sky were almost... no, they were exactly like that time Alex showed up on the horse.

"Like the last time."

I gasped. Blood rushed through my body and up to my head, instantly making me dizzy.

No, it can't be!

I turned.

If Honey hadn't also been looking at him, I would have thought I was hallucinating. He was standing a few metres behind me, squinting against the dying sunlight.

"May I join you?" he asked.

I nodded.

When he approached, his familiar scent surrounded me. I swallowed, grateful that I had no tears left to cry today.

He said, "Let's sit."

Clumsily, I went to a rock near the water and sat down. The stone was surprisingly cold for such a warm day. He sat next to me, close to me. I loved it... but my initial happiness quickly transformed into fear, because I didn't want him to disappear. Why was he here anyway? *I'm dreaming*, I thought. *I must be.*

But the stone under me was too real. This was not a dream.

"It's beautiful – how everything is lit up by the sun, and then extinguishes once it's gone," he said.

I couldn't reply, still puzzled that he was in front of me. A million thoughts rushed through my head. How was he here? Why? Perhaps my parents had made him come? Or maybe they'd been putting drugs into my food to relax me, and I was having the strangest, most vivid trip. Was he here to hurt me again, this time finally and forever?

I stared at him, my eyes wide open, my mouth agape.

The man of my life, the person my heart had been decaying for, the kindest and most genuine soul in this mad world, my ex-boyfriend — Alexander Yanov was sitting next to me.

When Alex turned to look at me directly, I finally understood he wasn't a hallucination. Nor had he been forced to come here. Everything was there, in those ocean blue eyes I had been crying for. His eyes were shining with suppressed tears, too, and the sight of them almost made me lose my mind. I wanted to jump at him and hug him, but I was paralysed with fear. *Is he here to hurt me again? Or...* my stomach flipped. *Or for something else?*

"Once you were gone, my whole life turned into exasperating darkness. I haven't felt whole for a second the last couple of months," Alex said.

It took time for my mind to process that. My eyes ran over him, eager to remember all his marks and features: his sandy blonde hair, his strong hands and rough fingers, those wide shoulders where I used to sleep peacefully, his arms that could lift me like a feather, the mole on his neck I liked to kiss, even the curve of his earlobe that I remembered by heart, the way he positioned his legs while he sat. Everything was there.

"I can't live like this any longer, Jane," he said, his voice almost breaking. He swallowed and continued, "I wish I could say I was sorry, but I cannot. I never hated you. I was fraught with anger, disappointment and pain. Those feelings took hold of me that last night in Berlin and numbed all my emotions towards you. I thought they would come back at some point, because having seen you, the state you were in in the hotel, I knew… I knew you were honest. I convinced myself that we would be fine, that everything would go back to normal after a couple of weeks once the tournament was over and we started a new life together – just two of us, away from those bastards. But, I couldn't stop seeing on you… everything that had taken place. Every time I looked at you, I saw a desirable woman everyone wanted. And couldn't help thinking how many of them had."

Turning my gaze away from him, I pushed back the tears and swallowed them like a colossal lump of wire.

"When I thought about leaving you, the feeling was worse," Alex continued. "Not because I was afraid of facing everyone, or perhaps that you would immediately go to Beller, but because I dreaded going to a home where you were not. Those two years, although terrible, I at least knew you were at home. That was selfish, but I couldn't cope with the situation any other way."

I knew what he was talking about. The same had been true for me all that time. Despite suffering every day, despite craving his touch and care, I still felt oddly satisfied to have him come home to me every night.

"I tried hating you. God knows how hard I tried. I told myself what every man in my shoes would – that I should move on, because somebody else would come along and fill the empty spot you left behind." I felt nausea at the thought of another woman with him. "However, that was out of the question. When some friends of the guys from the club tried talking to me, I felt repulsed, finding a billion flaws in them: their hair was too short, their skin too pale, their eyes too serious, their smile fake… They were all nothing compared to you. No matter how they looked. They were nothing."

Finally, warmth swam into my chest – a small, weak flame that relieved a bit of the clenching pain. I found the strength to look at him again.

"There was no way I could hate you." Alex stared out at the lake, looking close to tears. I could tell he had rehearsed this speech, that he had practised and battled for the right words. "But I couldn't reset my memory and get close to you again. Jane, I was afraid. I thought… I thought that if I tried to touch you, I'd be doing something wrong. You asked for that from the other men, so it must have been something I wasn't good at giving you. I thought if I even tried, you'd run away from me…to one of them."

Shock and disbelief broke through my paralysis, and I jumped off the stone. I knelt down in front of him and pressed a hand over his lips gently, putting a stop to the rest of his speech.

"Alexander, don't even dare think that, let alone say it out loud. Ever again." Alex closed his eyes and one tear spilled out, running down his cheek and sliding over my fingers. It took all my strength not to start crying. "What I did has nothing – listen to me – nothing to do with you. You were, you *are* a perfect friend, boyfriend, man. How you touched me, from that first day when you handed me your jersey and I felt your skin, to the modest kisses at Heathrow before that rainy afternoon in the hotel when we hit it off, and every next time... you were a perfect and loving man. You are what any woman could wish for." I sat back, inhaling deeply, drawing my fingers from his face. "I was the problem. I am the problem."

That was our first physical contact in months. My fingers on his lips. Damn, it felt divine. I tried to absorb it, commit it to memory, but when the reality hit me that perhaps this pleasant feeling would never happen again, I felt the familiar bile coming up my throat.

"We met at the wrong time," he said.

I met his eyes. "How do you mean?"

"You had been controlled by your father your whole life. You listened to him, feared him, made sure everything you did was appropriate and that he'd never be ashamed of you. Men didn't even approach you, they were so scared of him. We both know the difference between him and my father. Maria has never been under pressure like you. When we went to Germany, it was your first chance to unleash. It's ironic, because your father was there all the time, but those bastards planned well. And later, well, you went into it all by yourself. You liked the attention you were getting because you hadn't got it before."

He'd really thought about this. I stared at him in wonder, remembering what Gottfried told me that day near the end of the tournament: *You will keep searching for love in other men in order to compensate for what you missed out on when you were a child.*

"Am I wrong?" Alex asked, not without gentleness.

"No. It's just that..." I had to find the words. How had we never had this conversation before? "I love my father. I want him to be happy and proud. I'm his only child. That's my duty. He's given me everything. I am what I am because of him."

"Yes, that's true," he admitted. "But some things, he could've done differently. You needn't have been so frightened for most of your existence."

"It was necessary, Alex. Otherwise, I'd have disappointed—"

"Have Maria and I disappointed our parents?" he cut in. I fell silent. "Trust me, we were never afraid of them. We had arguments, disagreements, fights, but they gave us love and reassurance. We all knew that nothing we ever did would harm them, not really. The love of a parent isn't conditional." I shook with goosebumps. "He should've trusted you more, Jane. Then none of this madness would have happened."

My throat was dry. My next words were painful, as if they clawed their way out against my will. "We cannot blame him…"

"I know, we can't, but that doesn't mean he's not at fault. You, too. Because despite everything, you did have a will of your own."

"I'm sorry, Alex." My voice was shaky; my throat was raw. "If there was a way to turn back time and change things, I'd have done it a long time ago. Ever since we left Berlin, I've spent every minute of every day regretting what I'd done. And since I left Paris, it's been even worse, more intense. I thought it would pass. I prayed for it to pass, but it hasn't. Every day since we moved in together, I've been wishing that somehow I could make it up to you, correct my wrongdoings, and it's bloody killing me that I can't. I even thought… I even thought about reaching out to Matthias, only to make this pain stop, to make my parents stop worrying and looking at me as if I was made of glass. But I knew that would never work. It would never stop the pain. Not even temporarily. I swear, every morning, day, night, I beg for the life we had before Germany. Just you and me."

I fell apart again. The pain was excruciating, worsened by the fact that I had no idea what was going on. Why was he here? Why was he telling me all this? Was this some final confrontation to end it all, once and for good?

"I know," Alex said after a long pause.

I forced myself to look at him again.

"I know you could've gone to him every day since we arrived in Paris, and every day I wondered why you didn't." Alex turned to me, his face now serious and clear of tears. "After you said goodbye and got in the taxi that morning, I instantly understood what I had done. Once you were gone, thick darkness entered that house. I swear I could see it creeping in the corners, especially in the bedroom. I know I didn't come near you, but while you were there, hearing your breathing made it easier. Somehow, you were still mine, even though I couldn't make myself touch you." His serious expression deepened further, twisting into frustration. "I thought moving to a new city would change things, that I would finally move on. But the moment I walked into the apartment in Madrid, I realised that escaping Paris was in vain. I could see you everywhere, in every corner of every room, even though you'd never been there. It didn't help realising that you actually hadn't looked for Matthias or anyone else in all these months. It made me more aware of the mistake I had made. Sometimes I even hoped that you'd show up, tell me that you'd changed your mind and come to look for me, but I knew that was not possible. Not now that your parents are aware of how the situation between us is... was."

"They don't know," I managed to say.

It was his turn to ask, "How do you mean?"

"I only told them I had done something really bad and that your reaction was natural. I didn't mention the details. Dad was furious, of course, but I did everything in my power to keep him away from you. The main thing stopping him is that you've been protecting me all this time from the journalists. He appreciates that immensely."

"That part was more selfish than generous." Alex sighed. "I couldn't make myself say in public that you'd left me. I knew what havoc that would've caused, and I just wanted to avoid it and all the drama that goes with it. But mostly I didn't want to accept that we were not together."

"It counts, nonetheless."

"I guess, since he didn't kill me when he saw me."

"Yeah, that's the sign."

We both, finally, managed a weak twitch of the lips that resembled a smile. That was my Alex in front of me. I wished so badly that I could hug him.

"Jane, I can't live in that darkness anymore." He took a deep breath and exhaled painfully. "It's suffocating me from all sides, everywhere. The only place I can relax for a while is on the pitch, but the moment I'm off the grass, it presses on me mercilessly. God knows I tried to reset, to get you out of my mind, but it never worked. It's just gotten worse since the day you left." I almost nodded in agreement, knowing exactly how it felt. "I will never be able to move on, Jane. Remembering how you stayed by me, despite the fact that you could easily have gone to *him*, and remembering everything that we had been before that bloody month, I simply cannot hate you. I cannot make myself believe that the Jane I love is fake."

My chest squeezed in pain. *Love.* Not *loved.*

"She was never fake when it was about you," I said. "I never lied about my feelings for you. What I did while I wasn't with you came from some different part of me, a stone-cold part without feelings. A part I don't recognise. But whatever we did together, every minute we spent together, I was honest with you. You were the first and only man who swept me off my feet without a single word. Nobody has ever made me feel like you did that night at Wembley. Everything we have created together was pure, innocent, real. When I started loving you, I felt I had loved you before I'd even met you, because you were the perfect, wonderful soul I had been looking for. I know I screwed up like no woman has ever screwed up. So know that I have no reason to lie to you again. By leaving Paris, I lost everything. I've been trying desperately to start living again, but I'm not able to. I can, however, swear on my life, my father, mother, friends, everything and everyone, that I loved you with all my soul, I still do, and I will never be able to move on without you."

The weight of the words I'd just uttered pressed me into the ground. I started sobbing, gasping and crying again. My vision blurred so that I couldn't see him anymore.

And again, I didn't know what was happening. Why was he here? Why were we putting each other through this? Weren't those two years enough? After this encounter, I would go back to the corpse I was when I arrived in Texas, or even worse. Why would—

"I came for you, Jane."

*****

I don't know how long it took me to comprehend what I'd heard, even my breathing, clean my eyes and face with the sleeve of my jumper, and look at him – seconds, perhaps, or maybe minutes.

His ocean-blue eyes were full of love, sorrow and warmth when I met them. "I know we've suffered a lot. But life, separated, is not doing any good to either of us. If you think we can still move on, together, and be what we once were, come with me. Come with me to Madrid, Jane."

As every word slid out of his mouth, I took it in like a desperate wanderer devouring drops of water in the desert. When Alex said my name with that familiar care and fondness, a new wave of tears overwhelmed me – tears of love, joy, and, finally, relief. I was too confused and stunned to move, but I saw his arm reaching out to me. The next moment, I was sitting in his lap, sobbing, shaking, squeezing him, running my hands over his back and through his hair while his strong arms encircled me entirely. His scent was all around me, creating a bubble of comfort. For so long, I'd known I needed his touch to feel better; now that it had finally come, I felt as if I were drinking out of a well of youth, life and health. His face pressed against my neck, and the feeling of his breath on my bare skin brought me back to life.

Still, I was afraid to rush.

"Alex, are you for real? Are you truly here?"

"Yes, love, I am." He was crying. "I am here, and I'm never letting you go again."

I had to take his face in my hands and look him in the eyes again to make sure that he was real, that those words came from him. It was him. He was there, full of love and care. My Alex. He was true.

I squeezed him with all the power in my body. We stayed there, holding each other, as the sun fell out of the sky and the moon rose in its place. After crying for so long, I finally felt tired of all that pain. I wanted to sleep, and my eyes itched, fighting to close. But I was afraid that if I shut them, Alex would disappear – because he was a dream, or he changed his mind, or Dad kicked him off the ranch. So I blinked, fighting back the exhaustion.

Once darkness had fully fallen, we opened up even more. We both needed that to be able to move on. When a couple goes through what we had been through, they need the utmost confidence in each other – they need to know everything.

Alex knew most of it already. Before Germany, I was young, under protection for twenty years, devoid of proper attention from men. I didn't know what life was or that my reckless actions could bring about serious consequences. I thought nothing and no one could ever stop me, because nothing and no one ever had.

After Alex told me his point of view, I loved him even more (even though I thought it hardly possible to). He saw in me what he always wanted in a woman. Even if I was nowhere near as good-looking as I was, he'd still love me, he said. He loved how we talked, how I understood his jokes and stories from his childhood growing up in a country where not everything was legal and free of corruption – I understood, even though I shouldn't have because I had always lived in a bubble. Alex told me he'd felt even more sure about me after I met his parents and sister, who didn't adore me simply because I seemed nice, but rather because they had carefully observed how I talked to him and reacted to his touch in public, the stories he told, how I behaved at his games or when I wasn't with him. They still never suspected me of anything. They knew we had a problem, but they hadn't thought it was something serious. All this time, they believed that whatever it was, we could fix it, because we were meant for each other. I was thankful for all the forces that had painted this nice picture of me for them.

At the same time, we had both been telling ourselves to give up on each other and move on. But neither of us had the courage to take the first step. The curious public eye didn't make it easier, but even without it, it would have been the same. We spent four months apart, and instead of receding, the pain had been increasing, poisoning our minds and bodies.

"You know, I even tried to make up a scenario in which we would meet after the World Cup," Alex said. "I imagined that you did all that, perhaps were interested in Beller, but in that semi-final match, when I would win – because, well, we were a better team – you'd notice me. I'd probably do the same thing as at Wembley, and we'd hit it off. I'd get the trophy, and you, and it would be a nice summer fairy tale. Perhaps you'd still go on with Beller, but, somehow, I don't think it'd last for too long. Every time I played out that scenario in my mind, I couldn't help concluding that in the end, you and I would always find each other." He turned to me and smiled. "Is that crazy?"

I couldn't smile back. Adoration swelled up in my eyes, face and body. I sat in his lap, took his hand and put it on my heart, and placed my other hand on his face.

"I love you, Alexander Yanov. Forever and always. If you give me a chance, I will go above and beyond to make you happy. I will commit myself to you and you only. Not anyone else, not even my father. I will give my entire self to making you happy as you deserve..."

"Jane, I don't want you to—"

I put a finger on his lips. "I'm not saying I'll give up on anything or anyone. I will still love and respect my parents. But *you* will be my number one priority. If, by any chance Dad says 'Jane, you go with me here' and I think you won't like it, I won't go. I won't neglect my career and sit at home waiting for you with an apron on and lunch ready." Alex laughed softly at the image. "But I need you to live. Next to you, I am a better person. I grow."

He smiled, cupped my face in his big, strong hands. In the dark, I saw his eyes shining in the moonlight. Finally, I saw it. I felt it again.

"I need you, too. To live and exist. To fulfil my being," Alex said and drew me into a kiss.

Every nerve of my body reacted to the touch of his lips. First in surprise, because the sensation had been absent for years. But then our bodies remembered it all, and familiar excitement, bliss and tremors rushed through my blood vessels, absorbing me entirely. I hugged him harder, moaning with desire that had been suppressed for too long.

Finally, he was back. My Alex.

*****

It took three days of incessant negotiation and persuasion for Dad to allow Alex and me to come back together. Mom was reluctant, too, but she quickly took our side after seeing how my complexion had improved after just a few hours with Alex. She was the one who prevented Dad from attacking Alex the moment his arrival was announced by Sophie. Dad came down from his office furious as a lion and ready to kill with his bare hands. Thankfully, Sophie had informed Mom, too, who immediately called for Arnold, our ranch foreman. Arnold prevented any further incidents by separating my dad from Alex. I knew Alex was stronger than Dad and Arnold together, so I could only imagine how he felt unable to defend himself against the most dangerous man in the world. My love for him seemed to be increasing boundlessly.

The four of us sat in Dad's office. I was on the sofa, holding Alex's hand and afraid that if I let go for a single second, Dad might call our security workers to take him out. The conversation started with Dad shouting threats and *how-could-yous* at Alex, who kept silent while I defended him in a weak voice.

"Dad, I told you, it's not his fault—"

"Jane, have you seen yourself in the mirror over the past five months? You look half-dead. And I, your father, have been doomed to watch it every single day since you came here. Not this jealous kid here!"

I will never understand how Alex managed to stay calm with words like that being thrown at him. It went on and on, until, thankfully, Mom put an end to it.

"Brad, your daughter is not a saint," she said, interrupting another wave of anger directed at Alex. Dad fell silent, and all three of us looked at her. "I know how much you love her. *Your only daughter, your perfect Jane, your gem.* I am her mother. I love her, too," she said fiercely. "But you cannot turn a blind eye to what she did. The whole world saw it, for god's sake. You can't pretend she's completely innocent in this."

It hurt, even though I was grateful for it. My mother's words reminded me of my teenage days, when she'd reprimand me for not studying *something serious* so that I could continue what the two of them had begun, when she'd deprecate my modelling jobs and successes, when I wasn't a good enough daughter for her. But if her words would save Alex from Dad, I was thankful.

"Josephine, how can you say that?" Dad's furore still wasn't dissipating. "Can't you see what state she's in?"

"I can see she's significantly better since Alexander showed up here."

Surprisingly, Dad fell silent. Mom took a breath, and I knew she was about to say something atypical for her. She had always been a strong and powerful woman. Otherwise, Brad wouldn't love her and certainly wouldn't have married her; plus, she wouldn't be able to manage him. But she rarely let that strength rear its head – especially not in front of company. Mom approached Alex and me, but focused on him.

"Listen to me, Yanov. I know my daughter is difficult, hard-headed and complicated. I swear, when I met you, I thought, 'Oh my, this nice kid must have extremely strong nerves to control this wild beast.' But you seemed to manage. However, I was at that World Cup. I saw for myself what happened, and I see what has become of her. I don't justify her actions, but I'm her mother, and this stubborn, impulsive man is her father. We want all the best for her, despite everything. I can see how your presence here has already improved her health, so I believe it's best if you go on with what you have planned." Her eyes narrowed with holy fury. "*However*, if I don't see Jane improve over the next few weeks, and if I discover she is not happy with you, I swear on my life, I will put an end to you two."

We both swallowed, our hands sweating in each other's grip.

"Yes, Mrs Andersonn," Alex said. In any other situation, that would've made me laugh, but not then.

Just when I was thinking it wasn't fair for my mom to put all the blame and responsibility on Alex, she turned to me. "And you, Jane. I believe you have grown up in the last couple of months and that you understand the gravity and weight of your actions. You had always been careful about how you behaved…but that summer, something got into your head and you went berserk. You always managed to get away with anything because this man protected you." She pointed at Dad, who was watching this exchange with something akin to amusement. "But no more, Jane. You are not a child. You are a woman. You were a woman then, too. You should've known better. But we can't cry over spilled milk, so we must move on. I hope you are aware of your behaviour and that in the future you will take full responsibility for it." I opened my mouth to protest, but she cut me off before I spoke. "Yes, I understand you did that already when you suffered in Paris for two years. But this is the real recompense – to do the right thing now. Not just do wrong and feel bad. If you fail, you two are over, I promise you this: I'm not going to watch you go through bulimia, depression and breakdowns again."

I was flabbergasted by her speech, but more than anything, I was impressed. Alex squeezed my hand.

"Yes, Mom," I uttered.

She then straightened up and turned to Brad, who was bent on his desk, observing her admiringly.

"Do you have anything to add?" she asked him.

Dad cleared his throat. "Nothing at all. I couldn't have said it better."

Alex and I exhaled in relief. The discussion was soon over, and this time Alex and I understood we were either to give our best to work things out, or the next breakup would be our last one.

I finally felt hunger, and for the first time in months, the thought of food didn't evoke nausea. I was shy to suggest it, so I thanked the heavens when Sophie, god bless her, knocked and announced that her dinner had been waiting for us, and Mom suggested we show respect to the hardworking woman.

I felt like a little five-year-old when I saw how impressed and relieved Dad and Mom were seeing me finish my plate of fish and steamed vegetables, my first proper meal in weeks. At first, Dad didn't want to allow Alex to sleep at the ranch, but seeing how white my face went at the suggestion of Alex leaving for the night, he changed his mind. I was afraid that if I separated from Alex for even five minutes, he might never come back, or perhaps everything would turn out to be a dream. Thankfully, that wasn't the case.

That first night together after five terrible months of separation – two years of it, really – had some magic to it. Sophie, excited that I had finally eaten something other than blended vegetables without vomiting, prepared us hot chocolate and butter cookies, and we snuggled under the blanket in my bed. "Make sure you finish them all, or you're not leaving this room," Sophie said affectionately before closing the door.

When we were alone, I sat in Alex's lap and hugged him, loving the feeling of his arms all around me. I needed to stay there for some more time, to persuade my mind he was really there, gentle, loving and kind, like before Paris. My body seemed to be drawing energy and strength from his, which was amazingly firmer and even more muscular than the last time I'd touched him. It excited me, but it also made me sad because it reminded me why he had spent so much time in the gym – it was all the free time he would otherwise have spent with me.

"Tell me about Madrid," I asked, and he did, in the soothing voice of an audiobook storyteller. He shared with me all the nice details he could remember: the weather, the architecture of the city, the warmth with which the club management and members welcomed him, the spacious and bright apartment in Barrio Salamanca, the car that came with the contract as well, the shopping streets, old-fashioned restaurants on the Plaza Mayor, little antique shops where he'd bought a few pieces and paintings, the parks he went running through, the Manzanares River by which he liked to walk. I'd been in Madrid before, so I could mostly picture what he described to me, which intensified my excitement that this beautiful city would be our new home, the place where we would start over again, the blank page on which we would write only pleasant, wonderful memories.

Sometime far after midnight, feeling exhausted after what had felt like the longest day of the year so far, we decided to go for a bath – together, since we didn't want to lose sight of each other for a second. He was filling the bathtub with water, adding the scented salts and removing his clothes. Behind his back, I was doing the same, but shyly. I felt like we were about to have sex for the first time. After being emotionally distant for two and a half years, even this simple step had the taste of something new.

Excited at that, I wrapped myself in my bathrobe until he finished drawing the bath and undressing. When he turned, I slowly removed the white robe, my skin trembling in anticipation of being against his.

But when he saw me, the look on his face instantly changed. I shook with fear. "For god's sake," Alex gasped.

Then I remembered. He wasn't disgusted by my body. He wasn't remembering how many other men had once touched it. I was so joyous and happy that he was back, that I'd completely forgotten that I was now barely forty-two kg. A corpse.

"What have I done..." he whispered.

I dropped the bathrobe to the floor and approached him, placing my arms over his neck. "No, Alex, it's alright."

"It's not alright. Have you seen yourself?" He was crying. "I don't know how I haven't noticed it before." He hugged me, carefully, as if he feared he'd break me. Large tears ran down his reddening cheeks.

It was my turn to be strong. I made him sit in the hot water, and I placed myself in his lap, encircling him with my legs, my hands in his hair. He hid his face in my half-wet hair. "I swear I didn't see it until now," he sobbed guiltily.

"Of course, you didn't. There was no chance for that."

"I am so sorry, Jane."

I took his face between my palms. "Listen to me, Alexander. Nothing, absolutely nothing, is your fault. All this that you see – I've done this to myself. Me and only me. It's alright now. You are here. You came for me. The nightmare is over."

The bath was so pleasant, and our bodies were so exhausted from all the stress, apologies, tears, joys and thankfulness, that when we left it and hid under the blankets, naked, we fell into a twelve-hour dreamless sleep. When I put my head on his chest and felt his arm on my back, I finally felt utterly, purely, entirely happy like I hadn't been since July, almost three years ago.

*****

One week later, we were on a plane to Madrid. Dad wanted to keep us longer at the ranch so that he could see for himself how Alex treated me, but Alex had to go back to Spain for two important games. The best goalkeeper in the world wasn't supposed to miss out on much for personal reasons. "Not even when they include your precious daughter," Mom told Dad jokingly, which again softened him.

I was shining with happiness and radiating positivity. I wore my new best dress that covered all the sharp edges of my hips, knees and shoulders. I had already arranged a meeting with a doctor in Madrid who would examine me to see if everything was alright after so much neglect and malnourishment; then I was scheduled with a nutritionist and a personal trainer. I was thrilled to get back into the best shape possible. I had everything now that I had Alex back.

When I phoned the girls to tell them the good news, they started shouting and screaming. Angie even disappeared into the kitchen, only to come back a few seconds later spraying champagne all over the room.

"Lana, do you think I'm ready to take some opportunities now?" I asked her. Though I'd considered my career dead, it actually had some life left – the papers had never stopped writing about me, especially about my absence. Lana, still my personal manager, had been dealing with all the inquiries and offers that kept coming despite everything.

"Finally, you're asking." She was grinning hugely. "There's a huge pile of offers I could say yes to right now and you'd be busy for the next ten years."

I squeaked with joy. "Alright. Pick the best three. We'll do them one by one, in between my training and the time I spend with my man."

Our arrival in Madrid was quiet and unnoticed; I was grateful to whoever was responsible for that. Relaxed, we drove to Alex's apartment close to his team's training grounds. Two more players from his team lived with their girlfriends in the same building, so I decided to say hi as soon as I settled.

Since Alex was scheduled to have extensive daily training, we thought it was best to have the girls with me those first few days. I was still afraid that everything was some hallucination or a dream induced by some strong drugs my parents had gotten for me. Having Bea, Lana and Angie around most of the time Alex was away was a lifesaver. We went for endless shopping sprees, bought decorations and furniture for the apartment, visited hidden coffee shops and salons, and even took photos with fans who recognised us but weren't too intruding or aggressive. Everything was coming back to normal.

The girls didn't stay with us in the apartment, even though there was space. They wanted to give us privacy and freedom to continue where we had left off. A couple of times, they left before Alex was back from training; in those few minutes of being alone, I would be again overcome with fear that he was not coming back. I would start imagining that he must have given up on everything. However, when the front door would creak open, I'd jump from the sofa and run to welcome him like an excited puppy.

One week after we arrived in Madrid, I was finally convinced that there was nothing to worry about, that my man was there to stay. It was Sunday, and he was playing an important game in the Spanish league. I attended it – the first one after Germany. Needless to say, it caused havoc on the stands. Lana was with me as support for my big comeback. (Bea and Angie had to return to London for work.) I made sure I looked impeccable in an orange dress that covered all my deficiencies and professionally done hair and makeup. Later on, when we went through the photos from the game, we saw I looked wonderful; but it was not because of the dress, but rather how truly, sincerely happy I was within.

The game was excellent for Alex's team, who won 2–0 against their big enemy. Towards the end, heavy clouds covered the open stadium and thick showers made sure every inch of my dress was soaked. I could've gone off the stands, but that was out of the question. My man was there in the rain, so I was in the rain, too.

When the final whistle sounded, I couldn't take my eyes off of Alex, who looked magnificent – his jersey wet and stuck to his perfect body, his hair now the colour of dark sand. After he chatted and greeted the other players, he started towards the tunnel, but then turned to look for me. I knew he was remembering I was actually there for a change. He then removed his jersey and walked towards me. My insides swirled with excitement. I knew what was on his mind. This was another step in our new beginning. He would do the same thing he had done at Wembley.

When Alex jumped over the fence and pressed the green jersey into my hands, I was beaming, not stunned like that time.

He cupped my face. "I missed you, Jane," he whispered into my ear, where no camera or bystander could pick it up.

My heart was about to pound its way out of the chest. We were so enthralled in each other that everything around us was muted. Only later would we see what a show we were for the people at the stadium – and the whole world, in fact. That badass, cliché, perfect couple: footballer and model, happy together again.

Back in the apartment, Lana stayed with me until Alex returned from the post-match press conference. We were skimming through the articles that were already rolling in – loving them and the public's reaction that was so positive at the sight of the two of us bristling with joy in each other's company – when I heard the front door. Lana packed up rapidly, congratulated Alex on the win and disappeared before we could invite her for a drink or snack. She didn't even let me escort her to the door.

When Lana was gone, Alex and I were standing in the middle of the living room. Barefoot and in pyjamas, I felt sensitive, exposed, full of desire for him and his touch. In his team tracksuit, Alex was smiling at me, his face drawn with determination and longing. For me.

"Are you hungry?" I half-whispered, goosebumps spreading all over me at the thought that this man would sleep in the same bed as me.

"Not at all, thank you," he replied.

I recognised that shine in his wonderful, ocean-blue eyes, and I blushed. "Should I fix you a hot bath?"

"No, darling. You can just get ready for bed." He dropped his bag to the floor and approached me. His hand went to my back, pulling me to his chest. Our eye contact didn't drop. He kissed me. A wildfire burned throughout my insides.

"Alright," I said quietly. "I'll wait for you."

"Please do."

My legs and joints were jelly from all the expectation – for a moment, I worried I might trip over the carpet on my way to the bedroom. Fortunately, I didn't.

When I closed the door behind me, I crouched, inhaled deeply ten times and started thinking. We hadn't made love for such a long time. Did I even know how to do it? How should I behave? I wanted him. My whole body ached for him. But should I show it or not? Should I give him everything I had been dreaming of, or be calm and let him do whatever he wanted with me? Should I wear sexy lace or regular underwear? Maybe sexy wasn't appropriate. But if I wore something everyday, perhaps he'd think I didn't want to dress up for him.

Burning with contradictory thoughts, I went to the bathroom and washed my face with ice-cold water. I looked at myself in the mirror. "Be how you feel, Jane. You cannot be fake with him," I said aloud.

I removed my pyjamas and stayed in simple, white, cotton underwear. I switched all the lights off except for one bedside lamp, which I diffused as much as possible so he couldn't see on my face how terrified I was, and I hid under the blanket.

When Alex came in, I didn't speak. I only observed him putting away his clothes. He kept only his boxers on; I sighed loudly. I was nervous with lust, frightened by the fire rising in my lower belly. He crawled into bed, and my breathing accelerated. My ears were deafened by the rushing of blood through my body as my heart pumped harder and harder. The moment he took me by the arm and turned me to face him, my body electrified. I stared at his eyes that shone with love, and I couldn't help diving into the beauty of his closeness. His hair, his chest, his scent, everything in my view was perfect. Like he always had been. I touched his smooth skin, enjoying its feel under my fingertips, while he drew a finger from the corner of my eye, over my cheek, lips, jawline, neck, down past my breast, my nipple, stopping on my waist. I couldn't stay still. I moved under his arm and pulled myself into his lap. We straightened, and he now relied on the back of the bed, his hands on my shoulder blades as he pressed his lips onto mine.

My limbs were shaking, wanting to take all of him in. But he didn't seem to want to rush, although I could feel at the bottom of my belly how much he wanted me. We didn't talk; we communicated with our eyes. He unlatched my bra and helped me out of it. I felt vulnerable, but more than anything I felt lustful. Gently, he put a hand in my hair and relaxed me back on his arm, so that he could place kisses over my neck and down the line where my cleavage used to be. I was shaking with desire. When he sucked my nipples, one after the other and back again in perfect waves, knowing exactly how I liked it, I couldn't help moaning. I felt a tear form in the corner of my eye and slide down my cheekbone. His touch was pure bliss, and I came in several waves.

I wanted to respond equally, to give him the same amount of pleasure, to show him that I had missed him and wanted him all this time. But he didn't let me. He was the leader now. And I didn't mind. I loved it all, as I had always loved whatever he would do to my body.

He placed me on my back and then lay over me, his muscular arms pressed solidly against both my sides. I shivered at the sight of this man's strength and power that he could exercise over me. At the same time, I felt scared – what if he stopped again? It wouldn't be completely unexpected. What would I do then?

Alex kissed my forehead, my nose, my cheeks, the corners of my lips, my chin, then my waiting lips. He moved down to my neck again, covered my breasts with more kisses, moved around my navel. I was a thousand degrees hot and wondering how my skin wasn't melting. With his tongue, Alex drew a line over my belly before moving even further downwards. I felt his warm fingers on the side of my hips and thighs. Slowly, he slid my underwear down my legs, and then he removed his boxers, too.

My breathing was intermittent with moans, but in my mind, fear still wafted around. I closed my eyes, begging him not to stop, not to get scared or dejected again. I wasn't sure I would be able to take it after all this.

I felt him lay over me, surrounding me again with his colossal arms. He patted my hair.

"Jane…"

I forced my eyes open. Alex was there, those ocean-blue eyes in mine. My fears and worries dispersed. He was mine, as he had been a long time ago. As he would always be. Regardless of everything. Despite everything.

With new confidence, similar to that of the old Jane Andersonn, I moved under him and let him enter me.

It hurt slightly, as if I were a virgin, for many reasons: I hadn't been touched for too long, and he hadn't been that excited for the same time. I wanted to smile, to laugh hysterically, to cry in this insignificant pain worth worlds of pleasure. I was sensitive, vibrant; every move he made pushed me higher towards the pinnacle of the utmost bliss. My body wasn't sure if it could take it all, but my mind knew it would – because it used to, years ago.

When I felt brave and strong enough, I moved under him, changing the rhythm and putting us another step closer to the orgasm we both craved. We started swaying together, as if dancing perfectly synchronised. Whatever was happening in me, I saw the same in the depth of his eyes. Only a moment more and we reached the top, simultaneously, the same length, same breath. The familiar liquid bliss dispersed through me and I began crying with joy.

When he relaxed onto me, I hugged him as hard as my muscle-less body was capable of. He was indeed back. My Alex. And I was his – fully, only his.

CHAPTER 3

It took three months of regular eating and exercise to get back to a weight and shape I was satisfied with. I would've put on the weight faster, had it not been for my health problems. As expected, my blood results came back bad, as did the exams on the general state of my body. But I wasn't scared. I took responsibility for my actions, as Mom said, and did everything required to recover and be the Jane Andersonn everyone knew.

Lana arranged a couple of interviews and short projects to ease me back in, and I enjoyed doing them even more than I'd hoped. To be on the safe side, she made sure nobody could ask any detailed questions about the weight loss or my absence for the previous two years. Only shallow questions were allowed, to which the answers were only specific enough to satisfy – Paris hadn't gone down very well with me; I felt lost being away from London and my friends; I found the language extremely difficult; I was upset by the articles following the World Cup and the incident with Matthias, which was only a friendly congratulation for the trophy; all of these situations took a large toll on me and my health. I understood my overt friendliness had been perceived in the wrong way, which wasn't fair to the amazing boyfriend I had, so I had to quiet down for a while.

However, in this new, Spanish chapter, one thing was different from before – all my arrangements, jobs and interviews were now organised around Alex and his games. Alex's matches were my number one priority, whenever and wherever he played, whether in Spain or with the Ukrainian national team. I knew it contradicted the independent woman I had always striven to be. But the months in Texas had shown me who I was without him. With him, though – with him I could conquer the world again.

Lana chose projects for me carefully. I did one at a time, exercised, ate a proper diet, slept and rested, and accompanied my man wherever he went. I was back on magazine covers, shopping mall windows and even runways, and he was proud of me. I also took up a project with a Ukrainian pop group, appearing in their music videos and helping expose them to an audience outside the borders of their country. As I had been doing before, I continued learning basic Ukrainian so I could manage a couple of simple sentences when I visited or met Alex's friends. I wanted from every part of my heart to make him happy. His family was over the moon to see that everything between us was alright again. I will never stop being thankful to Alex for not telling them about our secret breakup and the reasons behind it. He successfully covered it all up, and I loved him immensely. This man was perfect.

We spent two weeks in Texas over the summer. That was Dad's requirement – he wanted to see for himself how I was doing. After he approved of my new look and constantly joyous mood, we were "allowed" to spend some time in Ukraine with Alex's family. Soon afterwards, the new football season started. To my immense relief, none of the players I had been involved with were moved to Alex's team, or any team in Spain. For now, there was only Paulo Reis, playing for the best team of Valencia, with whom I had spent only one extremely wild night induced by Portuguese wine. There were a couple of games, though, when Alex played against Robin Braam's and Friedrich Larsson's team, but they ended peacefully, without any uncomfortable inconveniences.

As for the situation in Germany, Rolf Gottfried was still the coach of the national team – and still a very good one. He never suffered after what he said about me in the semi-final against Ukraine, and most of the media in the country firmly believed him. Dad tried to go after him, but the furthest he managed was to get Gottfried fined for slander, which he disgustedly refused. To add insult to injury, the media was also on Matthias's side. They still wrote about us as star-crossed lovers who had secretly been together throughout the World Cup month, and that Alex was the main bad guy who wouldn't let us be together. That stemmed, of course, from the fact that they couldn't forgive him for not stepping down in front of their legendary goalkeeper, Dieter Lahrmann, who they desperately wanted to get the Golden Glove at his last tournament. Alex hadn't cared about that; he had just kept winning every possible award he could get.

What troubled me more than anything was, of course, Matthias. That man never gave up. Judging by Alex's behaviour, he never found any of the letters Matthias sent to me in Paris – god bless Agnes. In Texas, Matthias had no way of reaching me. However, a couple of weeks after we arrived in Spain, I started receiving flowers and messages. Thankfully, I managed to read and dispose of them before Alex ever saw them. I couldn't reply to anything, not that I was now a faithful and loving girlfriend. I was not getting involved in that story again. Matthias even found ways of reaching me through my email and phone number, and even though I always ignored and blocked him, he kept getting new emails and numbers.

His persistence troubled me beyond the threat it posed to my relationship; it was plain to see from Matthias's words that he still cared. Since rekindling things with Alex, I had been repeating to myself that that crazy man was indeed out of my mind. I had nothing to do with him. Surely, he would have to stop at some point. However, the weeks dragged into months, and Matthias didn't recede – quite the opposite. I expected something from him at least once a week. Lana was working hard to control who had my personal information and prevent sharing it, but Matthias always found a way. "Damn German thoroughness," she said with an irritated exhale once, almost making me laugh.

Surprisingly, Alex and I talked about him, from time to time. It was always Alex who'd broach the topic, and I'd reply. I didn't want to avoid it, even though it was uncomfortable in the beginning. Alex deserved honesty from me, and that was what I gave him.

"Jane, I have to ask you something," Alex said one evening while we were sitting on the balcony, the busy city swarming under us. "I just want to be sure about it, to understand you."

"Go ahead, Love." I didn't even suspect what he'd say.

"What are your feelings for Beller now?"

I swallowed hard and squirmed under the blanket. "I feel sorry for him."

"So you believe that he still has feelings for you?"

"I don't know for sure, but it seems like that. What made you think of him?"

Now he inhaled. "I'm sure you've figured out I came to Madrid slightly abruptly by cancelling my contract in Paris early. You can probably guess the reason for that."

"I have and I can." Of course, he didn't want to be forced to work and become friends with Matthias's best friend.

"When Schwimmer came to meet the players, he was all friendly and kind. Then he waited for the two of us to be alone, and then he asked me about you, worriedly, as a friend. But I knew that, at the same time, he was inquiring for Beller. He told me there was nothing wrong with letting go of things that didn't work, that I would destroy both of our lives if I stuck to it."

I was angry that Ben had spoken like that to Alex. I knew he was worried, for Matthias mostly, and probably for me, but he needn't have attacked Alex.

"What did you tell him?" I asked.

"To mind his own business."

"That was the best answer."

Alex managed a weak smile. "I was surprised, though. It's one thing when a guy just wants to have sex. It's completely different when he's worried about the girl years later. He seems to truly care for you." There was no trace of anger in his voice.

I refrained from correcting him that I hadn't had sex with Matthias. What we did have was more, worse than that.

"He just needs to get over me," I said. "Once he meets his match, he will."

Alex caught my hand. "Somehow, I doubt it'll happen soon. It's been three years since then and he's still stuck."

"Well, that's his problem, isn't it? Right now I can only feel sorry for him. He is a good person. He deserves to be happy." My heart squeezed in pain.

"Is that all you think of him now?" He turned to look me in the eyes.

I knew I mustn't lie, not for a single word. "I feel terribly sorry for having given him hope then." I swallowed hard again. Scenes with Matthias and me enjoying those few weeks in Germany flashed through my mind, and my heart cramped. I had been happy with him, truly happy. I hadn't faked it. I had cared. "The last time I saw him, he told me he'd never love anyone after me. I thought it was just what people say when they desperately want to keep someone. If it's true that he still cares, then I am a terrible person." My voice shook towards the end.

Alex squeezed my hand gently. "You are wonderful, Jane." He kissed my fingers. "The mistakes you made, you've been making up for them."

"Alex, it's never gonna be enough."

"Love, if I say it's enough, then it is." He smiled.

He had to be right. If he could love me after everything, then surely I must be truly making up for my wrongdoings.

However, it was just a matter of time before Alex would come across one of Matthias's messages. I suppose I knew, deep down, that the other shoe would drop. In late November, seven months after we got back together, Matthias was still incessant.

"You've got some mail, hun," Alex announced cheerily from the entrance door.

I didn't suspect anything. I was in the kitchen, mixing a vitamin concoction I still had to take on my doctor's orders.

"What does it say?" I came to the hall to welcome him.

"It's strange. Apart from the address, there's only your name, briefly." He passed it to me.

When I saw the handwriting and the abbreviated *Jane A.nn*, how *he* always addressed everything he'd sent to me after the World Cup, I went white.

"Love, are you okay?"

"It's Matthias. I'm sorry." My hands started shaking. I had to set my drink down so as not to drop it. Seeing the expression change on Alex's face, I shivered down to my bones.

He sighed with a resignation that broke my heart. "You two have a correspondence?"

"No...I mean...This is not the first letter. There's text messages, emails, flowers. He did it in Paris too. But I never reply to any of them." My voice was shaky, but it was honest. And he knew it.

He took another deep breath. "Why haven't you told me? We talk openly about him."

"We do, but after all this time...I don't know anymore if he really cares or he's making fun of us and wants to infuriate you."

"After all this time, I think he's probably serious and wants to infuriate me," he said with a brief, sour laugh.

"I'm sorry, Alex. I don't know what else to do. In Paris, our relationship was too fragile. I was certain that if I had mentioned Matthias, we would have broken up, so I kept silent. Since we moved to Madrid together, I thought it best to keep it secret until he gives up. Knowing Matthias, negating everything and telling him I don't care wouldn't help, wouldn't make him stop. He'd just feel encouraged to keep trying."

Alex suggested that we sit in the living room, for which I was grateful, because my legs felt weak under the pressure of the situation.

"Do you want to read it?" he asked.

"I always read them. To see how he is, but mostly in case he threatens to do something reckless."

"You're smart."

"Forewarned is forearmed."

We both smiled.

"Would you mind if I read it, too?" he asked.

I froze. But there was nothing to hide.

"I wouldn't," I replied, passing the envelope to him.

"Right now, it would make me the happiest and most relieved person on Earth if you just told me yourself that you are really happy, that this is what you want," Alex started reading out loud. *"I almost don't care if it's with him, since your health has clearly significantly improved over the past couple of months. I want you to be happy, but I want you to say it to me personally, not to act in the newspapers and smile as if everything has always been alright. I know you read all my letters and messages – I am begging you for a proper reply. Let's put aside that I miss you, that I wake up at night wondering where you are and what you are doing, whether you are alone, with your friends, parents or him. Let's put aside that nothing has changed for me since July 11th. I am fraught with worry. I need to hear coming from your lips that you are well and satisfied with, where and who you are with. Forever yours, MB."*

Tears were brimming in my eyes, but with a tremendous effort, I kept them there. Matthias was always emotional in his letters — a complete opposite to the irritating, hard-headed striker he was on the pitch — but these words felt so different, so much stronger now when spoken out loud, especially when that reader was Alex. I felt terribly sorry and terribly sad imagining what both of them were going through – because of me. When alone, I would read the letters, get emotional and throw them in the garbage. But now, in front of Alex, I wasn't sure how I should behave.

"Well, he sure is romantic," Alex broke the silence. "I give him respect for this. He truly cares."

"You think so?" I shuddered and blushed.

"From a man's point of view, this is not a joke. It's full of concern."

"And perhaps manipulation," I surprised myself by saying it, but I had to. I had to try to make Matthias look bad, at least in my eyes. I couldn't fall apart in front of Alex, who had understood me many times, maybe too many. I didn't want to push his limits.

He looked at me questioningly.

"Referring to my health and wellbeing in order to get what he wants," I explained. "Which in this case is a response."

Alex's eyes widened in surprise. "You sound so cold."

"I'm not. Those techniques are mentioned in books, TV shows, films, psychological papers. He may not even be aware he's using them."

"And how do you feel?"

I took another breath, controlling the tears and pushing them back. "I am sorry. I am terribly scared and sorry. Scared that he might do something to you, or himself. Sorry that I ever gave him hope." My voice shook with those last words.

Alex put the letter aside and took me by the hand. "Come here." He drew me over into his lap. "Don't be scared. Whatever he does, he can't hurt us. He definitely won't hurt *you*. And if he tries to do something to me, well, I can defend myself very well. As for himself, I guess there is nothing we can do about that. He has to find a way to deal with his life, to find a purpose without you. And as for you feeling sorry, I guess only you know how difficult that is, and nothing I say or do can erase it, although I wish I could. However, I'll be by your side, Jane, forever." His hand was at the back of my head, massaging my scalp, which soothed and relaxed me instantly.

"Will you ever cease to amaze me, Alex?" I whispered, brimming with love for him.

In return, he kissed me, sending vibrations throughout my limbs and chest.

"One last thing, Jane," he said, seriously but without anger. "Don't hide anything from me that has to do with him. There is no other way I can fully trust you."

I looked him in the eyes, feeling guilty, and saw that he wasn't jealous. No. He was mature, reasonable and confident. I would never hide anything from him again.

Bea and Harold Dare had been doing great from the moment they hit it off in Germany. They were another footballer-meets-model fairy tale, although Bea got an offer for a sitcom and stopped her modelling career for a while. The sitcom was supposed to be for only a year, but the show got a huge audience who demanded more, so acting had become her primary job. She enjoyed it, especially since she played a role of a smart older sister, which she had always been to me. Filming took place in London, and Harold played there all the time, so they moved in together shortly after the World Cup in Germany was over. I wasn't there, so there was no reason for her to stay in our old apartment. The place I'd called home was empty, but we all stayed there whenever we met in London.

When you think about it, it's humorous, almost unbelievable – Bea and I, best friends, both found our perfect men in footballers, and goalkeepers at that. In many ways, Harold was similar to Alex, but he was way more impulsive and temperamental when he played. Alex could keep calm even in the most stressful minutes of the game, and he had only gotten better at that since the incident in Germany that cost Ukraine the final. This disposition has helped his teams win numerous titles. Harold, on the other side, lost his mind every now and then, sometimes even starting fistfights. With Bea, though, he was like a sweet teddy bear. I teased him that one day I might have to call the police and report him for disturbing the peace, because sooner or later he'd have to show his wild face at home, too.

"No way," Harold replied, pulling Bea into a bear hug. "Simply because this woman is a witch. She has some magic to control me."

I was beyond happy for the two of them.

"He will propose to her soon," Alex said one evening after we saw them off at the airport.

My heart jumped. "He told you that?"

"He never mentioned anything, but I feel it's gonna happen. Just wait."

And it did. During Christmastime, they went to spend a few days with her family in Pittsburgh. Harold couldn't have been more romantic – on Christmas Day, after breakfast, while the fire crackled and snow whitened the suburb, he went on one knee and asked Bea to accompany him for the rest of their lives, in front of her whole family. It was magical. We needn't have had to be there to know it. When she called Angie, Lana and me immediately afterwards to retell everything, we were all screaming and jumping around. The ring was a diamond that looked as if it had waited only for her hand to wear it.

They tried to keep it a secret, but, of course, their attempts were in vain. Soon after the holidays, the whole world was talking about one of the greatest upcoming weddings in England that year.

In the meantime, Alex and I celebrated Christmas with our parents. Alex wanted to be the host and show my family he could take care of me and everything in our home. He insisted that Dad and Mom stay with us in the apartment, rather than in a hotel like his. We took them around Spain as much as we could and enjoyed the mild, snow-free winter. For New Year's Eve, we went to Andorra to experience a bit of cold and skiing. Alex arranged a stay in some beautiful picturesque bungalows that Dad was truly impressed with. Those days were full of mulled wine, snowball fights and laughter, and our parents getting to know each other more. I felt as if I was exactly where I belonged, that everything was as it should be.

Normally, a few days into the new year, the Andersonns would already be creating plans for the upcoming weeks and preparing to go back to work. However, this time, Alex mysteriously insisted on delaying it all. His reasons became clear on January 7th, when we found another set of presents under our tall tree in Madrid. I hadn't forgotten this was when Ukrainians celebrate Christmas, but nobody, myself included, had thought to hope for a replay. It was another joyful night; the apartment shook with traditional Ukrainian music and the scent of wine and horilka.

I loved Alex, more and more, endlessly, seeing how hard he was trying to make my parents like him and to make me the happiest woman there was.

On one occasion, Alex took his parents to look for a gift for his sister, Maria, while I stayed alone with mine. We were drinking tea when Dad suddenly said, "He really is a proper host, obviously a family man. I'm sure he'll be an excellent father."

I choked on my tea, sending the hot liquid up into my nose. Mom laughed, taking the mug from my hands.

"What?" Dad asked innocently.

"N-nothing," I spluttered. "I know Alex has everything to be a perfect father."
But I couldn't say anything else. Other words felt fit to follow: family, kids, motherhood...I could clearly imagine having it all with Alex, but certainly not anytime soon. I was turning twenty-four in May, and I still wanted Alex just for myself. We had at least two years of lost time to make up for. I wanted us to travel more, enjoy ourselves, be responsible only for one another. A child was a huge no. What kind of mother would I be anyway?

And then, for a millisecond, another question flashed: What kind of father would Matthias be?

I was ashamed of the thought and pushed it out of my mind quickly. That story was over. In spite of all his persistent letters, I didn't give in. We were forever over, and it was time Matthias understood it.

*****

The year we kicked off in Andorra was the year of another World Cup, this time in territory unfamiliar to all of us – Brazil. I'd been there only a few times for work, and Alex never had. Dad did have some partners there, so he knew the area between Rio and São Paulo. He still planned to attend the whole event, from beginning till end.

This time, I didn't worry about going to different games. I'd made up my mind that I would be with Alex all the time, except for perhaps an occasional English match with my parents. No Germans, no Italians, Portuguese, Dutch, no one.

They all qualified, of course. What came as an extreme relief was that the Germans got randomly picked for the first group again, group A, while Ukraine ended up in the last one, H. Statistically, the only chances they had of meeting would be in the final, which, I hoped, would never occur. I prayed that somebody would kick them out before, so that Alex and I, and the whole of Ukraine actually, wouldn't have to go through that enormous stress.

To make sure I really wouldn't get a chance to do anything stupid at the tournament, I started organising with Lana day by day what I would be doing in Brazil. I had Alex's game schedule and the English team's, too, and in-between matches we squeezed in plans for autograph signings; visits to local schools, markets and beaches; talks with small businesses that I could help; short football games where I could gift footballs, goal nets and posts for schools and training campuses, and even provide scholarships in Europe for the most talented boys and girls. Lana was going nuts trying to manage all that, but she was happy. "She'd rather be doing that than covering your ass when you hop on a plane to get a fuck," Angie joked, getting a pillow in the face from me and a look of reproach from Bea.

Another thing I wanted to organise was specifically for Alex. I wanted to show his people how much I cared for him and loved him, because throughout Ukraine there were still masses who disliked me and openly blamed me for the bronze medal their team had taken home in Germany when they could've had gold. And they were right. That was why I planned to make sure all the stands in the Ukrainian matches were full of Ukrainians. I knew how people there struggled. A trip to Brazil for many was an impossible mission. I wanted to make it real. I was about to provide 10,000 plane tickets for the Ukrainian matches at the World Cup.

I made all the calculations myself before suggesting it to Lana, whose brain exploded, knowing she'd have to deal with another mountain of logistics because when I wanted something, nothing could stop me. She calmly advised me to talk to some of Alex's friends before and discuss the best way to do it, so I chose Nikolay Pavlov, who still played in the national team as well as for a team in Barcelona, so it was a short trek to meet him.

"You want to do *what*?"

It took Nikolay half an hour to understand, but we quickly got down to planning everything in detail. First, we'd announce a competition – whoever wanted to go for the tournament would have to write a short essay of maximum eleven sentences saying so and why. Transport would be provided, accommodation and match tickets would be on them.

We opened the competition in March, with a deadline at the end of the month. In April, we'd announce all 10,000 names. Officially, it was all Nikolay's idea. He wanted to do something for his people. My name was not mentioned anywhere.

Lana managed things with a Ukrainian interpreter because she couldn't handle it all by herself, and with the language barrier abolished, everything went faster. I didn't do much, except provide the funds. I was proud that I didn't have to borrow anything from Dad or Mom. My work over all these years had enabled me to do this giant venture all by myself.

In order to cover up the hours I spent locked up in our apartment's small office, talking to Lana on the phone, I also organised a second competition to transport the most avid English fans to and from Brazil in two A380 airplanes. This competition was based on photos of fans in jerseys, presenting how much they loved the sport. By organising this, I could hide all my involvement in the Ukrainian giveaway from Alex.

In April, the names were announced, and in May, the final preparations started. Most of the leagues were reaching their last rounds, and Alex and Nikolay were invited onto the biggest sports show in the country one week before the flight to São Paulo. Nikolay and I agreed that he would explain everything then, and I was brimming with joy and excitement, looking forward to seeing Alex's face once he found it all out.

*****

May, however, didn't start well for me. The first weekend of the month, Alex had an early morning training before an important match on home soil in Madrid. He left before I woke up, so I was having coffee and running through the latest news in the fashion industry and, of course, peeking at the tabloids, expecting, like every other day, that I'd read something commending me or the latest promotion I'd done.

This time, as soon as I opened the news page, a colossal title in bold black letters flashed at me.

"I'D GLADLY WELCOME ALEX BACK. JANE'S NOT GIVING HIM THE RESPECT HE DESERVES," SAYS NATASHA MILANOVA.

I almost dropped my coffee mug. First, I saw red, and then, white.

Of course, I knew who Natasha Milanova was. What I didn't know was that she still mattered – to Alex or to anyone. She had once been Alex's girlfriend, the one his friends referred to as "the blonde he dated for barely a year, but it didn't work out so they broke up on friendly terms." There had never been any more discussion than that. Alex had only mentioned her once. I knew from his story that she was a kind, calm girl, who worked as an assistant at her university. They hadn't even been in touch. She didn't matter. She wasn't supposed to matter.

So why had somebody talked to her? I scrolled in a panic to see all the world tabloids full of the same brief interview with her, in which she insults me openly for what I had done in Germany! How could she think she had the right and freedom to do so? Didn't she know who I was? I was Jane Andersonn. I could crush her between my two fingers and make her smaller than a grain of sand! How dare she speak after all this time, after Alex and I had been together four and a half years?

Tears of rage brimmed in my eyes, but I controlled them as I read the short interview until the end. She missed Alex. She'd welcome him back as soon as he realised I was not the right woman for him. She had always thought I was a bad idea, knowing how kind Alex was, that "a spoiled British brat with inclination to drinking" would never appreciate and understand a man like him. I read three more tabloids, then two in Italian and three in Spanish. All of them were exactly the same, copied and translated word by word. I wanted to blow fire at the laptop, hoping that somehow it'd reach those ludicrous articles and burn them out of existence. Lana called me, but I didn't pick up at first. After the sixth time, I did.

"Calm down, Jane. You have to talk to Alex first…"

"Have you read what she said?" I hissed.

"I have, every single word, and it's suspicious—"

"What's suspicious, Lana? There is nothing suspicious. She can't have been clearer in her statements, that bitch!"

"Listen to me. Don't do anything stupid. Wait for Alex to return. Something is not right here."

I wanted to drop the call, but Lana pivoted to discussing the arrangements I had to finish before I got on the plane to São Paulo. I knew she was just distracting me from doing something reckless. I replied briefly and curtly, conjuring up ways I could make this stupid blonde pay for what she had done, and also musing on what compelled her to say these gross things now, after all this time. *Alex and she had something recently! It must be that!*

"Is that all, Lana?" I asked, already irritated by the string of unimportant questions she was asking just to keep me on the phone.

"Promise me you won't do anything."

I didn't reply straight away. Then, I heard the door open. "Alex is back."

Taking a deep breath, I put the phone down with shaking hands. When I stood up, I realised my entire body was shaking, too. I crossed my arms and stood in the middle of the living room, waiting for him as if he had done something terribly bad. Which...maybe he had. I didn't know. On the other hand, didn't he have all the right to, after what I had done to him? I was the one without the option of being jealous. I had committed my fair share of unforgivable acts. If he had done something similar, with his ex-girlfriend, he had all the right to.

Still, the thought of him, my Alex, with another woman – it made my insides boil. He was mine and only mine. I was the best-looking woman in the world. Any other would be a downgrade for him and a defeat for me. That some average chick could take my guy to her bed...it nauseated me.

When Alex entered the living room, I knew straight away from his face that he had already read it. He was red in the face and panting – he had rushed home.

"Jane, it's all a misunderstanding," he said, but he stopped there, realising how it sounded.

I stumped over the parqueted floor to him and hissed in his face, *"Have you had something with her since we met?"*

"No, Jane, of course not," he said calmly.

It was the truth.

Instead of receding, my rage increased. I stepped back, an eruption of emotions rising in me. "How DARE she talk about us like that!" I screamed.

He approached me, folding me in his arms. "Love, it's not what you think."

I gave him a piercing look.

"Damn it, I'm so clumsy with these situations. I keep saying the wrong sentences."

I tried to push out of his hug, but he didn't let me.

"Natasha and I haven't been in touch for years, not since we broke up. She doesn't bear a grudge, she moved on with her life."

"How do you explain the interview, then?"

"It's not an interview. They caught her by surprise and surrounded her. She said a few sentences, but nothing similar to what they wrote."

"How do you know all this?" I scrutinised him with my eyes.

"She called me while I was on the way."

"Why does she have your number?"

"She felt terrible after seeing the articles, so she called my parents to explain what had actually happened. They gave her my number."

I wanted to be angry at him for being so calm and composed. The thought of him talking to his ex-girlfriend, who had caused this disgusting turmoil, infuriated me.

"I thought she knew her place," I hissed again. "What could she have said to be misinterpreted like this? It can't be far from the truth."

"It is. She said I'm a nice guy who deserves all possible love and respect, especially being in the spotlight incessantly. They took that and twister her words into the statements that are out there."

I was silent for a while. What he said made complete sense. That's what tabloid journalists did. It was nothing unusual. They had done worse to me, us, other people.

As a cautious relief washed over me, my muscles still weren't loosening. "What are we gonna do now?" I asked, my shoulders tense under Alex's touch.

"Nothing. We continue being happy together. I told Natasha that if anyone bothered her again, she should threaten them with lawyers and police, and I'd help her with that."

"You'd help her?" I hissed again.

He laughed.

"What's funny?" I hit him in the chest.

"You're incredibly cute when you're jealous."

A wave of feelings overwhelmed me. He could've been disapproving of me for being angry at him for nothing, considering I had *actually* done something terribly bad to him. He could've told me to calm down, waited until I did and then changed the topic, since cheating, even when theoretical, was an uncomfortable thing to talk about between us, because of me.

Instead, he disregarded my mistakes and told me I was cute in my mad jealousy.

I loved him.

"I'm not jealous," I whispered through a smile, relaxing on his chest.

"Of course not. Except, the fire brigade is downstairs since you set off all the alarms with your furore." He kissed me on the head.

"Don't tease me. I was ready to kill you both."

"Your expression when I walked in was priceless. I actually might ask her to do this more often." Alex chuckled again.

I raised my head to look him in the eyes. "Don't even think about it." I knew this conversation was somehow pointless. Matthias and I had been filling up the newspapers for the past four years, and Alex had every right to want to kill us both, too. However, here he was, making this situation so ordinary, as if we were an ordinary couple who had these ordinary occurrences. I loved him even more for that, so I took part in the show.

"Or what?" He kissed my nose.

"Or I'll break your arms and then your only career will be as a Hummel model."

He caught me by the waist and lifted me off the floor. "And if I now make love to you and show you you're the only woman in my life?"

I hugged his hips with my legs, grinning with satisfaction. "Then I'll break only one arm."

He kissed me as he carried me towards the bedroom, chasing away all the thoughts that had distraught me that morning. He proved to me again that he was a wonderful, mature, conscious, caring man. My perfect man.

*****

The episode with Natasha Milanova wasn't the only turmoil that fell upon us in May. We quickly forgot about it, busy with the end of the Spanish league and preparations for Brazil. One day, Alex came home from his training in the evening; I had ordered a light dinner to surprise him. He only had two games left with his team to play, and then we'd go to Kiev for final settlements and the flight to São Paulo. I noticed he didn't eat much, even though the food was delicious, but I assumed he was exhausted. The last couple of weeks had been truly tough on him. When he wasn't playing games, he was training with his team, and when not that, he was in the gym.

We moved to the balcony, and I brought us some sangria. I took his hand in mine and started massaging it how he liked it, but he was unusually silent and tense. I started blabbering about the conversation the girls and I had had that day, about how and where we'd meet in São Paulo and the first thing we'd do, when he interrupted me.

"Jane, I actually wanted to talk to you about it," he said gravely. I didn't like the tone of his voice. "I've given it a lot of thought, and I think it's the best that you don't go with me."

His words bounced around in my ears and head, but I couldn't process them.

"H-how do you mean, Alex? Not to go where?" Childishly, stupidly, I hoped I misunderstood.

"To Brazil. I think you should stay in London. Or here."

Although it was a hot May evening, my blood temperature dropped to zero. I wanted to say so many things, to rebel, to scream, to yell at him. He couldn't ask me for something like this. I, Jane Andersonn, couldn't skip the World Cup, not when my boyfriend—the best goalkeeper in the world—would be there. My girls would be there. My parents. Even random English and Ukrainian people I'd never met but helped would be there. How could I stay in London?

I didn't say any of those. Something else dawned on me. Something worse.

"You don't trust me, Alex?"

My body felt cold and clammy. I didn't need his answer. I knew it. All that we had been building since we got back together, in this wonderful, unforgettable, beautiful year, it all fell apart into pieces, unfixable smithereens. How could he do this? After everything I'd done. I'd loved him. My whole body and mind had been entirely his since he picked me up from Texas. And in seconds, it was unravelled. I had been deluding myself. We were never going to be the same; we'd never have full trust in each other.

Who could blame him? Who would forgive what I had done? Ben Schwimmer was right. Matthias was right, too. This relationship should've been over that night in Berlin. Why had we done this to each other?

"I trust you with every other thing, Jane, but not with this one," Alex finally said. "I've been extremely worried and anxious about this. I'm afraid I wouldn't be able to give my best at the tournament. The boys and my country don't deserve another disappointment like that one in Germany."

"I can't blame you," I said without looking at him. I didn't dare speak more. All that was on my mind was, *this is it.* We were now one step from breaking up, this time forever, and I wasn't sure how my brain, body and soul would take it. Again.

Wordlessly, I stood up and went to our bedroom. The familiar bile and pain in my chest developed, spreading all over my body. It was terribly, frighteningly the same as that night in Paris, when I'd decided to leave. *No, you won't be a living corpse again, Jane. Not again,* I said to myself. *You mustn't do it. For your parents. For your friends.*

To busy my mind, I started jotting down mental notes about what I would do in the morning, what I would pack, tell the girls, Dad and Mom. Poor Lana would kill me – all her work over the last few months would be in vain. I'd have to tell Nikolay not to mention my name anywhere. He could take all the credit. I'd go to London, talk to the girls and then see what to do next. I could not become a skeleton again.

I was lying in bed in the dark, my eyes wide open, when Alex entered the room. He removed his clothes, but I didn't dare look at him. I was afraid I'd start crying. However, when he lay next to me, all my determination sank.

"I'm sorry, Jane. I had to tell you," he said in a gentle voice.

"I completely understand. No need to apologise," I tried to sound as dispassionate as possible, but my voice obviously shook. He was looking at me, I could feel it, but he didn't say anything. There was nothing to say.

Neither of us slept much that night, but Alex had to get ready and go to training early in the morning. I pretended to be sleeping until he left, and then mechanically got up, showered and sat down to eat. The smell of food woke in me the familiar disgust and nausea, so I gave up on it. I'd try later. Then I sat on the balcony with a notebook and started writing up bullet points about what I should do.

First of all, I must wait for him to play his next game, which was the following evening. Saying anything before could affect his performance. Waiting for the following weekend and his last game was out of the question, because I knew I wouldn't be able to handle it. So tomorrow evening, after he came home – because I wouldn't attend that one, I was not putting myself through that – I would tell him everything, take my documents and leave, this time for good.

Second, I would go to London and cry with the girls, staying there as long as I needed with Lana and Angie around, who'd push me to eat and exercise. Then I'd skip that bloody World Cup and spend the whole summer somewhere far away, in Australia or New Zealand, away from everyone's prying eyes.

Third, I'd meet my parents and explain everything. I'd take up acting classes and a serious, professional mentor, and start aiming for an

Oscar. That had never been my wish. I was satisfied with my modelling career and my occasional film roles. I knew very well that getting an Oscar was next to impossible because, still, I owed most of my job success to my family name; plus, my acting was nowhere near Meryl Streep, Jane Fonda or Cate Blanchett. But since this challenge was near impossible, it was the best thing I could dive into after breaking up with Alex. I needed something to focus all my mind, body and soul on, to recover from that loss.

After writing up my plan, I went back into the kitchen and forced down my throat some eggs and avocado toast, and then I went to the gym in the building.

When Alex returned, he, of course, noticed I was not in a good mood. He tried to cheer me up, but in vain. All I could think of was the inevitable, coming up in slightly more than twenty-four hours. The lump in my throat felt harder and larger with every passing minute, but I didn't collapse or cry. Instead, I continued my routine around the house mechanically.

Later that evening, I vomited the dinner, and then the lunch. Alex was worried and knocked on the bathroom door, but I didn't let him in. I kept saying that everything was fine. I didn't want him to think for a single second that I was trying to blackmail him with my health. He suggested we watch a movie, but I refused and went to bed. He came to bed soon afterwards – I heard him sneak in, my back turned to him, again pretending to be sleeping. He hugged me close, spooning me, and I put all my power into not letting out a single sob, knowing that was the last hug I would get from him. The next morning, if I had gotten up before him, he'd have seen that my pillow had a large stain from a night full of tears.

"I'll see you at the stadium then," Alex said, packing to leave for the match.

"Erm… I'm not coming. I'm sorry."

He stopped in the middle of putting his sneakers on and looked at me. "Jane…"

"I can't. I may vomit any time again, so better not to embarrass you, or myself." *What a lame excuse, Jane. You could've thought up something better.*

He straightened up and took my face in between his palms. I closed my eyes tight, preventing any tears from bursting out. "Alright. I'll miss you," he said, placing a kiss on my forehead.

"Good luck," I managed to whisper. He left and I went to the gym again.

When I finished my workout, the match hadn't even started, so I went to a nearby hotel to swim in their enclosed pool. I had to keep my body busy so that my mind stayed as stable as possible. A twenty-minute swim, half an hour in the sauna, swim again, thirty-minute sauna, one more round of swimming...

When I checked the time again, the match was over – Alex's team had won. I went back to the apartment and took a bath. I was in the kitchen making a protein shake when I heard him at the door.

"Congratulations," I said quietly when he came in. He looked damn attractive, tired from a long day, his hair still wet from the shower. Normally, he'd never be too tired to have sex with me. Now, I believed it was the same, only that was not an option anymore.

"Thank you." He reached for my shake and took a few gulps. I knew he did it to get closer to me. "Could we have a word after I change?"

I shuddered. "Of course. I'll fix some tea."

"No, I'll fix it. You go and wait for me on the balcony."

I took my shake and left. I was snuggled on the outdoor sofa, curled under the blanket since the breezy, late-spring evening was strangely chilly. I sipped the protein liquid, praying it would stay down in my stomach. I needed strength for what was coming. Alex was out not even half an hour afterwards, two matching mugs in his hands. We always used those mugs for our balcony time, even when we drank wine. They were a gift from his sister – a football mug and a red court shoe mug that clicked perfectly when placed next to each other. He rested them on the table and sat next to me. *Why did he do that?* I was thinking. He should've taken the chair. I needed distance for this. He placed his arm over my shoulders. Damn it. Why was he doing this? He certainly knew something was wrong.

"I believe there is something you want to tell me, Jane," he said.

I didn't reply straight away. I collected my thoughts for a minute or so, fighting the urge to squirm underneath his patient, heavy arm on my shoulder. He waited patiently. Then, I took a deep breath, exhaled and moved under his arm to face him, trying to be as cold and devoid of emotion as possible. Knowing what I had to do, I began reciting my speech.

"Alex, I think I should go to London. This time forever. You don't trust me, and we both know that's not good. I can't blame you. You have every right not to trust me on anything I say or do. But we're both mature enough to know that that is not a good sign – not for a friendship, let alone the serious relationship we have been building. I am terribly sorry, because…" My voice shook. "…because I love you, immensely, unconditionally, but like this we're either already nearing the end or we'll never be entirely happy. Therefore, I'm gonna leave in the morning. I'm sorry. I'm sorry that I cannot take this. I'm sorry that I'm not the girl you want and deserve."

I looked away, concealing the first, most persistent tears and hoping that he wouldn't say anything that could possibly hurt me more. When he didn't, even after a considerable amount of time in shared silence, I stood up, ready to march back inside. *I might even take a flight this evening*, I thought, if there was any.

"Jane," he called after me. I stopped dead in my tracks, my eyes now blurred with painful, hot tears. "Remember that night, before you left last time?"

I turned, my face now distorted by the emotions fighting within me. I mumbled a stifled, "Yes."

"After I fought with my parents, I talked to them. They told me about love, commitment and work in a relationship, and I made up my mind then. I wanted to give us another try."

I stopped crying instantly and a cold sweat covered me. Was he really saying what I was hearing him say?

"I was ready to turn a new page, leave behind all my anger, frustration, distrust, doubts, everything. That night, finally, I was ready. However, when I saw how determined you were to go, I thought it was truly over, that I had done enough damage – that it couldn't be fixed, nothing I said or did that night would make up for the two years we lost. I thought there was no love in you left for me after everything you'd gone through, and I stood no chance of ever being important in your life again. I decided to let you go."

I was still standing, though my legs were now wooden and I felt a strong breeze could have toppled me. This was a revelation. If I only had known, that night in Paris…if he only had said something, anything, I would've run to his arms, forgiven him for anything, as if there was anything for me to forgive.

"The moment you left, I knew I was wrong," he continued, "and that was reaffirmed every single day I had to live without you. I couldn't believe how much I missed you, how much I couldn't lead a normal life without you. You have no idea how many times I regretted not having said anything then." Alex stood up. A tremor passed over my body – he almost always did that to me when we were close. He took me in his arms, holding my back so that I couldn't retreat. As if I had wanted to. As if I could. I was immobile, glued in place. "I am not making the same mistake again, Jane." He was gravely serious. I saw it in his eyes. "I am not letting you go. I love you, immensely and unconditionally. And I trust you." He said it effortlessly, without pausing.

"Alex, are you sure?" I stammered. "I am not blackmailing you. We are not kids. It's reasonable if you don't have confidence in me—"

He placed a finger over my lips, electrifying my whole body. "I love you, I trust you and I have confidence in you. You are the woman of my life, Jane Andersonn. You've proven that over a billion times so far. I'm not losing you again."

He smiled, and then he kissed me, clearing away all my fears, doubts, concerns and uncertainties. I almost cried in relief. Instead, I hugged him hard and returned the kiss, excitement rushing rapidly through all my nerves, relieving a wish that had been concealed for days.

"Yanov, next time you frighten me like this, with insinuations of a breakup, I swear, the world will host a funeral for its best goalkeeper while I'm hiding somewhere in Southeast Asia."

Alex put a hand under my shirt while I played with his hair, swimming in his eyes. "No, Jane, no more leaving, breakups, mistrust or anything of the sort. You're my woman and I'm your man, through and through."

"I love you, Alex."

"I love you, Jane."

*****

The first Wednesday in June, one week before the Ukrainian national team was scheduled to depart Kiev for Brazil, Alex, Nikolay and Vlad Starovski were guests on the biggest sports talk show in their country. By then, it was in every sports newspaper, journal and magazine – a high belief in this Eastern European team that had shocked the world four years ago. The statistics spoke well of them, comparing them to all the strongest opponents. Almost everywhere, the odds were in the Ukrainian team's favour – except in the case of Germans; the percentage was slightly more in the favour of Die Mannschaft. Alex, I knew it, promised himself to fix that.

Nikolay and I decided that was the moment for him to tell the truth about the competition we had organised and awarded. I was watching the show with Alex's parents and sister at their home in Kiev, excited like a little girl and waiting to see their reaction, too, because they had no idea either.

"So, Nikolay, tell us about the charity competition you organised a few months ago," the host asked. "Why did you decide to do it, and how did you manage to organise everything in such a short time?"

My Ukrainian was pretty good at that time, so I understood most of their conversation.

Nikolay squirmed in his seat. "Yeah, that was a hell of a job. I am very happy and excited to be a part of it."

"A part of it? Aren't you the main guy?" the host asked.

"Actually, no. I'll be honest, since, well, I finally can." He purposefully took a dramatic pause. Everyone was staring at him, waiting for an explanation. "All this, the essays, plane tickets to Brazil and back, choosing the winners – it's mostly Jane Andersonn's doing."

Tanya and Olexiy turned to me, and Maria screamed. On the TV, the camera was on Alex, who was frozen. The host was also confused.

"Jane came up with the idea in February this year, but she wanted to keep it a secret as long as possible, because she was worried about how people might react. She didn't want it to be about her," Nikolay explained. "She asked me for help and advice, since she also wanted it to be a surprise for Alex. Her wonderful and hardworking team managed most of the bureaucracy and logistics. I'm literally ten percent involved in this. Jane wants to make sure that our stands in Brazil are loud, because she firmly believes, as I do, as do all of us, that we deserve that trophy and if some of our people cannot afford to be there to witness this history-making, they should be assisted."

The camera caught Alex again. He was shining smiling.

"Wait, wait, let's make it clear." The poor host was connecting everything. "You're saying that Jane is covering ninety percent of the cost of this venture?"

"That's correct."

The audience in the studio roared with screams and applause. The house of the Yanovs did, too. I was smiling, proud that I could do this much as Alex's family hugged me and thanked me in mixed English-Ukrainian. All our phones started ringing with messages and calls from everywhere. I already saw a notification from my news app that my name had appeared, but we had to focus on the TV show again.

"So, Alex," the host said when the studio finally calmed down, "what do you have to say about this?"

The audience roared again, seeing his smiling, joyous, proud face. "This is what you get when you date the best girl in the world," Alex managed, causing another wave of applause, laughter, screams and approving whistles and yells.

"You really had no idea about this?" the host asked when the studio calmed down again.

"Not at all. I mean, I was confused when Pavlov announced he was about to organise this. We were all thinking, *Wow, this boy is going on a big spending spree now that he moved to Spain*, because, well these things cost a lot."

"I could still do it by myself, you gigolo!" Nikolay intervened jokingly, to which everyone laughed again.

"I didn't suspect Jane at all," Alex continued. I wish I could have seen him in person as he said this, with a big, puppydog grin on his face. "I mean, she already booked planes for some English fans. I thought that was it with her craziness. When I asked her about Pavlov's project, she only replied, *Oh, Love, I'm only dealing with a dozen of really sweet kids who like football,*" he imitated my British accent, causing everyone to hold their bellies in laughter. "I had no idea she was about to send 10,000 Ukrainians to Brazil."

The world was in a frenzy about us. Once again, we were the perfect picture of a perfect couple. The articles about my surprise and Alex's reply – *This is what you get when you date the best girl in the world* – were in every possible media and were overwhelmingly positive. The Ukrainians finally loved me. I felt it in the days that followed the talk show, as Alex and I wandered Kiev. Wherever we showed up for coffee, lunch or last-minute shopping, we were greeted with love and praise. Alex shone with pride. I felt like the queen of the world.

We were invited for interviews and asked for comments about it, but we didn't have time to attend to all of them, since the World Cup was approaching at the speed of light. A new World Cup. A chance for Ukraine to finally win the gold it deserved. A chance for Alex to redeem himself after his mistake four years ago.

A chance for me to show that I was indeed Alex's faithful, perfect and loving girlfriend. Alex's, and only Alex's.

CHAPTER 4

On June 10th, I boarded the plane for São Paulo with Alex, his teammates and their wives and girlfriends. Including the stop in Amsterdam, the trip took eighteen hours. Bea, Lana and Angie opted to fly directly from London, and my parents from Dallas. We would all meet In São Paulo for the opening ceremony on the 13th, between – destiny had it – the host Brazil and the ever-so-present Germany.

To prepare myself and prevent any unfortunate meetings, I studied the groups and schedules for the Ukrainian, English and German teams. I knew every team's timeline by heart. Fortunately, I would be largely safe, apart from the first and, potentially, last day. The opening game was in São Paulo, where Alex and his team would face Chile five days later. That meant that Matthias and I would be in the same city at the same time for the first time since the previous World Cup (not including the four times he had come to play in Madrid, against teams that were not Alex's and that I, of course, didn't attend). The end of the tournament, according to numerous predictions, would see Germany and Ukraine in the final game in Rio. I had only to make sure nothing bad or disturbing happened on that first day, and on the last one.

When we arrived at our hotel, we went to the swimming pool immediately. Aside from being the beginning of the Cup, June 13th was also special for being Alex's twenty-fifth birthday. His teammates decided to celebrate every single day leading up to it, because when the competition kicked off, their strict diet, sleep and exercise plan would start. Thus we all ordered beer and cocktails straightaway and lounged on the chairs. We swam, jumped and screamed like a bunch of teenagers. We were in one of the most exciting countries in the world, a land of football! In South America! Of course, we let loose. The weather was wonderfully spring-like and humid, great music was blaring on the radio and we couldn't help joining in. Bea, Lana and Angie were with us, along with my, Bea's and Alex's parents.

This time, I got Alex a new phone as a gift, since his had battery issues. I had preloaded it with a thousand photos of us together, and me – dressed and naked. I had thought about adding reminders about birthdays and anniversaries, but he was good at that, which I admired him for. He even remembered the birth dates of his teammates and family members he hadn't seen for months.

Alex had also been creative with my birthday present three weeks earlier – he got me a set of candles, creams and bathing oils for many nights of absolute relaxation. When I moved in with him in Madrid, I drew lots of healing baths, since the doctor had advised it would be beneficial for my wellbeing. The first night Alex smelt the oils, he joined me, and afterwards whenever he could. Apart from the great sex in the water, our skin was also regenerated and our minds free of daily stress; it was as if those candles had some drugs in them. The set he found for my birthday was extraordinary. We knew as soon as I opened it because the scent spread throughout the whole apartment. We had already used it up and had to order more.

As the day drew to a close, we were overcome with jetlag, tiredness and alcohol, so we only had snacks at the pool bar and headed to our rooms at nine o'clock. I went to the bathroom, and as soon as I was alone, I remembered – Matthias was in the same city.

I hadn't completely forgotten about it. The media made sure to remind me, as much as we all tried to ignore it.

JANE AND MATTHIAS, PERHAPS TOO CLOSE AGAIN?

SO NEAR AND YET SO FAR

Magazines and blogs rang out with sensational headlines and photos of Matthias and me under the German flag four years ago. I asked Alex not to care, and he didn't. At least, he seemed not to. Nobody mattered apart from us. We were not letting them take away what belonged to Ukraine. Not even Matthias, with those gorgeous, divine, dark eyes full of furore, could sway me.

*****

On the first full day in São Paulo, Alex and his teammates went for a brief training to adjust to the climate and grass, while the girls and I spent time with fans who had come to watch them, since training viewings were approved for that day. I enjoyed myself from morning till evening, and not for a single second did I think about Matthias – where he was or if, perhaps, he was somewhere nearby. But I did when we reached the hotel, after I took a bath, had sex with Alex and lay in bed. I remembered that our hotels were only a kilometre or so apart, that maybe he had tried to send something to me again, that maybe he had seen me during the day but hadn't wanted to approach and put me in an uncomfortable situation.

I quickly pushed him out of my thoughts, feeling guilty, although I knew very well that I wasn't excited about seeing him. I was deathly frightened. I didn't know what a meeting with him would evoke in me. I had seen him in newspapers and videos, but not in person – not for four years. Live, it would be a completely different experience. Especially after how we had parted last time. Especially after all his letters and confessions of love and concern.

No matter what, I had to stay faithful, true and respectful to Alex. Matthias... he was just not supposed to be. Ever. Despite those coal-black eyes that once had adored me. How do they feel about me now?

*****

The day before the opening ceremony, Alex and I went out for some famous Brazilian barbecue. Neither of us had ever tried it, so we were excited – a feeling amplified by our eagerness for the tournament that was finally beginning the next day. We'd watch the opening game and then keep enjoying this wonderful city. I wore a knee-length burgundy-red dress that emphasised my waist and opened up at the neckline to show off my shoulders and breasts. I had help with my hair, but I did my makeup myself. Alex wore simple black trousers and a white shirt with a jacket.
"Hello, handsome," I couldn't refrain from saying.

"What's, up, gorgeous?" Alex took me into his arms and kissed me. "Let's go before I decide to destroy your hair."

We chuckled like teenagers and went for the door. Being a gentleman, Alex held the door, and I stepped out first.

I knew he was there before he spoke. I smelled his cologne. It was the same as four years ago.

"We need to talk."

It lasted only a second, because Alex stepped out of the room after me, but I could see him clearly, first in the corner of my eye, and then entirely. Matthias Beller seemed taller, somehow, perhaps skinnier, but definitely more muscular. The lines of his face were stronger and sharper than the last time I saw him. He seemed as if he were built only of muscles – probably as a consequence of an hours-long daily routine at the gym. Somehow, his eyes were even darker.

"You shouldn't be here," I managed to utter.

"We need to talk, Jane," he said, louder.

I was stunned. I couldn't reply. I only stared at him, absorbed by his Greek-statue-like beauty.

"I think she was clear," Alex said, stepping protectively in front of me.

I took Alex by the hand, out of love for him, but also to prevent him from doing anything reckless.

"No, she wasn't," Matthias persisted. "I've been trying to reach you for four years, Jane. We have to talk."

"You should've stopped a long time ago," I whispered weakly. The sound of his voice took me back through time. Once, I had enjoyed it so much, revelled in the compliments and love spoke to me. Now...now what? It awoke in me something. Memories, feelings, I didn't know. "We have nothing in common. There is nothing left worth any discussion," I added, surprised by how much it hurt to say it, even after all this time.

"There is plenty to talk about! You can't go against yourself, Jane!" He was stubborn.

"Listen, Beller, I am not going to let you upset my girlfriend," Alex raised his voice and moved to completely cover me so that I couldn't see Matthias any longer. "Please, leave us alone now. And leave her alone in future."

"No!" Matthias replied, loud and petulant. The two of them stood centimetres away from each other, firing off bullets from their eyes at each other. Alex with his bulky, large build, was bigger and taller, but Matthias didn't seem intimidated. "We have to talk about what happened then," Matthias said, looking Alex in the eyes. "Even you know it, Yanov."

I felt Alex's body shaking with controlled anger. I admired him for not losing his head. But I had to step in.

"Matthias," I pleaded, my voice hoarse. "It'd be better if you leave us alone. Whatever happened between us, it stayed there, in Berlin. Things are different now. There is nothing to talk about. I thought you understood that when I never replied to any of your messages. There is no need to keep dredging this up, to feed the papers with gossip. Let it go."

"Never! Jane, for god's sake! You expect me to forget about those two years this idiot here tortured and maltreated you!" At those words, Alex's hand, instinctive but restrained, caught Matthias by the shirt. But he didn't stop. "You couldn't move freely! He held you captive! You were a walking corpse, Jane! You expect me to let it go after you know how much I care about you?"

I was shocked that Alex didn't hit him then and there. He only held Matthias's shirt tightly, his face white. I was about to say something in Alex's defence, but there was no need.

"Beller, I'm not gonna repeat this again – I know what happened in Germany. I know it very well. Trust me, it's a hell of a burden to overcome. Those two years you observed on Jane – that's the toll it took on us. I also know what you did for her after the tournament was over, and I am grateful to you for that. Not many men would do the same. But if my girlfriend wanted to talk to you, look for you, go to you, she would've done so. I've never prevented or held her back. She can confirm that."

I didn't know who was more flabbergasted – Matthias or me. I glanced at Matthias over Alex's shoulder: What was it that he did after the competition? How had they not beaten each other bloody already? What was going on here?

I was impressed by Alex. He didn't talk like the jealous boy he had been in Germany when he complained about me going to their games. The person in front of me was a mature, responsible, self-confident man, sure of his qualities, aware of the truth and accepting it, facing it, dealing with it.

Matthias didn't say anything else. Alex let go of him and turned to leave, taking me by the hand. I only glanced at Matthias once to see he was looking after us, puzzled.

I let Alex lead me into the hotel lobby. My mind was blank, my head spinning fast, my heart pounding frantically. Once we were in the entrance hall, Alex suggested that we sit for a while. We took a small sofa and I snuggled into his arm.

"I'm sorry, Alex… I had no idea he'd try…"

"There's nothing to apologise for, Jane. He shouldn't be here."

"I'm impressed," I said shifting to look up at him. His expression was placid, almost amused.

"You thought I'd fight him?"

I nodded with a faint smile.

"Well, it's not that I didn't want to," he admitted. "But I thought it best to avoid any scandals. And if one of the best players on the German national team didn't show up for the opening game, that would definitely rise above the proportions of a regular scandal."

I let myself melt into his hug. "You're amazing. Truly. Every day you impress me more." He kissed me on the forehead. "By the way, since we're on the topic…I have to ask you – what is it you thanked him for?"

Alex inhaled. "He did a lot for you after the tournament was over. Gottfried went mental after you left Beller and came to look for me. He thought you'd leave me for Beller. He wanted to give everything to the papers, just to make you pay for not choosing him or Beller, and for getting away with everything, because, if you remember, it was all as I said – we stayed together, so nobody trusted a word about your relations with them. Gottfried wanted to give you up, but Beller confronted him. They had a huge quarrel, after which Beller was expelled from the national team." Something twisted in my stomach. "Gottfried still wanted to release his stories about you, but Beller threatened to make up some story about Gottfried having sex with underage girls, which would've been way worse than what he did with you. Apart from that, apparently, Beller being absent greatly affected the atmosphere in the team. The famous German Four were now three. The public and the Federation were furious that the golden boy, who had played a huge part in winning that trophy, was inexplicably missing. It's because of that pressure that Gottfried had to invite Beller back. Despite all their insistence that their players are equally good, they knew they needed Beller to get results. So Beller and Gottfried decided to bury the hatchet and move on. Now they are again like father and son."

I was paralysed with shock at this new, unbelievable information. "Matthias was kicked out of the national team?" I stammered. "That's...that's more important to him than the club he plays for."

"That's why I said many men wouldn't do what he had done."

"No, no, no. This can't be." I was being swallowed by too many feelings – I was ashamed, sorry, surprised, stunned that I hadn't known any of these before, angry at Alex for not having told me but also understanding because, why would he? "I feel terrible," I said. "I'm sorry, Alex. We shouldn't be talking about this. I'm just shocked. I had no idea..."

"Maybe I should've told you earlier, to get it over with."

"No, it's alright. But, how do you know? I hope it's not some public secret that only I wasn't aware of."

"No, of course not. It was Luca who heard first that Beller was out of the team. It sounded strange, so he investigated and it proved true. Some friends of his told him the situation on the team wasn't great because Schwimmer, Petrov and Krimm were pressuring Gottfried to make amends with Beller. When Schwimmer moved to Paris, he mentioned how Beller truly cared about you, because he had confronted his coach at a great cost. Once, when I played against Petrov, he tried to talk to me, but I avoided him. I only heard a few sentences – that Beller was suffering injustice because he was fighting to protect you. I put all the pieces together myself, confirmed with Luca and that's how it is."

I contemplated everything and then spoke. "So, they all think that you held me captive those two years? That you're some sort of a bad guy?"

"Seems like that."

"I'll talk to them. I'm gonna make it all clear. They can't spread stories like that."

"Jane." He placed his palm on my cheek. "I really don't care what they think of me. As I said to Beller – I am thankful for everything they did to protect you, but that's where my consideration for them ends. Don't feel guilty. Don't feel the need to justify anything to them. We are where we are because we managed to come out the other side of that story together. They don't matter."

Alex was right. None of them mattered. Not even Matthias, with his ever-so-loving dark eyes and arms I wanted to fall into.

I went for dinner with Alex, and we had a wonderful time. Brazilian barbecue was something different indeed. We were thankful we had the chance to try it there. All that meat, accompanied by good, local red wine, made us dizzy and full of reckless desire for each other. We couldn't wait to be back in the hotel. We started pulling clothes off each other when we entered the hall on our floor – I never found my white shawl afterwards. He kissed me everywhere, all over my face, neck, breasts and every patch of skin my dress did and didn't cover. That night, he was patient, which I admired him for, because I wanted him entirely, badly, and immediately. I loved him with all my body and mind. I gave him my kisses, my caresses, my touch. The hours trickled by as we enjoyed each other at peace, without having to worry about what we'd do the following day or if there was anything to attend. I came over and over again, absorbed in this man who loved me and whom I loved above everything.

However, when I woke up at the crack of dawn to have a sip of water, my first thought was of Matthias. How could I? How dare I be so happy when he, the man who adored me to the point of endangering his career, was a few kilometres away from me, alone, thinking about me? Because I was certain that was what he was doing. My Mati.

*****

The opening game of the FIFA World Cup started sharply at five o'clock at the Arena de São Paulo. Almost sixty-six thousand people attended it. Of course, they did. In this land of football, who'd dare miss this historical moment? Alex and I were there with our parents and friends. We wanted to experience the hospitality of the Brazilians, since Ukraine was scheduled to play its first game against Chile in this very city. We didn't care about the Germans.

At least, most of us didn't.

I couldn't *not* care.

When *Das Lied der Deutschen* started after the Brazilian national anthem, I had to summon all my strength not to start humming the melody or clapping in support. To make things worse, the camera closely recorded all the players during the song, finishing on Matthias, who stood the last in the line with his teammates.

Throughout the game, I tried my best to cheer for Luca Ferreira, Alex's best friend, but my eyes couldn't help wandering off to Matthias and his team. At moments, I felt as if I was back in time, four years ago, again attending the final game of the tournament. Only now, Alex was with me, I was his faithful girlfriend, and I controlled my shouts of support. Whenever I stifled a yell in favour of Germans, it felt like a knife stab in my stomach.

This year, Germany bore the statistics slightly better than the Ukrainians. While Milan Andreyevich kept most of his squad from the previous World Cup – making them an average of twenty-seven and a half years old. Rolf Gottfried hadn't hesitated to change his older players for younger ones, bringing the team average age under twenty-four. It didn't have to mean anything, because sometimes it was the experience of the players and their ability to remain cool-headed that mattered and won games. Gottfried's new, young players seemed to be pretty temperamental and impulsive.

And fast. The Brazilian defence was successfully broken after thirty-one minutes, in a combination of passes between Krimm, Petrov and Kevin Jäger, who scored the first goal of the tournament. He was only twenty and his talent and surge compared to Petrov's four years ago.

The German Four, mildly said, ruled European football. Matthias and Michael Krimm were still in Munich, both now aged twenty-eight. Matthias kept refusing offers to move out of Germany, and Michael Krimm made clear that he loved Munich and planned to finish his career there. On top of his great skills and commitment, Gottfried chose Krimm as the new captain of the national team a few months after they won the golden trophy, which was, admittedly, one of Gottfried's best decisions. Apart from being constantly serious, Krimm was unflappable, and when you have a team of mostly twenty-two-year olds, you need a leader who will keep them on the ground and level-headed.

Apart from that, surprising everyone, Krimm met a girl not long before the European championship two years ago and married her a couple of months later. She wasn't of exceptional beauty but seemed smart and accomplished. She owned a small business that sold handmade candles and house decorations, and she wasn't in Brazil because she was nine months pregnant. I was glad for him. The whole world was. Everyone was hoping and cheering for a boy, but the Krimms didn't want to announce the gender yet.

Lens Petrov, the eternal womaniser, was now twenty-four. He'd stayed in Munich for a year following the World Cup and then moved to London, where he played for two years before switching to Manchester. It was a bold move to jump from one rival club to another, but Petrov didn't seem to care, and neither did the fans, since he scored goals like a machine. The pinnacle of his career was yet to come.

Ben Schwimmer had stayed in Munich until he moved to Alex's team in Paris two years ago, where he still played. He was now twenty-five and seemed to be getting better and better with every week. His statistics proved that. He scored unusually frequently for a midfielder, and his assist numbers were also higher than average. He was the captain of the club, never missed a game and played almost the entire ninety minutes throughout the whole season. His price was constantly increasing. Officially, he wasn't dating anyone, but I heard tell he was a womaniser like Lens, although more covert.

They were the core of the German national team. Of course, Gottfried still boasted about how his players were equally skilled and that he wouldn't suffer if one or two or even three of them got injured, because there was always someone who could replace them. However, the German Four had brought good vibes, optimism and team spirit that were so cherished by their team. That was why without Matthias, nothing had been the same.

Together, they showed the fans on the stands and behind the screens—and the powerful host, too, the previous tournament finalist—that they were still extremely powerful and the statistics were fully justified. The Germans were never satisfied with one goal, or even a lead. They wanted more. That was how, in the seventy-second minute, a stray ball was caught by one of the new young players and passed to Krimm, who directed it at Beller, who scored, hitting the ball at an angle that the goalkeeper could do nothing about.

Alex and his friends swore, while I stayed deadly serious. I was stunned at how difficult it was to stay calm and even. How could I have been so stupid to think that I would be able to ignore Matthias so easily? That insane man. He was running around the pitch, waving to all sixty-five-thousand present people, looking extraordinarily handsome.

I slurped down the remainder of my beer, thanking god and all the forces who had pressured the Brazilian lawmakers to lift the ban on the sale of alcohol at football games. I immediately felt dizzy and nauseous – but better that than confused about Matthias in front of Alex, I thought.

As soon as the game was finished, we left the stands, eager to return to the hotel, have a swim in the enclosed pool and relax at dinner. From tomorrow on, the guys would be on a strict regimen.

Reaching the hotel proved difficult, due to the enormous traffic jams, but we didn't mind. It was all a part of the culture and experience that came along with this competition we all loved so much.

Alex and I went to our room to change into swimwear before joining the others by the pool. Not even a full minute after we entered the room – I hadn't even removed my shoes yet – there was a knock at the door. I opened it, and déjà vu hit me. Only, it wasn't déjà vu. It was all for real. As it had been the previous time.

An enormous bouquet of roses, all brilliant, vivid shades of pink, had been left on the floor in front of the room. I turned to Alex – we both already knew who it was from. I felt terrible seeing how anger clouded his face.

Still, my curiosity was stronger than my guilt, and I reached for the envelope placed in the flowers.

I've never doubted it, but after last night I am even more certain that I still love you. Perhaps more than ever.

We need to talk. You must agree it's high time. We didn't separate properly. I have so much to ask you. There are a million questions that need answers. Give me that chance. Please.

Forever yours, M.B.

I was fighting back tears with mixed success. Alex approached me, and I went white.

"I'm sorry," was the only thing I was able to say before passing him the note. I felt terrible. He needn't be going through this. He didn't deserve this stress.

Furiously, Alex crumpled the paper, but he didn't shout, didn't throw things around. Instead, he said, "It seems like I'll have to fight him to put in his head that he should leave you alone."

"Oh, Alex, I don't know. I'm not sure it would help."
I reached for the phone and quickly called housekeeping to come and take the flowers away. Their scent had already invaded the entire room, and I knew it would irritate both Alex and me.

"I should try."

I sat on the bed, my head bent in sadness and shame. He sat next to me.

"Do you want to talk to him?" he asked.

I looked him in the eyes, wishing I could dive into them and lose myself, wishing I weren't here right now, having this conversation. "If I knew that would solve this and keep him away, I would. But I highly doubt it."

He hugged me. "The next time I see him, I will talk to him," he said seriously. "Damn it. I want to break every bone in his body, but I agree with you...it wouldn't help. I'll try talking to him, explaining everything. With you, he doesn't listen. He only understands what he sees, and that is that you are beautiful and scared. He doesn't get that you're scared of him."

Stunned, I didn't reply right away. I had never thought about it that way. It was exactly like that. Matthias hadn't listened. Ever. Even in the beginning, when he asked me out, he was persistent until I accepted. He never took my no as an answer. It always had to be his way. Admittedly, that was something I understood – many things went my way, too. But all the big decisions were his. All except the last one, the biggest one, when I left him at the Olympic Stadium in Berlin, minutes after he'd won the World Cup, to come and be with this man. All these years, I'd never replied to his letters and calls, and he still persisted. Yesterday, I told him he shouldn't be looking for me. And as usual, he hadn't listened. Alex was right. He saw I was scared. He probably thought I was frightened of Alex. That was why he wasn't going to stop until...until I talked to him.

I didn't want to say it to Alex. I was afraid he might think that, deep in my heart, I actually wanted to meet Matthias. I couldn't hurt him over this again, so I put in my mind – I would not succumb to any of

Matthias's pressures, flowers, letters or anything. The pain he was causing with his love confessions and sad eyes, well, I'd have to get used to it.

"You can try that, Alex," I finally said. "But, again, I'm afraid it'd end up with a fight. Not because you're loose tempered, but because he's not reasonable."

"I know how to defend myself."

I chuckled. I loved him for being able to make me smile in almost any situation. "I know you do." I kissed him on the nose and drew my fingers through his hair, "I want you to know that I'm not okay with what he's been doing, that it makes me agitated, that it's nothing like four years ago. This time, they cannot sway me. I am yours and only yours. I swear on it."

Alex smiled and, with that gentleness that always astounded me, pushed a strand of hair from my face. "When you say it with those eyes, I'd believe that grass is blue."

"It is blue."

"Alright."

I laughed. "Come on, be serious." I sat in his lap. His hands under my dress made me forget all the worries of the day.

"I am serious, and I am seriously going to take you now."

It wasn't love-making. It was love-taking – desperate, eager, frenzied. My dress was on the floor in one piece, but his shirt lost a few buttons. I covered his perfect torso in kisses, feeling something stir in me as his firm abs, every muscle emphasised, cramped under my touch. When my lips and tongue moved lower, his hand in my hair squeezed almost hard enough to hurt me, but I didn't stop. I was full to bursting with some furore, some wild storm that I had to take out. We both were. We needed a vent. And this was the best.

Before he came, he pulled me by the hair, moving my head away from his groin, where I'd been whole-heartedly enjoying myself. For a moment, I was disappointed – until, in a rapid move, he placed me on my back, raised my legs over his shoulders and entered me. I screamed, absorbing all the beauty and bliss of the feeling he was giving me. I only had to move under him slightly before a forceful wave of orgasm shook my entire body. He saw it in my blurred eyes, let me enjoy it until the end. I saw him smile, confidently and with lust, and he then started thrusting into me, giving me more, taking himself, us, for another peak of bliss.

*****

Like last time, Alex's training took up most of his day. However, this time I didn't come up with any excuses to leave him. Other than the English team's games, of course. Matthew Vance, Dad's friend, was still the coach, but even if he wasn't, it was only natural that I attended the games with my parents and the girls.

This time, it was I who didn't want to leave Alex for too long. I knew it was for fear, although whether it was fear of what Matthias could do or fear of what I might do, I could not say. I didn't want to take any risks.

On the 15th of June, I left for Brasília with the girls. Bea was excited to meet up with Harold, as they hadn't seen each other for a week (the English team had gone straight to the host city where their first game would be). The three of us didn't stop teasing her for the entire two-hour flight.

"Come on, Bea, Alex and I used to see each other once a week before we started living together," I said.

"Yes, Darling," Angie said, "but those two have been living together from the beginning."

"We haven't," Bea defended. "We moved in after the first New Year's."

"Don't lie now," Lana intervened. "He spent every single night in your and Jane's apartment after we returned from Germany until the official move-in date you guys gave to the papers."

"Of course he did. That guy can make out seven times a day and still he'd go for more if he wasn't considerate to his woman."

"Angelina!" Bea was instantly all red.

"Come on. You two didn't get off of each other for at least two years."

"Damn it, I feel bad I missed all that," I said.

"You didn't miss anything, hun, they still do it quite regularly," Angie went on. "Actually, almost every time you think about bumping into them, surprising them, inviting them out for a drink – don't. They'll be busy."

Bea threw her travel pillow at her. "Let's not mention your sex appetite when you have a boyfriend."

"Not only when I have a boyfriend, girl."

I was doubled over, my stomach cramping from laughing so hard.

We were over-the-moon happy for Bea. Harold was everything she needed in a man. She was still getting used to the fact that she'd found somebody who complemented her in every possible sense; most of us are convinced those men don't exist until they show up. Their wedding was scheduled for mid-August in London this year, and we were counting down the days. Most of the preparations had been done. Their mothers offered to take care of everything. They didn't want to make it too grand, because all they cared about was having close family and friends around, but the papers were constantly gearing up for it, guaranteeing that it'd be one of the biggest weddings of the year.

In Brasília, we stayed in the same hotel as the English team. We arrived at lunchtime, and when the receptionist took us to the main restaurant, most of the players were already there, including Coach Vance – and Joshua Hadleigh, who, despite being with his wife, couldn't help staring at me.

I smiled at him innocently, trying to make the situation less awkward in front of the girl but somehow maliciously proud that I still provoked those reactions with men without even trying, without even uttering a word.

Harold was next to us in an instant.

"Girls, you come with us," he said, taking Bea by the waist and leading the way.

"Hun, don't do anything stupid," Angie whispered in my ear. "That poor woman doesn't deserve it."

"I promise, I won't." I winked at her and headed towards the large table where most of the players sat.

Half of the English players at the table were new names compared to four years ago. Harold, Joshua and Keaton Flanagan were still part of the national team. I greeted Keaton before taking my seat, and then turned to Joshua, who was still looking at me so unsubtly that, were I his wife, I'd break that plate over his head.

"Hello, Josh," I said. "Good to see you again at the World Cup." He went white. I could hear Angie stifling her laugh. The picture of civility, I turned to the woman and held out my hand. "Hello, Thea. Nice to meet you. Would you believe I'm gonna wear your dress tomorrow?"

That melted her. Thea Watkins Hadleigh was an admired and appreciated designer in the U.K. Her stores were in the bigger cities throughout the country. Being only twenty-five, she was considered highly successful in the fashion industry since she'd managed to break through at such a young age. Her family were well-off, too, and it went without saying that they had assisted her at the beginning. But no one could deny that she had talent and brains, and she was making a name for herself.

It wasn't a coincidence, of course, that I was wearing one of her dresses tomorrow. I had figured she'd come with Joshua to the tournament. Plus, the dresses she designed were indeed stunning and beautiful, and the first English game was a perfect occasion for me to wear a white and red one I had bought a couple of months ago.

Thea accepted my hand and smiled courteously. "Pleasure to meet you, Jane. Are you serious about the dress?"

"Of course."

"Then I'll make a call to have a couple thousand more sewn immediately."

We all laughed, including Joshua.

"You fox," Angie whispered, "I almost had a heart attack. I was sure you'd do something nasty."

"I'm not that girl anymore, Angie."

"No, but now you're a woman. I'd expect anything from you."

We didn't stay with them for long – I had to change and then go to a meet-and-greet Lana had organised for me. Bea stayed with Harold, so the three of us went out for a long and exciting day. I'd never been to Brasília before, and I wanted to do some sightseeing. But according to Lana's plan, that was scheduled for our next visit in two weeks, when England would play the third match of the group stage.

When we returned to the hotel at the end of the day, I was exhausted but fulfilled to have brought joy to so many young hearts. I invited the girls over for a late drink, because I felt I needed at least three glasses of good wine to completely relax. They came, and we talked excitedly about everything that had taken place that day. Lana was happy to tick off all the third-day tournament tasks. Angie was teasing ever-so-in-love Bea about being so defensive of Harold, who'd had an argument with one of the defensive players. I was happy, too, and while missing Alex, I was excited for tomorrow's game and grateful that my family were with me again for a month.

It felt good, being a faithful girlfriend.

*****

The game against Canada started pretty early, at one o'clock in the afternoon. It was scorching hot but wonderful. The Estádio Nacional could hold sixty-eight thousand people, and it seemed that all those seats were taken, which was a surprise since Canada had always cared more about hockey than football. They were definitely not among the favourite teams here.

The girls and I also got a chance to meet Harold's parents. They were a kind, elderly couple who adored Bea from the moment they saw her. They thought their son would either never marry or marry a gold-digger. Bea was more than he deserved, they joked.

Soon after the game started, Harold's, Bea's and my parents somehow got separated from us in the upper seats while the four of us screamed, yelled and cheered, waving our English flags – exactly like four years ago. I was jumping, singing, supporting, drinking beer, celebrating each of the three goals scored within the ninety minutes.

After the game ended, we retreated from the stands and headed towards the hotel, where we met the team for a light dinner. Dizzied by the additional wine I drank, I felt sleepy pretty early, so I went to my room. I had a flight back to São Paul in the morning; everyone else would stay, except for Lana and Angie, who wanted to be my company while Alex was at training.

For Lana, it was natural, since she worked almost 24/7 as my manager. Angie could've stayed with the English. I saw that she wanted to – she was eyeing the older brother of Duncan Fletcher, one of the players, who came to support his brother. The guy was a personal trainer with shoulders almost as wide as Alex's. Angie loved bulky guys. No wonder she liked him. Still, she came along with me.
"You didn't have to," I said on the plane the next day.

"No, I didn't. But don't worry about it. He'll get his chance the next time we meet." She winked.

"Come on." I nudged her. "Why are you here?"

She looked away, and I knew it was something uncomfortable. "I want to take care of you," she admitted, eyes trained on the scenery out the window.

My heart dropped. "You don't trust me? After all I've been through with Alex, without him, for him."

"I trust you." Angie turned to me, and I saw restrained anger in her eyes. "But I don't trust that man Beller. I saw him at the hotel in São Paulo while he was waiting for you, before he met you and Alex. Jane, that man is unnaturally, insanely obsessed with you. You have no idea what I told him, anything to get him to go away, to make him leave, and you know what he kept saying? That he loves you and he's not giving up. That I, as a good and responsible friend, should help set you free from Alex instead of supporting the prison sentence he's put on you."

I didn't know she had seen him that day. Still, I understood where her concern was coming from, and it infuriated me. How dare Matthias speak to my friend like this?

"Angie, you don't have to feel responsible for anything that happened to me in France. We've discussed it a hundred times. If I had wanted help, I would've searched for it. I needed to stay with Alex."

"I know. He just pushed my buttons with that stupid comment. But now I know that he's willing to do anything – literally anything – to reach you. Remember what a gentleman he used to be? Now, I feel like he'd step over dead bodies just to get to you. I didn't do anything while you lived in France, but at least I can be here. I can be around."

Perhaps she was right. After hearing that Matthias had got himself expelled from the national team because of me, it went without saying he was ready to do just about anything.

Didn't that mean he loved me more than anyone ever would?

CHAPTER 5

Back in São Paulo, the Ukrainians were getting ready for their first game. They would be facing Chile, which meant that their support may be in greater numbers than our fans. For this game it was estimated that in the huge Arena Corinthians, there were twenty-seven thousand Ukrainians. This game also started at one o'clock, in the day's strongest sun and heat, which in this part of Brazil didn't feel as harsh as in the north, with only 17 degrees on the scale, so for my debut, I wore denim shorts and Alex's jersey, with Ukrainian flags painted on my cheeks.

When the anthem was played, it was a moment for the movies. I held hands with Alex's mother and sister while we sang the lyrics that sent a clear message to our opponents in the following days, especially the Germans. It would be different this time. We wouldn't make the same mistakes. I wouldn't.

The Ukrainians, clad in yellow, started the match aggressive and on the attack. They were fresh and eager to show that they were even better than predicted. The Chilean team was also among the favourites, so the battle was harsh. I didn't sit down from the first whistle to the end of the forty-eighth minute, when the end of the first half was announced. It was still 0–0 and the ball possession was almost 50/50, with no great chances on either side. I knew Milan Andreyevich's team would do something in the remaining forty-five minutes. They didn't play to draw. They wanted all the points they could get. There was no counting, no fear of the opponent like the last time. Now, Ukraine knew they could take on anyone, since, well, they had done that four years ago. And the only reason they hadn't gotten the golden trophy then was the German coach. And Alex. And me.

I forced those thoughts out of my head. It wasn't the time to look troubled. My phone vibrated, and I checked it while waiting for the players to come out of the tunnel.

You are gorgeous. All the cameras seem to be on you. PS: You'd look way better with black-red-gold on your face, but I still want to take those cheeks in my hands and smudge them with kisses. ;)

I went cold and started sweating. Of course, he was watching the game on the TV. Flustered and instantly nervous, I let out a huff of frustration.

"What's wrong?" Lana asked. I passed her the phone. She rolled her eyes. "I'll block...oh, god."

"What?" Angie asked. She took the phone from Lana and started laughing maniacally. "That man is completely out of his mind."

"Let me see!" I took my phone back.

There was a new message under the original, followed by a picture with a bowl entirely full of SIM cards. *You can try blocking me. I'm ready. ;)*

I did something unforgivable – I smiled.

Lana was already shooting lasers at me with her eyes. I didn't know what to say, because I was immediately embarrassed, but Angie stepped in to my defence.

"Don't give her a lecture now. It's not the time. And who wouldn't laugh at something like this?"

"That's how it all started last time, Angelina," Lana hissed. "Give me that phone. He cannot buy that more numbers than your phone can block."

"It's okay, Lana. There's no point," I said. "I'm just gonna ignore him."

"Will you?"

I was too slow with my reply.

"See, Jane!"

"It's just text messages, Lana. Don't make a fuss over it."

The players were coming out of the tunnel now, so I didn't let her say anything. I knew what I was doing. What Matthias had done was funny. That was all. I'd even tell Alex. We'd laugh about it together.

The second half of the match was heated from the beginning. There were no substitutes, but the tempo was different, and it was accelerating every second. In the sixtieth minute, twenty-three-year-old Anatoliy Honchar, a new centre midfield, scored from twenty metres away from the posts, sending the ball precisely through a group of mixed yellow and red players. I screamed in unison with Alex's parents and sister, and the fans were jumping in support and exhilaration.

The excitement receded within minutes, replaced by a heavy fog of tension. Both teams now wanted to achieve something more – one team to equalise, the other to score again.

Ten minutes later it happened and, of course, my boyfriend wasn't the one taking the goal. This time, Andriy Barnik shot a goal that would earn millions of views on social media for its exceptionality. The ball bounced off three different feet within the penalty area before Barnik managed to jump high enough and hit it with his head, his back turned towards the goal. It was pure luck, coincidence, skill and talent.

Barnik was still referred to as "The Kid," although he was four years older than at the previous competition, where he got that nickname. After he was awarded the Best Young Player at the previous World Cup, he shot onto the lists of the highest-paid players in Europe. The best offer he got came from Liverpool, so he moved there. He was happy in England – he loved the weather and the people, he'd had a couple of relationships and was appreciated among the fans. In this tournament, he wanted to show he was still getting better and that his best time was yet to come.

The remaining twenty minutes of the game fell away in the blink of an eye. The Ukrainians attacked and defended in equal measure. No one scored on Alex. He was still the best goalkeeper in the world, with the best statistics to show for his extraordinary skills and talent; but he'd be the first to say he owed much to his teammates, who tried hard not to let the enemy players create too many dangerous chances that could end up as goals.

When the final whistle sounded, the result showed 2–0 for Ukraine, and we could all exhale in relief. Three points were ours. I followed Alex with my eyes as he walked from the goal to the tunnel, and sent him a kiss when he was near enough to see me. It was done with love, of course, but with a purpose, too. I wanted everyone to witness again how much I adored him. Everyone.

My phone vibrated again.

What do you think – if I text your boyfriend to tell him you were smiling most of the game because of me, would that destroy his mood?

I froze. My hands were clammy, and I worried the phone might slip out of them. How the hell did he get Alex's phone number? What was I going to do?

Yep, I think that's what I'm gonna do. Unless, of course, you reply to me. There you go, Jane. You can save your boyfriend a very bad day.

"Jane, don't!" Lana said when she saw me trying to type with shaking fingers.

"Lana, I have to. You don't understand."

If Lana or Angie spoke after that, I didn't hear them. My heart was in my ears as I slowly, painfully typed my reply.

- Are you blackmailing me now?

Wow! You answered! Why didn't I do this earlier? I am so stupid. I should've used this card years ago.

- It's actually very mature of you that you didn't. However, now I'd politely ask you not to. Ever.

Of course. If you meet me.

- You know that's not possible.

Why? Because we're not in the same city? Because you're constantly with Blondie? You know those are solvable problems.

- Matthias, you and I shouldn't meet. Please, don't write to Alex. Don't write to me anymore.

Alright. I'll call you when you return to the hotel.

- No!

Then I'll call Blondie.

- Matthias! Stop! I'll contact the police.

And tell them what? Come on, everyone cheers for us. You read the papers. I wouldn't be surprised if the police actually helped me.

- Stop joking! This is not funny! You are disturbing my peace and my life! Leave me alone! Leave us alone!

I will. But only when you say it to my face.

- It can't happen. You and I can never meet.

I'll explain to you over the phone why that's incorrect. I'll call you when you reach the hotel. You can choose – either you text me when you're alone, or I'll ring Blondie to tell him how much he sucks at football.

There was nothing else I could say.

- Alright. But we have a flight to Rio after they return to the hotel.

No problem. I'll call you when you're in Rio.

On the way to the hotel, I was silent. My brain was working fast, filtering through the dozens of emotions mixing in my head and heart. It would be difficult to hide this from Alex. What if I told him? I didn't want Matthias and him to talk. I didn't know what Matthias could say or do, but I was sure he could come up with something to make Alex angry, and I didn't want that. Not again. He'd already lost his head because of me once, and that cost him the gold medal for his country. I was not putting him in the same peril again. There was also no way I would be able to talk to Matthias while Alex was listening. Not even with my acting skills.

The only reasonable option was that I pick up the phone while Alex was sleeping or somewhere with his friends. Depending on how the call went, I'd decide whether I would tell Alex about it or not. I told the girls my decision.

As expected, Lana wanted to lecture me, but Angie stopped her whenever she opened her mouth. For the remainder of the cab ride, however, I could see Angie watching me closely.

Back in the hotel, I was packing when Alex came through the door. To mask my stress, I jumped at him and drew him into bed, not giving him a chance to notice that anything was strange. We only stopped when we'd be late unless he was showered and packed in fifteen minutes.

While I was waiting for him, I absentmindedly put some of his clothes into the suitcase, thinking through events and wondering if I was really doing the right thing. As Lana had said, this was how it started the previous time. I didn't want anything with Matthias then, but I ended up crazy about him. And now, now I was sure I shouldn't get close to him because...well, as he said, we hadn't separated properly. There were so many things unsaid. And when I saw him that day, in this very hotel, my heart jumped from something besides fear.

When we reached our rooms in Rio, I made sure Alex and I had another round of sex, this time under the shower, and then he said he was meeting the guys at the pool. They wanted to discuss something about the game between Morocco and South Korea, the other two teams in our group, that had finished with a draw. I said I would join them once I fixed my hair. He didn't suspect anything; my hair could sometimes take two hours to get completely presentable, and since he was far from an expert in hairstyling, he wouldn't know the difference between a five-second ponytail and properly styled waves.

As soon as I was ready and Alex was fifteen minutes gone, I texted *Now* to the unsaved number.

My phone rang.

I had to sit down and inhale deeply three times deeply before answering.

"Is that the most gorgeous woman in the world on the phone?" His deep voice and rough accent sent tremors down my spine.

"What do you want? Tell me fast. I have to go."

"To see you."

"Not possible. You know that. Why did you insist to call?" I was giving the utmost effort to sound cold and professional.

"To hear your voice while Blondie is not around."

"*Matthias,*" my frustration was rising, "in what language and how many times do I need to tell you? *Leave me alone.* Leave Alex alone. He's suffered enough already because of us. Please, stop."

"You've suffered, too. I've suffered. You left me at the pitch, Jane, with at least a billion people watching, and yet I don't get to hear some answers?"

What he said hurt. I felt the memory of that pain flash through me too – how much it hurt to let go of his hand, leaving for the unknown, unsure what Alex would do to me. That evening had gone better for me than I deserved. For Matthias, his ending was disputable. He took home that damn golden trophy, the most important in football. How many footballers get to achieve that? But he was also embarrassed, dumped by his greatest love, according to many. According to him.

"Why are you refusing to be fair with me?" he continued after I didn't speak. "If you don't care, as you say, why don't you meet me and tell me that?"

"I'm telling you now." My voice was pathetic, quivering.

"Why didn't you tell me, then? Not once during these four years? Was it so difficult to reply to a message?"

My breathing accelerated. "I respect Alex. I didn't want—"

"You can respect him for another hundred years, Jane, but you know very well what you feel about me."

I didn't want to answer that. "Tell me, what do I have to do to make you stop?"

"Meet me."

"Except for that."

"Listen, Jane Andersonn, I know you're used to getting what you want, but I am, too. That I let you do what you wanted that evening and go to that primitive idiot who locked you in the house for two years and made you look like a zombie is something I'll never forgive myself."

I couldn't be angry with him, as much as all my insides were trying. "Matthias, you couldn't have done anything. I had to go look for Alex. It was the only right thing to do. He never locked me up. Don't blame yourself for that."

"I do. Because I fucking love you and know that I would never do anything similar to you. Meet me, Jane. Show me you don't care. When I see that you don't care, I'll leave you alone, I promise."

"I have to go." I wanted this call over as soon as possible, because the sound of his voice evoked too many memories, too many emotions I wasn't allowed to feel, not now, not after all this time, not after everything Alex and I had gone through. "Please, don't threaten me with calling Alex. I would never forgive myself if he did something reckless and impulsive on the pitch again. Don't do it to him, Matthias, please. If you want to defeat him, do it like a man, properly, professionally, in the game. Not like your coach did."

I knew I surprised him by saying this, because he was silent for a long moment. I took the pause to contemplate the fact that, for one of the rare moments in my life, I, Jane Andersonn, was begging.

"Damn it. When you ask me like this, you hog-tie me," Matthias said after a while. "Alright. I promise I won't talk to Blondie, but that doesn't change the fact that I need to see you."

"No! And I have to go now. I'm running late."

"Let it be your way again. But I'm guessing you remember how stubborn I am?"

"I do." I didn't let him say anything else and hung up.

Damn it! Damn it! Damn it!

I ran to the bathroom to wash my face with cold water. I shouldn't feel like this. I shouldn't be so flustered about him. Yes, his voice excited everything in me, but isn't that only so natural? We used to have something. Something pure and beautiful. Something promising. There had never been any sex. How ironic! The greatest threat to my relationship, and we'd never even had sex. And he, being so hard-headed and persistent! Why was I so sure that he wouldn't leave me alone until we met?

If I really loved Alex, I shouldn't have a problem meeting Matthias and telling him that. So why was I so scared of being alone with him? He wouldn't drug me, rape me, hit me, or anything of the sort. If I stood in front of him and told him everything properly, perhaps he'd let me be, simply let me be with Alex. I was happy with Alex. I knew that. Matthias needed to know, too.

I fixed my makeup and hair and decided that I would keep avoiding the German as much as I could, at least until Ukraine made it through to the eighth final. Then, if he persisted or did something that could endanger Alex and his team, I would ask Alex for advice. I was not doing it alone this time. Nothing behind his back. Matthias could send a million butterflies fluttering around inside me with his voice and mysterious eyes, but I loved my perfect man. And I wasn't losing him again.

CHAPTER 6

Lana was trying her maniacal best to make me work every single minute I wasn't sleeping or with Alex. She wasn't angry, but she disapproved of me talking to Matthias. Angie was on my side – not that it made any difference when Lana passed me her tablet with a detailed plan for the day, even lunch and dinner breaks and Alex-comes-from-training breaks. I barely had time to breathe; I certainly didn't have time to give Matthias more than a passing thought.

On our first full day in Rio, Bea joined and the four of us went sightseeing. After a walk along the Copacabana and then Ipanema beach, I secretly hoped that we'd be able to sit somewhere I could peek at the game between Germany and Japan that was taking place. But Lana was adamant that we stick to the schedule, which, I knew, she had designed on purpose to keep me away from the TV. Later, I found out they had won 3–1. Good. Their new goalkeeper, Ewald Fuchs, wasn't like Alex.

Ewald Fuchs joined the national team one year after the European championship. Another goalkeeper had succeeded Dieter Lahrmann, but he also retired in short order. Ewald was a twenty-year-old wunderkind who many in Germany compared to Alex. However, the rest of the world saw he wasn't in Alex's league. He was gifted, perhaps, but not skilled. Alex was an exceptional, extraordinary combination of talent, hard work, sensitive reflexes, quick eyes and luck. Ewald had all of those qualities, but to a lower degree. Interestingly, though, he was extremely handsome, and charming, polite and charismatic to boot. Girls were losing it over his warm, grey, scrutinising eyes. He was loved by the national team, wanted by women and admired by the media. He certainly enjoyed nightlife and parties to the degree he could with his job, but he knew how to behave. And he was single. A deadly combination.

"I'd gladly shag him," Angie said for the umpteenth time. "Even though he's like, eight years younger."

"I bet he knows what he's doing," I added. "He seems to have gained some experience."

"Let's see. If we happen to be in the same city, I'm not wasting my chance."

"Unfortunately for you, I'll make sure that doesn't happen, so put your eyes on someone else," Lana added seriously.

"I agree," Bea jumped in.

Angie and I looked at them with comedic exasperation, rolling our eyes.

That day, June 20th, Alex and his teammates were scheduled to see two local primary schools whose pupils were exceptional in football competitions. They'd play a short game with the kids, do an autograph signing and take some photos, and then, in the afternoon, they'd be free for sightseeing. Lana organised an outing to go with them to see the symbol of Rio and Brazil – Christ the Redeemer. The following two days, the Ukrainian team would be busy at training, and the four of us would go to watch England play against Paraguay in Salvador, a city also on the Atlantic coast but two hours away from Rio by plane.

My family and I had never been particularly religious. We loved and respected holidays because they usually managed to bring us together, and they are a time when everyone felt cheerful and hopeful, regardless of circumstances. That was why, when I saw the tall statue of Christ, the awe I felt had nothing to do with religion. It was everything combined – the perfect, precise architecture, the grandiosity of its size, the hilltop where we stood, the sight of the city spread out under us, the sharp sun that cut through clouds down to the beaches and concrete streets and buildings, the unsteady ocean that disturbed the coast, the distant dispersed islands. Everything was pure magic.

Alex holding my hand made it all perfect.

I didn't want to spend much time away from him, so I agreed to leave after the England match and return to him in Rio in the early hours of the following day. Lana was happy to organise that, and I felt safer around him, although he was still away most of the day with his team and coach.

I couldn't tell anymore if I was afraid of myself or if I was worried that I might do something stupid if I were away from Alex. Nothing was like Germany four years ago, when I craved the attention coming from all those men who came to me, practically ready on a platter. My primary worry was the idea of being in Matthias's vicinity. I was afraid that once Alex was a couple hundred kilometres away, I'd start thinking differently, hoping that I could sort things out somehow, believing that I could manage on my own, or, worst of all – that I could do something again without anyone knowing. I was pretty sure Matthias suspected that, too, which explained his persistence.

That was why I kept close to Alex and behaved as he deserved – as his perfect girlfriend.

"I appreciate everything you've been doing, Jane." He murmured as he kissed me on the crown of my head the evening before the English game.

We were in bed, hugging, about to fall asleep, tired after a long and exciting day. I snuggled closer to his chest. I loved the feeling of his skin on mine.

"I care deeply about you." I kissed an old scratch on his hand he'd got while practising penalties. "I'm not letting anything or anyone get in the way like last time."

"I'm not that boy now, Love. Don't worry."

"You were a man even then, Alex. What happened was terrible. It would be too much for anyone."

He kissed me again, this time on my neck, sending goose bumps all over my body. "You're right, but it happened once. It won't again, I promise you. I promised that myself before we came here."

I turned to face him. His arms were draped across me, covering my whole back, and I knew I wouldn't be able to resist the urge to have him again, even though we were tired. "You know you're the best, most flawless man I've ever met?"

He smiled. "If you continue saying those things, I'm gonna strut around like a peacock."

"You already inspire awe, adoration and respect from everyone." My hand was on his back, moving slowly down to his leg. I tried to dig my nails in but couldn't manage to because, like always, it was as firm as a stone.

"Do you know what you inspire in me right now?" His fingers were in my hair, pulling me to a breathless kiss while I felt something else getting hard as a stone. "A wish to spend the whole night taking you in every possible way."

"That would certainly impede your training tomorrow. Your coach might be angry and demand we don't share the room anymore." I returned his kisses greedily.

"I have an idea," he said, effortlessly spreading my legs with his and climbing over me. "After this is over..." My breathing was already shallow with excitement. "We go on some secluded island here in Brazil, and we only drink cocktails and have sex, all day, every day?"

"Exactly."

He entered me easily and took me on a wild, familiar, rapturous roller coaster. He didn't want to finish fast, although I felt how easy it would have been to. He wanted to tease and torture me first, and then to love me, endlessly, prolonged, deeply, until I melted in it. And that's exactly what he did.

*****

After a fast breakfast, the girls and I left for the airport. We made it on time to meet my parents in the hotel near the stadium. The game was scheduled to start at four o'clock, and we had slightly more than two hours to have a drink in the hotel bar and head to the match.

I took a bath, put on a casual summer white dress with red roses, fixed my hair (in less than twenty minutes this time), applied some makeup and waited for my parents to pick me up from the room. Bea was going with her family, and Angie and Lana together.

I was surprised that Dad and Mom were late, but as they explained when we finally met, Dad had to make an urgent phone call regarding a big sale of some horses at the ranch. They looked gorgeous together, Dad in his grey suit and Mom in a dress matching the hue of his red tie.

We hugged, an occurrence that, once odd, had become more common since my arrival at the ranch in that decrepit state. We felt closer now than ever before. Even Dad.

"I missed you," I wasn't afraid to say anymore.

"We missed you, too," Dad replied as we headed downstairs. "You've been quite busy."

"Yes, Lana's making sure of that. But I enjoy it. São Paulo and Rio were a whole new world to me." We left the elevator and entered the vast entrance hall. "Plus, all the joyous faces of people we've met along the way – it fills me with happiness. Alex and I are together as much as we can be when he's not on the pitch. We talk, make plans—"

"You stay away from trouble."

"Brad!"

"It's okay, Mom." I blushed. "Dad has a point. I do stay away from trouble."

All three of us managed to laugh.

"Good afternoon. May I speak to you?"

We stopped dead in our tracks. An ice-cold sweat blanketed my body in an instant. Dad and Mom were flabbergasted, too. *No, no, no, no, no! This is not happening.*

"No, you may not talk to my daughter." Dad was the first to speak, emphasising every word.

I stared at Matthias in complete disbelief. My mind was overheating. Damn it! I was in Salvador. What did Lana say – where were they, Recife or something? That was like, a thousand kilometres from here! *He can't be here!*

"I actually wanted to talk to you, Mr Andersonn."

My heart felt like it had been frozen for several seconds. Since I miraculously hadn't dropped dead, I wondered deliriously if I was immortal.

"Matthias, for goodness' sake! Stop it!" I screamed. Mom took me by the hand.

Seeing how upset I was, Dad swelled in agitation. "Young man, I think my daughter is pretty clear. What are you doing here? I'm sure your coach doesn't approve of this."

"He doesn't know I'm here. I need to talk to you, Mr Andersonn. It's important and concerns the wellbeing of your daughter."

"In what way?" Dad asked.

Matthias looked at me. The sight of those determined eyes terrified me.

At the same time, I couldn't help seeing how much they adored me.

"I want only the best for her, and she knows that, but she refuses to listen. I need to talk to you, to explain everything, so you'll see I am not joking."

"Matthias," Mom intervened in a whisper. The last thing we needed was a public shouting match. "I understand that you have feelings for Jane. So why don't you respect hers?"

For a second, Matthias seemed moved by that. But he recovered quickly.

"Because sometimes we mistake love for guilt and responsibility," he replied, looking at me sadly.

I felt my legs and joints becoming jelly.

"Responsibility for what?" Dad asked.

"That's what I want to talk to you about."

I was staring at Matthias, surprised anew at how attractive I found him while simultaneously hoping that my eyes could begin firing off poison-tipped arrows. He was, as I remembered, a Greek statue, perfectly sculpted, his face adorned with splendid, faultless lines and the pleasing, complementary colours of his skin, mouth and eyes.

"Alright," Dad said after a brief pause. "I'll meet you here after the match."

His words punched the air out of my stomach and lungs.

"Dad, no!" I tried to rebel, but he raised a hand.

"Jane, I'll finish this, once and for all," he told me. Then he turned to Matthias again, whose dark eyes were wide with shock that Brad Andersonn had agreed to meet him. "We're in a hurry now."

"Alright. I'll wait," he said obligingly.

Mom took me by the hand and walked me out without another word. I turned back at the doorway to see if I had imagined all this, and my stomach dropped to see I hadn't. Matthias was still here, in the same city as me when he was supposed to be miles and miles away, watching us go, that self-confident, satisfactory smile on his lips. I wanted to charge back and smash a chair on his head.

- Are you completely out of your mind? I texted him the moment we were in the car.

Yes. For you. I thought you'd figured that out.

- Why are you playing games with my life and happiness? What will you tell Brad?

Exactly what happened four years ago. That Blondie took you captive to punish you, and that I am sincerely mad about you and want to be with you, but you are scared to leave the goalie.

- That's it. I'm putting you in a mental institution. Just wait until the match is over. Stay there, and I'll send some sanatorium staff to take you away.

Now you are making jokes.

We arrived at the Arena Fonte Nova, and I had to put my phone aside. Lana and Angie were waiting at the entrance, while Bea was with her and Harold's parents in the stands already.

"Girls, I need to talk to you," I hissed to Angie. She looked at me in concern. "It's serious."

She drew the letter "M" in the air with her finger. I nodded.

The moment the national anthems were over and the first whistle blew, I took my seat. I was between Mom and Lana, so I couldn't say much. It was difficult to concentrate on the excellent game when what was about to happen was hanging over my head like the executioner's blade.

I checked my phone some twenty minutes into the game and there was a message.

You can prevent me from talking to your father. You know how. ;)

- NO!

My chest clenched with contrasting feelings and duties. What was I to do? I had to protect my and Alex's happiness with all my power. If Matthias talked to my father, everything could go to ruin. I didn't know what he might tell him. Perhaps the entire truth, perhaps only the parts that suited him. Or maybe even something that had never taken place. Matthias knew very well there was nothing he could lose. He'd been kicked off the team once, and he was put back. He'd already lied to his coach to come and talk to me. He was ready for absolutely anything.

Well, then I take it you're leaving it up to me to save you from Blondie. Because you want to be saved. No problem, Darling. I'll talk to your father and sort it all out.

I waited until after half-time, when the girls and I went for a break away from our parents. I told them everything in one breath. They were furious.

"Let him do it," Lana said resolutely.

"Have you gone mad, too?" I gasped at her.

"No. You and Alex said it yourselves – after what Gottfried did at the previous tournament, after what you did, Alex and you stayed together. There is nothing, absolutely nothing any of them can do to separate you. And nobody Brad may believe more than Alex. Because you vouch for Alex. You see? Beller could tell your father just about anything, but if Alex says it's all lies and sticks to you, then Matthias has no chance of ruining anything."

"But what if he tells Dad something true, and Dad believes him? Many of the things I did there are true. If Matthias gives Dad details of how and when we met, how I avoided going back to Alex when I could, if he reminds him that I *suddenly* changed my attitude towards the Germans and cheered for them whole-heartedly, Dad may believe it all, no matter what Alex says."

"Jane," Bea cut in, "I believe your father would be on Alex's side no matter what. He's not stupid. He saw how Alex fought for you, how he cared for you, how he endured everything to prove he still really loves you. Your father approves of Alex to a great extent. Let Beller talk to him. He doesn't have any proof anyway."

"Or maybe he has," Angie said. We all looked at her. "Come on, Matthias knows all this. He also knows that if he infuriates Brad Andersonn, he's in for a lot of trouble. He probably knows or has something that Brad will believe."

"Oh, fuck," Lana said, her head in her hands. "Fuck, fuck, fuck!" She never swore. "Text messages." As soon as it dawned on me what she was talking about, I almost lost my balance. Lana continued, "A guy as infatuated as he is...I bet he kept all the messages you exchanged then, and I can also bet that you didn't hide your feelings in them. Am I correct?"

I couldn't reply, so I only nodded, as white and still as a wall.

"Then we have to prevent this meeting with Brad. At any cost," Angie said.

- Matthias, please, don't talk to my father. I tried for the last time, already knowing it was doomed.

Then you have to talk to me.

- If I do, will you promise you won't try to reach again any of my close family members, friends or Alex?

I promise.

- Alright.

I'm waiting for you. Room 1202. If you don't show up before 21h, I'll talk to Brad.

I wasn't sure if I should say what was on my mind, but at that moment, I thought it the best tactical move. He had emotions for me. I had to play that card.

- Don't threaten me. That's not how I remember you.
I sent it before I could think again about it, not knowing for sure if I was playing the game or was honest.

The guilty conscience that drove into my heart gave me the answer.

I couldn't wait for the match to be over. My legs were shaking constantly. I didn't cheer and celebrate the three goals England scored; I didn't remember the players who scored them. The game seemed to drag on forever. When the last whistle sounded after the ninety-fifth minute, I was the first to jump and push the others to leave.

Back in the car with Dad and Mom, they both noticed how stressed and absent-minded I was.

"Jane, I won't let him do anything to you and Alexander," Dad said, knowing exactly what was on my mind. "I'll put Beller in his place and make him finally go and find some other woman. Anything to make the stupid stories about you two stop." The thought of Matthias with some other woman immediately evoked nausea that bubbled from my stomach into my throat. "I will sort it all out."

"Dad, I think I should talk to him. I believe he's only doing this to get me to meet him. I've been refusing all this time, and now he's desperate."

"I'm curious as to what he has to say."

"Probably nothing important. God knows what he'll come up with, only to get you to make me talk to him. I think it's best that I do it straight away and finally get it over with."

Mom looked at me discerningly, and I knew she was aware that there were some things between Matthias and me that Dad, being a father, should not find out.

"She's right, Brad," she said. "Let her do the talking now, and if Beller insists again on meeting you, then you do it."

Dad pondered over it for a few moments. "You two are correct. Jane should deal with her own problems." He eyed me. "But, honey, if you need help, know that you're not alone."

I thanked both of them. Again, I found myself admiring Mom for having such a subtle power over him, Brad Andersonn.

I didn't want to waste time, but I still headed to my room first to take a quick shower, change into a clean dress and replenish my makeup and perfume. Did I do it to feel confident and strong in front of him, or was I trying to appear attractive and beguiling?

The guilty pang in my chest gave me the answer again.

The girls came to my room, where they'd wait until I came back to report what had happened. The three of them encouraged me as I swallowed hard, fixing my beige dress that tightly followed the line of my waist and legs to my knees.

I went to room 1202.

A million thoughts rummaged through my mind. What if this didn't help? What if Alex found out I'd met Matthias? What if Matthias threatened me with something I couldn't defend myself from? What if…

Nonetheless, when I stepped in front of the door, I gathered all the self-confidence I was able to before I knocked. I had it all planned in my head, like a movie scene: He'd open the door, I'd walk past him and avoid looking him in the eyes until the crucial moment, and then, with all my power and determination, I'd say I didn't love him and that he should leave me alone.

When he opened the door, the memory of four years ago hit me – when I went to the room he'd rented *for five minutes* to tell him it was all over – and I dumped my scenario in a shameful instant. His dark eyes were shining with excitement and joy, surprise and adoration. Paralysed, I stood there in the hall watching him until he extended his arm and drew me in. The moment he touched my skin, fire spread throughout my body.

I shrugged his hand off mine and stomped inside, more nervous than I'd expected to be in my craziest, guiltiest dreams.

"Alright, I don't have much time. Talk," I said robotically, my back turned to him.

When he didn't reply for an unusually long time, I turned. Matthias was standing, a considerable distance still between us, scrutinising me from head to toe. His hands were in his pockets, his dark hair messy, a black T-shirt pulled tight over his wide chest. With my eyes, I could trace the veins drawn over his strong, over-exercised arms, the denim of the dark jeans hugging his strong, perfect legs. There was stubble on his face, which was beautifully, maddeningly softened by the gentle, playful smile tugging at the corner of his mouth. He was cruelly, unforgivably, inexplicably attractive. The sight of him watching me like that, wanting me like that with his eyes…I was dizzy with fear, excitement, pride and the terrifying urge to run into his arms.

"You are beautiful," he said as I stared at him bluntly.

I fell apart. But I didn't cry.

"For god's sake, Matthias…" I whispered in a quivering voice.

He approached me.

"Don't touch me!" I screamed in fear. The thought of what I might feel under his fingers, what I might do, horrified me. This was a bad idea, an awfully stupid idea. I should never have come here. I hadn't thought it possible. All these feelings! How, after all this time? His hands were on my shoulders, and I tried to move away before my body could melt like it wanted to. I looked at the floor, at the lamp, at the curtain-drawn window, everywhere, anywhere, just not into those eyes that would make me do something reckless. "Don't put your hands on me…"

But it was too late. They were on my back, pulling me into a hug. "Calm down, baby. You know I won't do anything bad to you."

As a last effort, I put my hands between us and tried to push him away. But I was impossibly weak – I felt like my body was detached from my mind, like in a dream when all you want to do is run but your strength fails you.

His strong arms surrounded me, pulled me into his stone-solid chest that smelled familiar and seductive – a scent I prayed I had forgotten but still remembered. He was squeezing me tightly but without any real force, and his fingers were gentle, running over my back and through my hair. I felt the startling burn of tears threatening to form, but I didn't want to let myself cry. The old Jane Andersonn never cried. The new one only did in front of Alex and her father. Matthias, in spite of everything, could not see this side of me. Instead, I breathed heavily, my chest spasming with the sob that couldn't come.

"Let me go…" I tried. "This was a bad idea."

"No way I'm letting you go." He kissed my hair, pushing my repressed tears dangerously close to the surface. I squeezed his shirt and completely relaxed onto him. It felt good, after all the stress, to just let go. "I should've done this at the beginning. I should never have waited four years to get to you."

"No, no, no." I lifted my head. "You couldn't have done anything differently. Even this is a mistake. A terrible mistake."

He smiled. "I'm so enjoying this mistake, then."

"I'm only here because you threatened to hurt me." My voice was shaking. I didn't move under his arms; they felt too good. "You were ready to hurt me through my father."

"I'd never do that, Jane," he murmured, kissing my hair again. It felt wonderful.

However, the next second, I processed what he said.

"What?" I shouted.

"Come on," Matthias laughed. "Of course, I'd never tell anything to your father. How many times do I have to tell you that I'll never do anything that could possibly harm you?"

Furore took fear's place. I wasn't the poor little frightened emotional girl anymore. I was a bomb about to explode. With all my force, I pushed him away.

"You cunning, cheating bastard! I was scared to death! He was about to meet you! I barely prevented him!" I was screaming, but he was unmoved. The urge to slap him went out of my mind just as fast as it entered it. I couldn't fight him. At that moment, I thought it best to get lost, while I was still angry.

"I'm going!"

I started towards the door, but he stopped me, catching me by the arm.

"No!" His peaceful, gentle aura was supplanted by that oh-so-familiar desperation. "We have to talk, Jane. Since you're here, there's no way I'm going to let you go before we have a word."

I took a deep breath and looked furiously at his fingers squeezing my upper arm. He released it.

"Alright," I said through clenched teeth. "What do you want to know?"

"Everything, from the moment you left me until April last year, including why you didn't look for me while he was torturing you."

I wanted to remind him that Alex had never tortured me, but I knew it would be in vain, so I did as he asked.

"I returned to the hotel room. Alex was...well, devastated is a weak word. He shouted at me, I didn't even try to justify myself—"

"Did he hurt you?"

I remembered the lamp that flew past me and cut my upper arm. "No. He'd never do that."

"Oh, yes, I could see," Matthias mumbled angrily. "Go on."

"At one point, he told me I was the worst thing that had ever happened to him, and I couldn't handle it. I fell apart, in some kind of delirium. I couldn't stop crying. I almost suffocated, lying in broken glass and wood. It all seems like some vague, melodramatic movie now. When Alex saw how desperate I was, he suggested that we didn't break up but instead stay together, because that would protect us both. It would save us the colossal embarrassment I'd caused, since, well, my father's reputation would've been completely destroyed."

"Are you telling me that, even then, knowing that you had cheated on him with six other men, he still chose what was best for you, your father and him?" Matthias was in disbelief, his dark eyes searching mine for a lie.

"Yes."

"I can't believe that. He must be either mental, dumb or extremely vicious."

"He loves me, Matthias. That's why he chose *us* over himself."

"Sorry, but that's inconceivable."

I rolled my eyes. "It's not like we lived happily ever after when we left Germany."

"Alright. Go on."

I took a deep breath. Still, even the memory of those terrible two years made me nauseous. "What ensued in Paris…what you saw… it was guilt eating me alive. Plain and simple. And Alex…that was the natural reaction of a man whose woman betrayed him. He couldn't make himself touch me. At all." At this point, I sunk into the armchair at the corner of the hotel room. This conversation, this reminiscence took away an enormous portion of my energy.

"Are you completely honest now, Jane?" He crouched in front of me.

I raised my head to look him in the eye. "I am."

"You're saying that you two didn't have any kind of intercourse?"

"Yes, that's what I'm saying. Until April of last year," I confirmed in annoyance. "How could we? I'd had my share of fun behind his back. He was probably disgusted by it all. I was dirty." These words burnt my throat. "It was all a natural reaction. Still, no matter how much it hurt me, no matter how it destroyed me outside and inside, I couldn't help seeing on him how much he loved me, how much I'd hurt him. If I'd left after everything he'd done, everything he was doing for me, for my dad, I would've completely destroyed him. Even then, when I'd hurt him most, he thought more about me than about himself. And I loved him. I loved him before you, of course, but I loved him afterwards even more. He gave me back the life I'd squandered, the life that I didn't deserve. That's why I stayed."

Tears were now welling in my eyes, and with a heroic effort, I pushed them back. Going through everything again hurt so much. I didn't let myself think how Matthias must be feeling, hearing from me how wholly my heart belonged to another man.

"I would've given you everything, Jane. You only should've looked for me," he said, now seated on the floor in front of me.

"How can you say that?" I yelled. "Look at me! I slept with your coach. I slept with your best friend. I slept with three other men while I was meeting you. How can you even consider giving me anything but contempt?"

I could see on his face that it hurt him, but still, those eyes didn't hate me. "If Yanov can love you after everything, why do you think I can't?"

"He is…Alex is…" I wanted to say he was exceptional, extraordinary, divinely kind, a person whose heart had a great capacity to love and understand. But I couldn't make myself form those statements in front of Matthias. He was right, in a small way – if Alex could love me, which he did, why wouldn't Matthias be able to as well?

"He was just lucky to have met you first. I've said it a hundred times, and I'm saying it again," he continued. "Alright, I understand that you are thankful that he protected you then. If you'd broken up, your father would've been tremendously upset, and you and I would've been the story of the year, while Yanov would be publicly embarrassed. I get that. It would've been quite tough on him…"

"And not just for a couple of months or a year," I had to add. "He'd have been marked for life. Because I'm Jane Andersonn. Damn it. I can't really do whatever I want with my life. How paradoxical!" I hid my face in my hands.

"You can," he said gently. "You did it already."

"And look how it ended. I hurt you, I embarrassed the man I care about. I'd better stick to what my dad says I can and cannot do."

"Don't complicate it, Jane." He took my hands in his and looked at me with understanding, his lips curved in a tender smile while he talked. "Yes, you have that burden upon you, but we all do, in one way or another. In some small town, there is a daughter afraid to tell her parents she's in love with a man other than the one they plan for her. If she says anything, it'll be a disgrace for the family. She keeps quiet and ends up unhappy. Or she speaks up and there's a bit of tumult, but in the end, what matters is love. Love always prevails."

I knew then why I had fallen in love with him four years ago. I loved his romanticism, the passion with which he talked about what and who he cared for. He firmly believed it all. Still, I couldn't help being realistic.

"Please, tell me, then – how can you feel any love for me after what I did? Taking into account that even a man great as Alex couldn't come around for two years, that he needed to lose me in order to realise we should stick together, I am pretty sure you don't know what you're talking about." I raised my voice again. "Imagine that I never left you that night, that I'd stayed to celebrate the trophy with you, that we'd announced through the newspapers to Alex, his family and friends, to our parents and friends, that we were together. We would have been happy for some time. Your coach would've tried to spoil it, but we would've gotten away with it somehow. You would perhaps have forced it out of your mind that Lens fucked me while you were taking me out—"

"Jane..."

"We'd've been happy for six months, perhaps a year. And then maybe Gottfried would've dropped a crumb of doubt: *Do you really trust her? Come on, man, she fucked half a dozen people except for you. What makes you think she's faithful?* Or perhaps he wouldn't even have needed to say anything. You might've started thinking about it all yourself—"

"Jane..."

"And then you'd've started asking me questions – where I was, with whom, if it was true. You'd perhaps have gotten somebody to follow me, you'd have gone for trainings disturbed, maybe you'd even have avoided coming home because you wouldn't have been able to look at me without seeing what I had done—"

Gently, he placed a hand over my mouth, ending my delirium.

"Do you think I haven't thought about it, Jane? About every single detail you've just mentioned? God damn it, I have. And so much more. And you know what I concluded each time? That we would've worked out in the end."

I sighed. "You don't know what you're talking about."

"I believe I do, because I am the one who has been going through that over and over again. You think I didn't try hating you? I tried with all my body, mind and soul. In those first few weeks after you left Berlin, I was out of bed saying, out loud, 'Jane Andersonn is a monster. You don't need her. She doesn't deserve you.' I repeated that a million times during the day, and you know how I'd go to bed? Reading the messages we had exchanged and thinking through the moments we'd spent together, and I'd shout myself to sleep because at the end of each day I couldn't help concluding, believing, knowing that you hadn't faked your feelings for me." I tremored as another wave of pain ran through me. "And how do you think I felt every day, seeing you becoming a zombie next to him? There was something terribly wrong between you two. Everyone could see, but nobody spoke about it. It was driving me mad. And you made it worse by not replying to any of my letters."

"We were over. Or, at least, we should have been over, and I hoped that you'd figure that out if I ignored you."

"Hah," Matthias scoffed. "That didn't deter me from you. Ignoring me just made me more attracted to you."

"You are completely insane."

I stood up. I had to stop this. This conversation, this meeting, it wasn't going anywhere. I had to find some words that'd hurt him, anything to make him stop, and then leave quickly.

"Listen, Beller, let's end this now. I love Alex above everything, which means I will respect him and not meet you again. I want to remain loyal to him. I made mistakes in the past, and I'm not repeating them again. You should focus on finding a woman who can give you what I cannot, because I am already someone else's."

Proud of my speech, I looked at him, waiting to see pain on his face and then, finally, defeat.

However, there was only anger – anger mixed with affection. He grabbed me by the arms.

"You think I haven't tried being with other women? Do you know where it stopped each time? They'd say two words and I already couldn't stand them any longer, let alone touch them or take them to bed. And stop reciting me that bullshit you learnt by heart, or I'll put aside all my control and kiss you, which I'm only preventing myself from doing because I respect you and don't want to scare you. You know that!"

I was stunned. He was so close to me, his strong body, his perfect face. When he said the word *kiss*, my eyes looked down at his lips, imagining it, remembering clearly. We had kissed wonderfully, every time.

My body weakened. It wasn't shaking anymore. Instead, it relaxed in his arms. This man was not giving up, and I had no clue what to do or say to him.

"Tell me it was all fake for you, Jane," Matthias said calmly, taking me out of my daydreaming and reminiscence. "If you tell me now you were just playing with me, that you didn't mean any of the things you said and did for me then, I'll leave you alone. It's that easy."

Lava spread from my head all over my body. I had the key to this door. I could close it shut, lock it and never turn back again. Alex and I could finally be happy without anyone disturbing us, without this wretched reckless man going after us incessantly. All I had to do was lie. One more time. All I had to do was look him in those eyes, those coal-black eyes that always devoured me with adoration, and lie to him that I never cared.

But I couldn't make myself. Not even after all this time. Not even for Alex and my sake.

I still cared. And hated myself for it.

He smiled, which threw me off-balance. His hands still held my arms, and I seriously considered leaning onto him as my body again grew weak, when he said, "Go out with me, Jane."

Shock twisted my face as my pupils widened anew. He chuckled, drawing me into a hug, pressing my body onto his. "You think these petty four years changed anything between us? You think time has lessened what we feel for each other? Come out with me and see for yourself."

"You are crazy," I stuttered, fighting my way out of his hug I'd unforgivably enjoyed. "That will never happen."

"Why? Are you scared of what you'll discover? That you perhaps loved him but what you feel for me is way beyond that?"

"Shut up," I whispered.

"I'm not telling you to leave him. I'm only asking you to go out with me, that we have a chit-chat, so that you know where you stand with your feelings. We deserve that after everything we've gone through."

"Alex doesn't deserve that. I won't do anything behind his back. No way am I going anywhere with you. I know where I stand with my emotions. I love my man who now trusts me completely, despite everything I did to him, and I plan on not failing him."

I wanted to infuriate him, to make him so upset with me that he might finally start to hate me, but my strong words didn't produce their intended effect. Instead, he approached me. A table was behind me, so I couldn't move back. He put a finger on my cheek and ran it down my face. It was like a slow match that set me on fire.

"Why don't you give yourself a chance to be happy, Jane?"

I closed my eyes, enjoying his touch. "Because I am happy. And I've already had enough chances," I whispered. "Alex and I suffered a lot to have the happiness we have now. I won't squander that."

"You think you are happy, but you're scared to think about what we could have, what we could be." He cupped my cheek, his other hand on my waist, and I quivered all over. "I will never hate you, Jane. What I told you that night you left me still holds true – there won't be any other woman. Only you. I'd never hurt you." His breath was on my face, intoxicating me. "I'd do anything for you."

I wet my lips to receive the kiss, but his lips ended on my forehead instead. I knew at that moment everything he had said about us was true.

"I know you would," I said, barely audible.

He pressed me to his chest, and I hugged him with all my force, trying not to feel terribly guilty for what I was doing and instead enjoy the moment, the touch, as I held back the tears burning behind my eyes.

"Why don't you give me the chance, then?" he asked.

I took a deep breath, gathering all the energy from every cell in my body and gently pushed him away. "I can't, Mati. I can't leave him."

I left before he had the chance to do or say anything, but I was still surprised that he didn't prevent me from leaving – perhaps he was confused and paralysed by the strength of his emotions. I knew I was completely out of my mind and barely standing on my heels, but still I ran down the hall, not turning, not looking back.

I returned to three pairs of curious eyes that then shifted to worry. Bea, Lana and Angie looked at me, confused, without a clue what to say.

"Tomorrow. Everything tomorrow." I managed to form a few words.

They stood up to leave. Bea turned at the door.

"Jane, don't give yourself space for any irrational thoughts."

"Too late, Bea. I'm all irrational."

CHAPTER 7

After an early, quiet breakfast, the girls and I said goodbye to my and Bea's parents and left for Rio de Janeiro – Ukraine would be playing South Korea there the following day. This time, Bea decided to go with us, since Harold would spend most of his time in training anyway. My mood didn't change much after I woke up. I hadn't managed to get a good sleep. I wanted to explain it away as jet lag, but there was no use. My parents knew I had met Matthias, and I didn't dare lie in front of them. They didn't ask many questions. Before we left, Dad only said that I should take care and we'd talk when we met in Manaus in a few days, where England was playing their last group game against Greece.

On the plane, I couldn't say anything. The girls were chitchatting while I only sat by the window and thought – what the hell was I going to do?

One thing was for certain – I had to tell Alex. The very thought of him suspecting me again evoked all the unpleasant memories from France, so I ruled out any lying to him straight away. I would tell him I'd talked to Matthias, but not until his match against South Korea was over. Until that evening, I would pretend everything was perfectly fine.

First, I had to pour it all out to the girls. "My room," I mumbled when we checked in at the hotel.

I knew I shouldn't drink, but I was also aware that in order to meet my boyfriend and appear as if everything was alright, I needed a bit of encouragement. I took a shot of whiskey from the minibar. When the girls entered the room, they saw me standing by the window, the small bottle of liquor in my hand, and not one of them made a joke about it. Not even Angie. She came to me and took the bottle away from me, gently, like I was a spooked animal.

"Tell me what's up," she demanded.

I sat on my bed and retold everything, A to Z, from the moment he opened the door till I shut the same door behind me. They listened without interrupting. Even when I was finished, they still didn't speak.

"I'm so terribly confused." I had to interrupt the silence. "I know I want Alex, I love Alex. I don't doubt it for a single second. What I don't know is why I get so flustered in Matthias's presence. Damn it, when he gets near, I feel like I want to touch him, let him hug me, enjoy him completely. I don't know how to get rid of that feeling. I thought it'd be gone after all this time, but no. I swear – every time he touched me, I had to fight the urge to dive between his arms."

The girls pondered in silence for a moment longer. I saw them exchange a look, and then, in unison, they stood against me – or on my side, I couldn't tell in the moment.

"You mustn't see him again," Angie said. "No matter what he says or how he threatens you, you mustn't be alone with him. He told you he wouldn't say anything to your father, so we know you're safe. Now it's up to you to keep avoiding him. At some point, he'll have to stop."

"Angie is right," Bea agreed. "By meeting him again, you risk losing Alex, even though he loves you. I believe he's more cautious than last time. I'm afraid if he suspects you even once, you may lose him forever." The very thought of that was a knife in my heart; Bea must have seen that on my face, since she pivoted away from the subject quickly. "Let's not talk about that. What's important is I firmly believe Matthias is not the man for you, regardless of what he claims."

"How can you be so sure?" I asked, desperate.

"Because you are both forces of nature. You're two burning fires that create a storm, an earthquake. It's exciting at the beginning, but it ends in catastrophe. You're obviously passionately attracted to each other, but your energies are too strong. They don't match; they clash. I can easily imagine you two beating each other to bruises occasionally, then ending up in bed, and then doing the same again. He's used to getting what he wants, and you're used to it, too. And what's worse, you get what you want in identical ways – with force, attitude, protrusion, aggression. That's not a good combination, Jane. With Alex, it's different. You two complement each other in everything. His attitude and behaviour are tailored to match and control yours. That's love. You and Beller, that's futureless passion."

I absorbed each and every word she said, and I knew it was true.

"Yes," I said, which felt like a weak response to Bea's near-poetic evaluation of my core self. "But...how do I get over this? I can't have a passionate moment with Matthias and still be with Alex."

"That's what a relationship is," Lana said. "You choose now, Jane – either you choose the man who knows all of you, the best and worst, and still adores you entirely. Or you indulge in an affair with one who idealises you."

"How can we be sure it's just an illusion he has of me, when he's been stuck on me for all this time?"

"Of course, he's stuck on you," Angie said. "You've been the most beautiful woman in the world since you turned seventeen, and you dumped him at the World Cup final. We'll never gauge what's in his head, but I've got a pretty good guess."

"I know two things for sure," Lana added. "You have to stay away from him. And you're not alone. Alex told you, your father told you. You have us. You can do this, Jane. But only if you want to."

Do I want to?

"We'd better get ready," Lana said, getting up before I could respond. "Otherwise, we'll be late for the tour of the Tijuca National Park, after which we'll check out the Sugarloaf cable car and end the day with drinks at the Copacabana."

"Damn it, girl, where do you get all that energy?" Angie asked, sighing.

Lana didn't reply; instead, she looked at me.

*****

The match between Ukraine and South Korea was at one o'clock. The sun was sharp but not merciless. Winter at this part of Brazil felt like early spring in Europe so the weather didn't affect the tempo of the game. Both teams acquired several good chances for a shoot at their opponent. However, by the end of the first half, only one ball had gone into the net, and it wasn't behind Alex's back.

During the break, I gulped down a pint of beer. When we returned to the stands, I was dizzy with energy and optimism, just like the thirty-thousand Ukrainian fans who tirelessly shouted and sang. The second goal occurred seven minutes before the last whistle, again scored by the players in yellow. My boyfriend's sheet was still clean.

When we and the players returned to the hotel, we had little time to celebrate, since we immediately packed and left for the airport to go to São Paulo again. The last game of the group stage was scheduled there against Morocco in four days' time.

Both Alex and I were dead tired, so we slept on the plane, missing the entirety of that short flight between the two big cities. I was grateful that Coach Andreyevich would let the players rest until tomorrow afternoon, so Alex and I could spend some relaxed time together.

I avoided checking my phone those few days, and for good reason. Matthias didn't miss any opportunity to tell me how he was waiting for his answer, to say how I was mistaking guilt for love and how we both deserved answers. I didn't reply to any of his messages.

The evening we arrived in São Paulo, I didn't want to tell Alex anything. He was exhausted and happy about the win, and I didn't want to spoil that with Matthias. I also didn't want to deprive myself of our always wonderful post-victory sex. I admired how he always found the energy to get excited in bed with me, to take me with force and strength after an extremely demanding day at work. That night, he behaved as if that short nap on the plane was a proper nine-hour sleep. His kisses were wanting, possessive, wild. He bit me everywhere, over my neck, breasts, hips, the insides of my thighs, and when I couldn't help moaning loudly, he made me straddle him. I arched back, enjoying him fully, and came forcefully. He didn't, so he lifted me, pressing my back against the wall as I encircled him with my legs. And holding me as if I was light as a feather, he entered me again and again.

During the night, we woke up. At first, I thought it was a wonderful dream, his fingers teasing me, but when he entered me, I screamed, realising it was all true. And I enjoyed it – greedily, shamelessly enjoyed it.

*****

Alex spent the following afternoon with his teammates while the girls and I explored the city. We visited the Sé Cathedral, where we signed autographs, talked to fans and gave away Ukrainian and English jerseys, scarves and signed flags. Then we moved on to refresh in Ibirapuera Park, again meeting hordes of avid football lovers. For a late dinner, we stopped in the vibrant Paulista Avenue, the awake and bustling centre of the city. I knew Lana wanted to sit somewhere without a TV, but since we were in Brazil during the football World Cup, that was impossible. When we took our table, the second half of the match between Germany and Algeria had just started. Luckily, at the same time, Brazil played Japan, so the crowd watched that game more animatedly and on much larger TVs.

I did my best to ignore the game Matthias played. I ordered food and wine, and tried to tune out the commentator. I even turned my back to the speakers and the screen. The meal took time to arrive because the place was so crowded with visitors. It wasn't an uptight, expensive restaurant, but rather a nice, decent-looking bar, so we didn't complain.

When I finally indulged Lana in conversation about our plans for the upcoming few days – since we would visit a few more Brazilian cities –

a goal was scored. And although the commentating was in Portuguese, nobody could not hear the exhilarated voice announcing the scorer: *"BELLER!"*

"These people won't let us live," Lana said, annoyed, stabbing her chunk of chicken breast.

"Lana, we can't do anything about it," Bea told her. "It's better that you stop stressing. We are in a land of football, during the world's largest football tournament, of which the Germans are the current champions. There is nothing you can do."

Through gritted teeth, Lana agreed, and we did our best to talk about anything but football. In the end, the result was 3–1 for Germany, which still put Ewald Fuchs further behind Alex, with two conceded goals in total so far. Good enough for the end of the evening.

Afterwards, we strolled along the avenue before heading back to the hotel, entirely exhausted. I was thinking only about the hot bath I'd take and the hotel's soft bed sheets, when I remembered I still had to tell Alex about Matthias. The following evening I was leaving with the girls to Manaus for the England–Greece match, and I didn't have much time.

When we entered the reception hall, the lady who welcomed us told me the Ukrainians were by the pool, so I went straight away to greet Alex and tell him I'd be waiting for him upstairs. He was already there by the time I got out of the shower. I kissed him the way I couldn't in front of his teammates because they'd tease him for days afterwards.

"I missed you, busy girl." His hands were already under my bathrobe, finding my sore back and shoulders. "Come here, you need a proper massage."

Any woman who has spent a whole day in high heels knows how much love a sentence like this means.

I let him gently squeeze every muscle along my spine, every muscle he knew how to touch perfectly, and although I enjoyed it immensely, I straightened up before I reached the stage when I'd be too sleepy to form sentences.

"Love, there is something I have to tell you," I began. "I apologise…it's not pleasant, but I don't want to hide it from you."

He caught my hands and started rubbing my palms. Dear lord, how much I loved him.

"Tell me."

"Matthias met my parents and me that day we were in Salvador. I didn't want to tell you anything before your match. Honestly, this moment was perfect, so I'd gladly not have spoiled it, but I had to tell you. I don't know what to do."

I relayed everything to him, every detail – apart from my strange feelings for that damned German. Alex listened carefully, without interrupting, and when I finished, he sighed.

"I guess I'll have to fight him after all."

"No, Alex, please don't." I took his hand in mine. "If I was sure I could deal with this myself, without you knowing, I'd do it and tell you after the tournament. But since he went straight up to Brad and Josephine, I don't know what he's capable of next. I don't know how he's managing to do all this, but it's insane. I don't know what to do. He promised he wouldn't try to reach anyone close to me any longer, but I don't know how much I can rely on that. I just...I don't know."

He was silent for a few minutes, pondering it all, before he spoke. "I'll have to talk to him myself." My heart stopped. "And it'll be best if you're there, too."

A chill ran up my legs. "You mean like, a confrontation? With the three of us?"

"Yes. If only I meet him, well, then you know how that'll end. And he'll still believe I'm preventing you from going to him. But if we meet him together, the chances that I break his jaw are lower, and if you're there to confirm what I'm saying, that he's disturbing you, us, then he'll finally give up."

A vision of that meeting flashed in front of my eyes and pushed bile up my throat. But I knew he was right. I couldn't refuse this proposal.

"But you'll have to be really persistent and cold with him," Alex added. "I know and understand that you're sorry. But if you show it, if he sees it, he'll perceive it as love, and then we'll be back at square one."

I swallowed hard. How was I to tell Matthias I didn't care any longer, that I'd never actually cared enough? How was I to lie?

If I wanted to keep this wonderful man who I loved above all, I had to.

"Alright," I agreed. "We'll do that. The first chance we get."

Alex caught and kissed my hand. "Deal. We'll do it together. You, in the meantime, take care. If he touches you, I swear I'll kill him and I won't feel a damned thing."

I chuckled. "You mean, you'll take your gloves off, kill him, and go out on the pitch without blinking an eye?"

"Exactly. My pulse wouldn't even change. It goes without saying that beating him now is, somehow, natural. I'm a hundred percent sure it wouldn't affect my focus for any game."

I laughed, already seeing this problem disappearing. He'd convinced me.

He started removing his clothes.

"Alex," I breathed, and he turned to me. "You are the most exceptional man I've ever met. I love you."

He bent over to kiss me. "I love you, too."

*****

"That's not a bad idea," Bea said on the plane to Manaus. This trip was one of the longest at the tournament – a four-hour flight from São Paulo, since Manaus was the capital of the state of Amazonas, up in the north-west of Brazil. "But this time, you're the one who'll have the most difficult job."

I shuddered.

"Yes. No matter what Alex tells him, he'll still act upon your reaction," Lana added. "You'll have to look him in the eyes and tell him it's all over."

Nausea again rushed up my throat.

"Don't be a weakling now!" Angie stepped in. "You've done quite a lot of shit, darling, and Alex is beyond wonderful for tolerating it and sorting it out this way. Do you have any idea how difficult it must be for a man to meet his woman's ex-lover? Still, Alex is being reasonable and doing it with you because he knows doing it alone wouldn't produce any solutions. At the same time, he knows that you can't do much alone either."

"Which you *should* be able to," Bea added with raised brows.

"How do you mean?" I asked belligerently.

"For some wild, imperceivable, unfathomable reason, when you're on your own, you can't tell Matthias to let you be," she explained. "You love Alex, and that can't be more obvious, but when you meet that irrational German, you somehow forget all about yourself and Alex, and you succumb to him. Alex probably understands that and believes that while you're with him, you may be able to gather the strength to tell Matthias to leave you alone."

"But when it happens this time," Angie stepped in again, "you'll have to really say it and mean it. We hope you understand that."

My body felt feverish, hot and cold at the same time. I looked at Angie with desperate eyes, rendered voiceless by a stone in my throat.

"Damn it, you stupid woman!" Angie yelled. "You still don't get it?"

"She doesn't," Lana said.

Angie approached me. "I love you, Jane, but what you've been doing with your life and to that wonderful man is beyond my comprehension."

"Anyone's comprehension," Lana added again.

"Don't be too tough on her," Bea defended me.

"Beatrice, if she can't tell Matthias to fuck off in front of Alex, that meeting had better not happen," Angie explained.

Silence ensued, during which I began to shake. Bea passed me a bottle of water, and I reluctantly took a sip.

"She's right, Jane," Lana said. "As your manager, I can tell you that this farce with Matthias is only good for publicity, popularity and money. You're lucky that Alex has been tolerating it all these years. But you have to make up your mind. You have to choose, Alex or Matthias, and then you have to tell one of them—"

"Matthias in this case," Angie interrupted.

"—you have to tell him to leave you alone, in such a way that he does it," Lana continued. "If you can't do it in front of Alex, then the three of you should never meet. Alex wouldn't take your reluctance any longer."

"Which means you have to sort it out yourself," Bea said.

I took a deep breath. "Yes, I understand. Either I say to Matthias's face that I don't care, with Alex by my side, or I tell him myself and make him stop chasing me."

*****

Manaus was a very different city from the previous ones we'd visited up until then, simply because it was the first one situated inland. I was grateful for the interesting, dispersed schedule the girls and I had; otherwise, I'd never have seen many Brazilian spots. When we landed, we took immediately to the streets. The plan for the day was to enjoy the traditional street food with other football supporters. After a couple of caipirinhas (Brazilian drinks similar to mojitos), we were all tipsy, full of pão de queijo[1], tired from wandering the streets of this genuine city and couldn't wait to return to the hotel.

Bea went to be with Harold, so Lana, Angie and I gathered for a quick recap of tomorrow's plan before hitting the hay. Since the flight back to São Paulo would take another four hours, we decided it was best to fly back on the day of the Ukrainian match against Morocco, which was the following day at five o'clock in the afternoon. We'd wake up early, head for the airport and make it on time. As soon as I lay in bed, I fell asleep immediately, exhausted, without a single worry on my mind.

We all had breakfast together – us girls, my parents, and Bea's and Harold's parents. I sat with Lana and Angie while Bea was "being a good wifey" with Harold, as Angie teased her. As soon as I finished eating, I went to my room to get ready to leave. The girls and I were supposed to go for a brief tour of the Rio Negro and Amazon rivers before heading to the Arena da Amazônia.

During the tour, I didn't think once about men. That was how much it took my breath away. Floating over the dark surface of the water was a surreal, beautiful experience, especially when the boat stood at a point where the black Rio Negro joined brownish Amazon River. The difference of the colours was incredible and unmistakeable. I was aware that we were finally seeing something we had only studied in school. The smell of life – from the forest, the water, the city – was mesmerising, and as we headed towards the shore, the echoes from the football fans across the city reached us, a hush that turned into a roar the closer we got. The entire area felt alive with some new magic.

We arrived at the stadium almost late, so we grabbed some snacks and water there to fight the humidity, still buzzing with excitement about the previous half of the day. My parents were there, as were Bea's and Harold's. The stands weren't entirely full, but the atmosphere was great regardless. We sang, waved flags, jumped, and shouted the names of the players who passed the ball towards the Greek goal. The first half was calm, but the second was a show to behold. Joshua Hadleigh scored the first goal of the game in the fifty-ninth minute, and Simon Wade, another new defender on the team, followed in his path twelve minutes later.

Soon, the game was over and we were heading back to the hotel. Matthew Vance had told Dad that we should meet them for dinner, so I had my evening already planned. I only wanted to give Alex a call before going to sleep.

---

[1] Small bread buns filled with cheese. (Portuguese)

I took a car with Dad and Mom because I assumed they wanted to talk about what I had done regarding Matthias. As I sat across from them in the vast van, Dad took out a bottle of cold water, opened it and passed it to me.

"What did you manage to do with the German?" He didn't hesitate. He never does.

I drank half of the bottle and commenced my story, which was the same version I had told Alex – accurate but deprived of my emotions and strange behaviour.

"You know what, Jane?" Dad was annoyed. "If this continues for much longer, I'll sort it out my way."

The storm in his eyes looked familiar.

"Dad, please, no..."

"I've had enough of these stories about you two, and he still persists despite everything you do or say. It can't go on like this. Next time Beller bothers you, tell him that either he stops or your father will make sure this is his last World Cup. If I can't get him out of every possible team, then I'll get somebody to injure him badly so he'll never be able to run again."

"Brad, for goodness' sake!" Mom shouted in disapproval instead of me. I was paralysed with fear. "Don't even think about doing something cruel like that. The poor boy is only in love."

"The poor boy is mad and attacking the peace of my family. Do you expect me to watch it and do nothing?"

"No, but you don't have to go that far. You can't destroy someone else's life to protect ours."

"And he can?" Dad wasn't calming down.

"Dad, please, let's wait. I completely understand you." My voice shook. "But we can't inflict something as serious as the end of a career on somebody who doesn't mean anything bad."

He looked at me discerningly. I knew I looked desperate, but I hoped that, counterintuitively, my desperation would calm him down. I couldn't allow any more harm to fall upon Matthias after how much I had hurt him.

It worked; Dad gave up his anger.

"Alright. Let's see what will come of this. But if your way doesn't work...we'll see. You're not alone, Jane."

I took him by the hand. "I know, Dad. Thank you."

As soon as we arrived at the hotel, I went to take a shower and change into a new dress. I fixed my hair and was ready within an hour. Lana and Angie picked me up from the room and we headed downstairs.

"I'm so excited," Angie squeaked. "Declan is here. I saw him today at the pool."

"You're talking about Duncan Fletcher's brother?" I asked.

"Exactly. That guy could serve as a sample in a biology class. Or an art class. I can bet every one of his muscles is perfectly trained."

"What matters is he knows how to use them."

"I'm sure he has it all." Angie was daydreaming, her eyes sparkling.

"See for yourself, then, and then let us know in the morning." I winked at her.

The restaurant was full when we arrived, so we took whatever free seats we could find. Bea was again with Harold, and Lana and Angie went to the Fletcher brothers' table, so I sat next to Keaton Flanagan and two other guys and their wives. Keaton had been at the previous tournament, so we reminisced about the English games I'd attended then and joked like old friends, even though we only knew each other from Germany and the newspapers. He was still single, though he changed girls regularly. He was considered the biggest womaniser on the team.

"Chances are I might be joining you in Madrid in the autumn," Keaton suddenly said. "I have a really good offer from Yanov's team that I'm inclined to accept," he answered my surprised look.

"That'd definitely be a new experience. You've never played outside of England, have you?"

"Correct. I'm not even sure I want now, 'cause I love Tottenham."

"Then don't. I'm telling you, there's no more beautiful city than London."

"You must love Yanov very much, since you moved for him."

"That's true. I can't complain, though. Madrid has wonderful weather the whole year round. But London is home. It always will be."

"Then push Yanov to move there. I know for sure that any Premier League team would gladly pay him whatever he asks."

"Good to know. It's not a bad idea, actually."

"Listen." He moved closer to me so that the others couldn't hear us. "There've been trustworthy rumours that a few German clubs want to present him with a very attractive offer at the end of the tournament. Have you heard about it?"

I went cold and clammy. "No. He's mentioned France and Italy, but not Germany."

"Probably 'cause he doesn't know anything yet. This is only between some coaches. I overheard Vance talking to somebody on the phone."

"I guess it's better that I don't tell Alex. Anyway, he'd never accept anything from them."

Keaton stirred in his seat. "Because of all the crap that happened with them?"

"That *has been* happening with them," I added, more to myself than to him.

This was a worthy piece of information. It was good for me to know, so I wouldn't be shocked when it came to light. I could never imagine Alex playing among those sharks. He'd never be comfortable there. He'd be successful and happy anywhere else, I was sure of that. He was loved in France – and in Spain, too. If he moved to Italy or England, or anywhere else, it'd be the same. Just not Germany.

The evening drew to a close, and some of the players, exhausted from the match, left for bed. I stayed up a bit later with the girls, though we were all tired. Angie's progress with the fitness trainer was more important. Soon, Bea left with Harold, and Lana and I were sitting at the table with a couple of the players' girlfriends when Angie approached us and, with a wink, insisted we leave.

"He was surprised I haven't watched *Pretty Woman*, so I suggested we watch it tonight," she told us on the way to the elevator. "Now I should get ready and expect him in my room within an hour."

"Why does he need an hour?" I asked, chuckling, happy for her.

"I don't know, but it's good, 'cause I need an hour. My room is a bit of a mess. I'd like to fix it and change into some proper minimal lace." She was all flustered.

"Is he interesting?" Lana asked. "You two seemed to be pretty engrossed in each other."

"Hell yeah! He studied physiotherapy, so he's always there to help Duncan and guide him in preventing serious injuries. That's one of the reasons he's here. He was offered a position on the medical team here, but he refused, since he's extremely busy with his job as a trainer. We talked about the people he trains, and...I know what you two are thinking, I thought the same, but no. The majority of his clients are men over the age of thirty. He says they take it more seriously and don't try to take him to bed."

Lana and I couldn't help laughing. "Which category are you?" I asked.

"I am the one who will take him to bed, but I'm not his client." She winked.

"Best of luck, then. Don't waste any minutes," Lana said. "And try not to be late for the plane tomorrow. Unless you want to end up with the *good wifey Beatrice* for a couple of days."

The laughter from the three of us rolled around the entrance hall, echoing. But the merriment was cut short when Angie suddenly stopped dead in her tracks.

"Goodness me!"

Lana and I followed her gaze, and I barely stayed on my feet when I saw what had surprised her. Coal-black eyes and black hair. He stood beside the reception, carefully watching us. Insane. He was completely, absolutely insane.

Fire ignited in my head.

"Girls, go," I hissed. "I'll sort this out."

"Are you sure you don't want us to be around, just in case?" Lana's voice was quivery.

"Don't worry. He won't do anything to me. If he tries, I'll scream my heart out and put him in jail."

He was smiling now, the bastard. I left Angie and Lana and stomped over the tiles, making my heels heard in the lobby.

"What on earth are you doing here?" I barely controlled myself from shouting. Matthias smiled and put his finger over my lips to silence me, but I hit his hand away. "Don't touch me like that in public!"

"Then take me somewhere I can. Or give me my answer now." He said it simply, as if it was the easiest thing in the world.

"What goddamn answer do you want? I told you already – I am not going out with you anywhere. Now get lost, before somebody sees us."

"I'm not going until you give me a proper answer. It's up to you now if anyone will see me."

I wanted to slap him across his self-conscious, satisfied face. But I had to think rationally. If anyone saw him – not even us together, him alone was enough – they'd know immediately he was there because of me. They'd probably conclude he was *with* me, too, and then the articles and rumours would spread faster than I could reach Alex. I couldn't risk it.

"Come to my room, 1006," I whispered. "And take the stairs."

He knew I said it to be malicious, but he didn't complain that he'd have to climb ten floors. He only smiled again self-satisfactorily. And underneath the anger boiling inside me, I couldn't help perceiving another heat burning its way through my insides. The guilty, shameful perception that his smug face was just as charming and attractive as it was infuriating.

I entered the elevator, my insides twisting with excitement, fear and sadness. We were about to be alone again, and this was the chance we had all been waiting for. I should tell him to leave me alone. I should be cold, strict and determined. After tonight, he should never again look for me.

Lana and Angie were waiting in front of my room, and I felt sorry that Angie was squandering the time she could be using to get ready for the fitness trainer.

"Girls, it's alright. I'll talk to him," I said.

"Talk to him where?" Angie asked.

"There," I pointed at the door of my room. They looked at me in a way that could freeze flowers. "I know, but where else? I can't allow anyone to see us downstairs. Or anywhere. This is the most privacy we can get."

Lana rolled her eyes. "Be careful. I'll be nearby. If he tries something, scream. If you don't call me within an hour, I'll come with security."

"We have a deal. Now, go and relax – especially you, Angie, you deserve this. Don't let me spoil it."

They hugged me in support and left.

I entered the room and left the door ajar. I felt the urge to take another shot of whiskey, but I'd already had a pretty good amount of alcohol, so that would be more of a hindrance than encouragement. I also thought about removing my shoes, but I decided on the contrary, because they gave me more confidence. I needed to be strong. I would recite the speech to him; I wouldn't give him a chance to talk; I would make him leave. He was an idiot to have come here. Yet again, he had wasted his time.

I was standing next to the window, observing the lively streets swarmed with tourists below, when I heard the door open. I waited until he closed the door to turn around.

Why did he have to be so brutally handsome?

"How many times do I have to tell you to leave me alone?" I asked.

He didn't reply straight away. Instead, he walked across the room. With every step he took closer to me, I shook more, and when he stopped, I could feel the electricity between us. We didn't drop eye contact for a second. By the time he stood a few centimetres from me, I had lost every single piece of confidence I'd had.

In a sudden, lightning movement, he caught me with one arm. His hand was now in my hair, my body pressed to his.

"You know when I'll stop?" I felt his breath on my face. "When you stop shaking like this in my presence." His dark eyes were shining with perseverance and attraction; everything about him was an invitation, soliciting me to lean in closer. "You keep blabbering that I should leave you alone, and all the while your whole body quivers before I even touch your skin. Once that stops, once you really stop caring, then I'll retreat."

He was completely right. But as for when would it all stop – if ever – I had no clue. I felt no more control over my body in that moment than I could control the weather. I had believed so fully that we were over. However, these last few days had showed me something different. What was I to do now?

"I'm not letting you go anywhere, and I'm not leaving tonight until you give me the proper answer," he added, gently massaging my scalp. My joints melted under his touch.

"Matthias, please." I had never sounded so weak. "I can't go anywhere with you. I can't do it to him…"

"Yes, you can."

"Where would we go anyway? How? When? I can't disappear like I did before. If he suspects anything, I'll be in great trouble, both with him and my parents. I can't make the mistakes I made before. Please, Matthias, let it go."

"I can't let it go. I tried, and it didn't work for four too-long years. We need to sort some things out, Jane."

"We talked about it last time." My voice was desperate. My body enjoyed his touch. He put his other hand on my back, threatening me to give in. "Don't be crazy anymore. You're risking too much by going after me. Your coach can give you some serious problems. You're five hours away from where you're actually supposed to be!"

"Yes, but I told you before – I'd take a ten-hour flight to spend one hour with you. And don't worry about my coach and my status in the team. I can take care of that. *You* need to take care of something else."

He saw I was melting in his arms, and he enjoyed it. The same way I enjoyed it.

My knees clicked and I almost lost my balance, so I relied on him entirely. I was grabbing his shirt, pressing my cheeks against his chest. The sound of his heart thudded against my ear. His cologne was everywhere around me. His hands massaged my entire back. I closed my eyes. I had no idea what to do, what to say, how to behave to make him leave, how not to do something stupid that night.

"Look at me," Matthias said in a tone that was enchanting, so masculine, deep and attractive, that I had to fight with the utmost strength to defy it, because I was sure that if I faced those eyes again, they'd hypnotise me and make me do whatever he wanted. I shut my eyes tightly and squeezed his shirt harder, but he took my chin between his thumb and forefinger. "Look at me, Jane."

I couldn't resist. A heavy cloud of fear blanketed me, paralysing me, making me dependent solely on him. I was right. Those eyes did have some dark magic in them. And they were close – dangerously, improperly close. Too close. He drew a finger up to my hair, parting a strand away from my face, and then dragged it past my eyebrow and down my cheek. Then he cupped my face with his strong hand. Semiconsciously, I closed my eyes again and rested my face there. It felt divine, blissful.

"No, Jane, open your eyes," Matthias said quietly, almost whispering. "I want you to look at me while I'm kissing you. I want you to see what I've been talking about all this time."

My temperature rose to a thousand degrees. Stepping back was nowhere near my mind. My stomach twisted with emotion and expectation. His hand moved, pulling me closer to him. I parted my lips, vaguely aware that they were dry but too far gone to remember what I should do about that. There was no need; he was determined to do it all by himself. The moment his lips touched mine, I felt thrown back through time but simultaneously felt as if not a single minute had passed since our last kiss.

When he sucked my upper lip, I moaned. When he sucked the lower one and then bit it slightly, I almost cried with the desire to have more. I could feel each hair on my body standing on end under his influence, each nerve surging alive, ready to receive and remember all of the sensations he was about to give me.

My hands couldn't keep calm and ran to his hair, to those long strands I once had played with. When he covered my mouth entirely, I clenched my fingers, affected by the sudden surge of the moment and its strength. Desire and passion spread throughout me, and as I moved with him, we could both feel and see how much I had missed it, how much I wanted it all, in spite of everything I had said. He wasn't holding me against him anymore – I was pressing myself to him, wishing to absorb his warmth, his scent, to keep the traces of his touch on my skin. The prolonged kiss was a ride I couldn't get off of, during which we both sighed and moaned with lust that had been sustained and suppressed for too long.

When our foreheads touched so that our lungs could get some air, we panted and listened to our hearts thudding loudly.

"Do you believe me now that nothing's over yet?" he whispered.

"I do," I whispered back. "But this still means it mustn't continue."

"I don't know how to stop it, Jane," he said desperately. "See how strong it is? I don't know how to live without it."

I raised my head to look him in the eyes. I adored everything about him, including that stubbornness that had brought him here. "This is reckless. We are reckless."

"Yes. And I love it," he said confidently, drawing a smile out of me. "Go out with me, Jane."

That question again. It was the same as the last time, only now we were in a completely different place – four years older, and our emotions four years stronger, preserved by wanting and longing, and now reignited. I knew the answer would be the same.

"Alright," I said, my heart fluttering like a thirteen-year-old girl's. Again.

He grinned and kissed me on the forehead. "You've just made me the happiest man in the world. And it's not a cliché, it's true." I smiled shyly. "And don't for a second feel bad about accepting it. I wouldn't have left you at peace until you did."

I nudged him in the ribs, to which he replied by kissing me again.

"Now tell me – where, when and how?" I asked, still snuggled comfortably in his arms.

"I'll tell you as soon as everything's ready to the minutest detail. Don't worry about it."

"Fine, just don't make it a dodgy nightclub. I'm not falling for that card again."

"Don't worry. It will be nothing of the sort."

He had to leave within minutes. His flight back to Belo Horizonte was the last one of the day, and he had to be at the airport within an hour or risk missing it and being absent from another training.

When Matthias let me go, it felt disappointing, empty, but I still floated on my legs. He closed the door behind him, and I threw myself on the bed, allowing myself a couple of minutes of pure happiness and excitement.

But as soon as those moments had elapsed, the sudden sense of guilt reminded me of everything I was doing was wrong. Horribly wrong.

I hesitated to call Lana, embarrassed at what I was about to tell her. But the phone rang, and glancing at the clock I saw it was exactly an hour after we'd separated. I told her to come, prepared to lie about one crucial part of the meeting, but when she sat on the bed next to me, I knew I couldn't.

"There was nothing else I could say, Lana. That feeling, it was insane how strong it was. If I'd refused, he'd still be here in this room."

"And what do you think you'll achieve by going out with him?" she asked patiently, although I knew she was disappointed and furious inside.

"That I will see it's a mistake, that it's not as strong as it seemed a while ago, that he's arrogant and annoying. Then I'd be able to tell him I don't care."

"That's a valid point. I only hope it happens."

I asked her to stay with me tonight. I was scared of the sadness that overcame me. I didn't want another sleepless night after which I'd wake up with a stone in my throat. Instead, we watched an action movie with Chris Hemsworth that lulled us into sleep.

I didn't call Alex.

CHAPTER 8

When the alarm went off, I robotically woke up, got dressed, applied makeup and fixed my hair. I was surprised I had slept dreamlessly and felt well-rested; however, there was little time to ponder everything that had taken place.

Lana and I decided to skip breakfast and have our first coffee on the plane, where we'd summarise the events of the night. We waited impatiently for Angie in the entrance hall, assuming she had an exciting story to tell us. But when she showed up, we couldn't decipher anything from her expression.

We didn't talk much on the way to the airport or as we boarded the plane. Finally, when we took off and once the flight attendants left us, Angie demanded that I tell her everything. When I finished recounting the previous night's events, her only comment was: "Girl, you're going to your doom."

"What else could I have said or done?" I asked desperately. I couldn't bring myself to apologise – that would be too close to admitting I'd done something wrong.

"I don't know. I really don't know."

"Are you gonna tell Alex?" Lana asked.

I had thought about it and, although it was insane and cruel, decided that it would be best to stick to my non-lying policy. "Yes, I'll tell him," I stuttered. "Everything except the kiss, of course."

"He'll go nuts," Angie said.

"I know, but if I don't say anything and he finds out anyway, from the newspapers or someone who may have seen Matthias, I'd have a colossal problem."

"True," Lana agreed. "Let's see how he'll react to that and what he'll advise you. Perhaps you may manage not to meet Beller after all."

The thought of that saddened me. I did want to meet him.

"Yes, you're right. Nothing is set in stone. Just because I agreed to meet him, that doesn't mean I actually will," I said, in spite of my thoughts. "He knows that meeting here, outside of his country and home territory, will not be easy at all. I won't risk even a one-percent chance that anyone sees us. If he wants to take me out, he'll have to plan every single possible detail, from the lighting in the room to what I'll wear."

"You think he won't do that?" Lana asked through a thin veil of scorn.

I knew the answer. "I know he'll try. I hope he'll fail." I sighed. "I hope he won't succeed, so I have good reason to refuse him."

They nodded understandingly, and we finished our coffee and breakfast in silence. I was going through Alex's timetable for the day: He was playing against Morocco at five in the afternoon. The next day, we would probably take a plane to Salvador, where they'd play against Belgium if they end up the first in the group – which was most certainly the case. That meant I could tell him about Matthias tomorrow on the plane, since tonight we'd probably celebrate going through to the eighth-finals.

"Wait, what about your night?" I asked Angie when I snapped out of my planning reverie. "You're not very vocal about it."

"Yeah, Jane's right," Lana agreed. "Don't tell us the sex was bad?"

Surprisingly, Angie chuckled. "There was no sex."

"What?" Lana and I said simultaneously, our mouths agape for two reasons: Angie hadn't slept with the guy she had been aiming to, and she was not upset about it.

"I wanted. I tried," she explained, "but he didn't give in."

"He resisted you?" I was in disbelief.

"Barely." She laughed at our still-baffled expressions. "Oh, he was hard, don't doubt that," she explained, "it's just that he didn't want to *just fuck me*." We sighed and giggled. "Yep. He said he seriously liked me, that he'd been offered sex numerous times since they arrived in Brazil, and he wasn't looking for that. He wants to take it slow with me."

"But, how often in life do you get a chance to have wild sex in the middle of Amazonia?" I asked disappointedly.

"I know. That's exactly what I told him, but he was adamant. No sex."

"Then what did you do?" Lana asked.

"We watched *Pretty Woman*, kissed and cuddled, and slept." She shone. I was glad for her. "He insisted that I stay with Bea, but I refused. Said I wanted to be with you two."

"That's lovely," Lana said. "So you'll meet in a few days in Brasilia?"

"Exactly. And I made him promise he'd take me to bed then, otherwise no more meetings." We burst out laughing. "I'm serious. This night was sweet, but I need to know what package I'm getting. If he's useless in bed, no romance can keep me interested."

"Makes sense. Better to find it all out at the beginning," I said.

"Exactly. Imagine we date, and after a month, it turns out he knows nothing – just lies down and expects me to do everything. Then the World Cup is already over, and I could have experienced a dozen other guys. No way I'm letting that happen."

We laughed and joked until we landed in São Paulo. Angie cheered me up for sure, and getting off the plane, I felt more prepared to meet Alex. The good thing was that we would see each other only after the game, because the players would already have left by the time we'd reach the hotel. In the meantime, I'd do my best not to think about Matthias and our encounter last night. I packed him in a little box, as I did with Alex four years ago, and kicked him out of my brain.

*****

The game against Morocco was the last one in the group stage. Group G, whose competitors we'd face, was already decided – Norway was first with three wins, while Belgium was second. Depending on how we played today and how Chile played against South Korea, we'd face one of the two. Statistics and expert opinions largely agreed that we'd be first and take on Belgium in the next round – which, at the same time, meant that we'd be on the opposite side of the table from Germany. The only chance we had of playing against each other was in the finals, or in the game for third place. Thankfully.

We changed quickly and headed to the stadium. Alex's parents and sister were waiting for us there. Everyone was certain Ukraine would win the game, which was why my parents had decided to skip it and move along with the English team. Still, I enjoyed the atmosphere in São Paulo, with it being the biggest city in Brazil and welcoming the highest number of tourists (along with Rio). The music in the streets and bars was excellent, and the vibe at the Arena Corinthians was somehow even more electric. When we came to the stands, the fans were already fired up, singing and chanting their hearts out.

Milan Andreyevich's team wore yellow and the opponents red. I had a yellow dress exactly the same hue as the jerseys, and I proudly sang the anthem with the rest of the Eastern European crowd. Nobody would ever say that anything was wrong at that moment, that I'd been in a compromising situation the night before. Nobody would doubt that I was Alex's.

The Moroccans were good opponents, despite being terribly unlucky in this game. They needed to win – and Chile to lose, with a significant goal difference – and they were truly giving their best efforts to achieve that. But it was in vain. They could pass the Ukrainian first line, but the defence was impenetrable. They couldn't reach Alex enough to even have a chance at a goal. The shots they had were easy for him and not dangerous at all.

On the other side, the Ukrainian forwards attacked furiously, passing the ball between each other with skill and luck. They started scoring in the forty-fourth minute, with Barnik taking the lead, and their run continued in the second half, when Lev Zahara, a defender, Ivan Rostov, a midfield, and Pavlov scored three more times. The game finished decisively after ninety-two minutes.

The news hit soon after that Chile had won against South Korea 2–1. The final results put Ukraine in first place in the group, and Chile second. We'd face Belgium, they Norway. Tomorrow, we'd go to Salvador, where the game would take place in five days.

I returned to the hotel before Alex. My heart swelled at the sight of the TVs in the hotel lobby playing live post-game interviews with Alex and his teammates. I knew this was a big achievement for them. Despite what they had accomplished four years ago, Ukraine was still not considered a football force, ranking with Italy, Spain, the Netherlands and Germany. They were usually described as a group of lucky, extremely talented boys, led by an exceptional, committed and educated coach – a combination that would never be repeated again. Most acknowledge that they would've won the previous Cup if it hadn't been for the German coach and his vice.

Now Ukraine was here again, showing great results and giving hope to their country that they could win it now. Most likely, this was their last chance. By the next Cup, most of these excellent players would be too old to play, probably even retired. A lot was expected from them now. I stood in the lobby for a spell, watching them explain all that to the curious and impatient journalists on TV.

My phone buzzed. It was Matthias texting me again to say how beautiful I looked at the game. I didn't reply. The part of my brain that was allowed to think about him was now locked away with tape over its ears, eyes and mouth. I'd reply tomorrow or the day after tomorrow. Not tonight. Not when I was about to be the perfect girlfriend for my perfect, winning boyfriend.

I took a shower and went to bed. I skimmed through my full email inbox and some articles, trying my best to stay awake. When Alex entered the room, I was cuddled under the blanket, almost paralysed with exhaustion.

"Congratulations to the best goalkeeper in the world," I said weakly.

"Oh, you poor thing." He dropped his gym bag and approached me. When he sat next to me on the bed, I hugged him and drew him into a kiss. "Let's just sleep. We'll celebrate tomorrow. Trust me, I'm dead tired, too. Those interviews seemed never-ending, but Milan wanted us to stay until no one had any more questions."

"Of course. They love you guys. You should give them as much as you can."

"I'd rather be with you, chilling in bed." He kissed me on the forehead.

"Come, then."

He removed his clothes and joined me within minutes. I hugged him, placing my head on his chest. Everything was normal, natural. Next to him, sleeping in the same bed, listening to his heart and breathing, I was calm. Happy. I loved him for this peace he gave me so simply and smoothly, so easily.

*****

Thankfully, the flight to Salvador wasn't early in the morning, so Alex's team, Lana, Angie and I had a late breakfast and took off from São Paulo around two o'clock in the afternoon. We hadn't had time for sightseeing in Salvador before, since the girls and I were there for barely one day a week ago at the English game against Paraguay. Fortunately, the team also had an afternoon off to relax, so Lana and a few Ukrainian players were organising what we'd do and see in the remaining few hours before sunset.

On the plane, I managed to take Alex to Nikolay's empty first-class suite, threatening jokingly that no one should get anywhere near it unless they wanted to disturb us at an…inconvenient moment.

Alex knew it wasn't sex I drew him there for. He felt through my cold and sweaty palm that I needed to talk.

"Something happened with Beller?" he asked as soon as the door was closed.

Seeing his concerned face, I instantly felt terrible. Terrible for accepting Matthias's invitation, for kissing him, for feeling what I felt then. I went white, and my hands started shaking. Alex didn't suspect anything. He only grew angry.

"What did that bastard do?" he hissed, love and care in his voice. He squeezed my hands, but instead of making me feel better, it only heightened my disgust for myself.

I managed to squeeze his hand back. "He came to see me in Manaus. He was standing at the hotel reception, refusing to leave until I talked to him."

"Again? Putting you at risk like that! I hate that he chooses to go after you when I'm not around. The coward."

"I don't know what to think of it, Alex. What he's doing with his coach and team can't be described as cowardly. But I only want this to stop," I said honestly.

"So you talked to him?" he said, more confirming than asking. His voice carried no judgement or blame – another twist of the knife.

"I had no choice. He didn't want to leave, and the English team were there. I didn't want to risk anyone seeing him. But...something else happened." I took another deep breath, seeing how his colour changed. "He insisted that we meet again, go for lunch or something."

Alex was infuriated beyond measure, and I knew I would have to lie – to properly, sincerely, deeply, strongly, convincingly, just like four years ago, *lie*. I let my voice quiver, prepared a couple of tears in the corners of my eyes and weakened my grasp on his fist until he realised and carefully cupped mine. And then I took a deep, shaky breath, and looked him in his stormy, ocean-blue eyes.

"There was no way of getting away from him that night until I said yes."

The effect that produced gave me not pleasure, but it was what I wanted, what I intended. He believed me. Rage spurred throughout his whole body.

"This is it. I'll sort this out myself."

"Alex, please, don't do anything yet—"

"Jane, he was about to physically hurt you. What do you expect me to do?"

"What you feel is the right thing to do. But you must not impede the success of your team." I played the card that I knew would bring him to reason and do as I said. He had disappointed his team once. He wouldn't do it again. He'd promised to them, to himself, that he wouldn't. "First of all – if you do something reckless, I'll never forgive myself. It would be a repetition of something that I already can't forgive myself for, and I know you feel the same. I told you this because I didn't want you to find out from somebody else and then think I'm doing something behind your back again. I'm not. I never will." I managed to keep my voice even.

"Second of all – you must focus on your games and training. If he hops on a plane for a four-hour flight to disturb me, you mustn't neglect your team the same, 'cause then, if something happens at the Ukrainian game, you'll always have something to blame yourself for." He listened to me, his furore receding, leaving his alert and tense body. I loved how I could calm him. When he got enraged, he was like a colossal beast, but under my touch and voice, he became calm and attentive. "If you two happen to meet, I would love for no violence to occur. But it is up to you to decide. I can't demand anything of you regarding that."

"I can promise you there will be some violence. And that's an understatement."

I smiled faintly. "Thirdly, Alex – I only said yes to get him out of the room. It doesn't mean we'll actually ever go anywhere."

"I know. But what it does mean is that he'll persist in chasing you."

He spoke the truth, and that excited and scared me at the same time. "Probably, yes, but we'll see along the way how best to respond to that without affecting the Ukrainian performance or causing any scandals." I caught his hand and squeezed it tightly. "What I can promise you for sure is that I'll do everything in my power to keep them away from us – and you, primarily. You just have to promise me that no matter what Matthias says or does, once you step on that pitch, in your head, there will only be space for football."

He was silent for a moment and then, finally, smiled. "I bet every man in the world would die to hear these words from their woman." He drew my hand to his lips and kissed it. "I promise that I won't let them affect my concentration for the game like last time."

I kissed him on the cheek. "We'll be World Cup winners, then."

*****

The afternoon in Salvador was colourful and adventurous. After checking in at the hotel, we got on the team bus and headed to visit a primary school that had outstanding results in regional football competitions. What was supposed to be a meet and greet turned into an hour-long football game. Even Lana, Angie and I took part, because the school had a very strong and successful girls' team, too. We played mixed and I was the goalkeeper, for obvious reasons. It was more fun than I'd expected. I managed to block a couple of shots, but the majority ended up in the net; we all got a good laugh in at my expense for how terrible I was.

It felt incredible to laugh and play so unselfconsciously. The children's honest joy made me understand something. I could do this forever – making them and their peers happy as they were now. I *should* do this, instead of thinking about a man who was strictly prohibited for me. If I put all my efforts and free time into meeting and talking to these kids, who had big dreams in small, underdeveloped environments, I could make their lives more hopeful, and mine clearer and freer.

"You've drifted off?" Alex's voice floated in. We were still on the old school pitch.

"I was just...thinking about how what little we do makes them so happy," I replied. "If...if I had done something similar in Germany, perhaps—"

"Hey, no," he stopped me. "Don't go back to that." He hugged me and kissed on the crown of my head, to which nearby kids giggled. "We'll do it now. Together. As much as we can."

I kissed his hand. "Thank you."

Close to sunset, we left the school to go for dinner in one of the city's more famous restaurants. The food was exceptional, to the point that we all collectively agreed to meet the next day for a prolonged session at the gym.

When we returned to the hotel, I was too tired to look at my phone. I also anticipated that Matthias had sent me something, so I decided to check it in the morning. I had enough thoughts knocking around in my head at the moment; I scarcely needed to make it even harder on me.

Alex and I had a shower, during which we couldn't refrain from a slow but wild session that exhausted us even more. He knew exactly how to treat my body and mind. When he foamed up the shower gel and started massaging it into my back and shoulders, he kneaded out most of the tension and stress I'd collected since the morning. I closed my eyes and let him squeeze my muscles. His hands, however, quickly moved to my breasts and started squeezing them, too, focusing on my nipples, which got hard instantly. Wordlessly, I turned around and pressed myself up against his crotch, instantly confirming he was more than ready to enter me. As he massaged me, I placed him inside me and we both moaned in unison, shaken by the wave of sensitivity with which my tight insides reacted to him. With my back to him, I couldn't see his face, but the sighs I heard divulged the absolute pleasure we shared. I moved slowly, enjoying every second of the sensations I was receiving. He was still not giving up on my breasts; in fact, he squeezed them harder. I led him to start thrusting into me, first slowly, and then wilder and faster, until we came together and almost dropped down to the shower floor.

I turned around and leaned into his chest, and he covered me with his arms.

"Now I expect you to carry me to bed, snuggle up with me and not wake up until noon," I whispered.

"Whatever you say, my love." He kissed me on the forehead and did as I said.

*****

I was immensely thankful to Alex for silencing his alarm as soon as it sounded. When I woke up slightly past noon, the bed was empty except for a note on his pillow, accompanied by a rose.
See you at lunchtime. xxx
Well, lunchtime was almost here.

I stretched lazily and took a look at my phone. It was loaded with messages that I'd need hours to reply to. I skimmed through the list, consciously looking for an unsaved phone number. I told myself it was only for the sake of precaution, but the guilt clenching my heart betrayed my true intentions. When I found it, my heart leapt.

I guess you're coming to watch England in Brasília?

It was sent yesterday while we were on our flight to Salvador.

- Yes. I replied.

It bothered me that he didn't answer within a few minutes. I went for a quick shower, expecting some reply when I got out of the bathroom, but there was nothing. That wasn't like him. Or perhaps he'd gotten upset and given up?

My phone rang. It was Alex, telling me he was almost at the hotel and I could meet him in the restaurant. I put on a breezy orange summer dress and headed downstairs. Lana and Angie joined me within minutes. The moment we sat at the table, I understood why Matthias hadn't written to me yet – he was playing against Spain in Belo Horizonte.

"I'll get them to change the channel," Lana said immediately, seeing my stricken expression.

"You can't, Lana. It's the first game of the eighth-finals and the only game on at the moment," I replied, trying to conceal the wicked happiness bubbling inside me.

She knew exactly how I felt and scrutinised me with her eyes disapprovingly. "Alright, but sit here where you can't see the screen."

"Of course." I changed seats obligingly.

Alex and his teammates arrived shortly, and he, Andriy Barnik and Lev Zahara joined us at the table. They saw the game that was on and couldn't help watching it, both out of professionalism and subdued hatred. I hoped without hope that Spain would win so that Germany and Matthias had no reason to stay longer in Brazil, which would definitely make everything easier for me. It helped to see that the forces on the pitch were even throughout the first half. However, by the second part of the game, Germany had created a number of really good chances that were followed by enough good luck to result in two beautiful goals. The scorers were Ben Schwimmer and Kevin Jäger, with Matthias assisting both of them.

Only after the last whistle did we realise that the table had been silent for a while. All six of us were watching. When the camera started focusing on each player, I purposefully started up a conversation about Ukraine's game against Belgium three days from now.

At the previous World Cup, we had battled Belgium for third place and defeated them 3–0. Now they were raging for revenge. Milan Andreyevich had been stressing the importance of this match since we ended up first in the group. The Belgians would do everything in their power to reach the quarterfinals.

Because of that, I had something special planned for Alex on the match day. Lana and Angie jumped to help me the second I said what was on my mind, and now, while the boys were discussing the potential dangerous tactics their next opponents could make, the three of us exchanged knowing glances.

After lunch, I went up with Alex to the gym – it was on his schedule and I wanted to join him – after which he left for training again and I decided to join the girls by the pool.

We hadn't been there for an hour when Lana's phone rang. The call was brief.

"It's here!" she squeaked.

She didn't need to say anything else. All three of us jumped from our loungers and ran to my room. A conspicuously dressed lady and her assistant had arrived with a package that I couldn't wait to open.

Within seconds, a large, luxurious, lustrously wild Carnival costume in the colours of the Ukrainian flag was in front of us.

"I love it!" I screamed in awe. "This is going to be astounding! What a show I'm going to give!"

"I bet you will," the creator of the fantasia[2] said in slow, sweet English. "Now you'd better try it so that we see if there is anything that needs adjustment."

The lady, Barbara, had made the costume for me. She was a local designer Lana had discovered online. When Lana reached out to her, the poor woman thought we were frauds at first, but Lana patiently convinced her otherwise. Sewing a costume this exuberant and lavish would normally take weeks, but she accepted to do it within ten days because it was for me and, well, because "You don't get lucky like this every day," as Barbara had said.

Now, as she assisted me in putting it on, I saw it was a hell of a job.

"Please, would you come to the match?" I asked. "Honestly, I thought my girls and I would be able to pull this off together, but now I see I'd look ridiculous without professional assistance. This is pure art in which we have no knowledge at all."

"You think I'd let you wear my creation improperly?" she laughed, her expert fingers sliding needles everywhere around my hips where the most adjustments were needed. "Of course, I'll be there."

The headpiece was the most challenging part. We decided to change it for a smaller one. The initial one Barbara had prepared was extravagantly big, and while it fit my head, knowing how passionate I got during football games, there was a high danger that the decoration wouldn't stay on. We made a plan for Barbara to come the day before, when we'd return from Brasília after the English match, and bring the smaller headpiece and the adjusted bottom part of the costume that was too low in the front and too tight on the sides.

"This is a great idea, Jane," Angie said when Barbara and her colleague left. "Alex will love it."

"And the world will love it, too," Lana added. "I can already see the headlines – *The Perfect Couple Reaffirmed*."

We laughed. "You really think like a ruthless manager." I threw a cushion at her.

---

[2] Fantasia - Portuguese word for the costume for the Carnival in Rio.

Alex was about to return from his evening training, so the girls left me alone. I used that brief free time to check my phone and was guiltily excited to see the reply from the unsaved number.

Alright then. So tomorrow we go out. When do you land?

My heart started beating faster. He was truly insane.

- Go out where?

In Brasília, of course.

- You're out of your mind.

We agreed on that a long time ago. When will you be in the city?

- Around two p.m.

Great. I'll pick you up at four.

- You're behaving as if we're going for a normal date and that it's completely fine if somebody sees me entering a car! With you!

I was simultaneously angry, upset and exhilarated. A smile danced on my lips.

We're not kids. I know what I'm doing, and I'll repeat myself – I'll never do something that could harm you. So tomorrow, at exactly four o'clock, start walking towards the main entrance of your hotel. I'll be in a blue BMW. You sit in the front and we go. Agreed?

All my insides twirled.

- Where are we going?

That's a secret.

- Would you give me a hint so that I can stop worrying?

You can stop worrying, and I won't give you a hint. It's a surprise.

- Isn't four o'clock a little bit too early?

Spending time with you can never be too early or too late. ;)

I smiled but decided to keep my cold facade. - *Alright. But I have to be back in the hotel by a decent time. I'm meeting my parents in the morning for breakfast and then we're going to the game. I can't afford to look tired.*

Don't worry. I took care of everything.

I hesitated with my reply. I didn't want to say anything. I didn't want to prolong the conversation, because that would show him how damn excited I was about it all, and I wasn't supposed to be. Terrible, devilish guilt was eating my insides like acid, although I was all girlishly flustered.

P.S. Wear something calm. ;)

Damn it! I couldn't stifle a laugh or prevent my heart from jumping again.

- I do have something like that in my suitcase.

But not like last time. Those white jeans attracted attention.

Did he really remember those details?

- Alright. No jeans this time.

What are you up to now?

Argh! How could he initiate a conversation like two normal, ordinary people dating when we were everything except that?

- I'm in my room. The girls just left. I had to keep cold.

Did you watch the game today?

I lied. - *No. I was busy.*

Then I guess you've heard that we're playing the Italians next. Tough.

- Well, it's your turn now to have a more difficult side of the table.

xD You're cruel. But we'll manage them all. I assure you we'll be in the finals.

- Good luck with that.

Is Blondie there?

Why the hell was he bringing Alex up?

- He's just about to return.

Why are you so stiff then?

- Because we're not supposed to have a friendly chat.

There are many things we are and are not supposed to do, Jane.

I knew I could interpret this in a hundred different emotional, naughty ways. That was why I didn't reply, too submerged in my colourful thoughts, too fraught with guilt.

I'll relax you a bit. You're too anxious, arrived on my phone ten minutes later.

Needless to say, I jumped from the bed, imagining all the crazy things that could have crossed his mind.

- What do you mean? I typed with shaking fingers.

He didn't reply within a minute.

- Matthias? Still nothing.

It was already almost eight, and Alex could get back to the room any time. I didn't want to text him and risk him suspecting anything. This was his typical time to return. So why wasn't he here yet? Perhaps he'd stayed back half an hour with his coach and teammates to discuss something.

Twenty minutes of uneasiness later, there was a knock on the door. I immediately knew it was some kind of delivery, and I could almost bet on my life it would be flowers from the crazy bastard.

When I opened the door, the courier passed me a light, wrapped package the size of a football. I thanked him, looked down the hallway and breathed out in relief on seeing that Alex was absent. I then retreated to the room and started unpacking the delivery with the speedy fingers of a little girl on Christmas.

It was a teddy bear. A little, beige teddy bear wearing a white T-shirt saying *I miss you*. He was small, easy to hide in a suitcase or purse. There was also a note, of course.

I can't wait to see you tomorrow, the most gorgeous woman in the universe.

Stupidly, I smelt the toy, hoping that his scent would be there, which wasn't the case. The bear smelled fresh, oceanic, peaceful. I could lie and say that the it was a gift from a fan the girls and I had met during the day. Alex would believe it, but I wouldn't be able to look at myself in the mirror if I did that.

I didn't know how I still could, even now.

I pushed the teddy bear into my suitcase, making sure enough clothes were on top of it and that Alex would only find it if he was really looking for something, which he never did.

Less stiff now? :)

I was lying in bed again. - *I swear, tomorrow I'll slap you once for every time you stressed me out over the past few days and shortened my life.*

I'm looking forward to it.

- *Thank you. He is cute.*

Alex entered the room at that moment, and I jumped to greet him, tossing my phone aside in feigned disinterest. For a second, I was ashamed at how leisurely and quickly I had done it. Despite my skills being four years rusty, I again had managed to pack one man in a mental box and throw him out of my mind to focus on another.

I smiled generously at Alex, remembering the fantasia I'd wear in the colours of the Ukrainian flag in his next match and imagining how happy and proud that would make him.

"Hey, big boy. Where have you been all this time?" I hung around his neck.

"Honestly, trying to escape my dictator coach and come back to sleep on your breasts for ten hours straight." He kissed me on the forehead, dropping his bag to the floor.

"Let's do it, then. Hungry?"

"Not at all. Let's go to bed. Do you really have to go tomorrow?"

"Unfortunately, I can't avoid it. It's England."

"Alright, alright. I tried."

I kissed him on the cheek and went to get ready for bed. Before I joined him, I glanced at my phone one more time.

Nineteen hours, thirteen minutes till we meet. Goodnight, petite little Jane.

*****

The flight to Brasília took exactly two hours. On the plane, we had breakfast and coffee. I told Lana and Angie what had taken place the evening before. I had to, because I needed someone to take care of the teddy bear. I didn't want to risk having it in the same room with Alex again.

Lana was stubborn.

"I can take it," she said. "But it'll end up down the chute of the hotel. If not burnt on the balcony."

"How could you..." I complained but gave up quickly. I then gave sad eyes to my other friend, who didn't have much choice.

"Alright, I'll take care of it," Angie grumbled. "Only because I don't want you and Alex to fight over a stupid toy."

"Thanks, Angie. Just make sure you tell something to Declan if he stumbles into your room these days," I said.

"Oh, you're right, I should." She narrowed her eyes at me. "You're still a damn good liar. Thinking about everything."

"That's why I've never been caught." I winked.

"Don't you wink here," Lana said, annoyed. "You *were* caught. And not just caught. You were observed and monitored for a long time, because there is something that coach knew then, and perhaps still knows. You shouldn't be going out with that hardheaded prick today. Not just because it's not good for you and your *finally stable* relationship but also because I can bet that, same as the last time, Gottfried knows much more than we think. And he can use it any time."

"No, Lana," Angie stepped in, "I think the old man has given up. Come on, look at Alex and Jane. They've stayed together after everything. I don't think he'll waste his energy." I wanted to thank her, but she continued, speaking to Lana strictly as if I wasn't there at all. "However, I also don't think that he'll need to intervene – Jane and Matthias will fuck up everything themselves."

I took a deep breath. "I see that neither of you will ever understand me – unless perhaps the same happens to you one day."

"What, the *same*?" Lana hissed, frustrated. She was, I could tell, exerting a tremendous effort stopping herself from raising her voice and causing a scene. "You're going out with a man you had an affair with, while you still have a wonderful boyfriend who you claim you love."

"I..." My voice shook. "I'm afraid I have really strong feelings for Matthias, too."

"You don't! 'Cause you can't! Do we have to spell it out for you like you're fifteen? You two spent a very brief time together, hiding from everyone. Then you didn't see each other for four full years. Whatever you may feel is an illusion. It's unreal, based on something, someone that doesn't exist. I can bet that if you spent seven days together, you'd realise you've been living in deception."

What she said made sense. However, she wasn't the one experiencing those feelings. She could never know.

"I wish it was deception, Lana. That's why I'm going today."

They gave up, knowing they stood no chance. No matter what they said, I'd still do it my way. If they refused to be my alibi – I told Alex I'd be with them in the spa the whole afternoon – they'd just make it all much more complicated for all of us. So they agreed. When we parted ways, I felt both pairs of judgemental eyes on my back. But I paid them no mind; I had a date to get ready for.

Every hour closer to the meeting, Matthias texted me. *Four hours, thirteen minutes. Three hours, thirteen minutes. Two hours...*

Once I started getting ready, my heart began pumping fast. I was sweating to the point that I had to take a shower and listen to a few minutes of calming music. A quarter past three, he wrote: *On my way. Will text you when to go down.*

I was naked then, my makeup and hair ready, avoiding getting into a little black A-line dress because I still sweated every time I saw his number on my phone screen. *This is it,* I thought. *Put that dress on, woman, and kill it. You can't be afraid anymore.*

- *Alright. I'm ready.* I texted back.

Exactly at 3:54, he texted me back.
Go down and wait by the elevator.

My body began shaking and my heart was trying to pump its way out of my body. I ignored it because, well, I had no other option. I reapplied a rose-induced perfume that was strong enough to deal with the heat outside (plus, I wanted to be on the safe side, because I still didn't know where we were going). I covered my hair with a blue floral scarf, put on large sunglasses that covered almost half of my face, took my frame bag and left the room.

I wasn't alone in the elevator, but the elderly couple didn't pay much attention to me, which meant I did a good job concealing my identity.

The moment I stepped out into the spacious entrance hall, I picked up my phone as it vibrated.

I'm driving in. Start walking towards the door. I'll stop, you enter and we go same second.

I felt as if I were in a James Bond film; if I hadn't been so stressed, I'd have told him that.

I started walking with surprising confidence. The hall was busy with football fans from all over the world. Nobody paid attention to the shawled girl in a simple black dress, yet I felt as if all eyes were on me, as if everyone had gone silent and only the clicking of my heels could be heard throughout the cavernous lobby.

When I saw the blue BMW out front, tremors flew up my arms and legs, but I didn't change the rhythm of my steps, nor the pace of my breathing. I had to remain calm until I entered that car.

I passed through the large rotating door and into the Brazilian heat. The windows of the BMW were dark, so I couldn't see inside. For a millisecond, I thought, *What if this isn't Matthias, but someone else?* Was I about to make a fool of myself? Was I walking into my doom, as Angie had said?

However, there was no space for hesitation or mistakes. It was a blue BMW, as he had said. It could be no one else. A concierge materialised next to me and opened the door. I thanked him with a brief nod. He didn't know who I was, and I didn't want to expose myself now at the last step with my voice and accent.

The moment I sat in the black leathered seat, I knew I was in the right place – his cologne was already in every crevice of the inside of the rented car. The door closed, and we continued along the cobblestoned road towards the exit. I didn't remove my glasses or shawl. I didn't even dare look at him. Out of my peripheral vision, I could only see the black of his hair. I noticed he was wearing sunglasses, too. My hands were shaking, so I clutched my bag until my fingers went white.

Matthias also didn't talk, but I could feel his smile. There was no music coming off the radio; the silence pressed on my chest, almost preventing me from breathing. As soon as we drove into the street and joined the traffic, I couldn't keep quiet anymore.

"Is this even legal?"

"What?" His voice tilted with humour. He hadn't been expecting that question.

Why did he have such an attractive voice? I said, "Tinted windows."

"For you and me, today, it is legal," he replied simply, still smiling.

He removed his glasses and put them in the compartment under the radio. I did the same with both my glasses and scarf, although I wanted to stay hidden under it all, afraid to be so close to him. *Alright, Jane, pluck up your courage,* I told myself. *You're not a lost little girl. You weren't four years ago. You mustn't be now. Look at him. Face him. Get what you came for. Prove to yourself and him that you two are not what he believes you to be.*

I took a deep, silent breath and turned to observe his profile. He wore dark jeans and a black shirt. He was simply and divinely handsome, especially with one hand on the steering wheel. His face had a day-old beard that made him terribly attractive. Four years ago, I remembered, his face had always been soft, always freshly shaven. Now he was twenty-eight and a hell of a man – a man who didn't need to shave to impress a woman, and instead bloody impressed her with his seemingly careless stubble. I began imagining it, rough under my fingertips, or on my cheeks, or over some other parts of my skin, which caused me to start sweating again. He turned to look at me in that moment, taking me by surprise. It was like he could read my thoughts.

I didn't manage to say anything until his gaze had been on me for too long. "For goodness' sake, Matthias, you must watch where you drive!" I was mildly aware we were at a red light. But still...

He didn't even blink, let alone return his eyes to the road. He only smiled, like the bad boy I had fallen for. "You look beautiful, Jane."

I knew I was going red, because I felt my blood reaching a boiling point. The light turned green and he, thankfully, returned his eyes to the road, giving me time to pull myself together. *Come on, Jane. What did you say to yourself a few seconds ago?*

I took a deep, silent breath. "Thank you," I said, trying to sound unmoved. "You look good, too."

He laughed, confident and self-aware, evoking all the familiar feelings – when I'd wanted to slap him across that overly self-satisfied face, when his air had excited and charmed me. "That's a huge compliment. You've never said that."

"I haven't?"

"No, otherwise I'd have remembered it."

"Well, I certainly meant to say it, at times." I knew at the very same moment that I shouldn't have said that, but I couldn't have helped it. He was gorgeous, and he was there because of me. I couldn't be rude or lie.

He laughed again. I loved the sound. It almost made me laugh, too, every time – just to be in on the joke, just to feel closer to him.

"So, where are we going?" I asked, purposefully changing the topic.

"You'll find out soon," he replied predictably. I sighed, and he caught it. "I swear on my parents that nothing bad stands a chance of happening to you."

"Alright. I guess I don't have any other option now but to trust you."

"You don't have to guess. You can trust me."

"Since you jumped in front of my father, I've been reluctant to."

"I told you already – I'd never have said anything to him. It was just a way to make you talk to me. That beast of a man believes everything you say. He'd have cut my head off before I even got to the part where we went out for the first time."

I laughed thinly, still a bit tense. "You looked rather convincing that day, both to me and him."

"I would have done anything just to make you speak to me."

"Yeah, I can see. I know..." I ended the sentence with nothing else to say, sadly, trying to count how many reckless things he'd done for me at this World Cup.

Suddenly, he pulled over. Cars and pedestrians swarmed past us on the street. I went cold instantly, trying to remind myself the car had extremely dark windows. "What are you—"

He took my hand in his. "Jane, it's me. Matthias." He kissed my knuckles, slowly, sending tremors all over my skin, reaching every nerve within my body, even the marrow of my spine. "Look at me."

Although scared as a gazelle, I faced those dark eyes and saw they were filled with warmth.

"I am still that same man you met four years ago. I haven't changed a bit. I only love you more." He kissed the back of my hand again, and I closed my eyes, my emotions battling each other to the death. "It's only the two of us in the world right now. You can be that happy, fluttery girl I know. The girl you are." Again, his lips were on my skin. "I know you probably feel guilt at being here, but try not to. I wouldn't have left you at peace until you agreed to meet me, and also, you know you actually want to be here. Whether that's right or wrong is rather dubious now. We're here to find out."

Instead of an answer, I squeezed his hand and nodded, swallowing back tears, my emotions, Alex, everything that was screaming in my head that I shouldn't be here. I told myself there was no other way now – I was here, with him, with the man who loved me enough to commit an insane number of irrationalities; the man who evoked in me the trembling of my heart, skin, nerves; who confused my breathing and my basic postulates of judgement. Since there was no going back, I had better accept the ride and enjoy this time we had together.

I took another deep breath. "Have you got any drinks here?"

He laughed again: "Sure, I do." He let go of my hand to turn and get a bottle from the back seat of the car. "This is *cachaça*[3], white rum, typical of Brazil. Forty-eight percent alcohol."

I glanced at the transparent liquid and prayed for it to give me relief. "Pass it over."

---

3 *Cachaça*, Portuguese, pronounced as ka-'sha-sah

He opened the bottle and gave it to me. I took a big gulp, without smelling or tasting it with my tongue, expecting standard rum. In the next moment, I suppressed a spluttering cough, which manifested with a few tears. "T-this is pure alcohol."

He chuckled.

"But I like it," I added. "You've tried it?"

"Yes, many times."

"You're not gonna have some now?"

"No, thank you. This month it's prohibited, remember?"

I sniffed jokingly. "You finally got to take me out and you'll still respect your off-the-pitch rules?"

He laughed. Gosh, what an attractive laugh he had! I took another gulp of *cachaça*.

"Hun, you're extremely important to me, but around football, I don't compromise."

I wanted to ask him if that meant that football was before me on his list of priorities, because if that was the case, he should turn around and drop me back at the hotel so that I didn't waste my time with him, since, obviously, Alex had compromised football for me four years ago when he lost his head and received three goals because of this man's coach. However, I bit my tongue. I knew better than most women how much football mattered. Football had been there for these men before me and would stay forever, regardless of what happens with me. It was the number one priority. I was trying to nail that into Alex's head, too. This man knew his core values. I had no right to complain.

"Alright. Why have you got a whole bottle, then? Just for me? You want to get me drunk and kidnap me?" I joked and took another sip. It burned my throat but it warmed my insides, flushing out the thought of Alex and helping me enjoy these minutes with Matthias that I had longed for.

"I don't need to get you drunk to kidnap you," he replied, smiling. "Perhaps, soon, I won't even need to kidnap you to make you come with me." He turned to wink at me. "This is only a gesture of Brazilian hospitality."

"Thank you. I like it." I closed the bottle and put it next to my feet. Our day had only just started, and I didn't need to get drunk in the first half hour. "Tell me about the guys. Update me first hand."

"Most of it you know from the newspapers. But if you want the information closest to truth, Lens is still the same – all about girls, night clubs and games. Ben is somewhat similar, though he's growing tired of constantly being in relationships that don't fulfil him. We all sense he'll settle down soon. Friedrich and Debora are still doing fine. Michael's had the most changes in his life."

"Yup, I remember reading he met Victoria not long before the Euro two years ago."

With a mane of curly hair that reached her hips, Michael Krimm's wife wasn't particularly pretty, but her eyes were big, calming and friendly. Most importantly, Michael was head over heels for her, and he showed it in his own particular, composed way. They always held hands or his arm would be around her; he hid her from tabloids or any kind of attention; and as the media had respected him before, they respected him again when he found his significant other.

"Yes, they hit it off immediately. He has never been happier than since they met. They're expecting Krimm Junior these days."

I jumped in my seat. "So it's definitely a boy?"

"They've been hiding it pretty well, but yes. It's a new football star. We're still debating the name."

"Who's 'we'?"

"What's that question, Jane? We are not only the German Four for the journalists. We're a family."

"Anyway, why are Ben, Lens and you debating the name of Michael and Victoria's kid?" I laughed.

"We'll be his godfathers."

"All three of you?"

"Well, Lens was already Michael's best man at the wedding, so technically only Ben and me."

"Choose well, then."

"I always do." He took my hand from my lap and drew it to his lips. Goosebumps covered me instantly, and for a precious couple of seconds, I felt as if we were a normal, ordinary couple driving through a city, happy to be together, discussing friends' matters and making jokes. It felt blissful and fulfilling.

He dropped my hand to point at an unusual, white, half-sphere-shaped building: "This is the Museu Nacional da República. It's an art museum. That grand building you see there is the Cathedral of Brasília."

"Are you sure?"

"One hundred percent." We drove past the religious building in silence while I admired it for its grandeur and extraordinary shape. "Soon we'll pass by the National Congress. That's one of the buildings that pops up first when you google Brasília."

He was right. I'd seen that modern construction before.

"In a few minutes we'll see the Bank of Brazil, then I'll drive you over the Juscelino Kubitschek bridge, and then we'll go for a random ride for you to see the coast of the Paranoá Lake."

"Wow! When I return, I'll be able to tell Lana everything about this place," I commented admiringly.

"Exactly. Did you know that Brasília was planned in the shape of a plane? The residential areas are on the wings, while the main government buildings are along the fuselage."

I stared at him. "Matthias, did you study a Bädeker[4] before taking me out?"

He returned my gaze and mesmerised me with his smile. "No."

"How come you know all this, then?"

"I've done my homework."

"You just said you didn't go through a guidebook."

"You're incredibly cute when you're confused and relaxed." Again, he took my hand and kissed it. "I missed you."

Matthias was looking at the road in front of him, more focused now since the traffic had become denser. There was no need for me to say anything. He did nothing to show me he required it.

Still, I said it.

"I missed you, too." And it wasn't the *cucaracha*, or whatever the name of the rum was. I truly felt it.

He looked at me and smiled again, kissing my hand once more, this time not letting it go. "It's part of the surprise," he added.

"What?" I'd drifted off for a second.

"Why I know so much about this city."

"Ahem. So I can dare guess you are nowhere near as familiar with the other host cities?"

"Exactly, I'm not."

"I'm looking forward to discovering your secret then."

We both laughed, and he drove on, showing and describing buildings to me as I observed them, enjoying the sound of his voice and the cute accent in which he pronounced the Portuguese names of the monuments and streets.

After two hours or so of driving, we headed away from the busy city streets toward a calmer area.

---

[4] A Bädecker is a guide book, however usually it refers to a series of guide books published by the German publisher Karl Bädeker.

"Wherever you're taking me," I said, "Please, bear in mind that I have to be back in the hotel at an appropriate time. The match tomorrow is at one o'clock and I have to meet my parents and the others early."

"Don't worry. My flight back to Rio is at nine tomorrow, so I'll have to leave around seven in the morning."

That calmed me down. He wouldn't risk not being back for his training on time – not when he had escaped for one day already. I knew it.

Still, I wondered what the surprise was. We were in an area with reduced traffic, and it was already getting dark. The colour of the sky was charmingly rose gold. I wished we could be on some hill together, watching the sunset. Was that the surprise?

He parked in front of one of the entrances of a colossal block of buildings.

"We're here," he announced.

"Where?"

"You'll see in a matter of minutes."

A thousand wild thoughts reverberated through my head. This was much too public. What was on his mind? What had he been preparing? What if a bunch of journalists were inside waiting to make our secret relationship – or however this could be defined – public?

"Jane." He'd noticed my breathing accelerate. "I'd never…"

"I know."

He smiled. "Let's go; they're waiting for us."

My heart jumped again. "*They?*"

"You'll see."

He got out of the car and walked over to my side to open the door, but I did it myself. When I stepped out, I realised my legs were shaking. I took a deep breath, and he extended his hand. I accepted it, thankful.

Our BMW didn't stand out too much among the other cars parked in the vicinity, so I concluded the neighbourhood wasn't dodgy. It was probably an upper-middle-class residential area. Or perhaps this was a club, or a restaurant hidden from the many curious eyes this city was now full with.

"Do you trust me?" he asked, realising that my hands were shaking, too.

"I do."

It took me a millisecond to process how that sentence sounded coming out of my mouth. I could easily imagine us in front of a clerk, holding hands like this, giving our vows. It looked too good in my head; I had to disperse it.

"You'd never do anything to hurt me, but with your surprises, I'll end up with a chronic heart condition." I tried to crack a joke.

"Don't worry. So far they've all been good, right?"

We walked over to the entrance, a door labelled with the number twenty-seven, and he pressed a button on the intercom. Soon afterwards, a female voice answered with, "Ja, Matthias?"

"Wir sind hier,"[5] he replied.

There was a beep and the sound of a door unlocking, and we entered the building. While leading me through the hallway, Matthias was smiling, observing my utterly stunned face that was getting more and more confused. *Who is this woman? What's going on?* I thought.

"Are you taking me somewhere where they'll hold me captive forever?" I asked to break the silence in the elevator. He absorbed me with his eyes, sending goosebumps all over me.

"Why would I do that?" He wasn't touching me now, but I could almost feel his skin on mine. That's how piercingly he was looking at me.

"As revenge for everything."

"No, Jane. The only revenge I'd take on you would be in bed."

I burst out laughing. It felt good to be able to laugh about it, as if I had never slept with all those men while dating him.

On the seventh floor, I followed him out of the elevator and down a corridor until we reached door number seventy-three. He rang the bell and soon, as if she was waiting nearby, a middle-aged lady with red locks reaching her shoulders opened the door.

My first reaction was to smile, but before I managed, she gasped. She then covered her mouth with her hands and turned back to the living room. There was a commotion; several voices started talking all at the same time, and I could only distinguish two words through the mixture of German and Portuguese: *Jane Andersonn*.

I looked at Matthias, shocked. He only laughed and said, "Jane, meet the Brazilian part of my family."

I felt as though he'd splashed an enormous bucket of freezing cold water over my head and it was now sliding down my back, chest and legs.

"W-what?"

"Don't worry, they're not my parents." He put an arm around my shoulders. How could he be so casual? What was going on?

"Did they know I was coming?"

---

[5] We're here. (German)

"They knew I was bringing a special friend, but I didn't tell them her name."

"You weren't fair with them either," I admonished him.

"I like organising surprises for the people I care about," he said with a sly wink.

"Don't wink at me now. Have you gone nuts? What are you doing?"

"Introducing you to my family. And yes, I am nuts."

I sighed and turned to him, placing a palm on his cheek, hoping that'd bring reason to his unreasonable mind. "Mati, I'm not sure this is a good idea. Think of my status. I am officially with someone else," I whispered. "What will they say and think, having me here now? It could turn uncomfortable, and they'd have all the right to be rude to me."

He took both my hands in his warm, solid ones and kissed me on the forehead. "Don't worry, Jane. They're not like that. You'll see. I wouldn't have brought you here if I had any suspicions about them. They're my family and want me happy. When I suggested bringing a very important friend over, they all supposed it was a girlfriend I wanted to have privacy with and were willing to help as much as possible. They won't change their minds now for the worse just because that girl is you. I am sure the contrary will happen, in fact. Give them a chance."

"Mati, what if things go wrong?" I squeaked in a low voice. "After everything that's been in the papers about us, about how I'm a bitch who abandoned you but still has feelings for you which I don't renounce, about how I've been torturing you and keeping you on a leash—"

He put a finger on my lips: "About how we care for each other in spite of the time, distance and circumstances between us, and a million other headlines I could tell you now." He rubbed my shoulders. "Jane, they will like you, I guarantee. One hundred percent. If it makes you feel calmer, I promise we'll leave the moment the situation becomes uncomfortable or insulting. But that will not take place. Agree?"

I breathed in again and knew there was no other way. I was already there. He had obviously talked to them and organised this meeting, this dinner. I couldn't turn and leave simply because I was scared or because I was Alex Yanov's girlfriend. Matthias knew what he was doing. He wouldn't put us in danger.

"Alright," I said.

He kissed me on the forehead, and we walked into the apartment.

In front of us, there was a vast living room with three large sofas and two armchairs, a long dining table for at least fifteen people, and a couple of doors on the right side. It smelt of cosiness, warmth, welcome and home.

Apart from the red-haired woman, there was a middle-aged man (her husband), an elderly couple (definitely someone's parents), and two guys and a girl my age (their kids, I assumed). They all welcomed us, greeted Matthias in German, shook our hands and commented something – again in German – which I knew was about me because they were looking at me, their eyes shining in surprise. I didn't know what, if anything, to say, until – finally – one of the younger boys said in English, "So that girl is Jane Andersonn. No wonder you were so mysterious, Cousin."

We laughed collectively, and then it occurred to me. "Matthias, how am I gonna speak to them? I know nothing in German or Portuguese."

"Don't worry, I'll translate," he said, kissing me on the crown of my head.

"Espera! ¿Tu hablas español, Jane?" [6] asked the other boy. I confirmed, relief overflowing in me. "Then we're fine. We mostly understand Spanish and can manage some conversation," he explained in Spanish.

"Hey, that's not fair," Matthias said. "How will I understand anything, then?"

"Don't worry, I'll translate," I said, not intending it to be a joke, but it was. Everyone laughed. A pretty good outcome for the first minute with his family.

Mila, the redhead, ushered us to the dining table, mumbling something in Portuguese-Spanish about pork that she had prepared. Robert, her husband, a stout and strong man in his late forties, handed out drinks – more cachaça.

"Matthias, what exactly did you tell them before this dinner?" I whispered, still unsure whether to behave as his friend or girlfriend. They knew me, all of them. What I didn't know was whether they now believed all those articles that we had been together all these years, or whether Matthias had told them something else. In any case, kissing him or even holding hands in front of them at this moment felt odd, awkward and wrong.

"I told them I wanted to bring a girl over for dinner, that I wanted her somewhere quiet and relaxing where we wouldn't have to worry

---

[6] Wait! Jane, you speak Spanish, right? (Spanish)

about cameras and reporters. I also told them that she was not German, so I wanted to show her a bit of our tradition outside of Germany, that I care about her a lot, that she is very important and that it matters to me that they behave as if she was my chosen one, regardless of the circumstances they notice, because this girl is special and I want her to be comfortable and happy."

I melted in his words.

"You think they didn't suspect it was me? After all these years of us filling the tabloids."

"A long time ago, I told them it was just my trick to make Yanov angry. You're an inexhaustible source of inspiration for the reporters, while I only happened to be around in Germany and recklessly in love with you. I'm sure they didn't think it was you. Besides, why does it matter, anyway?"

"As long as they don't tell anyone, it doesn't."

"They won't. Not even their friends or neighbours know I'm their cousin. They like to keep a low profile."

He kissed me on the top of my head again, and I relaxed slightly. I turned around to absorb the place. Overall, it was quite dark, but the curtains were pulled closed, so I assumed that during the day the living room was full of light. The furniture was dark purple, and all the cupboards and bookshelves were traditional, old-style, painted in oak brown. I noticed some scented candles, but the smell was pleasantly pervasive and lived in the apartment – they lit them regularly, not only when they had guests coming over. Best of all, the aroma of sizzling meat wafted in from the kitchen. The ambience definitely calmed me. It wasn't just the cachaça. This home was humble and beautiful, and in the next moment, I felt glad for having come here with him.

"Thank you," I whispered in his ear. "May I hold your hand?"

He smiled charmingly, satisfied that he'd melted my anxiety and frosty attitude. "Of course, Schatzi." He cupped my frozen fingers and warmed them up instantly, sending waves of relief and heat throughout my chest. It was going to be fine. This was going to be perfectly alright. I was with him, and nothing inopportune would take place – quite the contrary.

I took up the role of a normal girlfriend, which was a natural part to play. It meant I needed to make my guy's family like me, or at least have a positive first impression of me. I turned to Robert, the head of the family, and asked in slow Spanish, "So, how are you related to the Bellers?"

He was happy to retell their story. Mila and their two sons assisted by translating some words into English when I didn't understand their Spanish counterparts. The girl there, Anabella, was the girlfriend of the older boy, Thomas; she also assisted, since her English was the most advanced (except for Matthias's, of course). That conversation was a wonderful and entertaining mash of languages, cultures, histories and experiences.

Robert explained to me that Mila's mother was a sister of Matthias's maternal grandmother. Before WWII began, Mila's mother married, and her husband got a farming opportunity in the south of Brazil. The sisters kept in touch despite the distance, time zones, months between letters (some of which never reached their intended receivers), expensive annual phone calls and the fact that they'd never see each other again. Matthias had always known about his cousins in Brasília whom he had paid the first visit to when he started making money from football. He was the first Beller from his grandmother's descendants to visit this branch of the family. They were distant cousins but great, invaluable friends, as Matthias said and they all confirmed. Mila's parents had first lived in Porto Alegre before moving to Brasilia for work, where she met her husband, Robert. His parents were Johan and Hannah, the elderly couple present, who spoke Spanish to me, asking me mostly about my life in Madrid and London. It was their lifelong dream to visit Europe for a multiple-month tour.

The children, Thomas and Lukas, were extremely engaging and polite. Thomas was my age and his girlfriend, Anabella, was a year younger. They both studied electrical engineering. Lukas, who was nineteen, had just begun his studies in journalism, specialising in politics and research.

"He wants to go to war zones and report the truth," Robert said. "We still hope that idea will fade out of his mind by the time he finishes his final year."

"Don't advise him against it too much," I said, "otherwise he might do it out of sheer stubbornness."

"She's right," Mila said. "You'd better support him and send him straight to Asia, and you'll see him switch to sports journalism and football games."

"I wouldn't mind that, once I'm missing a few limbs," Lukas said, and everyone laughed at his parents' half-astonished, half-joking faces.

After cachaça, we drank beer, all except Matthias, of course – a logical choice, considering the meal on the table was so quintessentially

German that even Matthias had to joke: "When I said *traditional*, I didn't mean the list of all the dishes that pop up when you google 'top ten German cuisines.'"

"Are you complaining about my cooking, little Beller brat?" Mila asked, putting another plate of potato dumplings and sauerkraut[7] on the table.

"Definitely not, Auntie. Bring it on!" Matthias apologised, taking another helping of beef stew.

The next minute, the tones of traditional German music jumped off the walls of the apartment, and Lukas sat down at the table, smiling like a boy who had done something naughty.

"What?" he answered Matthias's reproachful look. "You said *traditional.*"

"I'm gonna kill both of you," Matthias said, glancing from one brother to the other. "I bet all this is your doing."

"No complaints now, bro," replied Thomas. "You got what you asked for."

Everyone laughed.

"I'm sorry, Jane," Matthias whispered in my ear, "I didn't expect they'd go this far. If you're uncomfortable, I'll seriously ask them to stop."

I caught his hand under the table and squeezed it: "Don't worry, it's all beautiful so far. I'm enjoying myself."

He smiled. "So far. Let's see what else they have on their crazy minds. I knew they were silly, but I thought they'd refrain knowing that we'd have a special guest."

I smiled back. "It's all fine."

His eyes shone. Those mysterious, lively, coal-black eyes had stars in them; the sight of them spread a warm, liquid feeling through my stomach. I felt extreme joy at being able to draw that feeling from him. Over the past four years, he had mostly been photographed frowning or with angry, depressing thoughts written on his face. Seeing his face crinkling into a smile seemed like a privilege at the moment.

He kissed me on the shoulder and whispered again, "I am incredibly happy to have you here."

"I'm happy to be with you," I whispered back.

As everything mixed up – food, drinks, conversations, languages – I felt myself relaxing, melting into the comfort of the moment. Nobody asked me anything about Alex, or my friends, or anything from my "official life." I admired how naturally and spontaneously considerate they

---

[7] Fermented cabbage (German, but also common in English.)

all were, including the grandparents. They asked me about my job, education and interests; they inquired about where I loved working most, what I advocated for and what my thoughts were on the fashion industry and its various movements. It all felt completely ordinary.

I realised then that was one of the things that drew me to Matthias – that feeling of being ordinary. With him, because we had to hide, I could behave as if I was just Jane – not the Jane Andersonn with a double *n* at the end, not a member of that world-famous family who must watch every step she takes from the moment she wakes up until she goes to sleep. While with Matthias, I tasted what the normal life of a completely ordinary person looked like. Holding hands, family dinners, ordinary talk, no fear of anyone peeking through the window. I knew Matthias had taken care of everything. Not a single Andersonn worry was on my mind when I was with him.

Every day, I loved my life – apart from the two years in Paris – and I didn't long to change it for anything. But in these intimate moments with Matthias, it felt blissful, fulfilling, complete, enough with just two of us and nothing else. No football, no career, no cameras, no famous friends or mad coaches or parents…At that moment, I wanted it. I so desperately wanted to swap it all for this, to stay with Matthias in Brasília forever. Could he make it true if I voiced that wish at that moment?

"You want more beef roll, Jane?" Anabella asked, waking me from my daydream.

I refused, took a large gulp of beer and snuggled under Matthias's arm over my shoulders.

The evening progressed fast with all the laughter and chit-chat in four languages, and soon it was time for dessert.

"I didn't know if the mysterious guest preferred heavy or lighter cakes, so I made these two," Mila said, placing two enormous plates on the table. "But if I'd known you'd come, I'd have prepared something less sugary."

"No, Mila, don't worry. I'm not a calorie counter," I said, my mouth already drooling at the sight of her masterpieces. I instantly recognised the Black Forest cake, which I adored, though I'd only ever ordered it or eaten it at the confectionery. "I'm never refusing Schwarzwälder Kirschtorte, especially when it's homemade."

"Wow, you even pronounced it correctly!" Grandma Hannah exclaimed. "You can then take away that Zwetschgenkuchen, Mila."

I smirked at the equally delicious-looking cake.

"Plum cake," explained Lukas.

"I can try it, too," I said, excited like a kid visiting her grandparents after months of a no-sugar policy at home.

Everyone laughed. "I like your girl more and more, Matthias," Mila said, at which my heart stirred pleasantly, as if it was completely right that I was there, as if I was truly his girl.

I blushed and hid my face shyly in his shirt. He kissed my temple. "Me, too," he said, and I understood that, at least this evening, I truly was entirely his.

I raised my head to look at him. His eyes shone in perfect happiness, and in them, I could see the reflection of mine. He smiled and touched my nose with his, drawing both his arms over me. I wanted to melt and stay there forever.

He kissed my forehead, and just as I began imagining myself spending the whole night in his arms, Thomas interrupted us by suggesting a toast (probably trying to make the situation less romantic and more socially acceptable).

"What shall we drink to?" Robert asked.

"Just not football or any team in particular, please," Mila said.

"Alright, then to your Schwarzwälder Kirschtorte, Mum," Lukas said.

"Great idea," Anabella agreed.

"Let's try it first," Johan jumped in.

"Valid point," Thomas agreed and stood up from the table to help Mila cut the cake for the whole lot of us.

They let me try first and judge. One spoon was enough to conclude it was the best Black Forest cake I'd ever had.
"Huge cheers," I mumbled through a mouthful of cake, raising my beer to a chorus of laughter.

"You shouldn't mix sweets and alcohol," Matthias said in English, but his auntie understood.

"You, Beller brat, shut up and don't nag the girl. She doesn't have to worry about how many drinks she'll have just because you're scared of your coach," Mila said in a mix of German and Spanish, sending another wave of laughter over the table. "You haven't had a sip of our finest wine since you came for this tournament, and we've been saving it for you. Pff!"

"Don't be upset. He's just extremely professional," I defended him. "That's why he's among the best."

She rolled her eyes. "If he had one bottle of this red wine, he wouldn't need any of his chemical shakes and muscle relief gels until the end of the competition."

I turned to Matthias and said jokingly, "You should suggest that to your coach. Maybe he'd change his approach."

"That man, never."

"Then you must come here after the tournament to pay respect to your family and their efforts to save the best wine for you."

He paused for a second, and I knew what was on his mind. He needn't have said it, but he did. "I hope we will."

I didn't like being reminded of that, so I averted my gaze and, not sure what to do with my hands, took another gulp of beer.

"There might not be any left. Especially if he shows up as a loser," Thomas eased the tension.

Johan stood up then, having finished his cake, and walked over to the radio with its large speakers.

"I have an idea," he said. Everyone watched his every move curiously. "We should dance a bit."

All eight of us stared at him as if he was insane. "You funny old man," his wife said. "How do you think we'll move after all this food?"

"Very fast," he replied confidently.

"I completely agree," Anabella took his side. She downed her mug of beer and stood up from the table. "Ten more minutes to digest the food, and then we'll all dance."

Nobody objected, so neither could I. Despite doing my best to try most of the dishes Mila had prepared, I still had more alcohol (and sugar) than food in my stomach, meaning my confidence was sky-high. I was a semi-professional dancer after all. This shouldn't be too difficult.

What I didn't think was that the old man would play traditional music. German traditional music.

"No, Grandpa, seriously," Lukas rebelled.

"What's wrong with this music?" Hannah reprimanded him, leaving her chair to join her husband, who was already catching the rhythm.

"Grandma's right," Anabella stepped in. "We can kick it off with this and then change," she said in English so that only Matthias, Thomas, Lukas and I could understand.

In the beginning, I didn't even dare to smile as the two older couples joined hands and started dancing in a way I foggily remembered seeing four years ago at the opening of the World Cup in Berlin.

I'd never done much traditional dance, not even in England. I hadn't had the opportunity to learn, nor had I cared to. It would've proved useful now, I realised. If I was to repeat any of their moves, I was sure to look ridiculous.

Mila, Robert, Johan and Hannah looked at least a decade younger when they performed. They moved with zeal and pride, even though they'd just had a hearty dinner.

"Come on, we mustn't embarrass ourselves now," Thomas said, leaving his chair and holding out a hand to Anabella. Only Lukas, Matthias and I were still sitting.

"We'll watch and learn first," Lukas answered Thomas's pushy look. "I don't remember the last time I did this." Then he turned to me. "Sorry for this, Jane. If you don't want to take part, it's completely fine. I'll boycott them with you here."

"Yes, Jane," Matthias agreed. "I'll tell them to chill out and show some respect."

Their concern and understanding were lovely. "Thank you so much, both of you, but it's fine, really," I said honestly. "I actually enjoy this. It's a true German experience I won't get anywhere else."

"You know you'll have to take part unless you openly refuse this?" Lukas said.

I pondered it over for a second. *What to do? I can't evade this situation now. I'm already too deep in this affair. I'll go till the end.* "I'll join," I said, "I'm just hoping nobody will laugh at me."

"If they dare, I'll show them some videos from our previous family gatherings," Lukas reassured me.

"Thank you," I laughed.

The three of us then stood up and joined the dancing couples. A few seconds after we began, encouraged by the beer and great mood we'd collectively created, nothing mattered anymore. Neither I nor anyone else seemed to be bothered about the moves – if they were correct or not, funny or decent. All that was important was to jump to the rhythm of the bass and trumpet and to not stop.

I didn't let Matthias's hand go for a second. I hardly dropped his gaze, never dropped my smile. My cheeks hurt. He was beautifully handsome. His perfect, sharp face had something different to it, some charm now that it reflected pure happiness, not anger or sadness or aggression. This was my Mati: the one who made me laugh; the one who made me do crazy, extraordinary things I'd never dare do myself; the one who took the whole world, the sky full of stars, the universe, and put them in front of me, ahead of me, to decide which I wanted.

"This is nowhere near anything I expected you'd prepare," I said.

"I'm glad I managed to surprise you."

"You truly did, and positively at that. Despite how worried I was those few hours before coming down from my room, I'm happy, somehow. I'm at peace. And it's not the beer and sugar."

He held my hands tighter while I did a pirouette. "It makes me happy, relaxed and at peace to hear that," he said with a self-confident smile.

"You have a wonderful family. I was sceptical about how or if they'd accept me or treat me."

"I wouldn't have brought you here if I doubted them."

I smiled in response, and he kissed me on the forehead.

In the next second, Mila and Anabella interrupted us. "I've got a wonderful idea," Mila squeaked. "You two girls have to come with me."
I didn't have time to rebel or say anything. It felt odd to leave Matthias, but it would have been rude to refuse, so I looked at him, asking for approval, which he gave.

"Auntie, I hope you won't keep them for too long," he said. "Whatever's on your mind, Jane and I can't stay for more than two hours."

"Don't worry, Beller. We'll be back in a matter of minutes," Mila said, already dragging me over the improvised podium to one of the rooms.

Judging by the pictures on the walls, we were in Johan and Hannah's bedroom. Mila opened one of the wardrobes hurriedly and started rummaging through clothes.

"I know what's on your mind," Hannah said, entering the room and closing the door behind her. "Let me help you find them. We only have two that'd fit these skinny ladies. The others are too big."

Anabella and I still had no idea what they were talking about. We exchanged a nervous, quizzical look.

"The boys should have them on, too, don't you think?" Mila asked Hannah.

"Oh, that'd be so lovely! But only Thomas and Matthias, because their girls are here," Hannah agreed.

"You're completely right. Here." She withdrew her head from the wardrobe and passed a pile of brown-beige clothes to Hannah. "Take it to them and let Robert and Johan help them. Though they should know by now how to put them on."

"Oh, meu Deus," Anabella squeaked in Portuguese but I understood. "É isso que eu acho que é?[8]"

"Give me a second, darling," Mila said, entering the wardrobe again as Hannah shuffled back to the living room. Shortly after, Mila turned to us in delight, now carrying another pile of clothes, this time pretty and colourful.

"Dirndls!" Anabella jumped with joy and excitement.

"Dir-what?" I stuttered, but it was all becoming clear to me as Mila unfolded the first dress. It looked like something from an Oktoberfest advertisement. One was purple, the other burgundy red. They looked old, precious, high quality, luxurious and beautiful. I could imagine Mila – my age or her age now – wearing either of them and looking stunning.

"You girls should put them on and join your men," Mila said.

"Of course!" Anabella took the purple one and started removing her blouse. "Sorry, Jane, nothing personal, but I am shorter and skinnier than you, and this one is a smaller size."

"Yes, this used to be Hannah's. She was petite when she was young," Mila explained, passing me the red dirndl. "I used to wear this one. I still can, but it can be adjusted for you, too, Jane. It's good that you have some tits."

"I-I...I can't..." I hesitated. How on Earth was I going to wear German traditional clothes? I couldn't do that! Not to England, to Ukraine. To Alex!

"Why not?" Anabella asked, already squeezing into the dress. "We're only having fun for a few minutes."

"I can't, because..." I was at a loss for breath, almost forgetting how to speak Spanish. "I never...I've never even worn English or...or Ukrainian traditional clothes. I can't wear German ones now. It's not right."

Both Mila and Anabella were looking at me wide-eyed. I was expecting rage and admonishment. I knew I would ruin the whole evening, all of Matthias's effort, by refusing this. He was probably already dressed up out there in the living room, expecting to see me. But I couldn't take this step. My dad's face was crystal-clear in front of my eyes, and I could literally see the words above his head: *You've never worn anything similar from your country, and now this?* My heart froze in my chest. Alright, I was planning to wear the Brazilian Carnival costume, but that wasn't the same. This... This was betrayal in its purest form.

---

[8] Is this what I think it is? (Portuguese)

Mila wanted to say something but she seemed to have difficulty forming sentences in a way I understood, so she turned to Anabella, asking for assistance. I braced for their disappointment.

"Jane, we're so sorry," Anabella said instead, already fully dressed in her purple dirndl. "We weren't thinking. It's so rude of us."

Somehow, their discomfort felt worse than anger.

"No, it's fine. You didn't have any bad intentions. It's just me...I...I just can't."

I was ashamed. The weight of everything I had been doing the whole evening fell on me at once, and I felt the pressure of it crushing my chest. Nothing was their fault. They hadn't overdone anything, they hadn't gone to extremes. It was all my fault for having accepted Matthias's offer to come here in the first place. Sure, I couldn't have known Matthias would bring me to his wonderful, welcoming and hospitable family – who on Earth would expect he had such close cousins thousands of kilometres from Germany – but I should've refused before crossing the doorstep. Now I was in a situation that was the natural consequence of my actions. What an idiot I was.

Hannah entered the room. "Are you ladies finished? The boys are ready."

Mila and Anabella looked at me, waiting for my next move.

Cold sweat crept up my body. The next step was to get out of the room, face Matthias and the other men, tell them I would not wear a German dress and demand to leave as soon as possible. Then I'd wait in uncomfortable silence for Matthias to change back to his regular clothes, and we'd go, leaving them all sad, angry and feeling as if all their efforts had been in vain.

I couldn't do it. Not to them. Not to Matthias. Not after everything he had done for me. If my pride was in the game this time, I chose to throw it aside and do this for him. He deserved the evening he had so hard fought to organise. The last couple of hours were wonderful, and this burgundy dress would be the last touch, like a cherry on top of a very delicious Black Forest cake. Selfishly, I also thought that this was a unique opportunity for me. I was pretty sure I would never get another chance to wear German clothes. In any other circumstances, the Jane I had become wouldn't even dare wear an outfit in the colours of the black-red-gold flag. However, now we were in a private apartment, hidden from cameras, curious eyes and everyone who could ruin it all.

Wasn't the man who adored me waiting to see me in next room? I'd done so much wrong already; I could do this, too. For him. For us. God knew what would happen the next day. Or week. Or if anything would happen at all. This was our night, me and my Mati's. I could do one more reckless thing.

I sighed. "We're only having fun, after all. Would you ladies help me put the dress on properly?"

They smiled in relief and the tension vaporised.

I unzipped my dress and dropped it on the neatly made bed. Mila and Anabella were quick in assisting me. It didn't take much time; it wasn't as complicated as I thought, and Anabella was skilled as if she'd worn the same dress every day to university. I took a look in the mirror. The belt squeezed my waist well and exposed my breasts – perhaps too much for the occasion, but there was nothing I could do about it. The length was good, below the knees. Anabella and I wore the shoes we had come in that evening.

I looked beautiful. I couldn't deny it.

"Normally the hair goes in a bun or braids," Hannah said, "but let's not waste time on that. I don't even know where the pins and bands are, and you girls are gorgeous as you are now. Let's go. The boys are waiting."

I didn't protest. I liked my hair down and long. It covered my cleavage and somehow gave me a note of sex appeal that perhaps shouldn't be present in traditional wear, but it gave me reassurance and an extra boost of self-confidence.

Us girls in dirndls followed the older two women back to the living room, where the traditional music was playing loud. Matthias was talking to Johan while Robert, Lukas and Thomas busied themselves next to the radio, probably setting up a playlist. Johan saw us and nudged Matthias.

When Matthias turned, he was again that boy who'd stared at me, mesmerised in confusion and awe four years ago in front of the elevator in Berlin. He didn't move. He didn't react. He only consumed me entirely with his hungry, coal-black eyes that darted quickly over all of me and ended on my face.

I smiled, which encouraged him to defrost and smile back. I stepped toward him, and he did the same. When we were close enough, he took my hands in his and drew them to his lips. "You are enchanting," he said so that only I could hear.

"You're pretty handsome, too." I had seen him in lederhosen before, in the magazines – the players wore it when attending Oktoberfest – but never in person. They always looked the same to me; I'd never paid them attention, because I hadn't dared, because I shouldn't have. And now the man in front of me, holding me, that Greek statue I was mad about, was dressed in the traditional clothes of his country and looking handsome as hell, smiling at me as if he was about to marry me and take me to his small town to live happily ever after.

"Would you like to dance with me, mysterious lady?" He hugged me while a new song began in the background.

"There's no one else I'd love to dance with more now." I smiled and relaxed in his arms. He took me and swung around. "But I'm warning you," I added, "I still don't know a single step of anything you people dance."

"It's fine. We can watch Thomas and Anabella first, or we can improvise."

The music got louder, and I felt myself relaxing, my body easing, releasing the fear and tension and absorbing the rhythm. I gave myself a few seconds to look at what Thomas and Anabella were doing – they were excellent – and then tried to imitate them with my partner.

It wasn't so difficult. I danced, powered by the unique, warm atmosphere these wonderful, genuine people had created for me with their food, drinks, cake and songs. Everything they had given me mixed inside me and filled the air, flooding the room in revelry. We jumped, twisted, swung, and sang – in turns, together, with our partners. At one point, the whole family was on their feet, with the volume at its highest, carefree about everything and everyone. It felt like we were in a trance, all on drugs or in some unfathomable, unimaginable dream that was only distinguishable from reality by our burning feet.

Exhaustion eventually took hold. Only Thomas and Anabella, Matthias and I still danced. I clutched his upper arms, and his hands were on my waist. In that moment, he was the only man in existence, and in his dark, sparkling eyes I saw I was the only living thing that mattered to him. A vision presented itself to me, where I saw myself from above as if through the eyes of some cameraman. It was our perfect, fairy tale wedding – one day, in the near future, in a lovely, hidden German village, joined by our closest friends and family. And the two of us, just married, were dancing our souls and feet out, propelled by inexhaustible energy and a lust for life, drowning in our joy for each other.

It didn't feel odd anymore to kiss, hug or hold each other in front of everyone. On the contrary, it felt right. We were there with family, with people who cheered for and supported us. There was absolutely nothing that could go wrong or spoil this perfect moment. I gave in completely, not thinking about anything or anyone else but me and the man who held me as if he could never let me go.

I pirouetted one last time before falling on his chest. His hands were on my back, supporting me, holding me tight. Our foreheads and noses touched. We looked into each other's souls; we closed our eyes, smiling, panting and sweating from exhaustion and glee.

"I love you, Jane."

"I love you, Matthias."

We kissed as couples do on the altar, and if we'd had any rings with us then, no one would have been able to distinguish it from a legal wedding. I was fulfilled, joyous, ecstatic. I wanted him and he wanted me. I felt it in his touch, in the way he moved near and held me, in the way his fingers roamed my shoulder blades and hair, in the way he breathed when our lips separated for air. And I wanted him, I desperately wanted him to stay with me, to lay down with me that night, to wrap himself around me, to let me sleep on his chest.

I was about to voice that when a flash erupted in my peripheral vision. My heart skip a beat and my body seized, petrified in fear. I turned, praying it was just my over-imagination, to see Anabella with a polaroid camera, already taking out and drying a brand-new photo in the air.

"NO!" I screamed.

"Anabella, was tust du? Niemand darf herausfinden, dass sie heute Nacht hier war!"[9] Matthias shouted at her, almost as out of his mind as I was, reaching to grab the photo.

"I know, but I can bet on my arm that you'll thank me for this. Wait until it dries," she said, unmoved, as if she hadn't done anything unusual or wrong.

The music stopped, and unpleasant silence blanketed us for a long minute.

Finally, the photo dried. Matthias stared at it, not uttering a word. I reached out for it.

Anabella was right. In the polaroid, everything we felt, everything that was on our minds – every single emotion, wish, thought – was captured. We were completely and absolutely engrossed in each other. No one else existed in the world.

I turned to her. "Thank you," I whispered, ashamed at how I'd initially snapped.

---

[9] What are you doing? Nobody must find out she was here tonight. (German)

"You're welcome. Now let's take one where you're looking at the camera. This is a unique opportunity."

I looked at Matthias approvingly. "She's right. We don't have any photos together. We'll take great care of these."

He hugged me from behind and kissed me on the head. "I'll rent a safe in Switzerland and put them there, if that's what it takes."

I laughed while he placed his hands on my waist and his chin on my shoulder, posing for another shot.

The next photo was just as beautiful. We were love birds. Our pure happiness was visible all over our faces. We'd never been in a picture so close to each other. All those photos of us in the magazines were photoshopped. We had never been close in public, except on the eve of the final game of the tournament four years ago, but even then, we were covered with a German flag. This caption was priceless, invaluable. We looked gorgeous next to each other, a perfect fit – matched in stature, image and clothes. We radiated joy, adoration and infatuation as much as a photograph possibly could.

Not knowing how else to show her how thankful I was, I hugged Anabella, grateful that she'd helped us memorise this magical, surreal evening.

"You have no idea what you've just done for us," I whispered in English.

I didn't know what would happen with the two of us, but these photos were special, the first material treasure in our relationship. Everything we'd had up until then was gifts of the mind – thoughts, words, actions. There was nothing physical, except for those letters I had always thrown away like the flowers he'd sent. Now we had these two astonishingly perfect photographs to bear witness to this day. But even in my haze of joy, I knew very well I should keep them away from everyone at any cost.

"Jane, we should go," Matthias reminded me, responsible with time as always.

It wasn't too late, but the ride back to my hotel would take an hour, and we both needed some decent sleep. When I met my parents in the morning, I had to appear as if none of this had ever taken place. Matthias also couldn't miss his flight to Rio.

Therefore, sad and dismal, I went to Johan and Hannah's bedroom to change back into my black dress. I wasn't inebriated anymore. I was tired and in need of a hot shower and a soft bed; at the same time, I was on the brink of tears at the prospect of the evening ending.

Saying goodbye to this lovely, kind family proved extremely difficult. Mostly because I didn't know what to tell them. Matthias and

I...we were not certain at all. We had moved from a dead spot only slightly, microscopically. I would almost certainly never see any of them again. This night was unique, one of a kind, unrepeatable. And as much as my heart yearned to scream this could be permanent, it knew, at least for the time being, that it was temporary. Any promises would be dangerous.

So I hugged each one of them and thanked them for the warmth and kindness they'd showed me unconditionally, unequivocally. When the door closed behind us, I felt a piece of me stayed with them in that apartment, to forever be taken care of, regardless of what I did with my life in the days to come.

I didn't say a word until we went out to the street. I was holding my barriers up with my utmost strength. I didn't want to start crying in front of him – not because of pride, but because he didn't deserve that. He had tried so hard to make me happy. He didn't need to see me cry. I was not allowed to ruin everything.

The fresh air cooled my face, and I inhaled deeply, taking in courage. We still held hands.

"This was one of the most beautiful outings you could have done for me," I said, floating in his mystifying darkness.

He smiled and touched my cheek. "I want to kiss you, but I'm holding myself back because we're outside."

Back into bloody hiding. "I wish I'd said it a minute ago."

He smiled. "Let's get into the car."

It took us almost an hour to return to the hotel. Our fingers were intertwined the whole way back. He noticed my mood receding and talked to me, gently, as if telling a bedtime story to a child. I loved him for that. He understood my fears, concerns and sadness without my having to voice them. He soothed me, even managing to make me laugh by the end of the trip.

Matthias pulled over at the corner a block away from the hotel. I looked at him, confused.

"Is this the part where the drug starts to work and you kidnap me?"

He laughed and cupped my face. "No, darling, I just need to give you instructions on how to leave the car when I drop you off. And I also wanted to kiss you one more time before saying goodnight."

I was puzzled. "Instructions?"

"Yes. Put your scarf back on, and I'll drive in and stop for a second. You wait for the concierge to open the door – don't open it yourself, that'd be suspicious – then step out and go, without turning back. You got it?"

My world fell apart. "But...where are you going?" Previously. he'd slept in my hotel. I expected the same now.

"I booked everything at the airport, the hotel and the car, because the flight is early and I can't risk being late. Plus," he sighed, "I didn't want to compromise you. If anyone sees me, they'll instantly know who I'm here for."

Seeing his expression change, I knew that all my disappointment, misery and heartache were written on my face. I couldn't imagine sleeping without him this night. Not after everything. I thanked all saints and gods that Alex was nowhere near; I wouldn't have been able to lay next to him after a meeting like this. But the next most frightening thought was me sleeping alone.

I looked away, pushing back tears and telling myself I had to be brave. He was right. He shouldn't sleep in the same hotel. It would be extremely dangerous and reckless for both of us.

Matthias's hearty laugh pulled me from my grey thoughts. I looked at him, astonished. "Sorry, Jane, but your lower lip is shaking like a kid's when chocolate is taken from their hand."

I managed to smile, too. "The emotions are the same."

He patted my hair and looked at me with patience and adoration. "Jane, if you want me to stay, you only have to say so. I'll find a way."

Warmth filled my stomach and chest instantly. "Really?"

"Of course. If you tell me to jump off that Christ the Redeemer statue tomorrow, face-first, I'll do it without a second thought."

Now I laughed out loud. "Alright, then. I know what to say next time you piss me off." I took his hand with both of mine. "I only want you to hug me tonight. All night," I said quietly, longingly.

"We'll make it happen, then." He kissed my hands. "Go inside the hotel as I instructed you, straight to your room. Leave the door ajar. I'll park the car and come upstairs as inconspicuously as possible."

"You talk about these things as if you are pretty experienced. Makes me think—"

"I gained a lot of experience four years ago because I couldn't get one charming British girl out of my mind," he interrupted me.

"You're excellent with words, Beller. Let's go now."

It wasn't difficult to do as he said, although my legs still shook with fear and excitement. Nobody paid attention to me, even though the hall was full. I only breathed once I was alone in the elevator, and then again when I entered my room.

My phone was loaded with messages. I replied to Alex, telling him I'd enjoyed a wonderful, eventful afternoon with the girls, swallowing down the nausea that came with lying to him anew. Then I texted the girls that we'd meet in the morning and not tonight, and I'd tell them everything that had taken place – once my parents were out of sight.

I went for a quick shower and removed my makeup, mostly to kill the time, because every minute waiting for Matthias stretched endlessly. When I was clean and freshly coated with body mist, I realised it had been more than half an hour since we'd separated, and he still wasn't here. I began to worry. Maybe somebody saw him and now he was dealing with a bunch of curious and prying faces. Maybe they didn't allow him in the hotel. Maybe he got stuck in the emergency stairwell.

The sounds of the door opening slightly dispersed all my worries.

"I thought you weren't coming," I said when he closed the door.

"It took time to get rid of the car. They didn't let me in the garage because I looked suspicious." He laughed. "But now it's all sorted."

"How did you get through?" I giggled.

"Let's just say that the kind concierge very much cheers for me when it comes to you."

I approached him and touched his sharp, stubbled jaw. "I'm happy that you're finally here."

He hugged me and pressed me to his chest. "I assure you, I am happy, too."

I wore black underwear and a silk gown. Matthias's solid arms slid over the lace, massaging my back. I rested my head on his shoulder. He pressed his lips to my temple.

"Mati, I know I might be asking for too much, but let's not...let's not do it tonight. My head is swarming with emotions and everything that's happened, and my body is exhausted."

"You don't have to justify anything, Jane. Back in the car, you said you wanted hugs. And hugs you'll get."

I admired him more than ever. He was nowhere near upset. I felt it in his words. How on Earth did he possess such an abundance of patience for the complicated, difficult woman I was?

"Mati, are you for real?"

"Very real."

He carried me to bed while we kissed. I couldn't separate my lips from his. They were gentle, reassuring, loving. I removed my black gown and hid under the blanket, watching him remove his clothes. Yes, that was still my Greek statue. Perfect from every angle, every muscle trained to exhaustion, polished and sculpted to flawlessness. When he lay next to me, each nerve in my body stirred. I placed myself over him, absorbing his warmth, his mesmerising scent that was unchanged after these years. I felt on fire. Wishful. Lustful. Shameful.

I raised my head to kiss him, and what started as an innocent goodnight touch lengthened into a deep exchange of too-long-suppressed passion. He placed a hand on my breast and squeezed it gently. I moaned, asking for more. Skilfully, his fingers roamed over the black lace and then the skin of my arm, my back, my leg. I was ignited, drowning in the mass of pleasant feelings that overfilled me. He was perfect. His touch was right, sufficient, satisfying.

"Did you perhaps change your mind after you saw me almost naked?" he said when we stopped for air.

I giggled, and he joined me in laughter. The moment was killed; I was thankful to him for that. Nothing more was supposed to happen between us that night.

"You cocky Beller brat." I jokingly pushed him, but he hugged me stronger.

"Next time, Jane, I will make love to you all night." A shiver flew down my body, curling my toes. "Next time, when I don't have a seven a.m. wake-up call and a lethal coach to run to."

I couldn't say anything else, except, "We have a deal."

CHAPTER 9

Before we fell asleep, exhausted, I made Matthias promise he wouldn't leave without waking me, no matter how tired I was, even if I refused to open my eyes. As promised, he did so while he was putting on his clothes. To stop my heart from completely shattering, I started dressing, too.

"I don't know what to tell you without saying anything wrong," I stammered, sitting on the bed while he put his shoes on.

"You don't have to say anything." He straightened, and I approached him to snuggle under his arms. "Leave everything to me and show up where I tell you next." He kissed me. "Do we have a deal?"

I swam for a while in the dark lake of his eyes before answering. "We do."

He kissed me again, reluctant to move. "I'll keep both of those photos with me. I believe that's safest," he said.

"Yes, for now. Still, I would love to have one of them. When I figure out where I'll keep it."

I knew he wanted to add something that would remove the veil from our relationship's future, but out of respect for the beautiful simplicity of the moment – and awareness of its sensitivity – he didn't. He only kissed me one last time in farewell.

After he closed the door behind him, his scent was still so present in the room that I half-expected him to walk out of the bathroom or return with another surprise. I missed him so much already that it pained me.

Therefore, I didn't waste time. I ordered breakfast for four and texted the girls to come up to the room. I knew I'd need time to tell them everything, so I messaged my parents to say I'd meet them in the reception hall and we'd go to the stadium together. Lana and Angie arrived first, dressed up in jeans and white English jerseys, and then "good wifey Bea" made her appearance in shorts and Harold's goalkeeper shirt.

"What, am I the only one who wanted to wear a dress?" I commented.

"Perhaps you wanted to, but you won't," Lana replied. "I got a numberless one for you." She pulled a white jersey out of her bag.

Breakfast arrived, and when the table was set up, we sat and poured our coffee in a loaded silence. I took a sip of my coffee but could barely swallow it; I felt keenly aware of and overwhelmed by the prospect of telling them everything and no longer felt like drinking or eating anything.

"Do you want to start?" Bea asked, taking a bite of her toast.

"Wait." Angie raised her hand. "I want to eat at least one croissant before she begins. Otherwise, I sense I couldn't stomach my breakfast."

"That's not funny, Angelina," I replied, a little offended.

"Exactly – it's not funny at all." She devoured her croissant in silence, which confirmed my suspicions that the three of them were on the same side – and it wasn't mine. She nodded at me. "Now talk."

They didn't ask questions or let out any girly *oohs* and *awws*. In the beginning, they ate, but when I reached the part with Matthias's family, they gave up on food completely. Bea alone sipped her black coffee from time to time, her face a mirror of the other two's – a mask of shock and anger.

When I concluded my story by mentioning how he'd left not even an hour ago, the three of them remained silent, their expressions unchanged.

Angie was the first to move. She looked at her watch, probably checking how much time we had before the match, and then began: "Woman, you're playing with your life and luck. You almost lost Alex once—"

"Not almost," Bea intervened, and I could see she was equally as angry as Angie. "She *did* lose him. And he forgave the unforgivable." She was shooting sparks from her electric blue eyes at me.

"Exactly. And I wouldn't be so sure he'd do it again. You're going too far, Jane."

"I'm trying to understand you, Jane, but I keep failing to," Bea added. "We've talked this over so many times. So why am I saying to you, yet again, that Matthias Beller is bad for you? You should stay away from him. Those wonderful moments you have with him are just that – moments. In real life, out there, you two would fall apart in less than a year."

"How can you be so sure?" I snapped.

"Because you are too wild, too temperamental for each other. How can you not see, after all this time? You and Alex are like fire and water. You are wild and reckless and energetic. Alex is calm, composed, objective. He controls your spirit. He navigates you in the right direction, where you're happy and satisfied. On the other hand, Matthias is like oil. And you know what happens when fire and oil combine. It's all fun and games in the beginning, but at the first big hurdle, you'd fail. He's hard-headed, stubborn, audacious, aggressive, persistent – the same as you. You two would be a colossal disaster."

I was stunned at the comparison she'd just drawn for me, clearer than she'd ever said it. Comprehending everything, I looked blankly at the wall. Perhaps she was right. She probably was right. About everything. It made sense.

"Thank you," Angie said, breaking the silence.

"Girls," Lana spoke up, "you shouldn't be too harsh on her. This is not only her fault. Matthias is the one who keeps bringing it all up again. Jane had been fine and happy with Alex since they got back together, until this bloody tournament."

Tears were swelling in my eyes, but I had to suppress them. Weakly, I spoke in defence of myself. "His emotions are still there. I could see everything. It's not like he's bringing up something forgotten. For him, those feelings are as strong as they've ever been. I can guarantee that from the way he behaves with me."

"That's the strange, sad part," Angie said. "He should've gotten over you years ago."

"Yes, that's why I'm confused. But he hasn't gotten over me. Instead, he got expelled from the national team because of me, he fought with Gottfried because of me, he protected me even after I shamelessly left him in Berlin and now, he took me to his family. I am totally, absolutely confused. I am confident about Alex's love for me. But I can also see, I can *feel* that this man loves me, too. I just don't know what to do anymore. Whatever I decide, I have to make sure it's right – not for me or my wellbeing, but for the good of both of them. Especially Alex, who doesn't deserve to be hurt again."

"Don't you think that there's your answer, then?" Bea asked.

We all fell silent again.

I didn't want to hurt Alex again. I didn't want anyone or anything to hurt Alex ever again. After what we'd been through, after he'd conceded three goals and lost a World Cup semi-final because of me, after he hadn't shown up to officially take his Golden Glove because of me, after I'd embarrassed him on numerous occasions – he still forgave me. He came back for me. I knew he loved me and that he was the greatest man I'd ever meet. I would do anything for him.

For Matthias, I didn't feel the same. At least at that moment. That said enough in itself. I could not entertain those emotions any longer. This outing with him was a mistake, and it couldn't happen again.

It dawned on me what I was thinking. I met my friends' gazes in turn and nodded. Matthias and I must never, ever meet again. However much it hurt, it was the best for us. I'd been good without him. I'd been perfectly happy with Alex. Matthias had just brought mess into my life again. I had to cut him off. Once and for all.

*****

When we met my parents in the reception hall, a whole host of other people was with them – Bea's parents, Harold's parents and even Declan Fletcher, Angie's date. Everyone could see his face light up when he saw her, while her cheeks bloomed into a rosy blush. It made my heart leap.

Still, a large group like that made me anxious after everything that'd happened over the past fifteen hours or so. Absurdly, I worried they could see traces of Matthias on me. I breathed in, kissed my parents and politely greeted everyone else, and then we were ready to move.

As we headed towards the main exit, Mom caught me by the hand and inconspicuously separated us from the group.

"Jane, honey, are you alright?"

I looked at her, at a loss for what to say. How had she noticed anything? Not being close with my mother had worked in my favour before; I could lie to her without effort. Being close with her now, however, gave rise to new problems. "What do you mean?" I stammered.

"You look...drained."

"I...I guess I'm tired from the flight yesterday."

"I didn't mean exhausted or tired, but drained. Has something else happened recently?"

I looked into her light brown eyes that I hadn't inherited and saw I could have a good accomplice in them. "Something...has been going on, but I might tell you later. Anyway, I'm keeping everything under control."

She squeezed my hand. "Alright. Whatever it is, you can count on me. That man," she nodded towards Dad, "he doesn't have to know." She winked.

Warmth filled me, and I smiled at her, squeezing her hand back. "Thank you, Mom."

When we reached the stadium I did my best to enjoy the celebratory mood everyone was in. I didn't look at my phone even once, because I knew Matthias would text me to say he'd reached Rio, his hotel or whatever. As per my latest and freshest decision – that still threatened to send me into a crying fit in front of everyone – I didn't care about his whereabouts. We were not to meet again. Whatever happened last night was a beautiful memory, and it should stay in the past, in yesterday, in Brasília, forever.

I accepted the beer Declan treated us all to when we arrived. I tried not to look suspicious when I downed it in three sips and asked for another one. It helped me relax and shift my focus onto the upcoming match.

It was almost one o'clock in the afternoon and pleasantly hot – the perfect weather for a game. The players soon came out, lined up and sang the anthems. Paulo Reis was in the starting eleven. I hadn't talked to him since we last (and first) saw each other at the previous World Cup, and all these years he'd been kind enough not to try and get in touch with me. That firework adventure was left where it belonged – in a hotel room in Hannover. Since then, he'd even married and divorced and was now single again.

Thea Watkins-Hadleigh and a few other English players' wives and girlfriends sat close to us, so our part of the stadium was full of screams, cheers and songs. The game was fiery and aggressive from the first whistle. Both teams played in the same formation, with three strikers, so every two to three minutes the goalkeepers had dangerous situations to take care of.

Harold did great, and Bea was proud. When Harold would catch a difficult ball, the cameras turned to her and broadcast her joyous, exhilarated face on all the screens at the stadium and across the world. She was the girlfriend who stole the show that day. I was happy for her. She deserved it.

The first goal came from Keaton Flanagan, one minute before the end of the first half, sending us into half-time relieved and confident. The break ended fast, however, and I didn't get a chance to chat properly with anyone except to take a few photos with other wives and girls who we said hi to.

The game continued, and the Portuguese were determined to make it difficult. They fought as if they had nothing to lose – which they didn't – so even at the cost of yellow and red cards, they persisted in attacking our midfielders and defenders. Duncan Fletcher was hit badly in his calf in one clash, but after a couple of minutes of medical assistance, he was able to return to the game.

Our hearts jumped and skipped every few seconds, so we were grateful to Joshua Hadleigh when he increased the lead to 2–0 in the seventieth minute. Keaton accepted the ball sent from the last line of defence and hurried forward with Joshua following him briskly. Since Keaton faced two opposing players and a goalkeeper, he made sure they all focused on him before trickily passing the ball to Joshua on the left side, who took it on his chest and then shot mightily straight into the upper-right corner of the goal. The Portuguese goalkeeper stood no chance.

For a fleeting moment, I felt bad for Paulo Reis, who was about to miss yet another possibility of winning a World Cup. But he stood no chance anyway with Germany and Ukraine in his way, so he might as well leave the tournament now.

The English part of the stands was shuddering with the joy and power of thousands of jumping supporters. We knew nothing was over yet and anything could happen, but with twenty minutes to go and the ball possession 50/50, we were almost one-hundred percent sure we would not lose this game.

The players were tired and sweating as the clock ticked into the last ten minutes of the confrontation. Some of them were limping on cramped legs and had to step outside the pitch for a minute or two for relief. While Portugal had ten players on the grass, England saw its chance in the eighty-ninth minute and decided to try its luck; a swell of white jerseys rushed the opponent's goal with their full power. Simon Wade, one of the defenders, found himself in the perfect position with a clear path towards the net, and he didn't hesitate. He waved at Joshua, who sent him the ball. Simon didn't even calm it, instead positioned himself in a way he could send it precisely with a single move of his left foot – right between the posts.

The next moment, the whole Estádio Nacional roared – half of it in despair, the other half in exhilaration. It was 3–0 and definitively over.

We were singing, shouting and screaming, nearly drowning out the sound of the referee's final whistle. Though the result insinuated differently, England had come out of a tough game as victors. The next opponent would be either Norway or Chile, which we would find out later that evening.

It was almost three p.m. and I had no time to lose. Alex's game was tomorrow, and I'd promised to be back in Salvador tonight, after the English game. On top of that, I had to try on the fantasia that was supposed to be finished by now. I looked at Lana for support and she nodded, the same thing on her mind.

"Alright, Jane, say goodbye to everyone. Angelina, you too." She gave orders in a managerial way that was typical of her. "Beatrice, be a good wifey and go down to greet your man if you want to be on the same plane as us."

"Go where?" Bea was confused.

"Go down to the grass if you want to kiss Harold goodbye. He won and he deserves it, but we don't have time to wait for him to shower, finish with the press conference, etc. Go now or stay here, and you know you can't stay because Jane and I need you tomorrow."

"What's tomorrow except for Yanov's game?" Declan asked.

"You'll see, Handsome," Angie kissed him on the cheek. "We can't disclose anything now, so don't dare start any rumours."

"Alright, but..." He took her by the waist and whispered something in her ear, after which she went red with shyness. The next moment they were locked in a real, proper kiss.

I wanted to squeak but kept quiet because they didn't need extra attention. Lana helped Bea get down the stands, and for a moment, we all had to stop and stare at Harold and Bea romantically hugging each other at the side of the pitch. The cameras turned politely on them but then switched to the other celebrating players, giving them a bit of privacy and heightening the romance of the moment.

Lana then signalled for Angie and me to move, and we left the mass of excited fans. Bea was already waiting for us at the exit, and the four of us rushed to the airport, all still dressed as English cheerleaders.

"So, have you two gone public now?" I asked Angie, who'd been quiet until now, obviously on cloud nine.

"Kind of," she replied shyly, unusual for her.

"Before you...tested him?"

She laughed. "Yeah, I know it's not my typical self. But don't worry, before I kissed him I told him he'd have to perform really well to prove I didn't make a mistake."

We all laughed. "I'm sure he won't disappoint," Bea said.

"How are you so sure?" Angie asked her.

"Because that's how it is with someone your heart is all flustered about."

"Well, my heart is definitely flustered. But *his* has to be, too."

"It is."

"How do you know?"

"It is, Angie," I assured her. "Anyone with eyes can see that."

She reclined in her seat, cheerful as a teenage girl. "Alright, then. I trust you."

In the car on the way from the airport, I was glad to realise that the England–Portugal match had helped me push Matthias far from my mind. Even this morning seemed distant, as if the last time I'd seen or touched Matthias was a week ago. When I stood outside the door of Alex's room in Salvador, I felt completely ordinary, as if I hadn't done anything wrong, as if the previous evening with Matthias and his family hadn't taken place, even in my dreams.

As I entered the room, dragging my light trolley behind me, Alex was just coming out of the bathroom, fully naked and ruffling his hair with a towel. A familiar, warm excitement blanketed me at the sight of him, that mountain of muscles, so perfect and tall, with those blue eyes shining with joy.

"Damn, you're gorgeous," he said. "Except for the jersey, but it's forgivable."

I didn't expect that from him – my hair was a mess of dust and sweat, and I still wore denim shorts and a now-dirty white English jersey – but his comment reminded me that he could love me deeply in any state.

"What should I say?" I whispered, dropping my trolley to the floor and rushing to his embrace.

He held me easily with one arm while I wrapped my legs around him, my lips tightly pressed on his, absorbing his scent.

"Let's take this off." He stopped for a moment to put his hands under the jersey.

"Take it all off, and take me to shower," I sighed.

"As you wish." He bit my lip and set me on fire.

It didn't take more than fifteen minutes to have a shower and a firework session that ignited anew all my feelings for him. The water on my skin and Alex, in and around me, washed me clean of that bloody German who'd threatened to destroy it all. I promised myself I wouldn't let him do it. I was this man's and this man's only.

Alex suggested we have a light dinner in bed, watch a movie and sleep, but since I had to try on the fantasia costume one more time to make sure everything was in order, I persuaded him that I wasn't hungry and he should go with his friends (although my stomach almost betrayed me). He was curious about my plans but I brushed it off by saying the girls and I had a bunch of dresses we needed to try on to decide what we'd wear at the next couple of games. He trusted me, of course, and I kissed him goodbye. He promised to wait for me.

Barbara was in Lana's room, with Bea and Angie. At first sight, the costume looked completely the same as the previous time, but when I put it on with a good half-hour of help, I realised it was now perfect. Each part fit exactly as it should. When I saw myself in the mirror, I almost cried with joy. Matthias was nowhere on my mind. I only thought about how happy and proud Alex would be tomorrow once he saw me.

"I think it would be best if you show up in a regular dress for the first half," Barbara lined out her plan. "Don't get me wrong, nothing personal – I want Ukraine to win this one. But let's first see which way the wind is blowing. I don't want the world to watch you cry in my design." We all laughed. "Plus, dressing up here in the hotel would mean a lot of mess. Yanov would know before you even reach the stadium, because all the social networks would be flooded with your photos, right? It wouldn't be a surprise anymore. So let's dress you up during the break if the result is in your favour, or at least a draw."

"And if it's not?" Lana asked.

"We don't consider that," I said.

"I agree, but still. If it happens, we won't do anything at all. I'd rather return you the money than have the world talk about how my creations bring bad luck."

All five of us laughed again.

"We have a deal. So, tomorrow we do it at the stadium. Will fifteen minutes be enough?" I asked.

"I reckon twenty, but that's even better. Everyone will be back in the stands and the players on the pitch. They'll all be concentrated on the game, and then you show up, and *boom!*" Barbara ruffled the dress for emphasis and I giggled, barely able to turn from the mirror. She was like the director of an excellent movie.

"Sounds wonderful!" I jumped with joy.

In the room, Alex was awake and waiting, as promised, watching the highlights of the day's games. After England won against Portugal, Chile won against Norway 3–1, which meant England was taking on Chile in a couple of days in Fortaleza. We snuggled into each other and fell asleep before the highlights were even finished. A complete, fulfilling peace covered me in the shape of his arms.

*****

My parents flew in from Brasília to attend Alex's game, so we watched the first match of the day at the hotel when the boys had already left for the stadium. Today was the last day of the round of sixteen. The winner between Ireland and Paraguay would face Ukraine, who were expected to triumph over Belgium, the semi-finalists in the last World Cup who we'd defeated in the match for the third place. This clash would be fierce, but most of us were confident that Alex's team would prevail. They were stronger than they'd been four years ago, while the Belgian team's statistics had slightly deteriorated since.

It was 1–1 between Ireland and Paraguay when we left for the Arena Fonte Nova, but when we arrived at the stadium, the match had finished 3–1 for the Irish. Still, regardless of the opponent, I was sure that the Ukrainians would reach the finals this time. Germany was a shoo-in on the opposite side of the table; there was no one else to parallel them.

As we found our place in the stands, I was boiling inside. Not because of the heat outside – the weather was perfect – but with excitement. I was about to give a show to the world for my Alex, and I mustn't make any mistakes.

Lana must have seen my knee bouncing in anxiety as I stared out at the pitch, going through everything that could go wrong (I had a strong image of me falling over into the row in front), because she nudged me and passed me a small bottle of a transparent spirit.
"From Mr Olexiy Yanov," she explained. "He brought a box of these from Ukraine."

I opened it eagerly and took a sip without sniffing, recognising instantly the strong and vicious horilka. "Thanks," I said, my eyesight blurring for a second and freezing goosebumps covering me from the strength of the drink, and a cold sweat followed. I took another bracing swig of the horilka and pasted a smile on my face as the players jogged out onto the pitch.

The anthems played out, and the match kicked off. Watching the ball dart back and forth across the field, I began stressing and reviewing what might happen if Alex took a goal. That would be his first at this tournament, so he wouldn't break his record from the previous competition. That was the least bad thing. The second was that, well, his team would be at the brink of expulsion, in the eighth-finals, which we had never considered an option. The third outcome would be that my surprise would be destroyed without a chance of ever happening again. Wherever the next World Cup took place, it certainly wouldn't be Brazil any time soon. The costume would be a complete waste. I didn't want that. I could picture myself perfectly, cheering for my man while he was winning on the pitch. That's what would happen – no use entertaining any other scenarios. I focused with all my might on keeping my thoughts from straying, on being present here, supporting the Ukrainians, alongside thousands of other wives, girlfriends, families and fans. They had to score the opener.

I didn't sit much for those first thirty-five minutes. The moments of action were sequential, one after another, with barely a ten-second break in between each other. Then, finally, a few moments into the thirty-sixth minute, Nikolay Pavlov accepted a long ball sent all the way from Alex, squeezed past two Belgian defenders and rushed forward as if his life depended on the outcome of this run. All the remaining players rapidly joined him on the Belgian half of the pitch, some eager to help, some to prevent him from scoring any way they could. The former ones didn't need to do anything. The latter ones failed. He scored, with a volley that surprised the goalkeeper by heading towards the right corner but ending in the left. The goal was a masterpiece.

Our side of the stadium roared in unison. I screamed my heart out and jumped to hug Alex's parents and sister and then everyone else, relief overflowing in me. Now I could definitely go on with my surprise.

It was incredible how it had played out – completely unexpected, even for Alex, who'd aimed for the front but hadn't thought for a second Nikolay would run with it like that. None of the players did. Just Nikolay, now smiling viciously in his typical confident manner, strutting around like a peacock while his teammates hugged and congratulated him. At this pace, he was on track to be the top scorer of the tournament. This was his fourth goal; he was now equal with Joshua Hadleigh.

When the celebration was over, the remaining ten minutes plus additional time were action-packed and passed rapidly. The desperate Belgians tried to score a comeback goal so that they could begin the next half with confidence. However, their efforts didn't go past Alex. He was magnificent, defending everything. The shots weren't extremely dangerous, but they were constant and coming from all sides and players. Even the defensemen and midfielders tried to score. Alex caught every ball.

I wanted it to be a good sign for the remainder of the match, so when the referee announced the end of the first half, I didn't hesitate and rushed away.

The girls followed me. Barbara had told us to meet in front of the door to a large office belonging to one of the stadium advertising managers, who kindly and excitedly agreed to help us. We went straight there, avoiding the groups of people flowing into the hallway from all sides. Barbara was waiting, and all five of us went inside and locked the door.

Apart from the assistant who had accompanied Barbara before, there was another woman, a makeup artist who specialised in preparing Carnival dancers.

"I couldn't just let you go out there incomplete," Barbara said. "I know you girls simply cannot manage this makeup in such a short time."

I had to hug her. "Thank you for thinking of everything."

She chuckled. "Girl, don't thank me. I'm doing this for my benefit, too. If everything goes well and your boyfriend's team wins, my business is going to soar."

We all laughed and then, knowing there wasn't time to spare, started my silly venture.

The costume itself wasn't too complicated, since we all worked together and fast. However, the head decoration took more time than expected. It simply didn't want to stand. Wearing this meant I had to dance – I couldn't be out there standing still as a stone – but the piece didn't stay in my hair, regardless of the number of pins and hairspray the group of women wielded.

"*Faça a maquiagem dela enquanto estou consertando isso,*"[10] Barbara said to Daniela, the makeup artist. I initially didn't understand until Daniela opened her box and sat in front of me, beginning to apply the eye makeup.

I glanced at my watch. "Barbara, the game is starting now. Can I go without the headpiece?"

"No way," she replied strictly. "Give me a few minutes. As I told you before, you'll show up there at the perfect time."

I trusted her and let Daniela finish her job, counting in my head how much of the game I would miss and what Alex and my parents would think about me not being there.

After less than ten minutes, Daniela exclaimed, "Done!" and closed her box.

"Excellent," Barbara turned to us and approached me to place the complicated headpiece. This time, however, it went on easily. She attached it with only a few pins. It was so tight I knew I would have a headache after an hour or so, but I didn't care. All that mattered was that it stood and would stay standing, no matter how much I danced and jumped.

"You're a true master of your craft," I said when I stood up and marvelled at myself in the mirror. "This is divine."

---

[10] "Do her makeup while I'm fixing this."

They did an outstanding job – outperforming my already high expectations. The blue and yellow suited me perfectly and matched my long, dark-brown hair. The golden high heels I'd changed into were as stunning as they were comfortable. My nerves had evaporated altogether. I was ready to take on the entire stadium with its 48,700 spectators.

As I walked down the tunnel – one foot in front of the other, feeling like I was walking in slow motion, preparing myself like a showgirl about to step onstage – I could hear the roar of the fans, their chanting and feet thumping on the floor like thunder. I could also distinguish the voice of the English commentator, who was guiding the raucous crowd through another attack and Alex's defence. My stomach stirred while I stepped confidently, every inch closer to the magic on the pitch.

When the sharp sun fell on my face, I had to close my eyes and then smirk. I took a look at the grass and then the board with the result to avoid an unpleasant surprise – no change, thank god – and then quietly continued to my seat a few rows up with Bea, Lana and Angie behind me. At first, no one noticed anything until I reached the vicinity of my and Alex's parents. But when they saw me, everyone did.

In an instant, I was on the big screen – a crazy, irrational and extremely devoted Ukrainian fan girl – and I heard screams and shouts of approval in the distance. I caught the eye of a few nearby supporters and smiled, and when they realised it was me, they roared in awe, carrying along the remainder of the stadium. It was magical.

Thankfully, some particularly dedicated fans had brought along big remote speakers and had been playing music during the half-time break. They continued now, and I gave a little flourish and danced in time to the music, and the responsive cheers drowned out the song altogether.

From then on, every moment until the last whistle of the match was like a dream. Alex's parents were delighted to see me and applauded my act, my parents couldn't stop laughing, and I danced to the beautiful cacophony of music that was coming from all sides and mingling with the fever pitch of enthusiasm from the blue and yellow part of the stadium. Although he was far away, I felt the moment Alex saw me – not at the big screen, where I was projected every moment the ball was out of play – but on the stands, next to his parents, wearing the colours of his country. When the cameras captured him during a short break due to a foul on a Belgian player, he was still looking in our direction, smiling widely. This was the best thing I could've done for him today, I knew.

The atmosphere had heated up since my colourful reappearance. Between songs, chants and dances, I took time to snap photos with supporters as well as to pose for every camera directed at me. I was having a whale of a time and couldn't help thinking that it felt so natural, so right. This was what I was meant to be doing – to be there, wholeheartedly supporting my man. This was what I'd keep doing in future, I told myself. For Alex.

Finally, in the eighty-first minute, in the middle of the *Samba de Janeiro*, Lev Zahara passed the ball to Vlad Starovsky, who took it rapidly towards the front. Nikolay Pavlov and Andriy Barnik saw what he planned and ran forward, careful not to be offside. When the ball flew over the foremost Belgian defenders, they sprinted as fast as their legs could carry them, leaving everyone else behind. Andriy wanted to put another goal on his sheet, but the angle wasn't right. Therefore, he wasn't selfish; he shot the ball to Nikolay, who managed to place it sharply between the posts, in the corner out of the Belgian goalkeeper's reach.

For them, it was over. For us, the party continued.

Confident that the game was decided, the Ukrainian fans sang and chanted all the songs we could remember, united as a crowd, without a care about the stoppage time. We didn't even hear the final whistle. I knew it was over when Alex raised his hands in the air and removed his gloves. Another challenge was completed successfully; we were one step closer to achieving the dream.

Alex came as close as he could to the stands, beaming up at me. This time, there was no way for me to get down to the grass through strict security and the hordes of rowdy fans. Besides, Alex had post-game interviews to give. I waved at him, sending him a kiss captured by thousands of cameras. I already knew the photo would be iconic.

"Are you gonna change?" Bea asked.

"I'm not sure I want to. What do you girls think? Since I made this fabulous show, shall I go on with it until the end?"

"Hell yeah, you should!" Angie cheered supportively.

Buoyed by the moment, I took a large gulp of beer and went back up the stands to continue chatting and taking photos with the fans.

As it turned out, many of the people who came to talk to me were fans I'd helped bring to Brazil. They were of all ages, jobs and interests, from all parts of Ukraine, with one common passion – football. None of them would ever have been able to attend the tournament. I'd made their dreams come true. While talking to them and listening to all the praise and thanks, I felt I'd done another wonderful thing for Alex, something that made others think I was a wonderful person.

Wasn't that how it was supposed to be? Shouldn't partners make each other better people? With my guidance, Alex was the best goalkeeper in the world, becoming more easy going, confident and eloquent with the media. With his guidance, I was growing into the best version of myself; I was a better, kinder, more understanding, compassionate and emphatic individual. We were just right for each other.

Matthias had no space in my life with his brazenness and irrationality. Alex was the man in the room with me; Alex deserved the space he occupied.

During the ride to the hotel, I was physically exhausted but my mind was still sparkling with excitement. When I stepped out of the car in front of the rotating glass door, the porter immediately jumped to open the other, sliding door so that I could enter with my massive costume, which made me grin. I basically took up space like an American football player.

As the girls and I were joking with the hotel staff, Alex stepped out of the restaurant, dressed in denim shorts and a white short-sleeve shirt. "Hello to the most beautiful Carnival dancer I've ever seen," he said, charming as ever, sizing me up from head to toe. My stomach fluttered and a shiver ran down my spine, as if we'd just started dating.

"Hello, best goalkeeper in the world," I replied, aware that silence had fallen over the entrance hall. Everyone was looking at us. I walked over to him as if I were on a runway. "You changed."

"I didn't want to welcome you in a tracksuit." He put a hand on my bare waist. "We wouldn't match."

"Yanov, what are you saying? We always match."

He smiled. "You're right." My insides stirred at the shine in his eyes. "You made quite a show there, Andersonn."

"Did you like it?"

Instead of an answer, he hugged me and pressed me to his chest. His hand was gentle on my cheek. I closed my eyes, feeling his breath on my face. "I love you, Jane," he said seriously, "for everything you do for me. I love you to my core."

Guilt surged through me, but I didn't want to let it ruin the moment. I erased it from my thoughts. "I love you, Alex. Body and mind, I love you. I'd do anything for you."

Our lips connected, and he took me to a world where only our happiness existed, and nothing and no one else.

*****

"Lana, please, check these messages and delete them all if everyone's alive and in good health." I passed her my phone during our coffee break the following day.

After breakfast in bed, Alex had left for a light training session and I'd joined the girls. The Internet was swarmed with photos of me in the Rio Carnival costume alongside Alex, his teammates, our parents, fans and whoever happened to be in my proximity. It hadn't escaped me that it was the day after Matthias had done the impossible to create a romantic, intimate evening for me. I assumed he was furious, perhaps wanting an explanation, or perhaps wanting me sent to hell. I didn't want to know.

Satisfied with my request, Lana took my phone and scrolled through it. "There's nothing from Matthias," she said after a while.

That took me by surprise. "How do you mean?"

"The only two things he sent were *I am back in Rio. Have some great plans for the next meeting*, and *I carry your scent on my clothes. I terribly miss you.*"

I swallowed with difficulty, unsure how I felt. It was better that he hadn't reacted in a way that would affect my mood. But on the other side, if he was indifferent, then what had that whole family affair meant?

"I don't like it, but at least he hasn't fired some ugly language at you," said Angie. "Although I'm sure this is not the end."

"Let's just not think about it, please," said Bea. "Yesterday was one of the most beautiful days in Jane and Alex's life. Let's remember it like that."

"You're right, thank you." I caught her hand and she squeezed it with warmth.

"I just want you two to be happy and to enjoy what we all see you have." Bea stood up and hugged me. "Now, if you'll excuse me, I have to go and be with my fiancé."

We laughed collectively while Angie and Bea gathered up their handbags and trolleys, preparing to leave.

"I seriously can't wait for your wedding," I said. "That'll be the party of the year."

"I can't wait to call him my husband." She chuckled. "I know things won't be much different, but he's been more than a boyfriend or fiancé for years now. *Husband* seems so natural."

"August is almost here. After the Cup is over, you won't have time to go for coffee how busy you'll get with the preparations," Angie said.

"You're right. There are still so many errands to run, even with a very small and private wedding."

"It'll be perfect, don't stress about it," I assured her.

If it weren't for Declan Fletcher, Angie would have stayed with us. She seemed a little guilty, but I assured her I'd be fine with Lana, who was determined to defend me from Matthias by any means necessary if he decided to come over again. Anyway, we'd be reunited in barely two days. I wanted to stay with Alex as much as I could, which meant that on July 5th, when England would play Chile, Lana and I would take an early-morning flight to Fortaleza to watch the game, after which we'd return as quickly as possible to Salvador for the Ukraine–Ireland game on July 6th.

It was slightly terrifying to know that Alex's team was in the quarter-finals and that there were exactly ten days of the tournament left. We hoped to win the gold, which was equal parts ambitious and possible. Four years ago, we'd proven we were world-class footballers capable of reaching the finals. We'd reached the semis, even though we'd had to fight against many favourited, difficult teams. This time, luck was on our side, while the Germans had to struggle on the other side of the table. If everything went well, we'd meet them in the finals, which would be in two games.

That is, unless the Germans lost to Italy, who they were playing the same day England faced Chile. Or perhaps they'd lose to England in the semi-finals. I felt no joy at the prospect, but I also couldn't bear the thought of Ukraine and Germany being the last two teams standing, fighting for the Cup.

I shook it off, rubbing my temples to loosen the headache I felt due to all the overthinking. That's what it was – overthinking. I would support my man, to the end. It was that simple.

CHAPTER 10

The two days Alex and I spent together helped me recover from all the excitement and reload the energy I'd need for the remainder of the competition. His training started in the late mornings, so we didn't need to set alarms. It felt divine, waking up to a room lit up with sun-rays as I lay on his chest, in his arms. Alex was more self-assured now than he'd been four years ago. He didn't have bad dreams or anxiety about what might happen. He knew how hard he'd trained since moving to Paris and Madrid, that he'd won numerous awards every year, that he was at the top of his game. In his mind and muscles, he knew that he was not just good; he was an exceptional goalkeeper. Through the fluid certainty of his movements, the graceful slope of his muscles, he radiated self-confidence. I was in awe of him and how he'd grown so much from the excellent twenty-year-old boy I'd first met. He justified all the hopes his country had for him.

After his training, we went to the gym together. We challenged each other. He was better at lifting weights, of course, but we were a match on the treadmill and bike. He was faster, but I could perform cardio exercises for longer. The mocktails by the pool that followed were bliss, coupled with the cool, refreshing water that soothed our tired muscles.

We ran into Nikolay on the way back to our room.

"Are you gonna come down tonight after dinner? There'll be live music by the pool," said Nikolay.

"Live Brazilian music? Sounds like my cup of tea," I said, excited.

"Then we're going," said Alex without hesitation. "I can't miss seeing you dance in front of me," he whispered when we were alone once Nikolay left the elevator.

I kissed him in response.

He caught me around the waist and lifted me up; I hugged him with my arms and legs, and he carried me to the room.

*****

"You do love having all the attention on you, don't you?" Alex commented as he walked out of the bathroom to see me adjusting my clothes in front of the tall mirror. I had changed into an off-white tight skirt and top that managed to show a lot of skin without being overly vulgar.

I straightened up and, self-confident and aware of my good looks, turned in a circle to give him the opportunity to check me out entirely. "You don't like what you see?" I smirked. "If you want, I can change into a long, baggy dress."

He approached me and turned me back around to the mirror. He matched me perfectly in his white pants, but the sight of him shirtless and the first note of his cologne filled me with desire.

"I'm crazy about what I see." He kissed me on the nose.

I hugged him hard to extinguish the thirst that overwhelmed me. If we had sex again, we'd be late, and it'd be obvious why. I didn't want another round of teasing from Nikolay in front of everyone.

Down at the pool, the guys weren't drinking again, though Coach Milan Andreyevich had no objection to the rest of us doing so. I promised Alex I'd drink for him, so he only had to take care of me and prevent me from falling into the pool. The entire team was there, as well as Alex's parents and sister. By now, I could speak basic Ukrainian, so I chit-chatted with all the other girls and wives accompanying their partners. They were incredibly kind and understanding with me when I made the occasional mistake pronouncing some words or had trouble finding the right ones. Naturally, the more I drank, the better I spoke, making everyone laugh at my overconfident slips and slurs.

The music wasn't exclusively local. It started as such but transitioned into the popular hits of the time, while the DJ mixed in the sound of a stadium full of fans whenever he could, as if preparing us for the next challenge we'd face.

I did what I could do best at the moment – I danced my heart out. Gulping down cocktail after cocktail, I sweat it out in the magical night heat, swaying and singing along with the lyrics, whether I knew them or not. I was truly happy and proud to be there as Alex's girlfriend, and it reassured me even more that everyone else approved of me. As for the Ukrainians, they had forgiven me for everything I'd put Alex through. Now I could go on to feel pure, limitless joy with him.

And he loved me. I could see it in everything he did that evening – how he danced with me despite never being much of a dancer; how he touched my naked back, arms, shoulders and face; how he held me close; how he watched me while I talked to the others; how he worshipped me with his eyes while I swung with the tunes of the ever-changing music. I was a complete woman, a loved woman, thanks to him.

The party turned from the intended simple musical event to a night to remember. Lana and I, as experienced heavy drinkers, showed all the other girls how much alcohol they could actually handle. At one point, a couple of them jumped into the swimming pool, with their men joining them. Sometime after midnight, exhausted and with sore feet – I'd persistently worn my sandals, even though they'd been hurting me since early in the evening – I relied on Alex to lead me to the room.

"Where's Lana? Is she okay?" I murmured.

"Don't worry about her. She's being well taken care of."

"What do you mean?" I asked, curious but lacking the strength to raise my head from his shoulder.

"Lev is escorting her to the room."

"Hah, escorting! You're joking."

"He's a gentleman."

I couldn't help laughing. "Whose room?"

"Does it matter?"

"It doesn't. I just hope there won't be any trouble tomorrow." I sighed. I knew Lana. One-night stands weren't her thing, and Lev was a womaniser in the same rank as Nikolay Pavlov – except seven years younger. I didn't want her hurt, but then again, she was an adult. My brain could barely cope with itself that night, so I decided to wait for the morning to find out what had taken place.

"There shouldn't be trouble," Alex said. "Only you girls drank. We didn't. This night is a gift for us."

I screamed laughing. "You are such a predator."

"Of course, when I get to sleep in the same bed as you."

"And you're charming, too. Yes, take me to bed." I hung on his neck and he took me in his arms, as easy as lifting a feather, and carried me the rest of the way to the room.

When I woke up the next morning, I cursed at the pain in my legs and back. I reached for the tall glass of water on my bedside table and finished it in one go, dehydrated after all the alcohol the night before. Oh, my, it was a lot of liquid – litres and litres of cocktails, a kaleidoscope of colours. Then I remembered what'd followed after Alex and I returned to the room. Realised where the pain in my muscles was really coming from, I had to rapidly stifle a laugh so as not to wake him up. Even after almost five years years – or technically two, though I had been doing my utmost best to forget the time spent in France – he still managed to make our sex unique and wild, an original, unpredictable ride.

"You wanna join me for the gym today?" he asked when I was out of the shower.

"You wanna disable me completely so that I can't go anywhere tomorrow?"

"Maybe."

I removed my bathrobe and threw it at him. He jumped from the bed and appeared next to me in a second, fully awake and naked. Noticing he was aroused, I smiled. "I believe today we should skip the gym."

He spread my legs and carried me to the small shelf next to the curtained window.

"You are absolutely out of your mind," I said through a sigh as he entered me, maddeningly slow and patient.

"I'm not," he replied calmly, punctuating his words with kisses. "Nobody can see us. There's only a garden underneath the window."

"You've checked everything."

"Of course. Nothing and no one should disturb us."

With impressive restraint, he held himself back, moving inside me until I came twice and started begging him to stop. He continued, though, looking me in the eyes and making my whole body shake and quiver. This was, despite everything, lovemaking. We could no longer separate ourselves from it, whether slowly making out with foreplay or having wild, unhinged, uncontrolled sex. Whenever our bodies met, love was interwoven into every move. It's no surprise, then, that every orgasm we gave each other was strong, emotional, unique and unforgettable.

*****

"I can't wait to see Lana," I said over my toast and jam.

"I'll ask Lev for a report if you want to be on the safe side with him," Alex suggested.

"I'd appreciate that. Lana knows what she's doing, but I don't trust that guy."

He laughed. "Nobody trusts him. Don't worry, I'll talk to him."

I texted her as soon as Alex left for his training. Surprisingly, she replied straightaway that she'd meet me by the pool in a few minutes. I got into my swimsuit and found her already lounging in the sun, a lemonade in her hand and large sunglasses covering half of her face. I started to laugh but stifled it quickly seeing the serious line of her mouth.

"What's up? Don't tell me it was that bad?"

"Sit down here." Lana patted the lounge chair beside her. "You don't look much better either."

"Excuse me, I'm not hiding my face."

"Perhaps you didn't have as eventful a night."

I ordered a water and sat next to her. "I want to hear it all."

She removed her sunglasses and I could see how tired she was. "Damn it, the sun is too strong," she complained, putting them back on. "I didn't sleep...that is, *we* didn't sleep more than two hours. He's just left, straight for training."

I squeaked with happiness. "That's wonderful."

"Yup, it was memorable. While I'm completely exhausted and still inebriated, I am happy he met expectations. His reputation is deserved."

"I'm happy, too. So why do I feel a *but* floating in the air?"

She sipped her lemonade. "He wants to meet again tonight."

"What's bad about that? Just tell him we need to be up early and on the plane for the England game."

"That's what I said, but he started giving me fairy tales."

"What fairy tales?" I squeezed some lemon into my water.

"You know, typical guy stories. The ones they tell when they want to get you emotional and attached."

I gave her a piercing look, knowing what she meant but refusing to believe that Alex's teammate would do something like that to my friend.

"After our two hours of sleep, we hugged...I know," she added at my eye roll, "it just came natural, and I was drunk."

"But he wasn't, that bastard." The anger was rising in me.

"I know. Stupid of him, right? So after we woke up, we went for more, after which he said he'd never had it like that with anyone. I mean, yes, it was exceptional. But I wouldn't say anything like that to someone I'm just planning to...enjoy physically for some time."

"He's such a child!"

"Yeah, and I told him that, too. He insisted that we have breakfast together. I tried to refuse but the harder I fought to leave, the more adamant he was about not letting me go. We had another round before the food was delivered. Then I said he didn't need to tell me all those things, his performance was enough to make me come for more. I said that if he continued, he'd just ruin it all and make me want to slap him and regret I ever agreed to it."

"And...?"

"He didn't want to give up. He kept repeating the same bullshit like a machine: 'Lana, I'm not fooling around. This was wonderful, extraordinary. I've never experienced such a strong connection with anyone.' The worst part was that when I tried to leave furiously, he prevented me, and we had sex *again* – equally good, equally wild."

"Which means there may be something *you're* pushing down, perhaps?"

"Jane, he's six years younger than me and a dangerous womaniser. Whatever he feels or says might be true, might be temporary, or might be just stupid, reckless lies. I know that I don't want to get involved with such a man, and I'll tell him so tonight."

"So you agreed to meet again?"

"Yes, to clarify it all."

"Hm...*to clarify.*" We both laughed. "Okay, seriously. I'll talk to Alex and see what's going on with that kid. If he keeps bothering you, I'll personally put him in his place."

We clinked our glasses. "Thank you, Jane."

"But what?"

"What?"

"I feel another *but.*"

She sighed. "The sex was truly different, unheard of, beyond phenomenal. He was right, in a way. I just don't want to be fooled by some horny, immature boy."

I caught her hand. "You won't. I promise you that."

Finally, she smiled.

We moved to cool down in the pool, drafting the plan for tomorrow: We would get up at sunrise; hop on the plane; fly two hours to Fortaleza; meet Bea, Angie and my parents; and attend the game at five o'clock in the afternoon. Then the same was planned for the following day, when we would be back in Salvador in time for Alex's game against Ireland. I would need to plan my sleep well or risk fainting from a mix of tiredness and adrenaline.

My phone beeped. Expecting Alex to be coming back from his training, I instantly looked at it.

That was quite a performance you did out there. Though you'd look better in black, red and gold.

Lana saw me go white. "Don't tell me it's *him* again." I didn't answer. I just squeezed the phone in my hand. "Don't write anything back."

"You're right. I won't," I said quietly, putting the phone aside.

Half an hour later, while I was swimming and trying to kick the bloody German out of my thoughts, I heard the same beep.

I'll call you tonight at seven. If you don't pick up, I'll ring Blondie. Maybe I'll also send him those two photos we snapped. It's up to you.

I cried in despair, covering my mouth with my hand. I passed the phone to Lana when she worriedly asked me what was wrong. "Damn it, he can't give it a rest for two days, can he?"

"I-I'm sure he's bluffing with this," I said, my voice, quivering. "He's said so many times that he'd never hurt me. He won't do it."

"But you'd better take that call." Lana's voice was tight with anger. "We don't know how furious he may be now. You made quite a show there."

"You're right, but what should I tell Alex?"

"How do you mean, 'what should I tell Alex'? You tell him that you have to speak to your father, or Bea and Angie. You won't tell him the truth the evening before you're leaving and two days before his important game. Come on, I hate to say it, but lying is probably your best talent."

She was right. I mustn't upset Alex. It'd been days since he'd heard of any problems with Matthias. I supposed he thought everything was alright, that the German was out of sight and not bothering me. It had to stay that way.

Alright. We'll talk tonight. I replied coolly.

When he didn't answer back, I grew restless. It wasn't like him. That meant he was either gravely upset or planning something out of the ordinary, perhaps even dangerous.

No, Jane, I kept repeating to myself. *He told you so many times he'd keep you safe. He's already done so much for you without putting you at risk. He won't do anything now.* But. On the other hand, maybe he took my show in the stands as me spitting on everything he'd created for me the day before, all the effort he'd put in. I couldn't know until I spoke to him.

Doing as Lana told me, I managed to leave Alex with his teammates in the restaurant that evening, finishing my poor dinner a few minutes before seven and saying I was expecting a call from Angie and Bea to confirm some details for the following day. I wouldn't take long, I told Alex.

A minute after seven, my phone rang. I answered with shaking hands.

Matthias was silent for a moment, but I could hear his breathing. "I miss you," he suddenly said, catching me off guard. That was the last thing I'd expected to hear. After a day of imagining how furious he would be, I wasn't prepared for the gentleness of his voice. "It's been four days, but it feels like a year."

"Matthias—"

"We need to meet soon, Jane. I planned everything. If we lose tomorrow, I'll follow you wherever you go. If we win, I'll find a way to come and see you before the semi-final."

"Matthias, I thought you—"

"You thought I'd be angry for what you did at Blondie's match on Tuesday? Of course, I'm furious. I'm jealous. I wanted to fly there and drag you from the stadium, although everyone agreed unequivocally that you were the hottest, most beautiful Carnival dancer we'd ever seen."

I had a stone in my throat. I wanted to be upset with him, or for him to be upset with me. Not this. This was just making it more difficult. Again. "Matthias, you shouldn't be saying this to me. You should hate me and never want to see me again."

"If it was that easy, I would've done it years ago."

"Don't you see I'm trying to make it easy for you? Hate me, please. Give up on me. Don't go looking for me anymore. I'm not good for you."

"So you don't care for me at all? Everything that happened five days ago was a lie, was you acting?"

It felt as if my lips were sewn shut with iron wire. I couldn't make myself confirm his words. How could I lie to him about something so big? *Try, Jane,* I ordered myself. *Say it, even if you vomit afterwards.* "Yes, I pretended the entire day," I formed the words.

"Hah!" he barked out a laugh. "You can lie to Blondie like that, but not to me. Anyway, we'll discuss your costume show when we meet. I just wanted to tell you that, and we'll discuss some more important topics, once and for all. The tournament is ending, and I don't want the same scenario as last time. I want answers. I want the truth. "

I swallowed hard. "Of course."

"Jane?"

"Yes?"

"Don't talk to me like I'm a stranger. We're far more than that."

I sighed. "I know."

"I keep thinking about you, regardless of what you do, because I know what you feel when you're with me. I know that whatever you do for him is not your love. It's out of duty, and feelings of guilt. I know you're true and honest when we are together."

I took a deep breath, unsettled, my stomach flipping in nervousness. I didn't need to hear these confusing declarations that would only puzzle me more while my mind and emotions had already been stirred into a typhoon. What if he was right about all this?

No, he can't be. I knew very well how I felt about Alex. Matthias, he was just something I couldn't explain, something no one could explain. I'd tell him that.

"I'll see you soon, Jane."

"Alright."

"You won't wish me luck for tomorrow?"

"Oh, against Italy? Good luck," I said, keeping my voice measured even as anxious bile burned my throat. Deep inside, I wasn't sure what I wanted the outcome of that match to be. I had no wish to see the Ukrainians and Germans confront each other again. I didn't want another disaster to occur because of me. I didn't want the Ukrainian team to suffer, and I certainly didn't want it to be the Germans inflicting it. The last World Cup was enough for generations to come. Perhaps it'd be better for Matthias's team to end the competition soon. He'd be gone with them after I told him I wasn't interested in anything he had to offer me.

"Sleep well," he said.

"You, too."

"One more thing, Jane."

"Yes?"

"I'd never show Blondie our photos, you know that?"

"I do."

"Yet you agreed to talk to me?" I didn't reply. "Doesn't that tell you something?"

Without an answer, I ended the call, my hands shaking, suddenly scared of what he'd said. Yet again, he was right. Whether he was playing mind games with me, I wasn't certain.

Not knowing what to do or expect next, I began praying to any force out there that this insane man would just leave me alone. I prayed for whatever divine help I could get, because, obviously, I had no mental strength to get over him alone.

*****

"He did *what*?" Angie screamed so loud that every head in the café rose, looking for the source of the noise.

"Yep. He set up candles and wine. And then he insisted we meet for dinner after their match tomorrow," Lana was retelling last night's events.

"That little prick. He takes anything that moves to bed, and now he plays games like these?" Angie was unforgiving.

"I don't know what to think. I told him at least a dozen times yesterday that there was no need for all that. I actually said all that unnecessary romance and attention was annoying and freaking me out, that I'd leave and never meet him again."

"What did he do?"

"He threw the bottle and candles out into the hallway."

"And then?" I asked.

"Then we...you know."

The three of us couldn't help laughing.

"He's really sweet," Bea said. "Perhaps he's serious now."

"Come on," Lana rejected that option, "I'm older than him, and I'm Jane's friend. If there's anything he feels for me, it's the obligation to be gentlemanly because of Alex and Jane. He's a kid – he can't tell the difference between respect and genuine emotions."

"Maybe," Bea admitted. "But maybe we're mistaken. Has Alex collected any useful information?" She turned to me.

"No, he didn't have time alone with him yesterday, but he promised to do so today."

"Time will reveal all," Angie said. "In the meantime, enjoy the good sex."

"The unheard of, phenomenal, exceptional sex," I added, and we laughed again.

*****

I didn't want to follow the results of the Germany–Italy game until it was over, at which point I found out it had ended 3–2 for the German Four and their team. Their next opponent would be either England or Chile, depending on the outcome of the next game.

This meant that if my country won today, we'd meet Rolf Gottfried's team in four days in Belo Horizonte, where I'd definitely go with the girls and my parents.

Which meant that Matthias and I would again be in the same city at the same time, with Alex hundreds of kilometres away.

I mustn't think about it now, I told myself. If it happened, I'd take care of it. Somehow.

The Arena Castelão had 58,000, seats and all of them were occupied for this event. A slight majority belonged to the Chileans since, naturally, it was more convenient for them to travel to Brazil than for my fellow Englanders. Still, that didn't affect the atmosphere. The fans in white were shouting their lungs and hearts out, tirelessly waving flags and scarves. Dad was pretty confident about the game, so he spent most of the time chatting to his friends, while Mom was involved with their wives. I joined them for a few minutes but soon returned my attention to the pitch – at exactly the right time, forty minutes in, when the goal-scoring began.

A Chilean midfielder managed to pierce our defence and reach Harold Dare alone. It was one-on-one and the ball volleyed from his right foot into our net. There was little Harold could have done.

"It's far from over," I said confidently.
Joshua Hadleigh and Keaton Flanagan wouldn't give up easily. The Chilean team was good but not better than ours. We could see that in the clashes and fighting over the ball before this goal. I wanted to believe that we'd manage.

In the last minute of stoppage time, defender Duncan Fletcher – the brother of Angie's boyfriend – managed to run through to the front, take a pass from Hadleigh and successfully place the ball behind the enemy goalkeeper. We went for the break lighthearted.

The second half proved significantly more entertaining. The players returned to the grass reenergised like they'd had a power nap during halftime. There was a substitute on each side, and then the rush began. We took a lead in the opening minutes, but Chile levelled the playing field with a goal of their own within ten minutes. We clawed the lead back, though, when Flanagan scored unexpectedly from thirty metres back. The Chileans equalised it eight minutes later, but the goal was disallowed due to a literally ten-centimetres offside. Things were heating up; the fans and players alike were buzzing. As if that wasn't enough stress for the evening, in the eighty-eighth minute, Simon Wade, our defender, got aggressive with the opponent's striker and was handed a yellow card.

Finally, in the ninetieth minute, Wade compensated for his misstep by reaching the dangerous area near the Chilean goal and, with the help of

Keaton Flanagan, he managed to send the ball into the net with his head. It was now 4–2 and definitely over.

We returned to the hotel singing and drinking champagne on the way. We were in the semi-finals! That was one step better than at the previous tournament, when Ukraine won over England in another difficult game for me. This time it'd be the Germans, and I knew very well who I'd cheer for. I didn't want Alex facing off against Matthias in the finals. I didn't want another disaster caused by Gottfried and another disappointment for Alex. Despite the fact that the vicious coach had been quiet so far, I could bet he'd do something disgusting if required. My hope was that Alex was immune this time to any poisonous arrows that cruel coach could fire at him. With luck, Matthew Vance's team would take on the Germans with the same force and eagerness they presented today.

We all gathered in the restaurant for a quick dinner, and while I was on my second glass of red wine, all the TVs in the room began flashing the black-red-gold as the highlights of the day's other quarter-final game began.

It gave me malicious pleasure to see Rolf Gottfried losing his mind from the beginning of the game. Italy turned out to be a difficult opponent, probably the toughest Germany had met so far in the competition. His team couldn't complete enough passes to reach Italy's goalposts. Marco Moretti, the passionate player I'd had an intimate encounter with, didn't make it to this year's team. He'd suffered an injury a few years back and now played in the Middle East, at a different level. Still, this team was powerful and indomitable. They were simply everywhere – too densely positioned for Germany to make any headway.

I sipped my wine at watched the playback detailing how Germany's problems began when Ewald Fuchs, their young goalkeeper, couldn't defend an extremely forceful shot by one Italian forward. He evaluated the ball's trajectory well, but the shot was too strong for him to catch, so it went through his hands and shook the net wildly. It didn't look good for the world champions. The camera showed Team Captain Michael Krimm speaking calmly to his colleagues and repositioning them. Then, in the next scene, Matthias was shouting something to Lens Petrov, Leon Schneider and Friedrich Larsson, his face red with furore. Some ten minutes later, their plan made itself clear when Lens, Leon and Friedrich pushed the ball forward in one attack that played out at the speed of light. The entire Italian team was on their side, defending, but Matthias managed to squeeze through into position, his white jersey alone among four blue ones. Lens sent him the ball, and Matthias jumped with all his power and sent it behind the Italian keeper, equalising the score. It was a great shot; the highlights played it several times, from any angle they could find.

That goal took tremendous effort, and by the time the referee announced the end of the first half, all the players were red-faced and tired, in dire need of a break. The remainder of the clash didn't kick off in a way the German fans would appreciate. Even though Gottfried's team showed up on the pitch ready and ambitious, it took only one mistake from their centre for the Italian striker to get the ball and take it to the front by himself. Not waiting for his teammates to join him – and decidedly selfish and overambitious – the Italian player volleyed the ball from the right corner of the penalty area towards the German goalkeeper. His ambition paid off, and the ball sailed into the net. Even though I knew the final result, the sight of Matthias's hurt face on the TV made me grateful I hadn't had the chance to watch the game live. This didn't happen to his team often. For years, they'd been absolute favourites in every game they played, topping the group in every qualification. Leaving the World Cup in the quarter-finals was unimaginable for them. Now faced with it, their faces depicted despair.

In the eighty-third minute, however, after a series of high-quality attacks through which they justified their current title as the best national team on the planet, Artur Voigt, a twenty-two-year-old defender from a club in Dortmund, turned up at the right place at the right time. His goal brought relief and reignited hope for the German nation. My palms were sweating, and I noticed the restaurant had fallen almost silent, with everyone present watching the recap carefully.

The stoppage time was only two minutes; the deciding point would happen any minute. What I didn't expect was that it'd be scored by a goalkeeper. A corner was awarded to the Germans in the finishing few seconds. Ewald Fuchs decided to join his teammates, risking a simple counterattack that could bring disaster upon him and his country. The camera showed Rolf Gottfried holding his head in disapproval, but the young goalkeeper didn't even look at him once. I didn't want to know how he got penalised afterwards.

Michael Krimm shot the ball from the corner, and Leon Schneider tried to tip it off with his head but didn't jump high enough. However, Ewald did, and the next moment, the Italian net was shaking. Ewald turned and ran towards his coach, smiling innocently like a child, waiting for approval. Of course, he got it: Rolf hugged him as the rest of the players covered them in frantic celebration. The battle was over. They'd fought and hadn't disappointed. As usual, Germany had given the world a performance. It would be talked about all over the world for the next couple of days.

As I topped up my wine, it crossed my mind that perhaps this meant they weren't as strong as everyone thought. On the other side, maybe it just wasn't their day. We'd see in four days. When I'd be too close to Matthias again.

There was a knock on my door after the girls and I had parted ways. Although tired, I froze in fear. I'd had a good deal of late-night hotel surprises in my life. This could literally be anyone, but I prayed it wasn't Matthias. Anyone else, I'd be able to deal with properly. But not him.

A voice floated through the door.

"Hi, Honey, may I come in?"

"Mom..." I let her in, equal parts relieved and taken aback. "Of course. What's bringing you here so late?"

"I wanted to check up on you without Brad breathing down our necks."

She was bare-faced, wearing a T-shirt and tracksuit. *When I grow old, I want to look like her,* I thought with a smile.

"Makes sense. Thanks for finding the time."

"Don't thank me for that, Love." We sat on my bed and I snuggled under the duvet. "How's Alex?" she asked.

"He's great. Fully ready for tomorrow, and any next game. We're happy now, truly, honestly happy with each other."

"I'm really glad to hear that." She squeezed my hand. "And how's Matthias?"

My heart skipped a beat, but I still held her hand tight and took a deep breath. "Giving me some trouble."

"I thought so."

"How did you know?"

"Remember when I said you looked drained? Well, there's nothing and no one else that could be the reason for that, right?"

"Right." I didn't know how much I could tell her. "He...he's insisting that we meet, go for dinner and so on. I can't do that."

"Of course, you can't."

I immediately felt a prick of guilt. What would she tell me if she knew I'd already gone out with him?

"I don't know how to tell him to give up so that he eventually does."

"You have to really mean it."

I gave her a piercing look. Why did she talk to me like this?

"There's something rather romantic about you two," she went on to explain, "I don't think we can call it love, since you've never officially been together. To us beholders from the outside, it looks pure, innocent, grand, potentially perfect. In a way, it's probably addictive for you."

"What are you referring to?"

"Perhaps a part of you enjoys his attention and all the newspaper stories that go with it, so you're reluctant to tell him to stop once and for all."

"Mom, how can you...?" I wanted to be upset, but my voice was too weak.

"I am a woman, Jane, and I feel terrible for the mistakes I made with you that caused you to grow up without me. I could've taught you, advised you on so much."

I knew exactly what she meant, better than she knew herself. I'd made too many mistakes with men. Could it all have been different, had she been by my side during my sensitive teenage years? Well, no use crying over the spilt milk. She wasn't, and it was her fault. Perhaps now she could repair a part of the damage I'd made, even if she had no idea the extent of it. She was always beautiful, always had men courting her, but she never had had an affair.

"You think every man in the world is scared of Brad and won't approach me?" she continued, as if she'd read my mind. "Ever since we began seeing each other, there would be someone who'd invite me for a drink every now and then. Every time, I was crystal clear that I didn't want it. I'd emphasise that I love and appreciate my husband. Each one of them respected that, because I made them do so."

"You think I'm not firm enough with Matthias?"

"Four years ago, you weren't. You attended his games and parties, you laughed at his jokes and you made friends with him. You gave him hope. You should have left his vicinity the moment you understood his interest in you was serious."

"But Dad was going to those games and taking me with him, you remember!"

"Still, you went for those parties and a couple of matches alone. You shouldn't have done any of that."

I sighed, not knowing what to say.

"Honey, it's fine, because you were young, reckless and inexperienced. You craved attention and you enjoyed it. Luckily, you still have Alex after it all. Now you have to keep him, and to do so, you have to tell Matthias to stop."

I was trying to picture myself telling those coal-black eyes to leave me alone, strictly, emotionlessly, carelessly. Tears began swelling in my eyes. No, no, no, I mustn't cry now.

"Mom," I stammered, "I feel so sorry for him. The fact that he still goes after me means that his emotions are real. I don't know where to gather courage and hurt him by saying I will never care enough to be with him."

"You need to, Jane. Otherwise, he'll be stuck on you for years. He'll waste his youth and life."

Yes, but just the thought of Matthias with some other woman made me furious. I was a terrible, selfish woman. How dare I?

"I know you've probably gotten used to life with Alex. You two have known each other for almost five years. You know everything about each other – how you think, how you breathe, how your heart beats in certain situations. It may get mundane at times, but if you keep the sparkle, love and respect will stay forever. You don't need excitement from the outside. Alex doesn't need it because he loves you and only has eyes for you. You should be the same. You must fight that inner impulse to get attention from someone who's not your partner."

I took another deep breath and pushed the tears back. "How have you done it all these years?"

"I've always been aware that next to me, I have the most amazing, complete, accomplished man in the world who'd move mountains for me. I never took it for granted because I know his limits. I'm in awe of him. I've never thought he's entirely mine so that I can do whatever I want and he'll forgive me. I know my limits, too."

Well, that's your answer, Jane, I thought. *You've never known your limits. You still don't know them. You just keep playing, and you keep getting lucky. For now. You have to stop.*

"Think about it," she continued. "But I'm serious when I tell you that you have to let Matthias go. He seems like a good guy. He deserves happiness, not to commit his entire life to a dream, a fantasy. And Alex deserves to have a woman who'll love and care for him, who'll have eyes for him only."

I stretched my arms up to hug her and she hugged me back. I inhaled the scent of her soft, clean hair. She was right about everything, and I had to do as she said, as soon as possible. Now I was determined. I would finish this farce and finally be a proper girlfriend to Alex.

"Thanks for everything, Mom," I said while she was at the door, ready to leave.

"Most welcome, Honey. And one more thing – if it's gonna make you feel better: No matter what, when or where, Brad would never, ever have let you date Beller." My heart skipped a beat. "I remember him talking about it before Alex gave you his jersey. The only two options from the footballing world were Hadleigh and Krimm. Alex got lucky 'cause Brad hadn't heard about him before, and he's been proving himself over and over."

I laughed. "Michael Krimm? No way!"

"He's the most serious on the German team and an extremely successful sportsman. But too late."

I couldn't help laughing. "Alex it is then. Forever."

*****

It helped that I'd gone to bed early the night before, so waking up at sunrise again wasn't too bad. Still, I slept with my head against the window for most of the flight back to Salvador. The girls and I couldn't talk much since my parents were with us, and when we arrived in the hotel, there was no time left to tell them what I'd spoken with Mom about. The players were already at the stadium, so we sat in the hotel bar to watch the game between the Netherlands and Scotland to see who our opponent in the semi-finals would be if – when – we went through. The first half ended 1–1, but at the beginning of the second part, the Dutch managed to score and keep the lead until the end. We left for the Arena Fonte Nova immediately.

I didn't want to make a big show of myself at this game, so I wore a simple ensemble of denim shorts and Alex's jersey. One surprise was more than enough at this tournament. I didn't want anyone to say I was a chronic attention seeker.

Our seats were the same ones we'd taken a few days back in the match against Belgium, but this time some of Dad's Irish friends and business partners were joining us. I promised them I'd be polite and considerate, and they promised in return they wouldn't get upset over the outcome of the game whatever it might be.

However, I couldn't keep quiet when the Ukrainian fans began chanting the songs I knew. After all this time dating Alex and attending his games, I'd learnt almost all the favourites that were sung at the stands. Now their country was playing a quarter-final, the second one in their history, in the beautiful, faraway country of Brazil. They were making history again, and they were drunk with happiness.

Luca Ferreira was with us, too. He'd lost to the Netherlands a few days ago, which was a shame for Brazil but the Dutch had an excellent team. It was the hosts' bad luck to meet them so early in the competition and succumb to the force of their strikers. Luca was now committed to Alex's games until the end.

He was still Alex's best friend, although they'd played for different teams since Alex left the Ukrainian league. Luca stayed for another year in Kyiv before moving to England and then Italy. He was now one of the main stars of the best team in Rome, and he seemed happy there. He had a girlfriend, too, though she couldn't come to Brazil because of her job. She was a language teacher in a private school and didn't want to force her boss to give her a month's leave just because her boyfriend was a football player. I'd met her a couple of times and, she always seemed rather down to earth, humble and realistic. Luca's money and fame couldn't sway her into spending too much or rising above what she deemed appropriate and right.

Despite knowing all that, whenever I looked at him, I remembered our first encounter – that is, the first time I saw him – in his and Alex's apartment in Kyiv. Almost naked, he was the first man who'd stirred something improper in me since I met Alex. It all started with him back then. He had no idea.

He was still attractive, of course, but I couldn't care less. All the men I'd been with in Germany somehow made sure that I'd never think again about getting involved with Alex's best friend. Most likely, I was well aware of how much he cared about Alex and that he'd tell him immediately if he noticed me behaving distastefully. Therefore, after everything and all those years, Luca was always just a friend. He also didn't have a clue about what had taken place in Germany. He knew Alex and I were not really happy in France, but Alex never told him anything, for which I loved him immensely. Luca disapproved of my friendship with the Germans then, but it's not like he could do anything about it. When Alex and I got back together, he just accepted that everything was alright now.

After the national anthems, the game kicked off. It turned out dynamic from the first whistle. We played in yellow jerseys while the Irish wore their green ones. I'd been certain that Milan Andreyevich's team would take it easy at the beginning, using the early game to warm up so they could rush to score later. But the guys in green had different plans. They knew they were weaker, so they aimed to snatch as many goals from

Ukraine as soon as possible before they got tired or their opponents got wise to their style of play.

Things didn't go well for the Irish, but the game didn't go our way either. After forty-five minutes of incessant, aggressive fights over the ball, three yellow cards, at least a dozen dangerous shots at the Irish goalkeeper and the same number at Alex (who skilfully deflected them), the board still showed 0–0. My throat hurt from shouting and chanting, and I needed a drink to soothe it.

"You want a Guinness?" Dad's colleague held a can out to me.

"I am a fan, but not today, thank you," I politely refused, and he laughed with his friends.

Olexiy Yanov then took out a two-litre bottle of horilka and passed it around. It almost made me cry from how strong it was. The beer Luca got for us afterwards tasted like juice in comparison. I was thankful for it, though, because it relaxed me, and when the second half began, I'd forgotten that it could be Alex's last minutes at this tournament.

The Irish part of the stadium was the best supporters any team could possibly wish for. Almost all of them wore jerseys, and many had funny, unique hats and caps on. Smiles brightened their green, white and orange–painted faces as they waved flags and scarves and sang non-stop from the beginning of the game, perfectly synchronised. They danced and created perfectly choreographed Mexican waves. We were slightly jealous at first, but they motivated us to be louder and sing better on our side.

The deciding action came out of a corner near Alex's goal. Our defensemen successfully took the ball away from the dangerous zone, rocketing it over half of the pitch to the opposite side. The only two players in yellow were striker Nikolay Pavlov and midfielder Anatoliy Honchar. They didn't waste time. They rushed forward, not looking back to see if anyone would be there to support them, not needing anyone. Honchar gave the ball to Nikolay when two players threatened to take it away from him, and with possession now, Nikolay added extra speed to his already fired-up legs. Honchar did the same and paralleled the enemy defensive players.

Understanding that the Irish goalkeeper was confidently prepared in front of him, Nikolay's position was clear. He prayed that Honchar would be quick enough to use the moment of surprise they'd created. He shot the ball high towards him and waited.

With tremendous skill – and luck – Honchar calmed the ball instantly with his right foot and made a couple of rapid steps to dart ahead of the defence. It only took him a millisecond to prepare, collect all the force within his trained muscles, directed the ball to his right foot and shoot it as mightily as he could. And then he, like the twenty-four thousand of us on the stands, could do nothing but observe.

We all watched, mouths agape, as the Irish goalkeeper stretched his hands in the right way. The ball smashed his gloves but didn't stop; it was as strong as a bullet. The net shook.

My ears went deaf at the roar of the audience. Finally, it was 1–0. We were in the lead.

"That was a good one, I have to admit," said Dad's Guinness colleague. "One round on me?"

"Fine, but if you score next, we'll offer you Ukrainian vodka," I replied.

"No problem. Bring it on!"

The entire blue and yellow part of the stadium was standing now – jumping, actually – and singing their throats out. There were twenty minutes to go, but one goal was enough. We were already celebrating going to the semi-finals. If everything went according to plan, tomorrow we'd head to São Paulo, where the Dutch were awaiting us.

Nikolay Pavlov was twenty-nine at that World Cup. It was his third, and he intended to score as many goals as possible to set a record in Ukrainian history before the end of his career. Technically, he could play one more tournament like this to be the top scorer in his country. But Andriy Barnik was on a similar road – and five years younger – so Nikolay would first set a record that Andriy had to break. So far, he'd reached the goalposts successfully five times. The opening match was the only one where he didn't shake the opponent's net. Despite the fact that many of his peers were ready for retirement, Nikolay constantly proved with his energy and agility that he was far from that. Watching him fly over the pitch, especially in crucial moments, one would think there were at least five more years of top-class football ahead of him.

Thus, it was no surprise when Igor Krasinski and Lev Zahara organised a ball for him from the back line. Nikolay started towards the Irish goalposts at the speed of light, and Barnik followed. The way they exchanged the ball a couple of times looked easy and elegant, but it was the result of months and years of practice in pursuit of the standards of perfection that Coach Andreyevich set for them. The last one to touch the ball was Nikolay, sending it with his head to the unguarded upper-left corner of the goal.

The stadium roared and shook. It felt like a stampede was rampaging over it as Ukraine's fans yelled to be heard out of the atmosphere. Their team led 2–0 and it might as well have been over.

The Irish tried valiantly to pick up their game, but they were unable to get past the now-cemented Ukrainian wall of defence. Our guys had calmed down. The new aim was to keep Alex's sheet clean. Another record? Why not? Alex was the only goalkeeper at this stage who hadn't conceded any goals. We wanted it to stay like that.

Twenty minutes lengthened to what seemed an hour, but it was all in vain for the guys in green. When the two minutes of stoppage time expired, we were again jumping and threatening to knock the venue down in our glee. We were treated to another round of Guinness, after which we finished Mr Olexiy's horilka and headed back to the hotel, drugged with joy and pride.

CHAPTER 11

"I still can't believe it."

"Why not, Alex?"

"It's already the semi-finals. We are where we stopped last time, and it feels like only a few days have passed since we arrived in Brazil."

I snuggled under his arm and intertwined our fingers. "It's been a pretty turbulent month. No wonder it seems fast."

"It's crazy. We've seen and experienced so much here." Alex squeezed my hand, and I felt him shift slightly to look out the plane window. "I'm happy I got to know Luca's country better. He always reprimanded me for not finding time to come along and see his family. All this...visiting different cities, those school kids, future stars...I feel richer for the invaluable experience I've gained here."

"I couldn't agree more. Imagine how I feel – I got to see Amazonia!"

"I won't pretend I'm not jealous. But I hope we'll make time for a vacation over there."

"Of course, we will." I kissed his hand, and he returned the gesture by placing his lips on my hair.

"I don't want to jinx it, but I have a great feeling about all this, Jane," he murmured into my hair.

"About the tournament?"

"Yes. I know we still have to win against the Netherlands in three days, but I can clearly see us on Sunday in Rio, taking on the second-best team in the world."

"I can clearly see that, too." I raised my head to kiss him and then rested it back on his shoulder, where I fell asleep and did not awaken until we landed in São Paulo.

*****

After a nap in the hotel, Alex and I got ready to go down for dinner with his coach and teammates. I was comparing different earrings in the mirror against my outfit when Alex hugged me from behind and kissed the back of my neck.

"I talked to Lev about Lana," he said.

When he didn't elaborate, I turned and gave him a piercing look.

"I'm afraid I didn't find out anything you girls didn't already know." He shrugged. "He seemed to have been waiting for an opportunity to talk about her – when I asked him, he couldn't stop. He went pouring on about how something's different now, how she is exceptional, how mesmerising she is when she talks, how smart, elegant, eloquent, full of knowledge she is."

I sighed. "Are you sure he wasn't playing some game on you? Surely he knows you'll tell me everything and I'll tell her."

"I'm pretty sure he wasn't. I threatened him not to mess with my girl's friends the same way he does with other women, otherwise, he'll have problems with me. But he was persistent that Lana is not a joke for him."

"Well, that's not good news. I hope he'll give up after she tells him off. I just don't think it can work – the age difference is too big. He's an immature skirt-chaser, while Lana could be a CEO of a multi-million company."

"I know. But the two of them will have to sort it out themselves. We did our part." He pulled me into his arms, and my frustration melted. "Now, let's go. We don't want to be late."

*****

When are you coming to Belo Horizonte?

You are coming, right?

Jane, you can't miss the English game just because you're avoiding me.

If you don't come to the match, I will fly down to São Paulo and look for you. I'll take you out of your room if necessary.

You can't ignore me forever.

We have to meet, Jane. You know it.

I wasn't just ignoring him because I wanted to avoid him. I also didn't know what to reply back. Of course, I was going to attend the game between England and Germany in Belo Horizonte. But the idea of Matthias and me in the same city made me sick with worry. Alex would be hundreds of kilometres away, unable to protect me from Matthias – or myself. I was scared to answer anything. What could I possibly say? I couldn't meet him because I knew I wouldn't be able to tell him it was over between us the night before his semi-final match. It'd destroy him. It wasn't right.

On the other hand, if I didn't meet him this time, we probably wouldn't get a chance to meet at all with Alex at a safe distance. The moment the match finished, I had to rush with the girls on a plane and return to São Paulo because Alex had his semi-final the very next day. The last thing I wanted was Matthias coming to see me and facing Alex, perhaps even telling him something that could produce the same effect Coach Gottfried's yelling had last time.

All that taken into consideration, I knew the best choice was to see the crazy German now, when we'd be in the same city. I'd tell him everything I should have years ago, and if that affected his performance, well, it'd be payback for what happened to Alex.

- I am not avoiding you. I don't have time to be on my phone. Alex is always with me.

Then tell Blondie to give you some space to breathe and go train more, because he sucks.

Alright, I apologise. He doesn't suck. So, you're coming? When?

- Tuesday morning, before the game. I lied. We were going the day before the game because, naturally, Bea wanted to be with Harold and Angie wanted to be with Declan. Matthias just didn't need to know that.

And when are you leaving?

- Tuesday evening, after the game.

That doesn't leave any space for me.

- I'm afraid there's nothing I can do.

You know there is.

- I cannot, Matthias. The girls want to go on the day of the match, I can't risk anything with Alex now.

Alright, have it your way. But whatever happens, it's your decision.

- Are you threatening me again?

I'm not threatening you. I'm just telling you I won't let this tournament end before getting some answers from you. We'll meet, I promise you that. I'll follow you until we sit down for a proper talk. I hate it when you're pretending to be cold like this with me when I know everything, how you feel, how your heart beats when we're close to each other, how you tremble when we kiss. I'll put in your head that it's worth leaving that jealous blonde kid. He'll never love you as I do.

I shoved the phone into my bag without replying. Alex would return any time and I didn't want him to see me all excited, sad, flustered and worried. I took off my dress and went for a shower. All this hiding and secrets...it was exhausting. I couldn't wait for it to be over. Once the tournament finished, we'd all go to our respective homes, hopefully in a celebratory mood – my and Alex's parents, Bea and Harold, Angie and Declan, Alex and me. We'd go for a well-deserved vacation and then head back to London for the grandest wedding of the year when Bea would become Mrs Dare. Then a new football season would start and the Ukrainian boys would be spread across Europe; I'd start some new projects and work until Christmas, then another vacation, then more projects...

It'd be a wonderful, productive, eventful year, followed by another and then another. All with Alex by my side. Not Matthias.

When I got out of the shower, Alex was already back. I hid under the blanket and waited for him to join me. When I rested my head on his chest, the visions of our life were even clearer.

"I wish I didn't have to wake up early tomorrow," I said.

"I wish that, too." He kissed me on the hair. The weight of his hand on my back made all worries retreat. "Be careful tomorrow, Jane."

"You're saying that because of Beller?"

"Exactly. He'll try to talk to you, we both know that. Just stay safe and close to your parents and the girls."

I straightened up. "Alex, I don't want you to worry about me. You mustn't. Not before your important match."

"There's nothing I can do about it. I'll worry until you return, which is still before my important match."

"I'll be careful. In the meantime, promise me you'll train and make yourself so busy that you won't have time to think about what issues I might encounter there."

"Not an easy request."

I kissed him. "Please."

He kissed me back. "Alright."

*****

"You're not even considering giving him a chance after all the amazing sex you've had over the last couple of days?" Angie said on the plane, eyeing Lana over her large mug of coffee.

"No." Lana took a second croissant from the breakfast table.

"Not even after what Alex said about him?" Bea inquired.

"No. How come you girls don't understand?" she said, her mouth full. "The kid is just excited and confused because, well, because of the wild chemistry between us. There's nothing else. He'll understand that in a few weeks after the tournament is over and he goes on a vacation somewhere in the Caribbean when a bunch of young, desirable chicks start slithering all over him. He won't even remember me."

Angie waited for a moment before replying. "I'm not so sure about that. Why are you so stubborn? Why don't you give that kid a chance? Why do you have to act like a cold-hearted bitch who only wants good sex, when we all know you're not like that?"

Bea and I exchanged glances. Angie was blunt and a little crude, but she was on point. She only said what all three of us were thinking.

Lana swallowed her croissant. "Because I won't be another one on his list," she replied calmly, although I could sense she wanted to snap at us. "I won't give him a chance to make me fall in love and then hurt me, or worse – stay with me because I'm Jane's friend." My mouth went agape, but before I could say anything, she continued, "No, Jane, I don't have an issue with being known as your friend, or perhaps in your shadow or whatever. None of us do. If we did, we wouldn't have tagged along with you all these years. I'm only being realistic. Lev is not the man for me. If by some wild chance he is, then he'll have to spend more time proving it, because I'm not falling for someone for good sex only."

"*The unheard of, phenomenal, exceptional sex,*" I had to say after a brief silence, and we all laughed.

When we reached the hotel, Bea went to meet Harold and Angie to surprise Declan (he, like Matthias, thought we'd be coming on the match day). Lana and I went to our rooms to get ready for lunch with my parents. I wanted, as Alex had advised me, to stay close to my parents and the girls. From the moment we'd landed, I hadn't been able to shake the thrill and fear of knowing that Matthias was in the same city as me, this time for a valid reason. Even if we met, nobody would be able to say anything. He was here to play a game, while I was here to watch my country face his. If we met, it'd be nothing strange.

I wanted to slap myself for those thoughts. I shouldn't be wishing to see him at all. I shouldn't be finding excuses and reasons why it'd be ordinary. The weight of these feelings only cemented what I already knew – this was dangerous. It was time to finish it. Once and for all.

I agreed to meet Dad and Mom by the pool in the afternoon, after which they'd go for drinks with friends and I'd probably join them.

"If you want to avoid that," Lana said, "we can go through some projects that you'll be working on after Bea's wedding. There're plenty of emails and files to go through."

"I might do that. Their friends are fun when they talk about football. But when they switch to stocks, shares and real estate…"

"… which is always…"

"… then I just feel like an extra piece of furniture in the room, unable to comment on anything knowledgeably."

"Don't worry, then. It's sorted. I'll tell them these emails cannot wait."

We laughed like little girls who were accomplices in stealing cookies from our grandmother's pantry.

"Did you really think I wouldn't inspect every possible hotel in the city to see if you checked in?" A voice came from behind us. I jumped with fear and Lana screamed.

I recognised the voice instantly, but it took me a couple of seconds to find the source. The emergency exit door was ajar, and Matthias materialised in the frame. When he stepped out into the hallway, his cologne filled it. My stomach flipped.

Angry, still in shock and feeling sorry for Lana, I approached and slapped him with all my power.

"How dare you come here and disturb us?" I hissed, knowing very well I couldn't shout.

The hit had come unexpectedly; he looked equal parts puzzled and hurt.

"What else should I do, when you don't want to see me?" he said quietly and calmly.

I thought he'd be at least as explosive as me. But no, he was looking at me with those dark eyes, more disconsolate than ever.

There was a commotion behind us, probably caused by Lana's scream, and I knew I had to stop anyone from seeing us.

"My room," I said, tilting my head toward my room a couple of doors down, and both of them followed me. When we were safe inside, I turned. Lana still looked confused, while Matthias was staring at me again in his typical manner.

"Do you want to go?" I asked Lana.

"I'm not leaving you with him," she stammered.

"Come on, Lana, I'm not gonna hurt her," Matthias said.

"Not physically. But mentally and emotionally, yes!" she snapped.

"If you think I'm so dangerous, why didn't you save her from that idiot while he was torturing her physically and emotionally for two years?" he raised his voice.

"Matthias!" I intervened. "Stop blaming my friends for my decisions." But it was too late; I saw the shadow of guilt on Lana's face. "Listen, say something rude one more time to my friends and I'll—"

"You'll what?" he was close to shouting, his black eyes flashing in the dim light of my hotel room. "You'll do *what*, Jane? Tell me, please, what worse things are you capable of that you're not already doing to me? We spent a wonderful day together, you met my family, you enjoyed yourself with me, you were *you* with me, and then you just want to disappear and pretend nothing ever happened. Meanwhile, I can't get the pictures of us being happy together out of my mind. It already hurts like nothing I've ever experienced. Just fucking talk to me and let me know where we stand."

I went cold and unstable on my legs. I could feel my knees crumbling while my hands began to shake. What a terrible person I was. It hurt so much more coming from his mouth. For a while, I was stunned, unable to say a word in my defence. He didn't say anything that wasn't true.

Lana sniffed, making me feel even more horrid. "I'll go now because you two have to talk," she said quietly. "But Jane, don't forget you're meeting your parents in a few minutes. And later tonight, we've got work to do. If you need anything, just...let me know." With that, she rushed out, leaving me and Matthias alone in loaded silence.

We didn't move. We only devoured each other with our eyes. I realised I'd been scared and avoiding this meeting for a reason – he'd stirred up everything I'd stifled. Looking at him now, my body and skin ached for his touch. I could almost see the sparks that were firing off between us. I shouldn't be alone with him. I shouldn't have allowed him here. This was a mistake, and the consequences were potentially dreadful.

"Matthias, please," I finally managed to utter. "Don't talk in such a manner to my friends or family. They did nothing wrong. They couldn't have prevented me from staying with Alex."

He took a breath and approached me. I stepped back in fear. Still, he continued until his hands were on my cheeks. I was too scared to look him in the eyes, not now, when he was so close to me. Too close.

"I'm sorry, Jane. I just can't forgive myself for what you went through. I don't know how they can," he said sorrowfully.

"They know me, and they know they couldn't have done anything differently. They were trying hard. I kept them at bay."

"The same way you're keeping me now?"

I sighed, trying to escape his hands, trying to avert his touch that I so truly enjoyed. It made me shiver so strongly that I worried he might feel it.

"You can't throw away everything that happened in Brasília," he continued.

"I know. I can't," I said weakly. "We have to talk and make this right. What we did there should never have happened." I pushed his hands off me. "Don't get me wrong. I enjoyed it all. I loved every minute of it, but it shouldn't have happened." I was swallowing tears and pain. The sooner I finished this, the better. I'd recite everything, he'd go and we'd be forever over. Then I'd go see my parents, and by the time I realised how much pain I was in, I'd already be in São Paulo with Alex.

"Why shouldn't it? The fact that it did happen only means you're not completely fulfilled with him. You're wasting your life while you could actually be complete with me," he persisted.

"That's not true. I love him. I adore him. Not you. You and I are just a temporary delight, and we'd better understand it and move on."

"You don't mean it." He caught me by the arms again. "If you mean it, look me in the eyes and say that you hate me, that you don't care, that you want me gone."

How on Earth was I supposed to do that?

"Look at me, Jane."

His scent was everywhere around me. I took strength from every cell in my body to confront his dark eyes. They watched me, demandingly. "I...I hate you," I stammered. "I don't care. I want you out of my room." It sounded ridiculous.

He laughed, annoyed, not letting go of me. "You've got to try better than these murmurs."

I inhaled and said more loudly, "I hate you, I don't care about you, and I want you out of my room now."

"Slightly better, but still terrible. Come on, Jane, you love only Blondie, you forgave him for everything he did to you, and I'm here being an asshole and stalking you—"

"I hate you!" I screamed, my eyes trained on the ground. "I hate you, Matthias Beller." I forced his hands off my arms. "I don't care about you at all! Get out of my room now and never come back looking for me!"

I only dared to look at him when I finished.
He seemed completely unmoved. The playful curl of his lip, the casual arch of his shoulders – he looked as if I hadn't just thrown a bunch of terrible words to him. He stared at me, sizing me up. In a confounding contradiction, I wished both to throw myself in his arms and to hit him until he finally left.

"You're so damn beautiful," he suddenly said and closed the distance between us. He hugged me so that I had no way of escaping. I looked up into his face, inches from mine, and was mesmerised by the love and emotions for me it depicted. "And you're an excellent actress. I almost believed you! But you cannot hide what we have. It's so strong that the entire world sees it, even though you're someone else's girlfriend." His hand was in my hair, stroking my scalp and sending shivers down my spine. His voice softened, falling over me in a murmur. "Meet me tonight, after you say goodnight to your parents."

"Matthias, I can't—" The thought of it ignited my cold, clammy body.

"Why not? Because Lana won't let you? Come on, you can do whatever you want, Jane. You can meet me tonight, and we'll finally decide what to do about us."

"I told you already—"

"It doesn't count because it was lies."

"Why do you believe I'd say anything different if we meet this evening?"

"I'll make you speak only the truth." He kissed me unexpectedly, shortly. That brief touch set my nerves on fire. I wanted to rebel, to refuse, but he kissed me again. This time, it was prolonged, demanding, laden with wish and lust. And I returned it. It was so beautifully conquering; I couldn't not surrender to it. My body shook and ached when he stopped, disappointed his lips weren't on mine longer. "So, Jane. Tonight. Room 1000. That's the last floor."

I murmured a confirmation. My body and mind felt detached from each other. He kissed me in the same way again, and I couldn't resist diving in completely.

A knock on the door made me jump out of my skin.

"Jane, we're going down. Come on."

I froze with fear like never before in my life.

"Who's that man?" Matthias hissed.

"My father," I whispered back, pushing him towards the bathroom and closing him in there. "Dad, I'm not ready yet!" I fixed my hair quickly and went to open the door to face my parents. "I'm sorry, I was talking to Lana about some projects. I'll get ready and be downstairs in no time."

They didn't suspect anything. "Alright, see you there," Dad said, and they left.

When I shut the door, I leaned back on it, counting seconds and their steps, listening to make sure they didn't return. Matthias left the bathroom and I signalled to him to stay quiet. Still, he approached me and placed his hands on my waist.

"Tonight, Jane?"

The air he carried around himself was too strong for anyone to resist. I was sure it got him everything he wanted in life – the same way he got the answer he wanted from me that day.

"Yes, tonight," I agreed.

He smiled and kissed me, gently, carefully, fully, sucking my lips and showing me it wasn't just a one-sided feeling. I shivered and shook off goosebumps.

When he left, I knew very well it was all a mistake. Another one. I felt like an addict, cursing the drugs but unable to resist the high. Did I have a choice? Could I have done anything any other way? Tonight was my last chance to put an end to this, to us. This was my chance to defy whatever I could possibly feel for him – because it was strong and wild, yes, but it was also flammable and uncertain. While Alex…Alex was love.

Needless to say, I was completely unfocused while talking to my parents at the pool. I wished Lana had been there to help me out when I drifted away, but I had to deal with it on my own. "I'm fine. I'm just exhausted," I kept repeating. Unsuspecting and sympathetic, my parents suggested it'd be best if I skipped the night out with their friends. I agreed, saying I'd already had quite a few drinks with them that would send me to sleep early, but first Lana and I needed to discuss some job offers.

"Alright, just be ready for tomorrow. We're leaving at three for the stadium."

"Of course, Dad. By three I'll already have finished the spa and gym."

"Unless you sleep it all through," he joked.

Good. He trusted that I was tired, not anxious about meeting the crazy German on the top floor of the very same hotel we were lounging outside of.

I returned to my room and told Lana what the plan was. She was upset, of course, but not because I was ditching her for an evening out with a man – which was technically true – rather, she was certain nothing good would come of it. "I completely disagree, but if you come to me tomorrow morning and tell me it's all over between you two, I'll withdraw everything I said and apologise. Actually, it would be best if you tell me that tonight."

"I'll do everything in my power."

"How many times have I heard that, remind me?" I couldn't answer, instead looking at her like a guilty younger sister. "And why are you getting ready as if you're going on a date?"

"I want to feel confident when I stand in front of him and tell him everything."

"Or you want him to keep falling in love with you over and over again – to be blinded by your looks so that he doesn't hear what you're trying to make clear to him?"

I sighed. She knew me better than I knew myself. "No," I stuttered, "I only want to look decent when I walk out on him. I can't be shabby."

"It doesn't matter. What's important is what you'll tell him. This dress will just make it more difficult for him."

"It's a basic black dress," I rebelled.

She rolled her eyes. "I see there's no point arguing with you. Go now, so that you come back as soon as possible. If you need me, call me. Bea and Angie are also here. If he becomes violent, they'll get the guys—"

"Lana, he's not like that."

"How do you know anything about him, anyway?"

Sensing there was no winning here, I left her question unanswered. Taking only my clutch, phone and room key, I left. In the elevator, I texted Alex that I loved him. *I love you, too*, he replied, which squeezed my heart painfully. I swallowed the ache, his love, the image of him waiting for me alone in his bed, trusting fully in me. I pushed down everything before the elevator opened on the top floor of the hotel.

The hallway was long, but there weren't many doors in it – only three, actually: Rooms 1000, 1001 and 1002. A light beam was cast on the floor in front of the one I was supposed to enter. It was the farthest from the elevator, and I knew he'd left it ajar on purpose.

I was blinded by the chandelier lights inside Room 1000. It was dazzlingly illuminated like a sky of constant fireworks. It took my eyes a couple of seconds to adjust to the brightness. This room was far more luxurious than the others where we'd stayed. It was more spacious, with higher ceilings and larger windows, some of them even stretching from the floor. Everything was in hues of white, gold and burgundy red. It was a proper Presidential suite. The room was so big that when I ran over it with my eyes, I couldn't find Matthias at first, and I was momentarily terrified that I'd walked into the wrong place. But then he came into my view, walking in from an adjacent area separated only by an arch.

He smiled and stared at me. "Damn it, you're the most mesmerising woman on Earth."

I didn't reply; I just approached him coldly. Behind him, there was a wide, rectangular table set up for a dinner for two, with food neatly covered by domes, different wine glasses and champagne flutes next to plates, and an opulent candlestick.

"What is this?" I asked, a mixture of anger and excitement rising in me.

"It's a dinner table."

"Matthias, don't joke," I snapped. "We were supposed to just talk."

"Is that why you got dressed up?" He sized me up with a smirk.

I looked at him furiously. "I'm always dressed up, if you hadn't noticed."

"You are, of course. But tonight, something's different on you."

He didn't give me the chance to ask what, because he caught me by the arms and dragged me into a kiss. At first, I didn't defend myself, allowing myself that overpowering pleasure for a guiltily long moment. But then I pushed him away.
"Stop it," I hissed.

"Sit down, you need a drink to relax." He gestured to the table.

"Stop it, Matthias. This is not funny. We need to talk and make it short. I told you everything earlier today. What else do you want to know? Why have you forced me here? What do you want from me?"

His face became stern while I offloaded my frustration on him. He seemed pretty serious now. "The tournament will be over in less than a week," he said gravely. "We'll win it again. I don't want surprises like last time. I want to take you home because you belong with me. You're happy with me, and I'm not letting you go through another couple of years or even a lifetime in prison with that man. He may be good and true, a committed Prince Charming to everyone else, but he's not what you need. You and I, Jane – we are the perfect match you've been longing for. I want us to be together after this is over."

I turned my gaze away, gathering strength, preparing the sentences and clauses that would successfully refute everything he'd just said.

"Would you please take a seat?" he added. "This is not a conversation to be had standing."

I took one of the chairs. Matthias reached for a white wine bottle from the ice bucket and looked at me in question. I nodded, and he went on to open it and pour it.

Alright, Step One: I shouldn't get drunk. That would ruin everything I was supposed to do. Step Two: fighting and shouting at him would also produce zero effect. Loud words never reached him; in fact, he'd always won those arguments. Therefore, I had to be calm, composed and reasonable.

I took a sip of the delicious wine and put the glass back on the table, taking a deep breath. He was only looking at me, earnest and patient. It was on me to cut the silence.

"Thank you very much for the wine, it's excellent," I began. "However, I'm sorry about the food. I won't eat – I had snacks with my parents before I came."

"No problem, we've got enough wine."

"Matthias, tell me now, please, without hesitation, without drama, without lying – why do you want me? How can you want me after everything?"

He played with an empty glass in his fingers.
"Because from the moment I first saw you, I've known something about you is different. And because every time we meet, my feelings of attachment and infatuation for you are stronger. When we're together, when we talk, when we touch, I feel in every cell and nerve of my body

that it is right, that it is how it's supposed to be. What you did with those other men while seeing me – of course, it infuriated me. Of course, I was jealous. But it meant nothing, neither to them nor to you. I didn't need to put you through two years of pain to understand that—"

"Alex didn't—"

"Let me finish." I went quiet and sipped more wine. Matthias continued, "I know it seems unreasonable, and I've thought about it numerous times. I should hate you for cheating on me, too, for lying to me while you were also lying to Yanov. It should warn me of your character and make me stay away, but...the fact is, you were no one's woman then, Jane." I narrowed my eyes. "You cared about Yanov, but you two hadn't even been dating for a year then. You were more interested in what was going around you. You were collecting 'trophies,' if that's how we can refer to those idiots. You were their trophy, too. I beat the shit out of Lens when he explained to me how he could go after you knowing how mad I already was about you. He only wanted another trophy, he said. Same with Friedrich. Same with Rolf."

Those bastards went through my mind. Of course, I was a trophy for them. I just hoped they'd keep it to themselves forever. Coach Gottfried had unleashed once. Hopefully, he'd stay quiet, like the others.

"I thought a lot about it in the weeks following the tournament. How was I so sure about you, moments after I'd found out what had happened? When you ran down the stands to congratulate me, I was certain you'd already decided and were coming to stay with me forever. It was beyond beautiful – the sight of you approaching me with millions of flags waving around you when I'd just won the gold. I knew even then I'd forgiven you." He inhaled deeply. "I had no clue the worst years in my life were to commence."

Some urge of decency made me stretch out my hand to cover his. It didn't feel right to prevent it. "I'm sorry, Mati. I'm really sorry."

"I know you are. But what has made me angry every single night after you left is that you've always felt more sorry for him, and that it's won every single time. You can't leave him because you're sorry, because of what he'll go through after you break up, because of how the world will react to that, how they will support him and make fun of him. It's always been stronger than our love."

"Doesn't that tell you something?" I whispered. His eyes were despondent but I couldn't lie to him, not tonight, not now. "I'm not just sorry for Alex. I do love him. He's the most wonderful, caring and accomplished man. He's truly been making me happy. We've been through everything at such a young age. We've matured together. He's forgiven me. We've grown our destinies together." It hurt me to see Matthias in pain like this, but it was not the time to hide or sugar-coat anything. He needed to hear the truth so that he could let me go. No matter how much it devastated me; the time for selfishness was over. "You are special to me, you know that," I continued after he didn't speak. "When I said I loved you, it was true every time, and you know it. But it's a different kind of love. Trust me, I can imagine our life together sometimes, but in the long run, the more deeply I think about it, I realise it'd never work."

"Why wouldn't it?" He squeezed my hand. "Haven't I proven I'd do anything for you? Haven't I shown I'd do whatever you say or demand, to make you happy? I'd move to London to live with you, I'd even go to the U.S. if you decided to be closer to your parents or work there. I'd require my coach to never speak badly about you and instead to respect you like royalty. You gave me everything I thought a woman of this world could never possess. You have it all. You're intelligent, bright, brisk, funny, understanding, adventurous, lively and beyond gorgeous. I love everything about you, Jane."

I let go of his hand; his words hurt me too badly when paired with the warmth of his palm. "You don't get it," I said, taking the wine glass with shaky fingers. "You don't get anything."

"What is it that I don't get?" he shouted so loud that the brass dishes on the table tremored. I flinched. "You're right! I don't get what it is that prevents us from being openly together, since we're made to be so. And don't tell me it's your love for Yanov, because I don't trust it. When you love someone, you don't sleep with other men, and you don't put them in jail and torture their mental well-being. When you love someone, you fly over Amazonia without your coach knowing about it, and you sneak out to see them, exactly as the two of us have been doing since we arrived in Brazil. Why is it so hard to admit it, move on and leave bad habits behind?"

His explosive burst of frustration woke the dragon in me. I stood up and swatted my hand furiously across the table, knocking over the candlestick, some food and a wine bottle.

"Don't you *dare* twist my emotions that I so clearly drew out for you!" I screamed back at him. "And don't call Alex a bad habit, because he is far from that. He is so much more. He is a wonderful man who'd give his life for me, who's already sacrificed himself for me and for us. As for you and me – from the first day here, I've been telling you to give up and leave me alone. Every time we met, it was because you forced me and threatened to tell someone. And don't tell me you wouldn't, because I can see now that you are absolutely out of your mind and capable of anything. That's the difference between Alex and you! That's why I chose him and not you! He hasn't told anyone what I did to him. He kept it away from my parents, no matter how hard it was, to protect me, to protect us. While *you*, you'd destroy my life just to get me."

"I forced you?" he growled back. "I forced you to come?"

"Yes! Otherwise, I'd never even consider going anywhere with you. I'd never have been alone in a room with you, or anywhere close to you."

"Yet you loved that night out with me. And you are here again. Did you tell your boyfriend Mr Perfect that you were about to see me tonight?"

I hesitated for a second, catching my breath. "No, but only not to worry him."

"Yeah, sure!" He threw the chair between us at the wall, where it broke with a loud *crack*. "Damn it, Jane, you're still refusing to admit it." He caught me by the arms, tighter than he ever had. "You are here because you love me and want me. Look at you, you've been shaking from the moment you entered the room. Why do you keep lying to yourself?"

My blood pressure rose to a dangerous height. "It's passion, Matthias," I said. "Have you heard of that? What we feel is passion. It's not permanent. It's like a firework – it would be beautiful for some time but then die out and be forgotten in a couple of weeks." I removed his hands from me again. "So, what would you like to happen? That I break up with Alex and go public with you? That we go back to Germany, or London, and just ignore everything and everyone? Are you stupid? I am me because of the media and other people. I am a model, an actress. I'm on billboards and magazine covers, in shop windows and music videos. That's who I am and what I love doing. I'm useless at anything else. If people don't like me, I don't exist. What do you think would happen to me after I ditch Alex and go with you? I'll tell you what – the entire world would be against me. And *forget* about my parents. To put it shortly – Mom would perhaps talk to me, but I wouldn't be so sure about it, because Dad wouldn't allow her to. And *my dad*...ha! Killing me physically would be the only thing he wouldn't do. Apart from that, he'd made sure the world forgot he ever had a daughter. He'd blacklist my name and stop me from even trying to contact him or approach his house. Alex's life would be destroyed, because everyone would then know that I'd actually cheated on him with you, and they'd conclude I'd been doing it all these years. But fine, you don't care about him. You care about yourself. Only yourself. And you? Well, your life would be so much easier. You'd go on playing your football and keep getting great contracts and offers because the general public doesn't need to like you – you only need coaches to like you, and to score goals. And then what, Matthias? What would we do then? I wouldn't have any friends except Bea, Lana and Angie, I wouldn't have any work to do because nobody would hire me. When I'd go out, I'd only receive bad publicity and dirty looks. So let's say we'd get a large, secluded house somewhere, where I'd go crazy roaming around alone, because, well, my friends have their lives to live. You'd be the only person to love me and care about me. Perhaps we'd go for some dinners and events together, but the newspapers would want photos of only you, not with that slut Jane, so I'd stand on the side alone because nobody would ever want to talk to me, and even if some of them would, it'd be out of pity and courtesy towards you. Then what happens next? I'd become clingy and completely dependent on you and your love and attention. If you don't come home on time, I'd start thinking about who you're with or what you're doing. Jealousy would eat my common sense in a matter of weeks. And you know what else will happen? You'll start thinking about everything I did. Perhaps your coach will give you some mean hints – you know he's capable of it – and you'd slowly start despising me. You'd be sick of me and my possessive, needy attitude, and then you'd leave me and look for someone more decent and honest, more pure. There's no way our reality could live up to the fantasy you have been thinking of for the last four years. In this hypothetical miserable life you'd even resent me for having wasted years of your life chasing an impossible dream, knowing full well I'm capable of loving two men? And then what? My life would be destroyed, my parents' lives, Alex's life! I do deserve it, but not them. Is that what you want us to do? Is that what you think is right? Because of our passion?"

"It's not just passion, for goodness sake! You're saying all this, but there's so much you're not taking into consideration." I'd been shouting but his voice now was way louder. "You recited out all the bad scenarios, but what if the opposite happens, which I'm actually pretty sure of? What if we're made for each other? What if we're actually meant to be? What if this love's so strong it'll defeat all the anger your parents may feel, and all the bad comments and opinions we'll be bombarded with? What if you bloom by my side and begin getting more and more job offers because your appeal and energy can't be subdued? What if we become the new perfect couple, this time for something real, because you naturally go with me more than with him? What if your parents grow fond of me after seeing how much I care and how we complement each other? What if there is another woman out there waiting to be Yanov's perfect match, more than you, not because you're not perfect, but because he needs someone different? Are you going to be responsible for him never being entirely happy? What if everything falls into its right place after you become my woman in front of everyone?"

He took me into his arms and I had no way of escaping.

Tears and pain were burning my eyes and I fought my hardest to keep them from surfacing. The thought of Alex with another woman infuriated me. Just as the thought of the man in front of me with another woman did. Why was it so difficult to let him go?

"You have to give up on me, Matthias," I stuttered. "That'll never happen. It's all dreams and fantasies. You're not realistic."

He took my face in his hands and made me look into those tumultuous, coal-black eyes. "Do you know I have never given up on anything or anyone in my life, Jane? I'm not giving up on you because of some worries you've invented in your head."

"What would it take for you to set me free? What else should I say or do to make you understand we can't be together?" I said in a quivering voice.

"I want you, Jane," he whispered on my lips. "Even if the whole world falls apart into shards, I only need you."

There was immense strength in his words, immeasurable affection. I felt warmth and care for him, alongside an overwhelming urge to be closer, to feel his skin, his touch, to break forever this bond. His eyes were stormy, a hurricane of desperate joy that we were holding each other; and behind that, I saw roiling pain at all the words I'd said. I stretched up on my tiptoes just slightly, and he bent his head down so that he could kiss me, at first slowly and gently, and then deeply and committedly.

I spread my fingers over his back, drawing on his shirt, diving deeper into the kiss and relaxing into his hands that held my shoulders and hips. I gasped for air and continued, my eyes closed, absorbing the feeling of joy and the fire rising inside my chest that threatened to engulf my entire body. The urge we felt for each other had been stifled for too long; the surrender now came all at once, as a broken, defeated dam.

My hands found the buttons of his shirt and unfastened them one by one. When the fabric was somewhere on the floor along with the broken tableware, I put my fingers in his hair and bent on his solid body, shivering at every spot where his bare skin touched mine. He found the small zipper of my dress along my spine and moved it down, gliding with the entire surface of his hands over my back. I didn't know that touch would feel so divine. I surrendered to it entirely, twisting in the want for more.

I found his belt and opened it. His trousers found his shirt on the floor quickly. Our breathing accelerated dangerously. Finally, after all these years, we were about to do what was missing. We were going to make our relationship complete. After this, we'd know.

I shivered in excitement and fear, still not separating myself from his lips that so generously treated mine. His palms wandered over my shoulders and pushed aside the straps of the dress. It joined his clothes on the floor. He pressed my body to his and moaned between kisses. I understood him. It was almost painful, the want we had for each other.

Having stepped out of my sandals, I was now even shorter than him. He caught me by the hips and lifted me in the air. I hugged him with my legs and arms, diving head-first into this forbidden but necessary madness. He carried me towards the bed in the main room, which wasn't as destroyed as the one we'd just left. If his kisses had me brimming like this, I couldn't get out of my head what I'd feel in the next couple of hours.

He sat on the soft sheets and placed me in his lap. My breasts were level with his eyes now, so when I looked down at him, he returned the gaze, his eyes full of stars.

"You are perfect, Jane."

I knew what he meant. We had been almost naked like this before, but this time, the knowledge of what would follow added a special thread of magic to everything. He kissed my neck, slowly, patiently, carefully not to leave any marks, and then moved down towards my cleavage. He was gentle, making me moan and sigh and arch my back, demanding more. He kissed my breasts with worshipping lips, making me wonder how I could have avoided him all this time.

His fingers found the latch of my bra and disconnected it. For the first time that evening, I felt shy, as if I were a virgin being exposed in front of a man for the first time. In front of the man I had strong feelings for.

My body shook and tremored in pleasure and anticipation. His hands never let me escape too far from his lips, whose piercing touch was both cooling and burning my skin. He sucked my nipples carefully and greedily, taking his time, ignoring my screams. My fingers were running from his hair to his solid, smooth shoulder blades and back. The fire in the bottom of my belly felt like powerful, dangerous fuming lava, and I could sense he was equally excited. I gathered the courage to grab his face, separating his tongue from my sensitive skin.

Wordlessly, I kissed him, my eyes wide open. He understood what he needed to do.

Taking me easily by the thighs, Matthias placed me on my back, never disconnecting his mouth from mine. His hands lowered to the fabric of my underwear and slid them off slowly, sending goosebumps across every inch of my skin. I felt shyer than ever before, but at the same time, I was overwhelmed with desire. I let him walk his tongue over my body, from my neck to between my breasts, over my belly, my navel, and then lower, kissing each of my hipbones and going lower still. When he took hold of my knees to separate them, I began shaking with anticipation.

He saw it all, but for once, he didn't have that overly self-confident expression on his face. He was in a trance, in disbelief – like me – that all this was happening, that we were here, together, doing it all, making love, after so many long years.

Next, Matthias kissed my knee and started lining up touches, brushing his mouth up my inside thigh. Then he did the same on the other side, this time placing a rough touch on the warmest spot of my body. I yelled in desperation, completely overpowered by the guilty, animal sensuality that electrified me. I knew what he wanted to do, but I felt scared I'd shatter into smithereens if he did it. I didn't want that; I wanted our first time to be together, in unison.

Tenderly, I pulled his head up by his dark hair and made him stop. His eyes, momentarily confused, reached an immediate understanding when he met mine and saw the hunger in them. He was standing by the bed, so much taller than me even when I sat up. Without dropping eye contact, I reached for his boxers and moved them down, kissing his stone-solid abs. He knew what I wanted. He bent over me, encircling me with his arms as I stretched back on the bed. I spread my legs as he leaned into my hips. I thought I would burn out into ashes from the heat that emanated from us.

He stroked my hair and pushed a stray strand away from my face. "I love you, Jane. I always will."

It struck me harder than ever, because it was all true. I could clearly see it in his wonderful coal-black eyes, on his face that depicted only affection and fondness. I pulled him into an embrace, pressing my fingers into his firm shoulders, wishing I could hug him tight enough that our cells might fuse and we become one.

He moved his hips slowly and began entering me, easily, patiently. In the first instance, it filled me with bliss. It was beautiful; he was beautiful, so loving and caring. I stirred under him and let him relax onto me, into me, fully.

I moaned loudly from the all-encompassing wave of pleasure, pain, love, fulfilment and completeness that filled me entirely. I hadn't expected it would be this strong – my whole body went numb with ignited nerves.

He moved back, but I stopped him.

"No, Mati, please, stay there…" I panted. "Stay still in me for a while." When he placed himself fully again into me, I sighed again, absorbing all the wonderful, splendid emotions that his body was awakening in me.

He observed my face, smiling. "The number of nights I've dreamed about this…it's beyond infinite."

I smiled back. "I love you, Mati."

He kissed me on the forehead, then my nose and then my mouth. His lips on mine again, as we breathed as one, he began moving his hips, sending wave after wave after wave of luxurious delight over me, through us. My legs were clenched over his body while I sobbed his name and absorbed everything greedily, as if what he was giving me now was essential for my next breath. I came once strong, and then again, stronger, and *again*, even stronger, thinking my body would completely disconnect after he reached what he was aiming for.

When he roared in a voice I'd never heard from him before, a new surge of elation spread all over me, and I joined him. I felt him warm in my stomach, and the victorious sensation deepened my orgasm, too. When he hid his face in my tangled hair, I was still twitching in the remnants of bliss.

His body was fully over mine, and after a while, he shifted, making as if to move.

"No," I begged him again. "Stay in me."

"I'm not too heavy?"

"No, I enjoy it."

He laughed and pushed himself up only slightly, supporting his torso with his strong arms around me. "Can we have a heated-up argument like that again?" he asked.

I jokingly slapped him, keeping my hands on his face that was full of love for me. "We always have a heated-up argument when we meet."

"Yes, which means every time we can finish it like this, until we learn how to reach this no-clothes situation without arguing."

I burst out laughing. "What if we kill each other?"

"I won't let that happen. This is too good not to be availed of."

I laughed again and drew him into a kiss. "It was beautiful, Mati, unexpectedly beautiful. Different than…anything I've had before."

"I told you," he murmured through a kiss. "We need each other, Jane. It's inhumane how much."

I moved my lower back slightly but then felt a twitch in my stomach. He was moving, too. "No…" I whispered in a cracking voice.

"Yes." He smiled and kissed me. His hand found my breast and teased it until the arousal reignited in me.

Where all this was coming from, I didn't know. Perhaps it was due to all the years we'd been apart when we were supposed to be together. Was it possible that I'd made a grave mistake four years ago? Should I really have chosen this man instead of Alex, the wonderful being that he was? This was beyond sex, beyond lovemaking. It was everything two compatible souls could cherish and grow for each other. Had I been right or wrong for ditching it all because of my principles and protectiveness of an innocent man?

Matthias was already large in me, and he moved passionately, hungry for me, eager for our next peak of pleasure and bliss. I wanted to join this prohibited – or perhaps permitted – ride, not just to take it. So I pushed him aside and rolled on top of him, not separating our hips for a moment. He straightened up, hugging my back and pulling my hair while I rocked and swayed over him, my warm insides enveloping him, taking it fully, deeply, giving him all he could possibly ever want from a woman, because at the same time, I wanted to be the one who'd give him something he'd never forget, something he'd never have with anyone else.

His fingers in my hair made me arch my back so that he could dive into my breasts – not so gently this time. I loved it and demanded more, but he stopped when I heard his first loud moans. I felt his intense orgasm approaching, and I let myself loose again. He shouted my name, and after the liquid warmth filled me again, we crashed on the bedsheets fighting for air, holding hands tightly.

*****

When I awoke, my eyes flew open in fear that I'd slept for hours and missed my precious time with Matthias. We were cuddled up under the blanket, my head resting on his chest.

Awake, he looked down at me and chuckled, planting a kiss on my hair. "It's only been twenty minutes," he said, setting my mind at ease. "There's no happier man in the universe right now. I don't know if I'll ever sleep properly again."

"Don't joke like that. You have a game tomorrow." I was drawing over his solid chest with my fingers.

"I do. And I'll win, because of this. You cannot imagine the relief."

"You're right, I cannot." I sighed. "I still have the difficult part to do," I said before thinking better about it, surprising myself. It both was and wasn't a big surprise. It felt like I'd somehow forced my own hand; I couldn't go back to Alex after what I'd done with this man.

Matthias put his thumb and forefinger on my chin and titled my face up to look him in the eyes. "Don't worry, it'll all be fine. We'll do it together if necessary."

"We'll see." I swallowed hard, and the pain of everything that would follow once I admitted to Alex that we could not continue our lives together hit me hard in the belly and almost left me without air. I'd better not think about it now. "I'll talk to him after his final match. I'm not going to do anything that could affect Ukraine's outcome at this competition."

"Fair enough."

It all seemed like some vague, foggy dream. In Matthias's bed, talking about breaking up with Alex seemed easy and natural, like the right thing to do. All the love and feelings for Alex that I'd always cherished were still there, but a new one appeared – the feeling that he really didn't deserve me. A wonderful man like Alex Yanov deserved someone who'd be only his, who'd be able to shake off anyone else who courted her, who wouldn't give her body to anyone else but him. I loved him with my entire body and mind, and yet here I was with Matthias. Alex didn't deserve it.

"Mati, I'd like to know something." A question crossed my mind and I needed to force the painful thoughts out. "Why are you so idiotically stubborn?"

He laughed. "It's always brought me good. And you, too."

I scoffed. "It's brought me stress and tumult, but we'll talk about it some other time. Tell me, why are you so hard-headed? You're stubborn when you play, when you talk to your teammates and friends, and, of course, when it's about me?"

He straightened up and I watched his face while he talked.

"Honestly, I think it all started when I was nine and we got a new coach," he began. "I don't remember much of my life before that, but that crossroads I do remember, very clearly. I used to be a shy kid, actually—"

"Hah!" I couldn't suppress my laugh. "You're not being honest now."

"I am. You can ask my parents."

"Alright, go on."

"I was rather quiet but still played well. But that new coach seemed to hate me, at least that was how it looked to me then. Of course, a grown man has no reason to hate a kid he came to teach. Everyone noticed he was stricter with me than with others. If my friends made mistakes, he told them calmly what to correct and how, but with me, he had no patience, he always shouted."

"Did you tell your parents?"

"No. Everyone would have called me weak and soft. I was adamant on enduring it. It kept getting worse, though, which confused me greatly because I was becoming an excellent footballer and yet he always had something to reprimand me for. It went on for two years. I was the best in the school team, and also in the team where I trained with him – still, he always had something negative to point out. Until one day, when I exploded at him."

"What did you tell him?"

"'What do you want from me?'"

"And What did he say?"

"He said, 'I want you to be the leader, the main driver of your team, the one who pulls forward when everyone's down, and for that, you have to be made of steel. You must be strong, stubborn and persistent, because you have the potential for all that.' It stayed with me forever, every single word."

"Sorry, but you're not the captain of either Die Mannschaft or your club." I was confused.

"I'm not, but who's the guy who shouts most, argues with referees, always runs for balls that seem lost, and pushes others to try harder?"

I answered with a smile, understanding it better. "Was the coach still terrible to you after that?"

"Yes, but I wasn't affected by it anymore. His words only fuelled my energy and motivation. I learnt from him that if I wanted anything in life, I could have it. I was already the best in my generation. I wanted to reach the A-team – I managed it. I wanted to be a national player – I managed it. I wanted great sponsorship deals – I got them. Whichever girl I liked – I got her. So when I set my eyes on you, well, you know what happened." He caught both my hands and drew me to his chest. "You have no idea how happy I am now."

I kissed him instead of an answer, feeling his hands on my back already.

"I'm a bit thirsty," I said stirring between his hands. "What do you think we open that champagne you got?"

"Great idea. I'll get it!" He was already half out of the sheet.

"No, I'll get it," I said, pushing him back into bed. I wanted him to look at me while I walked naked around the room. I wanted him to see what he had, what woman was now by his side. "You're drinking tonight?"

I picked up the champagne bottle and one flute, and when I turned, I could see I was right – he was devouring me with his eyes.

"This night is special, I am," he said, still mesmerised as I approached him.

He sat on the edge of the bed, and it was now my turn to absorb his perfect, fully naked body. I passed him the bottle to open and held the glass for him to pour. The fresh champagne danced and bubbled inside. After taking a sip, I handed it to him and then stood between his legs. His free hand found my thigh and stroked it, sending pleasant shivers over my skin.

I could see fire in his eyes. He sipped the bubbly liquid and passed it back to me. The moment the glass was safe in my hands, he grabbed my breast and sucked at it roughly. I couldn't help letting out a stifled cry. He kept his mouth on me while his hand began sliding over my ass. I was already wet again, but I let him give me more of that bliss, drinking up his adoration like I drank the champagne. I finished the glass and threw it to the side, crossing my arms around his neck and guiding his lips over my breasts. Seeing how erect he was – and so focused on giving to me – I straddled his legs and sat on him, taking him in entirely.

He groaned again and hugged me with all his might. I moved aggressively, stoking the fire in his eyes, making him lose his head.

"Damn it, Jane, you are out of this world," he panted, looking me in the eyes. "I thought I already loved you the most a man could love a woman, but now I see it was just a trickle of what I feel now."

I laughed like a witch. "Is that your heart talking, or…?" I looked down.

He surprised me by standing up; I held my legs and arms around him tight.

"All of me, Jane."

He placed me on my back and entered me more deeply, roughly, demandingly, possessively, not for a moment neglecting my breasts or lips. I loved the sensations he invoked in me. I melted under him completely.

CHAPTER 12

It did feel odd, waking up in bed next to a man who wasn't Alex. Odd and wrong.

I didn't have time to ponder over it, because we both needed to rush – I to meet my friends, he for breakfast with the rest of the team – and we'd overslept, for obvious reasons.

"I wish we could have breakfast together like last time, without rushing," he said.

"There'll be time for that, don't worry. But for now, making it to your hotel on time is the most important," I replied, feigning cheerfulness.

He was in too much of a hurry to notice anything strange going on with me, for which I was thankful. I needed him full of the joy and enthusiasm he'd woken up with, and concentrated on the match that was taking place that day. I observed him as he put on his clothes. He was still that perfect, handsome Greek statue that I'd touched last night, the entire night. The same man who'd given me immense pleasure. But guilt began waking up, stirring in me like ingested poison. How could I do this to Alex?

I put on my clothes in between passionate kisses, each kiss reminding me why I'd succumbed to it all, why leaving Alex still made sense.

I let Matthias leave first, and then I left for my room ten minutes later to take a quick bath and prepare for the long day ahead. Immediately after the match, we'd take a flight back to São Paulo. There was no time to waste.

My legs and muscles hurt from the hours of wonderful sex, and my stomach roared to make its emptiness known, finally making me chuckle.

I called Lana to let her know I'd head down to the restaurant in a few minutes. She picked up instantly.

"No, honey, we're coming there," she said strictly, and I knew there was no point arguing. Instead, I ordered breakfast for everyone.

They arrived well before the room service did, and judging by how they stomped in on their heels, they were furious.

"Out," Lana demanded. "Spit it out, now. Everything."

"She doesn't need to spit out anything. It's obvious what happened," Angie stepped in, looking at me in a way that could freeze the sun.

"I...something happened," I began, "something significant. And I've made some decisions..."

I didn't feel a single drop of the certainty and confidence I had the evening before, when I'd talked it all through with Matthias. This reticent, fragile girl – who was she? Where was the woman I'd been last night?
I told the girls what'd happened, from the moment I stepped into his room, to the wine, the shouting, the kissing, the more shouting, the intercourse that followed and the rational decisions we'd come to. I couldn't stay with Alex any longer. It was the only right path for me to take.

"I...I cannot be with him," I stammered. "It doesn't make any sense. What happened with Matthias was something I've never had with anyone. It was wild and explosive, and wonderful. Apart from that, he's fought for me all this time, all these years, while he could have had any girl he wanted. Me going back to Alex after all this – what would it mean? I cheated on him four years ago. I cheated on him yesterday. He...he deserves better than me." Again that pang of jealousy at the thought of him with another woman, hugging her, kissing her, giving her what he was giving me. It was odd. And completely wrong. "I can't go on with him any longer. Matthias is the right one for me," I ended my speech quietly, not believing my own words at all, expecting the three women who knew me best to believe them.

Grave silence ensued. The girls stared at me, shocked, their faces twisted in disapproval and disbelief, sadness and anger. It lasted for too long, throwing me back again to the foggy morning with Matthias. Was it really the right thing that I was about to do?

Angie was the only one standing; Bea, Lana and I were sitting motionless at the untouched breakfast table. Angie approached me, her eyes firing off sparks. I felt scared, nervous like a trapped animal as she bent over me.

She slapped me. As hard as she could, or I was pretty sure, at least – I hadn't been slapped ever up until then. My head turned ninety degrees and the sound of the impact reverberated through the silent room. It wasn't the burning of my cheek that hurt me numb. It was the shock of what she'd done.

"*Are you out of your sick mind?*" Angie shouted, making the windows shudder. I turned back to look at Bea and Lana, who hadn't even blinked, and I knew they agreed. Angie was more infuriated than I'd ever seen her before. "That bloody unyielding imbecile gave you his dick, and now you want to throw away everything you've built with a wonderful man who loves you to death and who you love beyond that? Is that what you want to do?" She grabbed my shoulders and shook me. "*Is that what you want to do*, Jane? Did you forget Paris? Did you forget everything that happened there? You forgot you would rather have died of anorexia than leave Alex? You could have searched for this idiot then, but you didn't. Doesn't that tell you which one of them is more important? And do you remember those awful months in Dallas? You must not, but I do. You were crying every single day for Alex. For *him*, not for this hard-headed prick. If he truly loved you as much as he claims, he'd let you choose for yourself. He'd watch you be happy with the man who loves you with his heart and soul, and he'd respect your choices and not try to ruin them. Does Alex treat you bad? If he did, well, then I'd be the first one to encourage the cocky bastard to come and save you. But that's not the case. Let me tell you something that somebody should've told you a long time ago." A new wave of fear enveloped me. I was sure I wasn't ready for anything Angie would splash out on me now in this fist of furore. Her voice dropped to a low, vicious hiss. "*Matthias doesn't care about you.* He only wants you because you're the most beautiful woman in the world, and he can't get over the fact that you ditched and embarrassed him in front of millions and went for Alex, who, in his opinion, is of much lower value. He wants to cure his hurt pride by taking you from Alex. He wants to hurt him and prove himself. Matthias is a stubborn, irritating man who people love only because he scores goals. Apart from that, he doesn't have even one percent of the greatness that Alex possesses. If you're wondering why the sex was so good, well, it's not that deep. You two have built up that ridiculous longing for each other, and he's spread enough legs in his twenty-eight years of age to know what he's doing. It means nothing, and if you go with him, he'll ditch you in a year or two. He's not doing all this on purpose. He doesn't even see it. He thinks he's madly in love with you, but the fact is, he's just healing his inner wounds and traumas from god knows when, when he didn't get what he wanted. I'll say it again, Jane: If you choose Matthias, you're going to your doom, you foolish woman. You know why? Because your condition has a diagnosis. You're not the only one! I'm the same. Why do you think I keep jumping from bed to bed with different men? Significantly older, younger than me, anyone. Why do I start all my relationships with sex? Because my father was exactly like yours. He rarely hugged or praised me, I was constantly afraid of him and his disappointment, and I missed him. Gottfried was right when he said it last time – we just didn't realise then it was true. It's nothing to be ashamed of, but you have to learn to live with it and not succumb to it. You have to decide. Either you are single, trying all the men who come your way, or you are a committed and faithful woman. You can't go around messing up other people's lives."

She was right. I knew it that same moment. She was right about everything. That was what I was doing – walking around life, pretending to have a job and a purpose but living off my father's name and destroying lives. One thing I was certain of at that moment was that I loved Alex. He was my other half; he was the man for me. I'd nearly gone to my own grave with misery over not having Alex; something I could never say about Matthias. Perhaps we'd met too young, but I wasn't letting him go. Angie reminded me of all the reasons for that.

However, I thought of Matthias and everything wonderful we'd experienced last night, how much we loved – or thought we loved – each other, the thought of his elated face when I told him I'd break up with Alex, and those coal-black eyes that would turn devastated once I said to them I'd again changed my mind. It hurt me tremendously, and I surprised everyone by bursting into tears.

Angie was the first to hug me, and then Bea and Lana joined, too. They didn't interrupt me. I sobbed, yelled, coughed, shouted in a mutilated voice...every part of my body ached, physically as well as emotionally. I had to end this. I mustn't put myself in the same situation again. This had to be over.

After a while, when my tears dried up, I cleaned my face with tissues and took a few deep breaths.

And I made up my mind.

I'd see Alex that same evening. Then I'd know how I felt about him. Based on that, I'd decide whether I'd stay with him or go with Matthias. Whatever the decision, I'd wait for the end of the tournament. My heart pounded for only Matthias last night. If our love was real, then it'd be stronger than what Alex and I had built over almost five years. If I felt the smallest prickle of doubt when I faced Alex tonight, I wouldn't put him through any more cheating, and I'd go with Matthias, even if the whole world and my parents were against us. Alex was more important. He was worthy of someone who'd be fully his.

I didn't say that to the girls, but I assured them I was on the right track. They didn't want to inquire too much. Time was short, and we needed to start getting ready and making me look presentable for the world. Bea and Lana left to get ready in their rooms, but Angie brought her dress and makeup pouch and stayed with me. After I took a scalding-hot shower, she suggested she do a face treatment for me to remedy the swelling around my eyes from crying.

I was almost asleep under her fingers when she whispered, "I'm sorry if I was too tough on you. But you're my best friend. I love you."

I straightened up to give her a hug. "You are my older sister. You don't have to apologise for anything. Without the three of you, I'd be a completely lost cause."

*****

When I showed up to meet my parents in a strapless dark-red A-line dress and white sandals, I looked more stunning than I'd expected I could on such a day. Angie's help with my makeup and hair had paid off; whenever I passed by a mirror, I was assured I looked dazzling.

I was anxious about the match, of course, but knew I supported England wholeheartedly. I needed Germany away from Ukraine and Matthias out of my sight as soon as possible. On the other hand, I didn't want to see my country against Alex's in the final game. I behaved as if Milan Andreyevich's team had already won their ticket for the last day of the tournament, but only because I strongly believed they would win against the Dutch tomorrow.

Up in the stands, I accepted all the drinks that came our way. It helped a lot, especially during the national anthems. I was proudly singing mine and trying to ignore the joyous half of the Estadio Mineirão that sang *Das Lied der Deutschen*.

It was thunderous and wild after the first whistle. I avoided looking at Matthias, but he was so active, aggressive and magnetic that it was impossible not to see him. Matthias's spotlight on the big screen was rivalled only by Joshua Hadleigh, who used any chance he had to attack, and Simon Wade, who had numerous excellent saves in defence.

Nothing, however, could stop Michael Krimm from taking a long pass from the middle and heading alone through two English defencemen. He managed to trick them, feigning right and shooting left; the net behind Harold Dare's back shook.

We didn't want to despair too early. It was only the nineteenth minute and our team was playing equally well. That was confirmed when, five minutes later, Joshua Hadleigh and Keaton Flanagan rushed forward together, determined to attack and defeat the German goalkeeper, Ewald

Fuchs, who didn't stand a chance unprotected by his teammates from the last line. It was 1–1 and the first half was over.

I engaged in conversation with Bea's and Harold's parents, reassuring them that everything would be fine, although I wasn't so sure about it myself. Dad wasn't really happy, and I knew it was because he sensed the day wouldn't be easy. He was highly dubious about how it'd end – him and me both.

The players returned to the pitch while we were on our second beer. Coach Gottfried made one substitute, enhancing the attack; immediately afterwards, Coach Vance did the same. We were to expect high-quality combat.

We weren't given the battle straightaway; things kicked off unexpectedly slow, and for almost fifteen minutes, there wasn't a significant surge on either side. We assumed both teams were afraid to open up and attack with three forwards and a weaker middle and defence.

The English decided to throw down the gauntlet first. The idea they had was splendid, but it ended with a corner. The pause barely slowed the momentum, though, and England stayed on the attack, quickly transforming the corner kick into another shaking net behind Ewald Fuchs. The half of the stadium in white jumped in exhilaration and awe. We were now in the lead, thanks to an outstanding, beautiful goal by Joshua Hadleigh.

Gottfried was suspiciously quiet, while Matthias shouted at his fellow players, giving them directions together with Michael Krimm. When the game continued, none of the German players seemed upset, which was the correct thing to do. They mustn't lose it now if they wanted to win.

It was none other than Matthias who equalised the score twelve minutes later. With Lens and Ben on his sides, he ran forward against three English players and Harold Dare. Krimm joined them rapidly, and for a moment, the world saw a magnificent picture – the entire German Four together in the enemy's penalty box. The option of not scoring didn't exist.

Harold Dare was red in face. "He's losing his focus completely," Bea said in a shaky voice.

"Come on, he couldn't have done anything against the four of them," I replied.

"Yes, and that'll kill him. They can do this same move over and over again, ten times before the end of the match."

She was right. I didn't reply. I only prayed it all would end fair for both sides. Germany now was not the team that had struggled against Italy a few days back. They seemed strong and powerful, invincible and unyielding. Coach Vance was calm, as was Gottfried, but on both their faces we could see they didn't want to go into extra time. The only difference was Gottfried would have tolerated penalties, as those would suit only Matthias's team, since they had traditionally been superb at scoring them. Since Rolf Gottfried became the national coach, he'd never lost a match that went into shootouts. We didn't want this one to go there either. We wanted it over before the end of the ninetieth minute.

Seven minutes after Matthias's goal, Keaton Flanagan gave us hope. He slid past the two German midfielders and was joined by two other strikers. They were altogether too brisk in their passes for the puzzled defence of the enemy to keep up. After a few exchanges, the ball landed on Keaton's right foot, from where he sent it with all his force into the lower-left corner of Ewald Fuchs's goal.

I joined the girls and my parents in screams and shouts of awe and exhilaration, but I calmed myself down quicker than the rest of them, considerate of the fact that Matthias, still thinking I was with him, might see me and get upset. I thanked god and Keaton for bringing us this relief and continued cheering silently.

It turned out I'd celebrated too early. With only six minutes left to go, the Germans were not surrendering. Quite the contrary – they played as if they'd just stepped on the pitch after a good night's sleep. They didn't seem to be tired at all from running around for eighty minutes. In the true fashion of the German I knew best, the team were persistent, with no intention of letting this go so easily or letting England through to the finals over them. Michael Krimm, the intelligent, quick-witted captain, joined forces with two of his midfielders and Matthias, and they headed furiously towards Harold. Whenever some of our players tried to take the ball from them, they were unsuccessful and it'd be with another German the next second. The passes were short and quick, and Krimm was at the precisely right spot, jumping in to catch the ball on his head and direct it between the posts, where Harold had no chance of reaching. It was equal, again.

"It's not fair," Angie screamed. Bea was nonverbal, beyond sad and agitated.

"It's not, but they're good," Dad said. "We shouldn't have let them reach our box so easily."

"Brad!" Mom snapped, signalling Harold's parents' proximity with an exaggerated flick of her eyes.

"I didn't mean our goalkeeper was bad, but he can't do the job alone."

"The other boys are trying hard," Mom added.

"Yes, but it's not enough. These bastards are too strong," Dad replied.

Full of glee and fuelled by a surge of hope and elation, the Germans kept pressing on our exhausted and disillusioned group of players who, up until a few minutes ago, had believed their dream was coming true. Coach Vance tried giving them advice and guidance, but it was in vain. They seemed to have completely forgotten the game was still undecided and they could turn the result in their favour. Leon Schneider, a midfielder, didn't need much more than a solid high pass from Friedrich Larsson, far into our half of the pitch. He accepted the ball calmly and sent it towards Harold, again in a part of the goal he couldn't reach. It was the eighty-eighth minute and 4–3. It was over.

Bea was crying uncontrollably. I wished I could've stayed with her longer. Instead, we decided that Angie would, and Lana would go with my parents and me back to São Paulo. It hurt to see all the sad faces of my fellow English fans while the black-red-gold sections of the stands were singing and jumping with joy and pride. I quickly gathered my belongings and started behind my Dad and Mom, looking forward to getting out of this city that'd forever stay in my memory as the place where I had done something beautiful and unforgivable.

Before the plane took off, in order not to be suspicious, I texted Matthias congratulations and best wishes in Rio. It was right after pressing *send* that it dawned on me: Matthias would most probably face Alex there. It made me so nauseous that I spent most of the one-hour flight in the bathroom.

"You're not pregnant, are you?" Dad asked when I sat down and put on my seatbelt for landing.

I choked while Mom and Lana laughed. "Of course not," I replied.

"Brad, people also vomit because of bad food, air sickness or exhaustion," Mom explained.

"I know, but Jane's always had a good stomach, loads of energy and never suffered from air sickness." He looked at me perceptively.

"No, Dad, I'm definitely not pregnant," I reiterated.

"How do you know for sure?"

"I take care, trust me." I swallowed hard, embarrassed.

"Dear lord, Brad, look how pale she went," Mom said. "Don't talk to her like that just because you're excited to have grandchildren. There's plenty of time."

"Thank you, Mom." I smiled at her with gratitude.

Well, better that he thought I was pregnant than to suspect where I'd been last night.

When we arrived at the hotel, I politely said I wasn't in the mood to have any dinner and only wanted to see Alex. I knew he was waiting for me, even though it was almost midnight. I rushed to the room, dragging my small trolley behind, my heart pounding strong. This was to be the moment of decision. In the next few minutes, I'd know if I loved Alex for life.

In the next few seconds. The next few steps.

I opened the door. Alex was lying on the bed in his tracksuit, watching something on his laptop. I could hear a Ukrainian commentator and stadium shouts – he was preparing for tomorrow. When he saw me, he stood up, and it struck me again how perfect, handsome and complete he was. The way he looked at me told me everything – how much he loved, cared, waited, hoped and worried for me. From the warmth in his eyes at seeing me, from the way my heart warmed in turn, I knew this man was the only home I'd ever need.

The previous night flashed in its entirety over my eyes, clear as day. I felt terrible to have participated in it, but at the same time, I felt at peace with myself. I was certain then that if I hadn't done it, I'd never have known how much this man in front of me meant. He was perfect, loving, fulfilling, reassuring – I knew all that; I always had – and I could feel it emanating just by him looking at me with longing, understanding and patience. My Alex.

I dropped the trolley, slammed the door shut and rushed into his arms. He caught me on his chest, enveloping me in his large arms, hoping he'd never have to let me go.

"I hoped you'd come here in that dress. It suits you beautifully," he commented on the red dress I'd worn for the match.

"Thank you. I wish I'd had time to shower and everything, but we needed to rush."

"Come on, it matters more that you're back here."

I hugged him harder, fighting back tears of pain as I thought about Matthias and how he'd feel when I told him that, after everything, I still chose Alex – this time for good. Simultaneously, my heart clenched in relief as I felt overjoyed that I finally knew that I hadn't been mistaken even four years ago, that everything I'd done was right.

"Hey, what's wrong?" he asked when I sniffed. "What happened, Jane?" He placed a hand on my cheek, directing my face towards his with the gentlest touch when I didn't reply straight away.

I loved his ocean-blue eyes, the endless sea of them. I would forever. I knew it.

"It's over. Matthias and all that is over," I managed to say before bursting into tears. I couldn't admit everything to him, of course – I never would – but I needed to tell him a part of it at least so that I could unleash my soul and cry until I dried out. So much pain and trouble were boiling and rising in me, like a pot left unattended on the stove. I needed to warn him about it so that he didn't doubt me. I needed him to be with me, to hold me tight and reassure me while I finally, for the last time, closed that page with the black-eyed man who loved me, and who I loved, but not enough to fight against oceans and mountains to be with.

The story I told Alex was brief. I didn't want to extend it because it was a semi-lie, so by keeping it short, I could lie less and remember it better. I said I'd met Matthias because he insisted, that it all happened the night before, that he'd prepared a romantic dinner and poured out his soul to me. I said Matthias had told me all the reasons why I should come with him after the tournament, but that I was brief and resolute when I made it clear that I didn't love him, nor could I ever love him enough to give my life to him. I said had to repeat it a couple of times and listen to Matthias's sobs and pleas before he saw reasoned and accepted my decision, – and then he let me go. I cried while saying all that, explaining that I was so sorry to have made somebody so kind and good miserable – which was true – but that I also suffered because now I knew I'd lost forever a significant person in my life whose value I hadn't been aware of until the moment came that I needed to set him free.

*****

I woke up on Alex's chest. His scent reminded me where I was. Contrary to yesterday morning's feelings, it felt right to be here. The events of two days ago seemed distant and unreal, a figment of my imagination. It was all behind me, and knowing that made me feel light, though still with a wound on my heart. It'd take some time to completely heal.

I stirred on him, thinking he looked so beautiful when he slept. I put my leg over his belly, stretching, when I felt he was hard.
"You naughty…! I was certain you were asleep." I slapped him on the shoulder.

He laughed and opened his eyes. "I was until you started moving." He grabbed my leg and dragged me on top of him with one move.

"Aren't you afraid of having sex on the day of an important match?" I asked.

"Not at all. It'd calm me down."

"Alright, then – no need to convince me further," I said with a smirk, stroking my finger down his chest.

I placed him inside me, moaning instantly for the wonderful, overwhelming pleasure that spread within me. This was what I needed. This was love. This was the man I wanted.

He grabbed my breasts and let me lead. I didn't want to release us too fast and I was in a playful mood, so I moved my hips slowly, then rapidly, then slowly, kissing him in the short breaks when I'd let him stay still and twitch within me. He lost patience soon afterwards, as I'd hoped for and expected. He caught my back and pressed my breasts close to his face, where he kissed and sucked them greedily. He flipped me onto my back and slammed into me, making me scream at the strength of the multiple orgasms he awarded us.

"Now we're ready for the day," he announced hugging me.

"I couldn't agree more."

I loved him. He made me forget everything that had made me sad. He fulfilled me. He gave me what I needed and then more. And that's how it should be with the right person next to you.

*****

I headed for the fourth time to the Arena Corinthians with my parents, Lana, Mr and Mrs Yanov, and Alex's sister, Maria. The atmosphere promised to be memorable, and memorable it was – half of the over sixty-thousand capacity stadium was dressed in blue and yellow, giving the fans in orange a run for their money with the enthusiasm of their shouts and songs.

Robin Braam was not a part of the Dutch team due to an injury a couple of months ago, but even without him, his team was one of the strongest in the competition. They had stars who conquered European football and ruled Italian and English leagues; they had youth, experience, agility and perseverance. Yet their results up until now were worse-off compared to Ukraine's, for one reason only – the impenetrable Ukrainian goalkeeper and defence.

That was why when the game began, the Dutch started attacking fiercely, aiming to secure a goal and lead as soon as possible. Ukraine was slightly taken aback by the unexpected force rushing towards their centre line and Alex, but they quickly regained confidence and control of the game. It wasn't easy to defend against an opponent with such a historically strong offence, but they did their utmost. They had been preparing for years, building up to this tournament's performance. They'd been phenomenal in Germany, and while they hadn't won the medal they deserved, they'd since trained harder every day to reach the level they were now at. They looked way more composed, fortified and strong than the German team had last night.

The first half was coming to a close. The refreshing twenty-degree weather outside didn't impede the players' running and trains of thought – even nearing the halfway point, they were bright-eyed and quick-footed. The spectators at the stadium and watching on screens were being given quite a show; nobody seemed to prevail for a very long time, and each team seemed about to score any minute. The first goal was looming.

The Ukrainian defencemen won the ball from the Dutch midfield, and they sent it forward. Dmitro Kostyskyn, a new joiner at this tournament, accepted it and signalled Anatoliy Honchar and Andriy Barnik to join him. They headed forward confidently with a plan clear only in their heads – to us, what they were preparing seemed improbable. They neared the enemy's penalty box and began passing the ball between each other.

Suddenly, Nikolay Pavlov ran into the area, dangerously close to the goalkeeper but making sure he wasn't offside. Barnik shot the ball towards Nikolay, who turned, calmed it on his chest and then sent it with his right foot towards the goalkeeper. The keeper deflected the shot, but Nikolay was there to catch the rebound. He reacted quickly and made sure that this time, the net shook.

More than thirty-thousand souls applauded and roared with adoration for this brave, audacious man and with joy that we were in the lead against the omnipotent force of the *Oranje*.[11]

The first half ended, and I accepted the horilka passed on by Olexiy Yanov. I jumped and celebrated with the fans who were beyond exhilarated. It was happening. It was truly happening. We were halfway to the finals, halfway to where we'd deserved to be last time. Now, all that mattered was this year, and this tournament, when everything was going as it should.

---

[11] Oranje, one of the nicknames of the Dutch National Football Team.

"And what's even better? The Germans are waiting for us there!" shouted one ecstatic middle-aged man. "We'll kick their asses as they deserve."

What I'd feared most over the past month was about to happen in four days. I'd better brace myself for any possible outcome.

The players returned to the pitch when we were on our third drink. The cameras caught me while I was posing for a selfie with a group of girls dressed up in traditional Ukrainian clothes, against which my lily-yellow dress with blue flowers stood out. I looked pretty, but I still wished I'd been as ingenious as them. Those red-and-white dresses would definitely be good on me, and Alex would have been astounded and positively surprised.

Our focus returned to the game soon afterwards. The Dutch made all three substitutes while Coach Andreyevich kept his initial line-up.

"He doesn't want to rush. He wants to see how the boys will cope with these refreshed players in the middle and forward," Dad explained.

"Brad, you're an expert. You talk like a true, experienced coach," Mom teased him.

"Darling, I'm just English – football is the first thing we learn when we're born."

We all laughed. It turned out he was right. When Coach Andreyevich saw the Dutch manage to pierce through to Alex a couple of times, he decided not to risk it and strengthened the middle with one new player off the bench. In the next couple of minutes, the game regained its first-half grandeur. We were equal in pace with the orange team, and outdid them in persistence, never letting them come near Alex.

With thirteen minutes to go, the Netherlands became restless and panicky. They were losing, and the equaliser was nowhere on the horizon. They tried everything – tactical approaches, aggressive play, taking us by surprise, long balls from the middle of the pitch – but nothing went through Alex when it reached him. They were desperate.

Their desperation left us space for creativity. From the signs Milan Andreyevich was gesturing to his players, I understood he didn't want them to rush or try anything perilous but instead to remain calm and defend.

On the other side, I'd known Nikolay Pavlov long enough to be sure a 1–0 result was not sufficient for his ego. I knew he didn't want anyone to say later on that they'd squeezed through to the finals. He wanted to make sure the win was cemented and one hundred percent deserved. That was why he led one attack after another on the poor Dutch goalkeeper. Corner kick after corner kick followed, and the pressure was growing immeasurably fast. The minutes ticked off. Each one carried at least two attempts by the guys in yellow to score again. It was relentless.

Ten minutes to go. Another three attempts.

Nine minutes. Only Nikolay, Ivan Rostov and Anatoliy Honchar were in the forward position, struggling with the orange defence. Nikolay wanted to try everything by himself, but he knew the Dutch goalkeeper would likely defend. That was why he selflessly passed the ball to Anatoliy, who didn't hesitate for a second and sent it at a speed of light between the goalposts. The unfortunate Dutch keeper jumped to the right side but not far enough; the ball almost brushed his fingers and landed in the net behind his back. It was over now. Ukraine was in the finals of the World Cup.

I jumped and screamed my heart out, hugging Alex's parents and sister, my parents, and then any other fan who came my way. We sang; we chanted; we ordered more beer. The unbelievable was happening. My man was one step further than he'd ever gone. I was proud of him and what he'd made of himself over the past four years, what he'd helped his team achieve.

The remaining time until the referee's whistle was entertaining to behold, but it was obvious no big change would take place. The Dutch were exhausted, but beyond that, they were shocked at what'd fallen upon them. I saw them shaking their heads in disbelief and knew they genuinely hadn't expected this. They'd been overly self-confident. They'd forgotten the temperament these men possessed, that Ukrainians could make the impossible happen. And that they had the best goalkeeper in the world.

When we returned to the hotel, a live band was already waiting for us in the open restaurant next to the pool. (Olexiy Yanov had organised it along with the families of other players.) We were ready to celebrate the entire night until the flight to Rio tomorrow.

Rio, where Matthias already was. He'd probably even watched the game from there and seen me celebrating each of the goals and Alex's successful saves. He'd texted me but I hadn't opened the messages. No one and nothing would ruin this special evening that my man so deserved.

I went for a quick shower and changed into a knee-length blue summer dress. Although it was chilly outside, we were all warm with the joyous and victorious mood. I was gulping down one beer after another and already talking fluent Ukrainian to everyone around, sometimes even getting confused when I needed to speak to Lana in English. She wasn't as inebriated as me, mostly because she wanted to keep her head cool when the players arrived. She didn't want any more confusion with Lev.

When the receptionist announced the team bus had just parked in front, we headed to the entrance hall together with the musicians, who played *Samba de Janeiro* while we all danced and jumped, wild with happiness. The players were singing and shouting from the bus, and they kept the energy up as they entered the hotel. Nikolay began dancing and the other teammates joined him –even Coach Andreyevich, which was incredibly funny to watch.

Alex separated from the mad crowd and I was in his arms in a matter of seconds.

"You've made it, Love. You've reached the end. You got this!"

He swung me around. "I believed in it before the game, but when it actually happened, I still thought I was dreaming."

"You're not. It's all true. You took Ukraine to the final of the most prestigious competition in football."

"Whoa, when you say it like that, it does sound pretty impressive."

"It is." I kissed him. "And you should be proud of yourself for everything you've achieved."

"Well, to be honest, I am. When I see all of you happy like this, I am proud I've had a part in it."

I hugged him hard. "You were, are, and forever will be the best goalkeeper in the history of football."

"Erm...Lev Yashin[12] was pretty good, too. I wouldn't say—"

"He was before. Now it's you." I closed the argument with another kiss.

The night went on and on. Nobody seemed to get tired. I began feeling unendurable pain in my feet so I removed my sandals, but then my calves started cramping from all the dancing and jumping around. I noticed Lana trying to stay sober for some time while Lev Zahara was all over her. The whole party, he had eyes only for her. After a couple of hours, when she understood she was the only sober person in the vicinity except for the players, she gave up her resolution and joined us with champagne.

---

[12] Lev Ivanovich Yashin (1929–1990), a Soviet professional footballer, regarded by many as the best goalkeeper in the history of sport.

"Don't overthink it tonight. Enjoy yourself," I told her. She winked back, meaning she got my point and would let herself take what was being offered to her.

We stayed up a few hours past midnight. If the guys had been able to drink, we'd probably have partied until sunrise. But although Coach Andreyevich was proud and exuberant, he insisted they had to stay clean until next Sunday. "If we win the golden trophy, you won't have to be sober until the beginning of the season," he said.

"And we won't," Nikolay reassured him.

I couldn't wait to go for a shower. I was all sweaty and dirty, my hair completely tangled from dancing the entire evening. The hot water soothed my sore muscles like an immediate anaesthetic. Suddenly drowsy beyond belief, I closed my eyes and absorbed the relieving sensations. I was so tired that I couldn't even react when Alex's hands met my waist, startling me. He kissed me on the shoulders before moving so that he could stand under the shower. Damn it, he was handsome!

I thought I was beyond exhausted, but the sight of him ignited some hidden source of energy in me. He didn't want anything that night; I knew him. He was tired. I was. Most likely, he wasn't planning on touching me until perhaps tomorrow, if we had time before the flight. However, I couldn't resist. In front of me was the man of my life, perfect in every sense, with a body that invoked everything proper and improper in me.

I moved away from the water stream and kissed him on the lips. He smiled, his eyes closed sleepily, and returned the kiss, thinking that was it. I continued down to kiss his neck, then moved to his chest, his shoulders, his nipples, his rock-solid abs and lower, all the time scratching his back with my nails. He reacted to me almost instantly, and I smiled silently in encouragement. I played with him for some time, driving him crazy, before I took him in my mouth, inch by inch.

"Jane, let's go to the room," he panted.

"No."

"I want you."

"First I want you."

He squeezed my hair and let me finish what I'd begun. He enjoyed it. He loved it. I could hear how much, and it filled me with security and reassurance to know that I was the one giving him all that outrageous pleasure.

*****

"Bea and Angie will meet us in Brasília, they told me to tell you, if you don't mind?" Lana said on the plane on our way to Rio with the Ukrainian team. "Harold isn't taking that defeat well and Angie, well, she doesn't want to leave Bea alone when she can have Declan's company."

"Of course, no problem. We'll meet there tomorrow, right?"

"Where are you two going again?" Lev appeared next to our seats out of the blue.

"For the third-place match, England versus the Netherlands," I explained.

"Well, you're not going anywhere." He crouched next to Lana and touched her nose jokingly, aiming to kiss her, but she retreated.

"Who says?" she asked, defiant.

"Your boyfriend."

"And who's that?"

"I'll show you tonight."

She hit him on the shoulder and he left. Alex and I had to try hard not to laugh, especially when Lana turned back to us, her face blushing a deep red. "I'm sorry. He's annoying." She looked down at her coffee cup, playing with it.

"He's serious, Lana," Alex said. "I wouldn't be telling you this if I wasn't sure, but I've known him for a couple of years and I can assure you he is serious now. The rest is up to you."

Lana didn't want to argue with Alex, but I knew she was deeply confused. This man would have to keep trying if he wanted to win her over. He'd also have to work on himself much more than in the gym or on the pitch. We'd have to see if he was up to the task.

I wanted to stay with Alex as long as I could, which meant we'd take a flight to Brasilia the following evening. We'd watch the match next day and return to Rio immediately afterwards. I dreaded going up there again, dreaded being surrounded by all the fresh memories that the city held for me. I also worried about what might happen once I was alone. It'd be too risky for Matthias to follow me now, two days before the final game. On the other hand, Brasília was only two hours away. Crazy as he was, he could easily take a flight to come and see me while Alex wasn't anywhere near.

It was tremendously difficult to reply to his messages so that he didn't suspect anything. I forced myself to be cold, because lying anew felt gruelling and wrong. In a couple of texts, I explained that I didn't have time to talk or chat because I was always with someone, and he seemed to understand since the tone of his messages didn't change. The fact that Alex was my absolute priority now was strangely confirmed by Matthias not noticing something was bothering me. Because, truthfully, it wasn't. I was completely engrossed in Alex. Only in the moments when I had to talk to Matthias did I feel troubled. I was resolved to keep away from him until the tournament finished – and afterwards, forever.

*****

There was no point in Lana and me staying longer in Rio. In the last days approaching the final game, the guys had training after training, and when they weren't practising they needed rest. That was why only Lev disagreed with us leaving. In the end, he still reconciled with our decision and even saw us off with Alex.

"Is that your new boyfriend, Lana?" my father asked when we sat in the car.

"Dad!"

"What's wrong?" He raised his hands defensively while Mom and I laughed and Lana went red again.

"Nothing, Mr Andersonn," she said. "He's not my boyfriend. He thinks he is."

"Why does that matter, Dad?"

"I'm just asking. It's clear he's dumbfounded by you."

We all laughed, but I could see the shadow of a million doubts pass across Lana's face.

We met Bea, Angie and some members of the English team for dinner. Harold was there, of course, as well as Keaton Flanagan and Declan along with his brother, Duncan. I congratulated Keaton for the splendid two goals in the match with Germany and praised the other players for their excellent performance.

"Don't sugarcoat it, Jane. I was terrible," Harold said.

"Don't whine, Dare. They are just too good. There's nothing you could've done differently."

"Everyone keeps telling me that. Anyway, I'll watch the finals closely. I'll be there with B. If Alex doesn't take any shots from them, I swear I'll take private classes from him."

Everyone at the table laughed.

"Deal," I said. "I'll tell him to give you a special rate."

"But before that, you have to win the bronze medal tomorrow." Bea took hold of his hand, and he seemed slightly calmer.

I can't wait to see you.

- Same here.

Do you think tomorrow night would be possible? After you return?

- Perhaps. I'll try my best.

Jane?

- ?

I'm counting the minutes till the moment you come back to me.

- Me, too, Mati. I miss you.

I was disgusted by myself, but there was nothing else I could do differently. I had to lie to him for his own good. I needed both of these men, my men, to come to the Maracanã Stadium fully concentrated and in high spirits. Not distraught because of me. Not again.

*****

Being back in Brasília filled me with anxiety. Even though I knew it was highly improbable, I had a constant fear everywhere I went that some of the members of Matthias's family would ambush me to criticise and reprimand me for what I'd been doing to him. Of course, nothing of the sort happened. It was only my conscience playing with me, but all the same, I couldn't wait to be out of there.

This match began at five o'clock, giving us enough time to sleep in and get ready leisurely. The Estádio Nacional Mané Garrincha was roaring with exhilarated and excited fans when we arrived. I was slightly surprised at first, but then I realised that for my country, winning a bronze title was still an enormous success. I was glad the supporters felt the same way. The singing and chanting followed the players from the first whistle all the way to the end. The play was interesting, keeping our eyes glued to the pitch. The fans in orange were marvellous, and we paralleled them well.

The first half ended without any net being shaken but with the promise that something gripping would happen soon. We spent half-time getting intoxicated again and starting our celebration way before the game was over. Beer glasses were arriving one after another and couldn't be refused. But out on the pitch, the second half started so explosively that we soon forgot our drinks and focused completely on the grass.

Harold was the first to fail, and the Dutch were in the lead in the fiftieth minute. There was nothing much he could have done. He was one on one with the Dutch striker, and although he'd jumped in the right direction, he didn't make it on time.

I worried Harold might lose his self-confidence and award the enemy a goal or two more, but somehow, surprisingly, he composed himself fast and continued the game. Thea Watkins-Hadleigh was shouting her soul out, cheering her husband on as if he could hear her. Dad was also bellowing as if there was no tomorrow, alongside his friends and business partners. Even Lana and Angie were losing their heads screaming. I seemed to be the calmest one in the group.

The equaliser came in the sixty-ninth minute, the lead in the seventy-fifth, and the mic drop in the eighty-first. They were all scored by the players who'd joined the team over the past year – young footballers Austin Haley, Jason Peck and Kyle Mitchell. They sealed the fate of the Oranje, who could not cope with them successfully.

The medal award ceremony was emotional to watch. It was Coach Vance's first award with the national team. Whether he'd stay in that position, we were yet to see. According to Dad, he wouldn't mind, but it all depended on the Football Association. I was glad for Joshua, who deserved this shining moment in his career, and I was happy for the show-off Keaton Flanagan – this achievement would bring him a higher price on the market, which is exactly what he was aiming for. Of course, I was especially elated for Harold, who had just won a medal in the most important competition of his profession, weeks before his wedding.

Dad was emotional, too. "Thank god I've lived to see England winning something at a World Cup I was too young in 1966 to remember. It could've been better, but it will be once those Germans stop producing excellent players and your boyfriend retires." He gestured to me, and everyone laughed.

"Come on, you'll definitely see them winning gold," Mom said. "You'll live another thirty years for sure."

He agreed and hugged her. They looked twenty years younger. I wanted to look like that at their age. With Alex by my side.

I wished I could have stayed for the party in Brasília with my parents, but I wanted to be back to Alex as soon as possible. If I took the plane the next day, I wouldn't even see him before the match, and that was unacceptable. Lana and Angie both decided to go with me.

"You can stay with Declan and come tomorrow," I told Angie.

"It's fine. Half of them will join us tomorrow anyway, and to be honest, I'd rather fly with you in your fancy jet than be stuck on a plane with this lot of idiots who'll be dead drunk tomorrow morning."

"Makes sense," I agreed, laughing.

And so it was over, with no more pomp or circumstance. I left Brasília forever. When we took off, I stared through the plane window until the city lights completely disappeared, going through everything that had happened the last time I was there. I knew it wasn't good for me, but I couldn't help it ruminating.

I remembered Matthias's instructions on how to leave the hotel, the blue BMW, his cologne that hid in every wrinkle of that car – I was sure it still smelt of him. I remembered with fondness how he'd been a tour guide, how he'd talked to me as if we weren't doing anything wrong, making jokes and taking me by the hand to the mysterious building where his family lived. He'd introduced me to his family. I remembered the kind and genuine people who did their utmost to converse with me, who didn't judge me, who weren't rude to me when they had every right to be, who put in the effort to make me feel at home with the music and the dance…oh, the dance. I'd loved him. My entire being had loved him then. How he'd looked at me, absorbed me. How I'd lost myself in those eyes that, despite their darkness, were everything but unsafe. How was I going to go on without them? How, when he'd truly done everything he could to make me be with him, to choose him? Was I so terrible that his best wasn't enough? And those photos Anabella took of us. Where were they now? With him, probably. Was I ever going to see them again? What if I could take just one more look? Would they change my mind?

"Jane."

Even if they did, it wouldn't make any sense now. I'd decided, and I had to stick to it. I only hoped that this time, when I told him everything, it'd be the last time, that he'd finally move on and see that I was not the woman he'd been idealising all this time. His hatred would hurt, but better anger than his love that I couldn't indulge.

"Jane?"

Angie pulled me back from my daydream, and when I swallowed and felt pain in my throat and chest, I realised I was on the brink of tears again.

"What's up?" she asked.

"Nothing, I was just thinking…" I trailed off, unable to finish.

"About…him?"

I didn't need to answer. She saw my eyes, wide with suppressed pain.

She drew me into a hug. "Honey, it's fine. It's normal that it hurts, but you made the right decision, and you can continue living in peace with yourself knowing it. He… he'll stop hurting at one point."

"I hope, Angie. I truly hope. But I can't get what he said out of my head – that he's never given up on anything or anyone. It ludicrously flatters me, but it also fills me with fear. I have no idea what he might do once I refuse him again."

"If you make it so clear that he doesn't stand a chance anymore, he'll give up. You'll see. A real fighter wouldn't see it as a lost battle, but rather as a battle not worth fighting for. Don't get me wrong, I don't mean you're worthless," she squeezed my arm gently, "but if your heart is another man's, then there's no point for him to keep trying. Once he understands that, he'll set you free."

"We'll see. Tomorrow is the final day. Everything will be over tomorrow."

CHAPTER 13

"How do you feel?" I asked, combing my hair in front of the gilded hotel mirror.

"Definitely like the most excited man in the world...tied with twenty-four others, I guess," Alex replied casually.

I laughed. "You sound pretty calm."

"I'm not."

I put my comb down and went back to bed. "Alex, it won't be like the last time." I rested a hand on his stubbled cheek.

"That I know," he murmured, kissing my palm. "There's nothing they can do or say to make me lose my head like that. What I worry about is if they really are better."

"You were better last time, yet you lost and they took the trophy. If they are better this time and you still win, it'd be just a payback."

He smiled briefly. "I don't want to win that way. None of the guys do. We want to take the gold by showing that we are truly the best."

"Why do you doubt you are?"

"You've seen them play. They are precise to perfection, skilled, aggressive, decisive. We are all that, too...but also, to a large extent, lucky."

"You think luck has brought you to the Maracanã?"

He looked at me discerningly. "Not entirely, no. There's a lot of work behind it. Lots of sweating, training, planning, devising tactics, watching and analysing other teams' play."

"Exactly, and I'll just remind you that you haven't been scored on a single time at this tournament. Ewald Fuchs lost count in the quarterfinals already."

"Last time, I also hadn't been scored on until we faced them."

"They won't take it away from you this year. You saw their games against Italy and England. They're not as strong. They struggled."

"You're right."

"So there's nothing to worry about. Dreams do come true. You proved that when you won against the Dutch. You'll prove it tonight to your country, to the entire world. I just need you to remain focused at all times. Don't let them get to you, no matter how hard they try and with what means. Just be your brilliant self, deaf and blind to provocations, concentrated with your eyes and mind on the ball, not the player leading it. We'll take those gold medals home with us." I kissed him, first on his nose, then the lips.

He hugged me hard. "I love you. You're my best pre-match warm-up."

When he left, I took out a brand-new, white A-line dress I'd ordered. It was similar to the one I'd worn at the previous Cup final. I thought about changing colours but none other than white seemed appropriate. My high heels this time were deliberately mismatched, one blue and one yellow, a clear sign of who I supported, in case anyone doubted it.

- Good luck today. Be at your best. You got this.

Thank you, Love. Can't wait to get hold of that trophy and take you both home.

I didn't reply. I didn't have the stomach to.

I met the others at the hotel reception. It seemed that everyone I knew had come to cheer for my boyfriend's team. Bea and Harold, Angie and Declan, Duncan Fletcher, my parents, Bea's and Harold's parents as well, Mr and Mrs Yanov (of course), with Maria, Coach Vance and Luca Ferreira. There were many others whose faces I'd seen over the past month but couldn't connect to any names. Warmth snaked around my heart – I was on the right path. I'd chosen the right man.

We headed to the stadium in groups of four. The streets were flooded with confetti, flags, scarves, and, of course, thousands of fans blocking the traffic. We didn't stress about it. We'd left significantly ahead of time. Besides, if we got held up, nothing could keep me from the game. I'd run there if I had to. The girls and I were in the same limo and popped a bottle of champagne from the mini-fridge. It soothed my throat, and I made sure to have enough of it because up there on the stands I was certain I wouldn't be able to sip anything but water. My insides were already twisting. I'd almost vomited my breakfast after Alex left, but I forced myself to keep it down, aware that I'd need the energy today.

We made it with fifteen minutes to spare before the national anthems. I loved how I looked when the stadium's big screen caught me. I'd practised acting out emotions so many times and so well that now, decent joy and subtle excitement were the only two visible under scrutiny. No one could guess how worried and troubled I really was.

"Please, stay close to me," I whispered to the girls and they nodded.

The players began walking out on the pitch, and the stadium roared. I felt a drop of sweat sliding down my back, even though it wasn't so hot that day July 14th. I held Bea and Angie by the hands, unsure if I could stand up straight and stable on my own.

I recognised them all from that distance, even with their backs turned to us – the entire German team, playing in white, and Ukraine, again in yellow. They lined up next to one other, followed closely by a few beaming children who'd been given the opportunity to join for the anthems. Each player stood with a boy or a girl in front of them, the children's smiling faces emanating the purest happiness that they stood next to legends.

First up was the German national anthem, and I bet nobody present could shake off the goosebumps that covered us when the immeasurable mass of voices thundered the lyrics together with the players. The camera panned over each of their faces, and I had to bite my lips to refrain from showing any reaction. Matthias's eyes were full of zest and fire. He was so confident in himself and his team. For him, this match had already been decided.

No soul among the seventy-eight thousand attendees expected what came next. The next instrumental began, and the voices of all the present, proud Ukrainians rang out in unison, sending a tremendous echo throughout the stadium and farther. It was chilling and beautiful, the sound of that sweeping melody carrying through the crowd, borne forward with the overwhelming pride and honour of the Ukrainian fans and players. It made sense, I realised. The lyrics of the anthem made so much sense. Especially in this situation, when these two teams were confronting each other again, when yet again the only thing standing between these hardworking, devoted men and the cup that would fulfil a lifetime of effort – the only thing standing between them was the same foe as before. And to face that foe now, the team in yellow had returned – better, stronger, more confident, ready for revenge, to take what belonged to them, what had belonged to them even then.

I translated for the girls.

Ukraine is not yet dead, nor its glory and freedom,
Luck will still smile on us brother-Ukrainians.

Our enemies will die, as the dew does in the sunshine,
and we, too, brothers, we'll live happily in our land.[13]

This had to end well. It was the only right way.

The captains Michael Krimm and Vlad Starovski shook hands. The best referee in the tournament tossed a coin. The sides were decided. Alex and Ewald Fuchs went to their goalposts. The players dispersed around the fresh grass. The whistle pierced our ears loud and clear. And it began.

I couldn't sit still. Nobody could. White and yellow shirts mixed and bumped into each other rapidly and wildly. Not a single player hesitated. None of them were afraid. Neither of the teams had anything to lose. It was all on the line: a life of eternal glory or death in history.

Rolf Gottfried had his top stars on the pitch. Coach Andreyevich hadn't hesitated to do the same. They had identical formations and parried each other well. Most of the game played out around the centre – not so close to the keepers – which was an excellent warm-up for them, as well as for us, the supporters. Every person in the stands wanted to see a world-class football match, except for me. I wanted it to end fast, with the right team scoring enough goals.

Matthias and Lens seemed to be the main drivers of their team. They barked orders at their teammates and attacked mercilessly, causing the game to stop a couple of times for penalties within the first twenty minutes. Some scenes were painful to watch, especially on the slow-motion videos that replayed on the big screens. The Germans made sure not to be harsh enough to be given a red card – apart from that, they didn't seem to care. They were out for blood and glory.

On the other team, Nikolay Pavlov and Andriy Barnik weren't above the same tactics. They were not dirty players by nature, but seeing that they might be scored on soon and that the German defence was almost impenetrable, they opted for the attack in the same manner as Matthias and Lens. At the end of the day, not one of the twenty-two men on the pitch that afternoon had anything to lose. They only had to play safe enough not to get sent away.

Coach Andreyevich was mostly calm; he watched the game keenly, calling out to players as they'd come near from time to time. That

---

[13] Ще не вмерла України і слава, і воля,
Ще нам, браття молодії, усміхнеться доля.
Згинуть наші воріженьки, як роса на сонці.
Запануєм і ми, браття, у своїй сторонці.

was nothing unusual. What worried me was that Gottfried was calm, too. He started the game sitting on the bench, but soon afterwards, he moved to stand at the touchline, quietly observing the situation and contemplating. At first, I ignored it, but when the thirtieth minute went by and the result was still 0–0, his staring became sinister. My stomach stirred with nausea again. He was up to something.

I kept repeating to myself that it wasn't possible. He didn't know about Matthias and me. At least, that was what I thought. I had believed the same four years ago, and it turned out he'd known everything from the beginning. This time, however, Alex and the others were ready for anything Gottfried might come up with. I knew it. Still, his vicious eyes didn't look reassuring.

The defence of both teams began to falter some ten minutes before the break. It wasn't that the players were tired – I doubt they could physically feel tired, with the amount of adrenaline that was surely pumping through their veins. It was more that the strikers were learning about their opponent and finding ways to break through. The shouts and support from both sides of the stadium confirmed that.

The first dangerous attack and potential goal came from us. Volomin and Krasinski passed the ball between each other before sending it to Rostov in the middle. The forward players were already prepared, immersed between the German defencemen and onside. Ivan Rostov passed the ball to Nikolay, who suddenly began running at the speed of light. Anatoliy Honchar and Andriy Barnik paralleled him, reaching Nikolay in time to take his pass. The ball jumped off Anatoliy's head and got to Andriy, who calmed it on his chest and shot as fiercely as he could with his left foot towards the goal.

If it had gone anywhere else except straight to Ewald Fuchs, it would've shaken the net for sure. Roars of disappointment erupted over the stadium, soon followed by applause of support. Finally, the moment had come for some scoring.

Andriy got up from the grass quickly and regained his confidence. Despite coming up short this time around, Ukraine now saw that they could reach the rival's penalty box and take position for threatening shots. They were hungry for more excitement like this. After all, the people who'd travelled thousands of kilometres deserved to see a show here, in one of the most significant football venues in the world.

Three minutes later, Ben Schwimmer squeezed past defender Lev Zahara and came alarmingly close to Alex. His attempt wasn't as critical as Andriy's a few moments back, and Alex caught the ball without much trouble, but it was German's first shot on target. Now they knew they could break through our last line, too.

They didn't waste time. A minute later, Michael Krimm approached Alex and, from a close to thirty-metre distance, sent a rocket-powered ball straight at him. Alex caught it again, but on the replay, we saw how the air was knocked out of his lungs from the strength of the hit.

Three minutes later, Ivan Rostov managed to take the ball to the front, where Andriy Barnik was waiting for it. He headed towards the German goalkeeper alone, hoping that someone would follow. Captain Vlad Starovski and Nikolay did. Nikolay prepared to shoot once Andriy sent him the ball, but decided at the last minute to give it to Vlad, who stood six metres in front of the goal. Nobody breathed. It had to be a goal. From that distance, there was no chance he'd miss. The ball was already behind Ewald's back. He didn't manage to catch it.

However, Kevin Jäger showed up out of nowhere and knocked it away from the net with his head, preventing a goal. Again, roars of exasperation rumbled through the stadium.

Two minutes later, another commotion broke out in front of the German goal. It was the last seconds of the first half. Alex was the only Ukrainian on his side of the pitch. His teammates were using the last of their strength to finally score and go into the break with a lead. Ewald deflected one ball and Friedrich Larsson shot it away, but Sergey Lomin jumped in and kept the ball in play. Ben Schwimmer was now trying to get hold of it; he failed. Lev Zahara shot. Michael Krimm put his back between him and the goal. Andriy Barnik tried again; Ewald Fuchs deflected again. Racing to keep control, Nikolay caught the ball to take a shot – he didn't have the time to look – but Michael Krimm blocked it again, after which Lens Petrov finally kicked it high in the air and out of play.

The Germans could breathe with relief, but it was a temporary relief; every German supporter watching this confrontation understood now that their opponent was far better than anyone had anticipated. The only reason Ukraine hadn't scored just now was simply bad luck, and they didn't seem discouraged by it. When the referee announced the end of the first part of the game, the players in yellow walked confidently towards the tunnel, their faces firm and looking more reassured than they'd been forty-five minutes before. They now knew – the whole world knew – that they could defeat this invincible German machine.

I was grateful it wasn't visible on my dress that I was soaking wet from cold sweat that hadn't let up since the first whistle.

"Calm down, woman, I can see how pale you are through your makeup," Angie hissed in my ear. Of course, I was. Especially when I remembered what had happened at half-time on the last occasion these two teams had faced off.

I caught the fence in front of me and looked down at Alex, Matthias and Gottfried in turn, tracking their every movement. Gottfried was on the bench, not showing any signs of moving. Alex would have to pass by him for sure. I watched, all my senses focusing on them. Gottfried was talking to Ben and Leon Schneider now; Alex was only a few metres from them, walking with Ivan Rostov and Igor Krasinski. They were laughing, discussing something, not seeming to notice who was in their path. Matthias stood next to Gottfried, and I saw him glance at Alex and quickly return his gaze to his coach. When Alex and his teammates passed them, he looked up at me and smiled. I smiled back, and then he disappeared into the locker room.

Nothing happened. My fears were unfounded. I breathed out, able to finally fill my lungs with air as a colossal stone fell off my chest. Gottfried was still talking to Matthias and the others, and they retreated together. Matthias looked up to me, too, and smiled. I smiled back – with a cramp, but he couldn't notice that.

"This is going to be one of the best World Cup finals in history," Dad said. "I have to say, I'm thrilled to be here watching it live, and I'm proud that my son-in-law is part of this history."

Everyone laughed at his earnestness, including me, especially at how he'd referred to Alex as a member of his family already. I was glad that my choice made him proud and happy, but at this moment I got the most satisfaction at my dad's confirmation that this match was what it was supposed to be – a clash of two mighty sporting forces, not a war between two men.

I politely refused all the alcohol that kept arriving and only accepted water. I didn't know what would follow – nor did anyone else – and in case of some unprecedented circumstances, I didn't want to deal with nausea, too. I didn't talk much. I couldn't think about anything except those two men down there who were minutes away from entering the final combat. It might sound ridiculous to any regular person, but for all of us present there – the thousands of fans who breathed and screamed as one, along with the players and their entire team of coaches, managers, sponsors and medical staff – football was life. And that evening, that game and that golden trophy meant everything. Who won tonight mattered more than who lost yesterday or who'd be better next time. My heart knew that I wanted Alex to be the best one tonight. His team deserved it, and they'd showed the world that they were great enough, that the title wouldn't be a streak of luck or chance. I was well aware that Matthias's team was excellent, too. Of course, they were, with their wunderkinder – unassailable talents, boys who'd done miracles with the ball when they were sixteen, players who made football a form of art. If they composed themselves during this fifteen-minute rest, they could fight back and change the impression they'd left in the first half.

The players began walking out, white and yellow, one after another. My heartbeat accelerated. In forty-five minutes, everything would be decided.

All the Ukrainian players were on the pitch already, but some Germans were missing. Actually, the entire German Four was missing. I bent slightly over the fence, trying to see anything better, and a few seconds later, Gottfried came into view with all four of them and Leon Schneider.

Something was odd. Ben and Lens walked onto the pitch, leaving Leon, Michael, Matthias and their coach. Leon was smiling, which was strange, because Michael Krimm was yelling at Gottfried and Matthias. They were obviously disagreeing on something. Matthias tried to explain something to Michael, throwing his hands around, his dark eyes pleading, but Michael still didn't accept it. Leon tried, too, but Michael told him off even quicker. Then Gottfried began talking. Michael listened respectfully, then spoke and started removing his captain band. Matthias stopped him. They exchanged fire again, even angrier than before, and then Michael shook his head and stormed off, getting into position and staring at the grass in fury like he was trying to burn a hole in it.

What the hell was that all about? I wondered. German tempers flaring under pressure, or something more? There wasn't time to ruminate further; it was time to start. Gottfried said some final advice to Matthias and Leon, and they joined the others on the pitch. In the next second, the ultimate half of the World Cup final commenced.

The break had done the Ukrainians good. They seemed re-energised and fully rested for this confrontation. They were fast, covering every patch of the grass, and unyielding, not leaving any German player alone for the briefest second. In the first few minutes, they even managed to surprise their opponent and approach their posts at almost eleven metres. The Germans knew what they were doing, though, and there was always someone before Ewald Fuchs to take the ball to an area with less goalscoring potential. Friedrich Larsson was losing his head over Andriy

Barnik, who was built tiny and ran as fast as a bullet, easily swooshing around the German. In the short interruptions, we could see Friedrich crouched on the grass holding his head in frustration. Barnik had been awarded Best Young Player at the last tournament for good reason. He'd given them trouble even then.

On the other side, the German Four managed to create a number of splendid actions that were beautiful to watch (if you weren't a fan of Ukraine at that moment). They stabbed our middle line so powerfully that it took our players a huge amount of energy and effort to make up for their mistakes. Each of their three strikers – Matthias, Michael and Lens – got at least two opportunities to shoot at Alex. He defended all of them, catching some and boxing or deflecting most. His concentration was at its highest level.

Every time I saw his face on the big screen, I felt a palpable relief. He wasn't red or frantic, despite the number of offences he had to deal with. On the contrary, he was composed and focused, as if he'd been training his entire life for this match, learning how to do everything properly, perfectly, without making a single mistake.

That infuriated the Germans even more. However hard they tried, they couldn't score, and on top of that, they had to deal with constant attacks and counter-attacks from the guys in yellow, sometimes out of balls that seemed lost or out-of-bounds.

It made sense, then, in an infuriating way, when some fifteen minutes into the game they started making fouls – serious, painful fouls, unbecoming true and honest sportsmen. It became obvious pretty fast to everyone. The girls and I didn't need to hear Harold yelling "That's brutal!" to understand that the tempo of the game had shifted.

It started with their defensive players, who slid into the feet and legs of our strikers whenever they threatened to get near Ewald Fuchs's penalty box. Nikolay was the first victim, then Andriy Barnik, then Ivan Rostov, then Andriy again. That second time, Andriy shouted in agony so loudly that even we could hear in the stands. The culprit was Artur Voigt, a defender. He got a yellow card. We thought they'd stop after that punishment, but they didn't. Anatoliy Honchar was on the ground less than a minute later, but he bounced up pretending nothing had happened – he was dangerously close to the posts and on a mission. He shot, but Ewald caught the ball.

The next incident saw no other than two most temperamental players facing off on the pitch – Nikolay Pavlov and Lens Petrov. The majority of the Ukrainian team was in the offence. Nikolay was preparing to take a shot, his right foot already in the air, when Lens, realising there was no one else to stop him, slid and hit Nikolay's left calf, flattening him on the ground. It looked painful. It must have been agonising. Thousands gasped. We thought Nikolay's time on the pitch was done. He couldn't have remained unaffected by this.

The next second, he proved everyone wrong and jumped to his feet – faster than Lens, who also fell with him. He was red in the face and ready to fight. Lens had no clue how angry he'd made his opponent; when Nikolay shouted, it took him a couple of moments to regain his typical condescending air and stand straight to yell back in Nikolay's face. As they exchanged heated words, Nikolay was holding his arms next to his body in order not to grab and hit Lens. I'd seen him do this before – it was his way of preventing his overly impulsive self from entering a serious physical confrontation. Lens laughed in his face. I went cold. Nikolay pressed his forehead against Lens's. No, no, no, we didn't need a fistfight. We mustn't lose a player now.

Thanks to some divine power – or perhaps thanks just to Michael Krimm's level head – Michael approached and separated them. Andriy Barnik, Vlad Starovski and Ewald rushed in soon after, along with the referee, who was already taking the yellow card out. The guys were separated. Nikolay was upset, and Lens still laughing at him provokingly as the referee approached him and showed the card. Lens didn't rebel or obey; he only kept shouting at Nikolay until the referee told him something again. Finally, Lens walked off, throwing a final smirk over his shoulder.

It came as a great shock to everyone that Nikolay was still on his feet. He wasn't even limping, although I didn't doubt he was in pain. The game continued soon afterwards. They had a good chance from that free kick, but Friedrich Larsson sent the ball far out and our hopes at a goal were dashed again.

Literally two minutes later, Matthias started forward, accepting a pass from Ben. Lens and Michael were following him, tailed closely by the other players. They outnumbered the Ukrainians on this half of the field, and they wanted to use this unique opportunity. They all rushed straight towards Alex, who only had two teammates to assist him. It looked threatening. I almost closed my eyes, too scared to watch. The white jerseys passed the ball between each other, rapidly approaching Alex. Michael to Matthias to Ben to Lens to Michael to Leon to Matthias and finally to Leon again. It was dizzying. Leon kept going. He was in the penalty box, with only Alex and Igor Krasinski between him and the net. He had to score.

Sergey Lomin materialised and crashed into him, taking the ball off his foot – and taking Leon down with him, too. He saved it. He saved us from the goal. He saved Alex.

But at what cost?

Leon was on the ground, yelling in pain. On the big screen, it didn't look like acting. The clash was violent. Sergey had aimed for the ball but he couldn't have taken it except by force. My heart threatened to pound out of my chest. I squeezed Bea's and Angie's hands. The entire stadium was at a loss for breath. Coach Vance didn't say anything to explain. He didn't need to. It was obvious to everyone.

The Germans were awarded a penalty.

Time stopped, and then it lengthened. I went numb. I lost all feeling in my legs, but sitting was not an option – not now, when the entire Maracanã was on its feet, observing this historical moment.

No way. No way would they get away with this – that was the only thought my mind had space for. If Germany take the lead now, after the amazing game Ukraine had presented, they wouldn't stop. The morale of the Ukrainians would be shattered into a million pieces. They would try to come back, but it would be extremely difficult. This would kill their hopes. And the Germans…everyone knew how Germans took penalties. It was an international proverb – they always scored.

I wanted to scream in anger. This wasn't fair. Again.

Nobody around me said a word until Bea whispered, barely audible, "There's still hope. Players miss penalties. Keepers defend them."

"Germans don't miss," Lana replied gravely. "All German strikers have a hundred percent take on penalties over the past two seasons. I've checked."

I swallowed hard. Alex was on the big screen. Surprisingly, he didn't look upset or worried. Instead, he seemed focused and calm. I wondered what was going through his mind. He also had good statistics when it came to penalties, but still, he'd never taken any from a German. There was a commotion on the pitch. Sergey Lomin got handed a yellow card. Vlad Starovski tried to change the referee's mind, but we all knew it was in vain. The penalty was legit. The players in white talked amongst themselves. Alex was still alone, walking slowly from one post to the other like a predator in a cage. What was going through his mind?

Oh...who was going to take the penalty? That was what he was thinking about. It's what I was suddenly thinking about when the answer presented itself to me, like a premonition.

I began shaking uncontrollably. Angie and Bea squeezed my hands more tightly. I stared without blinking at the German crowd, and I knew. I prayed I was mistaken, but I knew. Who else? I still hoped Lens would be the one, but no...

No, no, no, no, no...

It was Matthias.

Of course. Who else would it be? He'd never miss this chance. Matthias jogged up, his face a picture of glee and confidence, so certain that Alex had already lost one battle from him. So much hatred had built up inside him over all these years. Why wouldn't he use this opportunity to humiliate Alex in front of everyone, in front of the world? He, Matthias Beller, could take Germany to the lead and eventual victory. He'd receive endless titles of praise and approval. He'd defeat the man he despised the most for the second time in a row.

Everyone watching all over the world was certain – once the Germans took the lead, they would do absolutely everything in their power to keep it.

Alex anticipated it. I knew it, even though his features didn't show any reaction. I knew it because I knew him. He stopped his slow pacing and stilled, waiting between the posts as Matthias approached the white penalty spot.

The thundering in my head intensified, and I realised the entire stadium was shouting and cheering – one half for Matthias, the other for Alex.

"Jane, get ready, you'll be in the news tonight regardless of your reaction," Angie said without the shadow of a joke. I squeezed her hand harder. I looked up to the screen, where my face flashed for a moment, and I was surprised at how calm and cold I appeared. Good. I needed to stay like that, for the sake of both of those men.

There was only Matthias and Alex now, and the ball between them. The other players retreated. Each and every German face was calm, a pre-emptive glee resting underneath a careful mask of stoicism. The Ukrainians were pale and waiting, preparing to react if necessary, though they all worried it wouldn't be.

Matthias emanated confidence. His coal-black eyes burned with elation. He smirked. Alex's face didn't move a millimetre. He stood on the line in the centre between the posts. The audience shouted their hearts out. The entire Maracanã was cheering the moment on. Millions of people watched this from their homes, so many of them awake at all hours of the night when they should be getting enough sleep for work or school, and I knew not a single one of them regretted a second they'd stayed up.

I took a deep breath, the deepest one I could. The referee whistled. Matthias evaluated for a moment, smirked again, jumped off – this would be a powerful hit – ran towards the white dot, reached it in three steps, swayed his stronger right foot and sent the ball volleying in a perfect curve to the far upper-right corner.

Alex didn't hesitate. The path of the ball was long. Could he jump that far? Nobody observing breathed. Matthias was looking at the ball he'd just fired out, waiting. Alex jumped once, and then a second time, his eyes on the ball and not on the player who sent it. He stretched. Would it be enough? I almost broke Bea's and Angie's fingers. The ball neared the posts, flying to the net – it only needed a few more centimetres.

But a pair of gloves was there to stop it.

Alex was on the ground, but just for a second. The next moment, he stood and looked to the ground, holding the ball victoriously in his hand. Then he turned towards the blue and yellow mass that went berserk in shock, disbelief and amazement.

He defended it. My Alex defended a powerful shot from Germany. From no other person than Matthias.

He didn't laugh. He didn't even celebrate. I loved him so much more for that. Even now, he was a considerate gentleman.

I didn't scream or shout, probably because I was too stunned to be aware of the magnitude of the events. I would be in the days that followed, but for now, I only hugged the girls and Alex's parents and sister, who cried with pride.

Matthias was on the brink of tears. I knew it because I knew how his face looked when he suffered. This time, he was in excruciating pain. His ego was shattered on the pitch, crushed in Alex's glove. He hadn't scored a penalty that he wasn't allowed to miss. He'd ruined his and his team's statistics. And he'd just made Alex great, inscribing him even deeper into the history of football. It was painful to watch, and not just for me.

"Oh, that poor boy. He'll never get over this," Mom said compassionately.

"Well, he was too big-headed and got what he deserved," Dad added.

"Brad, how can you be so heartless?"

"I'm just telling the truth. Hopefully, Yanov becomes his worst nightmare and he never dares come close to us again."

Dad was right again. Matthias's overconfidence did this, and Alex was already his biggest nightmare. This would only intensify once I told him in the next couple of hours that I wasn't going anywhere with him.

On the pitch, Alex was making his way up from the mountain of his teammates, who were jumping over him, whooping and celebrating and congratulating him. He still held the ball, which he finally passed on to the referee. All the while, he was still calm. Still focused. Still showing to everyone that he was definitely, unequivocally the best living goalkeeper.

Milan Andreyevich observed everything like a proud father, while Rolf Gottfried went completely white with fury. Whenever the camera caught him, he was either shouting or standing completely still, his lips pressed tight in agony, his eyes beady and frantic. His team had absolutely no control over the game.

Nikolay seemed to be inebriated with zeal and energy. So was Sergey Lomin, who'd caused the penalty, and so were Lev Zahara, captain Vlad Starovski, Andriy Barnik and the entire Ukrainian team. As soon as the referee whistled, they hunted the ball like starving predators. The Germans were still traumatised by what had happened, and this behaviour completely took them off-guard. The team in yellow showered them in attacks, one after another after another.

Until the sixty-eighth minute, that is, when Andriy Barnik and Nikolay Pavlov escaped all the opposing players and were the only two against Ewald Fuchs.

He didn't stand a chance.

Andriy could have taken the shot himself, but he didn't want to risk it. From his angle, the possibility was eighty percent. From Nikolay's, it was one hundred.

Ukraine was in the lead.

A miracle descended on Rio. It was a miracle that every football fan from this beautiful Eastern-European country had been praying for since the last World Cup. I couldn't help joining them as we shouted harder than we ever have, yelling like we didn't care about our next breath, ignoring the buzzing in our ears as we screamed our voices hoarse and our ears deaf. My legs regained confidence as I stomped on my heels, ignoring the pain.

Finally, Alex reacted, showing for a moment the man underneath the keeper. He ran to celebrate with his friends as they ran after Nikolay, who strutted around, brimming with pride. He ate a piece of the revenge cake, and it tasted delicious.

Gottfried was out of his mind. His players stood or sat motionless, in utter disbelief, thinking this must be just a very bad dream.

And a dream it was. A dream of millions, a dream of twenty-three boys and one coach and an entire country coming true.

The Ukrainians didn't want to lose momentum, so they took the ball back to the centre of the pitch and continued the game, eager to show more. With his defence, Alex had given them hope; he'd showed them they could do it. With his score, Nikolay confirmed it was all possible if they kept trying. Yes, the ever-so-dominant German team was good, but today, Ukraine could be better. In these last twenty minutes, they would be better.

The only composed player among the Germans now was Michael Krimm, who guided his players where to go and what to do. He seemed to have anticipated that the Ukrainians would keep pushing and wanted to avoid any more tragedies for his team. "He's sending them all to defence until they pull themselves together," Coach Vance said.

"As if that'll make any difference," I added and everyone laughed.

It did, but only in that there were now eleven players defending one goal. For the next five minutes, the ball didn't even cross to our side. Alex was standing alone, watching everything, composed and confident as ever, knowing he was the main cause of this ruckus in the strongest team in the world – up until now, at least.

A stray ball flew over to him. He caught it and sent it back to the German side where Igor Krasinski accepted it. Matthias tried to take it from him, but stood no chance alone against three defenders. Ukraine began another attack. It was the seventy-ninth minute. The boys in yellow still hadn't lost the adrenaline that was syringed into them by Alex. Again, all the players except Alex were packed into the German penalty box. One shot. A second. A third. The ball almost flew out, but Barnik reached it and sent it back to the anthill. Friedrich Larsson kicked it desperately behind his goal, hoping to stop it even if it meant a corner for Ukraine. Anatoliy Honchar apparently didn't want that free kick from the side, because he caught the ball and sent it back to where at least five of his teammates could hit it.

Vlad Starovski saw his chance. The others realised at once that he was in the best spot, and they all moved to protect him. He jumped high, aiming at the flying ball from Anatoliy and sending it towards the net with a sensational bicycle kick.

Ukraine's lead increased to 2–0.

My hearing failed for a second as I went temporarily deaf from the sound of the stadium. Bea was hugging me, then Angie, then Tanya Yanova, and then I couldn't keep track anymore. Just to make sure everything was legit, we watched the replay of the remarkable action each time it showed on the big screen. It was verified from every possible angle. No offside, no fouls. Everything was crystal clear and fair.

I believe that was what drove the Ukrainians that night, what gave them that surge and splendour, that winning energy and optimism. It was all fair. Even the penalty and Alex's way of dealing with it. The last time, Germany won with malicious tricks. This year was different. It was time for payback and revenge by simply being the best.

Gottfried stubbornly didn't want to substitute anyone. He let his starting team finish, perhaps because he was too proud, or perhaps because he still believed they could change something. When the game continued, some of the players – namely, the German Four and goalkeeper – regained their composure and made some trouble for Alex and his team. The experience the four of them had while playing together in Munich for many years was resurfaced now. When the German Four possessed the ball, they danced with it and it listened to them. They passed it between each other elegantly and precisely. Ben was the backbone in the midfield, Lens and Matthias the hot-heads who shot explosively, while Michael, thoughtful and unflappable as always, was seeking the perfect angle to shoot.

Nothing worked. Alex, with the help of his defencemen, managed to deflect everything.

On the other side, Ewald Fuchs was calm and focused – surprisingly so, since he was twenty-one and about to be blamed for his country's failure. Alex was the same age at the last Cup, I realised, feeling a swell of pity for the German goalkeeper. Ewald managed to deal successfully with a number of Ukrainian offences that came straight after the second goal. Coupled with the play of the German Four, Ewald's recent string of fortune seemed to sparkle some hope among the present fans. Germany was also famous for fighting till the end and changing the result in the final minutes. That seemed far from possible this night. It crossed my mind, though, that Gottfried or some other player – Lens, Leon Schneider or perhaps even Matthias – might begin some provocations to try their luck again. But it wasn't happening. Gottfried's players could scarcely hear him over the cheering mass of Ukrainian supporters who were already celebrating winning the trophy.

A victory which was less than ten minutes away.

As the Germans tried desperately to succeed in getting a goal past Alex, they also fought even more desperately against more Ukrainian attacks. The front line, led by Nikolay, didn't want to stop. A few players in white kicked our players too hard, earning two more yellow cards. Still, neither side was giving up – the Ukrainians rushing forward, the Germans defending with their bodies, legs, arms, everything.

There were four Ukrainians on the German half of the field, all of them defending. Ivan Rostov decided to try sending the ball towards Nikolay, who was jumping and waving, ready to accept it between two defensemen. Ivan shot but not strong enough. Dmitro Kostyskyn, who was behind enemy lines, managed to squeeze and jump above three players and send the ball with his head to the side where he hoped one of his team members would be.

It was too far and already too low, but Andriy Barnik didn't hesitate. If he wanted to score, this was the only way. Andriy surged forward, not aware of Leon Schneider, who was aiming at the ball with his foot, unaware of what Andriy was about to do. Leon's boot ended on Andriy's face – the cleats tore flesh as Andriy's head whipped sideways from the impact.

But not before Andriy hit the ball with his head, sending it to the net.

The net that was now shaking.

Three minutes before the end of the match, Ukraine led 3–0.

It was over.

Ukraine won the World Cup.

That was why Andriy jumped from the grass, ignoring the stream of blood gushing from his head and staining his jersey. His teammates ran after him to celebrate, while Leon sat on the grass, stupefied and horrified, his hands and white jersey smeared with blood. When the camera caught him, he was crying in utter despair.

The players jumped over Andriy, congratulating him while the stands echoed his name. He stood up, unaware of what a frightening and funny sight he was, drenched in blood and grinning in euphoria. Sergey Lomin was the first to pull him away from others and shepherd him to the medical staff, who began stitching his eyebrow and cheek.

The camera also caught Alex looking at the opposite goal and showing a number three with his hand. His friends had avenged him. This was a painful yet proper payback for the three goals they had scored against him before.

Gottfried wasn't upset anymore; he had passed that horizon. He was defeated, and there was absolutely nothing he could do about it.

Leon Schneider got a red card for kicking Andriy, but nobody cared.

The ball rolled from the centre dot, but nobody cared about that either.

It did hurt me to see them like that, Matthias and his friends. They were devastated. They could barely force themselves to finish those last few beyond-embarrassing minutes. Some of the players, when the camera caught them, were already crying. Others were dry-eyed but their faces were wrenched in despair. They weren't ready for this. Nobody was. Even Milan Andreyevich's team wasn't, until their goalkeeper defied the penalty. It was a night of miracles and dreams for these hardworking men, and nobody was going to take it away from them. Not anymore. It was their night.

When the referee let out the last whistle, the Ukrainian fans were already standing, so we started jumping, and I jumped with them. And I kept jumping, on and on, as the music began thundering – the *Samba de Janeiro*, again and again, percussive and jubilant. Each and every German dropped to the grass, as if they were the army of a defeated final boss from a video game. They were mortified, petrified, perturbed. It hurt seeing them like that, and I willed the cameras to return to the victors. Thankfully, they did, and when the big screen was swiftly populated by the ecstatic, overjoyed, exuberant and relieved Ukrainians, I remembered why I'd cheered for them in the first place. I remembered how badly losing had hurt four years ago, and I truly felt in my heart that this was proper restitution. They sang, ripping their jerseys off and swinging in the air; they carried Coach Milan on their shoulders around the pitch; they showered each other with water and champagne somebody passed on to them from the stands. Anatoliy Honchar suddenly had a large bottle of horilka in his hands and was drinking from the bottle, passing it around to his teammates.

When the adrenaline receded – only a little– they remembered their opponent who had given them and the world an excellent play, and they went around to shake hands. With extreme difficulty, Gottfried approached and congratulated each of our players. Michael Krimm, to set an example, led the other players to do the same. Leon Schneider was effusively apologising to Andriy for quite some time until Andriy finally took the horilka from Lev Zahara and forced it into Leon's hand, patting him on the back and reassuring him that everything was fine. I felt a swell of pride at the display of sportsmanship, watching these men take swigs of horilka in the wake of a cutthroat and career-defining match. Even Lens approached each Ukrainian to shake hands.

When Alex and Matthias stepped against each other, I went suddenly stiff, unable to move as the crowd swelled and jumped around me. Time stood still. Alex was slightly taller, but both of them were equally strong, exceptional footballers, immeasurable talents, great men. The camera zoomed in on them, a million flashes showering them from all sides. Their faces...Matthias was paper white, his eyes burning with pain, still hating the man in front of him. Alex was calm, victorious, but still humble. He was the first to hold his hand out. For an agonising moment, I watched as Matthias hesitated to reach out. But Alex said something briefly – I couldn't guess what – that made Matthias act professionally and accept the handshake. Then they turned from each other and walked away to their teams – one to despair, the other one to celebrate.

Ninety minutes ago, it seemed almost impossible that the Ukrainian team, with no World Cup victories to their name and an average age of twenty-seven and a half years, could take on the famous Die Mannschaft with an average age of less than twenty-four. Yet, it was all happening in front of our eyes. We were witnessing history.

I accepted all the showering compliments and praise, but I knew I needed to share this with Alex. My need to be with him was even more urgent when I noticed him greeting the fans behind one of the goals. My heart felt fit to explode. He truly was the most complete player, and I was sure that it wasn't just in my eyes. He was the most accomplished, well-rounded, considerate and honest man. I wanted to hug him, to be the first from the stands to congratulate him, before his parents, before his sister, before anyone.

I squeezed past Angie, Declan and everyone else on my way to the stairs. I could barely distinguish the steps, because fans were everywhere. Lana understood what I wanted to do and caught me by the hand.
"I'm with you!" she yelled.
I held her tight while pushing everyone in my path to the side. The celebration was so all-encompassing that I genuinely had to shove my way past, even though I knew if they had noticed me they would've all let me go. But I was happy to fight for it, to fight for this moment. With lots of effort and probably a few bruises that I'd see later, we reached the first row. Luckily, the last barrier separating the pitch from the stands wasn't too high. Lana waved at the nearest security and they helped me out. In a

matter of seconds, I was on the grass, my heels digging deep into the ground.

Nobody paid attention to me yet. Good. I wanted to surprise Alex. I saw some Germans in the corner of my eye – I recognised Ben and Leon – but I didn't stay long enough for them to say anything to me. Nor did I care. The only reason I was here was across the pitch, next to the goalposts. Somebody tried to catch my hand, I assumed it was another security, and then someone else yelled, I guessed for this person to let me go, so I pulled my way free and continued running, through the confetti, over bottles of water and towels, making sure I touched the ground with only my toes or else risk getting stuck or losing a heel.

When I separated from the crowd, a sudden volley of camera flashes blinded my peripheral vision. They'd noticed me. The flashes intensified as I got closer to Alex. I thought I could hear the stadium shout even louder than before, if that was at all possible.

Alex turned and saw me. His face now depicted the pure, honest joy that he deserved. I almost lost my breath crossing the distance between us, eager to extinguish it. When I finally reached him, my elation had taken hold of my body and it moved without my control, sending me into his arms.

He was ready for me, catching me covering me instantly with his wide, solid arms. He lifted me in the air and swung me around, diving his face into my hair.

"We did it, Jane! We won," he shouted placing his forehead on mine.

"You did it, Love. You did it, and then your friends followed," I said putting my hands on his cheeks.

He kissed me, long and deep. "Thank you, Jane. Thank you for all the motivation this morning. That thing you said – eyes and mind on the ball, not the player leading it. That was the key."

I smiled, although being reminded of Matthias still hurt, even in this situation when I felt invulnerable in my joy.
"I'm glad I helped," I said, brushing my fingers through his wet hair. "With me by your side, you'll definitely become better than Lev Yashin."

He laughed and kissed me again. "Speaking of that…"
He let me go for a moment, reaching to his shorts. I knew footballer shorts never had pockets, so I froze for a second, puzzled.

Until he took out a blue velvet box.
And went down on one knee.

"Alexander Yanov, you're not..." I screamed, feeling the weight of a world-full of eyes on us, unable to squeak out the rest of the sentence.

"I am." His smile was divine. He loved the way he astounded me; I love it, too. Never in my wildest dreams had I expected he'd do something like this. I hadn't even thought much about our marriage. We'd never talked about it. We lived together already, what else was there? I stayed frozen, focused on the perfect man beneath me and his blue eyes sparkling in the stadium lights. "Jane Andersonn, will you continue your life side-by-side with me, forever, as my wife and the only woman I'll ever love?"

My vision blurred. My legs got shaky. I swayed, suddenly dizzy.

This was it. My end with Matthias. My final beginning. My commitment to Alex. Could I do it? Of course, I could...but what I'd done with Matthias over the past few weeks flashed in front of my eyes like a very vivid movie. Where was he, anyway? Did he see us? Definitely. How could he not? The whole world was watching Alex and me now. Was he...perhaps? That person who'd tried to stop me...it could have been. How could I have missed him? What was he thinking now? The last time we'd met, I'd told him I'd leave Alex for him, and now...now Alex was looking at me with all the love and care in the world, his entire body and mind certain of me. Did he deserve someone like me? Was my *yes* good for him, if my *yes* was for forever?

Whatever the correct answer, I knew for sure that a *no* at the Maracanã after he'd won gold and was kneeling in front of me while the entire globe was watching...that was not an option.

I loved him. I truly did. And my first public tears – the tears of... joy probably... they brimmed from my eyes at this moment, spilling onto my cheeks. They somehow reassured me I was about to make the right decision.

Matthias, well, he'd have to take another devastating hit tonight. He'd survive. Without me by his side.

Because I was going by this man's side.

What else could I have said?

ABOUT THE AUTHOR

Jovana Iv was born in 1992, and lives and works in Southwest Asia. She studied English Language, Literature and Culture. So far she has written and published two short stories and a book *There Are Other Ways to Score* which is her debut novel and the prequel of *Potentially Settled Scores*.

You can find more about the author and her work on her Instagram profile *jovana.iv_*and Facebook page *There Are Other Ways to Score*.

www.ingramcontent.com/pod-product-compliance
Lightning Source LLC
Chambersburg PA
CBHW072350110726
47909CB00003B/662